·

Solomon's Table

John Hallam Lott

·

WebVivant Press

www.webvivantpress.com

·

Global Print Edition

ISBN: 978-1-908708-07-6

Published by WebVivant Press

www.webvivantpress.com

·

List of Characters

Tariq ibn Ziyad – Berber General and Governor of Tangiers

Izem – his Grandfather

Roderick – Duke of Beatica, Visigoth Pretender, later King

Egolina – his wife

Riccolo –his mother

Theudefrid – his father

King Egica – Visigoth monarch

Wittiza – his son

Idir – Neighbour to Izem

Menna – daughter of Idir, childhood friend of Tariq

Akeem – Berber warrior

Tala – Berber officer

Musa ibn Nusayr – Emir and Governor of All Ifriquya

Abd al-Aziz – his son

Count Julian – Byzantine Exarch of Septem

Florinda – his daughter

Kusaila – Berber chief

Asad – Elite Arab Guard Commander

Gunderic – Visigoth Archbishop

Tarif ibn Malik – Berber General

Al Walid – Caliph and head of Umayyad dynasty

Sulayman – his brother and successor

Pelayo – Visigoth Governor of Cordova and distant relative of Roderick

Askil – Berber General

Tamegrant – Servant of Julian and bodyguard to Florinda

Amayuu – Berber shipwright and engineer

Cyprian – Byzantine Merchant and associate of Count Julian

Camilla – his wife

Kunimund – Visigoth dissident

Geberic – Veteran Visigoth warrior

Byzantine or Roman Place Names

Cordova – Cordoba
Gades – Cadiz
Pomaria – Tlemcen
Septem – Ceuta
Arunda – Ronda
Elibyrge – Granada
Hispalis – Saville
Baelo Claudia – Balonia
Toletum – Toledo
Tarraconensis – Tarragona
Caesaraugusta – Zaragoza
Berytus – Beirut
Legia – Leon
Guadelete – Location not precisely known but probably close to Jerez de la Frontera

Chapter 1

Cordova, 680AD

The woman screamed. Her name was Riccolo and she was lying on bearskins on the floor of a former Roman villa. The villa was old and dilapidated, showing nothing of its former elegance. The chamber in which she was laid smelled of the farmyard. She screamed again. Her attendants, native Iberian slaves, looked at each other, their eyes devoid of sympathy. The birth was not going to be easy. Too bad! They would do what they had to in order to facilitate the delivery, but they were certainly not going to do anything to alleviate her suffering. Not for one of them. One of their oppressors. Her time would come. Until then they would stand expressionless and watch.

For two centuries and more they had existed under the Visigoth yoke. Many generations since then had accepted the new religion because the Christian faith had promised a more merciful subjugation, but it had turned out to be worse. Not that these three female servants had ever known anything different but, if the folk tales of their forebears were anything to go by, life under the Romans with their many Gods was easier than that which the Northern tribes had forced upon them with their one God. This Christian Church preyed upon the indigenous people of Hispania Ulterior, rather than prayed for them. The old Roman laws were applied disproportionately to a race they considered inferior and enslaved them mercilessly. So the women just watched and waited. Sure enough, the intervals between the screams diminished until, at a signal from the one appearing to be in charge they converged upon the figure, writhing on the stinking bearskins, her face channelling rivulets of tears and sweat. The final yell gave way to a convulsive groan and while two of the attendants held her shoulders, the other kneeled between the outstretched legs and pulled. It was over. Still kneeling, the birther took the cord between her teeth and bit hard. Two tied knots and, as if handing over nothing more valuable than a bag of flour, the squalling baby was passed over to its mother. These people lived and behaved like animals, reasoned the midwife, so why should they not be treated like them. Riccolo took the child and bared her breast. Roderick, that is what the boy would be called and christened as such, without delay, by the Bishop of Cordova. She had already lost three infants before they could be received into the Faith.

•

Ignorant or, more likely, ignoring the drama taking place in the villa behind him, the father of the new arrival was sitting on the banks of the Baetis, looking morosely at the autumnal river as it meandered past his feet. His name was Theudefrid and he was the grandson of a King, albeit a minor one. He was, however, conscious of his nobility and took care to dress in a way that set him apart from the natives who served him. Still Roman in style his attire, together with a number of their other customs, had been adopted from the Romans as the conquering Goth hordes swept them out of Southern Europe. What had not changed was the restless nomadic character that drove these tribes ever further away from their homeland. That essential gene remained in place long after succeeding generations had become "Romanised" and inter-bred with the indigenous population. It demonstrated itself as a tribal mentality, and it was this that was responsible for all the internecine rivalries, revolutions, and power struggles among the nobility that had made their home here in Hispania Ulterior or, as the Visigoths preferred to call it, Iberia.

Theudefrid had failed in his bid for power and so here he sat, plotting his next move. Which of his fellow nobles would ally themselves to his next coup and which would be more likely to rally their forces against him? His thoughts were interrupted by the sound of footsteps descending from the villa which was sited directly above the river. He did not bother to turn his head. It was the footsteps that were not heard which belonged to a potential assassin. A servant came up to him, bowed and informed him of his son's birth. Theudefrid barely acknowledged him or his news but sent him back to the villa for beer. It being brought to him, Theudefrid rose to his feet and started pacing the riverbank. A son at last. Perhaps another reason for regaining his status and power.

•

In Toletum, the city whose influence was so coveted by Theudefrid, King Egica was passing through his council chamber, a room richly furnished with priceless relics. Some of these antiques were said to have originated from the Temple of Solomon in Jerusalem. The artefacts, so legend had it, were originally the spoils of the Roman Emperor Titus when he conquered the Holy City some six hundred years earlier. They, in turn, had passed into the hands of the Vandals when they sacked Rome, changing hands once more when the Visigoths had replaced the Vandals. The beauty of these pieces meant little to any of these Northern tribes who valued utility above aesthetics but, to the newly Christianised Visigoths, their provenance had an almost spiritual significance. Thus it was, whenever Egica passed by the table, richly wrought of precious metals and jewels, he paused and marvelled as he always did, that this object had once been the property of King Solomon himself. These thoughts were interrupted by the entrance of a messenger bearing the news of Roderick's birth. Egica frowned. An heir to Theudefrid, a constant threat to his rule, was not good news. He summoned the captain of his guard. Now, perhaps, was a good time to remove that threat once and for all.

Chapter 2

Pomaria, Algeria, 695AD

The sheep were restless and had been all night. Now, in the pre-dawn hours, they continued to lift heads and turn as if trying to catch a threatening scent in the still air. When the threat came, it did as it always did, downwind and hugging the ground until ready to launch itself over the hurdle. It was in mid-air when the first spear sliced into its throat and the second, almost simultaneously, slipped cleanly through its ribs before its dead weight smashed into the ground, sending the flock into a bleating panic. It always took two spears. These Barbary lions could be enormous and allowed no room for error.

•

The tall old man in the shadows loosened the grip on his own spear and allowed himself a quiet chuckle, half relief and half pride at the skill of the boy who had killed the lion. The lad turned, "Was that all right, grandfather?"

"Indeed it was Tariq," replied the old man. "You are now what, seventeen? Tell me, why did you not make your first cast when the beast was on the ground, inside the pen? It would have been closer and less chance of a missed throw."

The boy moved over to the lion, a third spear held at the ready. His grandfather nodded his approval and took a step closer himself but there was no need of further caution. He repeated his question but still the boy gave no answer, crouching over the animal's head and running tentative fingers through the coarse black mane. The old man waited patiently and eventually the boy stood and turning said, "I thought it was only when the cat was in mid-air that it had less control over its movement. Just for those seconds, its feet off the ground; it was committed only to the leap and could not change its direction of attack."

Again a nod of approval from the old man who moved over to him, took his spear and asked when it was, exactly, that his grandson had come up with that idea. The boy looked puzzled, thought for a moment and said, "I think it was about two years ago, grandfather." This time it was the turn of the old man to stop and think. "Two years ago! Why Tariq, two years ago you were only…and even now you are only…" He studied the youth standing in front of him, quite unselfconscious, quite calm and unexcited after his kill. "It is true, the Prophet has made you strong and wise for your age but to plan for your first kill two years before you would be required to prove yourself, that is quite .." He considered the word "special". The boy shrugged off the compliment and replied, "Why do you think I could always beat boys older and bigger than I am? I found out when I was much younger that if I worked out my tactics beforehand then I nearly always won my fights."

"Ah!" interrupted his grandfather, "But how could you be sure that the other boy hadn't tactics of his own to employ against you?" Tariq shrugged his shoulders again. "The other thing I do is study all the other boys and after a while I get to know, or think I know, what their tactics are likely to be. It doesn't always work, of course it doesn't, but most of the time it does and now, because I nearly always win, nobody picks on me anymore." Delivered as a simple statement of fact, Izem, the boy's grandfather, could detect no trace of bravado in it. In fact, Tariq was much more interested in the lion than talking about himself and was busying himself by stretching out the tail to see how long it was. He looked up at Izem. "Have you ever killed a lion, grandfather?"

The old man nodded. "That's how I got my name. Didn't you know that Izem means lion?" Tariq replied, "Of course I did but it doesn't mean to say that you killed one, it could just mean that you have the character of a lion, that you are brave and .." he hesitated, "cunning." Izem laughed. "This one wasn't very cunning was he? He should have sniffed us out before leaping straight into the pen like he did, but yes, I have killed a lion. Only the one and I was much older than you are now and the lion was rather smaller than that beast that you have just killed. We must get some help to move him, the stock won't settle down until he's out of their way. Run back to the village and fetch Idir, he's strong enough. He'll be asleep mind you, so don't go charging in on him like that lion, otherwise you might end up like it did. Off you go, I'll stay here and look after the flock."

●

The boy, taking one of his spears, opened a hurdle, closing it carefully behind him. He made his way down the track leading to the village that represented home. His grandfather watched him make his way along the starlit track, wondering to himself for how much longer this small community would accommodate the precocious talents of this grandson of his. He set about shushing the flock and thinking how much things had changed since he and his grandfather had tended the village sheep. Most importantly, a new religion. He, like countless others of his ethnicity and generation, had been converted to Islam from the old tribal beliefs, and now most of the continent of North Ifriquya was under the Islamic control of the Umayyad Caliphate in Damascus. Izem was a boy when his tribe adopted the new faith which was to have such a profound effect on a way of life which, until then, had been largely nomadic and driven by familial traditions. Although loyal, he was becoming increasingly aware that his people, the Berber people, were very often perceived by the Caliphate as backward, second class and ranked very lowly in the minds of the Islamic hierarchy. Taxes were imposed disproportionately upon them and, worse, the enslavement of Berber believers, a proud, spirited race, was relatively common. Izem shook his head and could not help but wonder what the future might hold in store. Not for him, he was an old man and nearing the end of his days, but Tariq, mature beyond his years, intelligent and brave, what would it hold for him?

·

It took Tariq some half an hour to reach the first of the mean huts that formed the nucleus of his village but, long before he reached it, he sensed that all was not as it should be. The only noise he expected to hear was the barking of dogs before they picked up his familiar scent and the only light, that of the moon and stars, but no; now he could pick up the flickering light of torches and the voices of angry men. Perhaps he wouldn't have to wake Idir after all; for he was sure that one of the voices belonged to the very man he'd been sent to rouse. His first instinct was to go rushing straight for Idir's hut and tell him about the lion but this commotion at this time of night was unusual enough for him to stop in his tracks and wait. Quietly, and sheltered by the dwellings that lay in his path, he picked his way towards the direction of the altercation. Idir's voice he knew and that of Idir's wife, shrill and tinged with fear, but not the others. Authoritative, not loud but strange to his unpractised ear. Unfamiliar dialect, but then, any tongue not of his immediate locality was unfamiliar to him. He edged closer, clamouring dogs disguising the muted sound of his bare feet picking their way through debris strewn around the huts. The frenzied barking also prevented him from hearing the man coming up behind him, grabbing him by his hair and dragging him towards the sound of the voices.

Chapter 3

Pomaria, Algeria, 695AD

The grip on his hair was released but, before Tariq could turn around and identify his assailant, he was thrown violently to the ground into a circle of torches that, for the moment, blinded him. His unexpected and violent arrival appeared to have shocked everyone else as much as it did him, for his unceremonious entry into the gathering was greeted with silence. Not for long though. Whilst trying to lift himself up, he felt a powerful hand grip his chin and raise his head. He found himself forced to look into the face of a stranger whose black eyes reflected not so much anger, as Tariq had expected, but amusement.

"Well now, where did you find this one Akeem?"

The reply came in Berber but, like the first speaker, it was an accented Berber that Tariq had not previously encountered.

"Caught him skulking round the huts, Sir. Like a dog sniffing out a bitch on heat, Sir." "Ah," said the one who was obviously in command of the party, "that I very much doubt, looks far too innocent for that." He hauled Tariq to his feet, still holding on to his chin but before he could say more Idir, with whom he had been speaking earlier, pushed forward and, addressing Tariq directly, said,

"What are you doing here, why aren't you guarding the flock with your grandfather?" Tariq looked at the officer who released his hold in order that he could answer. "Grandfather sent me down to find you Idir. To ask you to come and help with the lion, because it's too heavy for us to manage on our own."

"Lion?"

Idir moved forward but was pushed back again by the soldier before he continued, "Izem has killed another lion has he?" He looked at the officer, not attempting to disguise the mockery in his voice.

"You see, here we kill lions, while you and your sort strut around trying to terrify simple village people. I told you, there's nothing here for the likes of you so why don't you take your rag-bag army back where you came from?"

There was no hint of amusement now in the officer's eyes as he unsheathed his blade and rested it gently against Idir's throat. Trying to defuse a situation which was apparently becoming threatening, Tariq intervened by bursting out that it was he and not his grandfather who had killed the lion. Another suspended moment of silence then, his eyes still locked with those of Idir, the officer said, "Lion or lion cub?"

"Lion Sir, a big one, his tail was this long."

Tariq extended his arms.

The officer instructed one of his men to watch Idir and turned to Tariq.

"Just how did you do that then?"

Tariq explained and the man looked at him, this time with real interest.

"How old are you son?"

Tariq told him and the officer thought for a second then, "Makes you a man now does it? Let's see just how much of one you are." Another pause while he looked around.

"You've already met Akeem; let's see how far you can get with him." He turned to his subordinate. "Do no more than put him in his place Akeem, don't kill him, he might yet be of use to us."

As he turned to Akeem, so did Tariq, who frowned.

"You want me to fight with him, Sir?"

"Why not?" came the reply. "You say you've already dispatched a fully grown lion tonight. Akeem might smell like one and he might be as nasty as one but I won't let him kill you, not like a lion would."

Tariq looked at Akeem for the first time. Not a very reassuring sight. Akeem was not especially tall but he was very powerfully built. Then Tariq started thinking fast. Coming at him from behind, as Akeem had, he could have grabbed his arm, his shoulder but no, he controlled him by grabbing his hair. Possibly that is what he'd try again. Which hand had he used, left or right?

"Come on then, not frightened are you?" taunted Akeem.

Idir attempted to intervene but was forcibly held back.

The two faced each other. Once again Idir tried to denounce the unfairness of the contest and again he was restrained by two of the strangers, soldiers or whatever it was they were supposed to be.

Tariq turned around so that he was standing slightly sideways to his opponent who, as he had predicted, swung a wicked right fist at Tariq's head. Tariq scarcely appeared to move as he swayed lightly out of range and, instantly, brought his bare heel up to Akeem's groin, kicking as hard as he could, the blow gaining impetus from the angle at which Tariq was standing. Akeem doubled up and as he did so, Tariq joined his hands, raised them above his head, took a pace forward and brought the double fist down onto the back of Akeem's unprotected neck. He dropped to the ground, groaning but not moving. Tariq was about to administer another kick to the man's head, thought again and stepped back, still ready to defend himself should Akeem recover. The officer let out a low whistle of appreciation and stepped between Tariq and his felled opponent.

"Who taught you to fight, boy?" Tariq gave one of his self deprecating shrugs.

"Nobody, Sir. I just do what my instincts tell me."

Idir shook off the restraining hands of his guards and said, "Told you so didn't I. We're real men here. That boy, as you call him, has killed a full grown lion and beaten one of your best men. All in the space of an hour so why don't you all just get off back where you came from and leave us alone."

The officer replied, not looking at Idir but still regarding Tariq, "Don't worry, we're going but he comes with us. He's wasted here and if you're honest with yourself, yes and to him, you know he is."

"Wasted!" Idir shouted back. "This is his home; he has responsibilities here, his grandfather, the stock. You think you can just march in here and take off our strongest and best youngsters, just so you can enslave them and force them to serve some fancy despot in whatever country you happen to represent?"

This time the officer diverted his attention to the irate Idir. Still he spoke softly but his authority was obvious.

"Believe me, I understand your problem. It is not so very long since that I was in your position. I was taken from my village but look at me. Yes, I was taken into slavery but now, although not a free man, I have a position and I am respected by my masters. We live in a time when there are more important matters to attend to than sheep. We need men like this one here and, whether you like it or not, he is coming with us, as are the others which my men are holding on the far side of the river which divides this place."

Idir glared at him but, before he could remonstrate further, Tariq spoke to him.

It was almost as though he, Tariq, was the elder and Idir the boy. Other things were changing. Cocks were crowing and the eastern sky was competing with the light from the flickering torches. The early morning chill was bringing with it a sense of calm to a scene which, hitherto, had been fraught with tension. All eyes were suddenly focussed on Tariq and even Akeem, now sitting up and rubbing the back of his neck, was straining to hear what Tariq was about to say. He spoke slowly and his words were carefully chosen.

"Idir, I know you mean well and have my interests at heart but I am going with these people." He indicated the soldiers with a sweep of his arm. "I always knew that I would leave the village to see what lay beyond it and now seems as good a time as any. Therefore I leave willingly and not as their prisoner. Please go now and help grandfather with the lion, he will be worried that I have not returned with you. Tell him too, that I will see him again. Tell him that is my promise and he is not to be concerned about me. Will you do that please?"

Idir looked mystified for a moment. Not apparently at Tariq's words but the maturity with which they were delivered. He nodded a reluctant agreement. The officer clapped his hands, signalling that it was time to leave but first he turned to Tariq, smiled and said, "We would have taken you anyway, you do know that don't you?"

Tariq grinned back, "Of course I did, but if you, as an enslaved man can get where you are, then so can I and then I'll have more freedom than I would if I'd stayed here."

The officer, whose name Tariq later learned was Tala, gave Tariq a long hard look before turning to Akeem, now upright although obviously in pain.

"What do you think Akeem, is this youth going to take my place?"

Akeem, massaging his tender balls, answered in his gruff dialect, "Pardon my saying so, your honour, but he'll go further, and pardon me again, but when he does I want to be with him. He'll be a good one to serve under, he will."

Tala gave a wry smile.

"Looks like I'll have to watch my back but don't worry lad, there's plenty of room for advancement in the service of my master, the Emir. Enough of that, it's time to move."

Thus saying, he mounted and led his foot soldiers towards the river that ran through the middle of Tariq's village. Tariq walked with Akeem at his side, intent on gleaning as much information as he could from him. Where were they going? Who was the Emir? What was an Emir, and what sort of life was likely to await him on reaching their destination? Before he could do so however, their progress was interrupted by Tala halting them with a raised hand. Even in the dawn light, it was difficult to see what was happening on the other side of the river but there was certainly a great deal of noise, amongst which Tariq's ear could clearly distinguish a voice he knew well, and it was clearly a voice in distress if not pain. He left Akeem's side, racing to the head of the column and reached the bridge before Tala's Barb could set a hoof on it.

Chapter 4

Pomaria

Having reached the other side of the bridge, Tariq stopped because he could no longer hear the cries. He cocked an ear but all he could make out was the sound of the tidal river washing against the banks, the sharp tap of hooves on the timbers behind him and the assorted grunts and snorts of waking domestic animals. He tried to recapture the sounds and the direction from which they had come but he was not that familiar with this side of his village. His own side, which he knew like the back of his hand, was far less developed than this. Devoted exclusively to the old rural tribal lifestyle it was generations away from what went on here where commercial activity was thriving, particularly that of the leather industry, the smell of which hung in the air and was offensively alien to Tariq's senses. A maze of alleys confronted him, lined haphazardly with dwellings, workshops and tanning yards all with their attendant animal shelters. Most had been thrown together from local materials and the remains of the old Roman buildings, the dawn light displaying a bizarre mixture of mud bricks interspersed with fine mosaic tiles and shards of discarded pottery. It was the river that was responsible for this sudden explosion of commercial activity. Easily navigable, goods could quickly and cheaply be transported down to the open sea and thence to regions of which Tariq hadn't even heard.

•

The sound of footsteps interrupted his concentration and he turned to see Tala, leading his mount, followed by Akeem and the others and, to his surprise, Idir, who had apparently followed of his own free will. Idir moved to his side.

"What is it Tariq, what have you …?"

Tariq held up a hand.

"Quiet Idir, I thought I heard…"

Idir caught hold of his shoulders and spun him round.

"You thought you heard what Tariq, was it Menna? Was it her voice that you heard?"

Menna was Idir's only daughter, scarcely more than a child and, like a lot of the younger children from their side of the river, living and working in this new and developing half of their village. This they were more than happy to do. For one thing, it was much more exciting, lots of new things to see and experience but, equally important, paid work for unskilled small hands was easily found.

Idir, getting no response, shook Tariq to elicit an answer. Tariq, calm and unemotional, gently gripped Idir's wrists and removed his hands from his shoulders.

"I don't know Idir, I honestly don't. I thought I heard a voice that could have been hers but, on the other hand, there are so many other voices and noises it could have been anybody."

Hardly had he finished speaking when a figure, little more than a shadow, could be discerned emerging from one of the labyrinthine alleys and speeding in the direction of the bridge. Behind it, a much more substantial figure was giving chase and gaining but, with a final spurt, the slight figure of a girl sprinted across the lane leading to the bridge and, with a shriek of relief, threw herself into the arms of Idir. Her pursuer, one of Tala's men, was on them almost immediately and, within seconds, his dagger was at Idir's throat. Before anything else could happen, Tala, handing his horse to one of his men, stepped forward, motioning the man with the weapon to step back. The man reluctantly did so. Tala turned to Idir.

"What is it about you that make my men want to slit your gullet?"

Idir, clutching the girl, glowered at him.

"My daughter, he was after my daughter."

The girl, whose initial sobbing had subsided, gasped out, "He was going to take me away, father, and he…he touched me."

This time it was Tariq's turn to intervene, before Idir lost control.

"Tala", he said, almost as if he'd known the officer for years, " She is Idir's only daughter and if he thinks that she's been assaulted by this man, he has every right to be angry. The girl is only twelve."

Tala turned on the soldier who had been chasing the girl.

"Is this true? Your job, on this side of the river, was the same as ours on that side."

He gestured to the bank from which they had just crossed. He went on, "To take those suitable to serve our master and your orders were quite clear. You use force if you have to but that is all. How they respect us is not important, for our force, for our knowledge, whatever, but their respect is important if they are to be integrated as the Emir wishes. By your behaviour you have shamed us. Akeem, take him out of my sight and do what you must, only do it quickly."

The man, not young, not old and with a skin of somewhat lighter hue than his compatriots, offered no resistance when Akeem took him by the arm and drew him along the river bank and down into the tall reeds some way upstream. A few minutes later Akeem emerged alone then, his sword sheathed. Tala turned to Tariq.

"One of the doubtful privileges of rank. You have to do things which can be repugnant to your natural feelings."

Tariq looked at him.

"And what about Akeem and his natural feelings?"

Tala allowed himself a rueful smile.

"He doesn't have any! But he's loyal – or at least he was until you came on the scene."

Tariq continued to look at him questioningly but Tala abruptly turned his back on him and announced that, if they were to catch the morning tide, they had better start getting ready to embark. One of his men lifted a horn and blew a single long note, which was immediately answered by another and soon, around a long bend in the river, two barges came into view, propelled by four oarsmen in each.

•

By this time the rest of Tala's men appeared on the river bank, bringing with them a dozen terrified looking souls, all from this side of the river. Tariq, it appeared, was the only victim to be taken from the other side. He asked why this was. Tala was brief.

"All this lot have learned some sort of skill or other while working in the trades they practise here. To be honest with you, we didn't expect to find anybody worth taking on the other side. That is, until you turned up."

"What about Menna?" Idir growled, holding the girl, still upset, tightly to him.

Tala didn't even look at him.

"She comes with us."

"Oh no she doesn't, she stays here with me."

"If you don't let go of her, I will have you killed *then* she will come with us."

Idir looked wildly around as if expecting help. Tariq held out both his hands to her.

"Leave her with me Idir, I'll look after her."

Idir clutched her even more closely and so tightly that her sobbing was cut off for lack of air.

"What do you mean, you'll look after her? You're in the same boat as she is. You're just another slave, albeit a willing one and that's something else I can't understand. You always appeared to be a bit above the rest of us and now you're happy to be at the beck and call of someone you don't know, never even heard of and, most likely, won't respect."

Tariq shook his head.

"I have already explained, Idir. I have no choice, none of us has, and since I have no choice I shall just have to make the best of my life that I can. What did I have to look forward to over there?" He jerked his thumb in the direction of the straggly group of buildings on the other side of the bridge.

"And look at him." This time a gesture to Tala who was making an effort to remain patient. "He was a slave and look at him now. So, leave Menna in my care. We've known each other all our lives and I'll make sure that she doesn't come to any harm."

Idir looked uncertain but loosened his hold on the girl who, still sniffing back tears, looked from him to Tariq and back to her father before giving a tiny nod of acquiescence. Idir was still not sure and started to protest again until Akeem stepped forward and announced in his gruff manner that, if anyone was stupid enough to threaten the girl, they would have to answer to him as well.

Tala shook his head and muttered, almost inaudibly, that the sooner his men were back in strict military training, the better. He then ordered that they board the barges and be on their way.

•

The first thing to embark was his horse and, from the care with which he organised the operation, this was obviously regarded by him as the most valuable item in the manifest. The prisoners, unshackled but closely supervised, were split between the two barges, as were their guards. Tariq was in the second vessel with Akeem and between them, Menna who, after waving to her grieving father, dried her eyes, snuggled up to Tariq and went to sleep.

Idir, though, couldn't resist one last taunt. As they drew away from the bank and into the current he shouted, "Common barges! Is that the best you can manage. I would have expected fearsome looking vessels of war."

Tala turned and good humouredly shouted back, "You would have seen us coming then, wouldn't you? And by the time we'd landed, you'd have all run off to the hills. As it was, we were just two commercial barges, coming to pick up stuff from the tanneries."

Akeem, glancing at Tariq, noticed from his expression that even that fact hadn't escaped his notice.

Four oars pushed them out from the banks and were then employed to keep them steady as they drifted down river on the ebb tide. Once out in the basin and thence to the sea, the primitive sails were hoisted and, hugging the coastline, they tacked slowly west.

Keeping his voice low, so as not to disturb Menna, Tariq spoke to Akeem.

"What is the name of this place we are being taken to?"

Akeem replied, somewhat less discreetly, "The barges will take us as far as a small port called Tetouan and from there we travel on foot to a place called Tangier, where the Emir has his headquarters. After that, it's up to him where you go but, if he takes to you and I think that he will, you will go wherever he goes. Very busy man, the Emir and a very able General."

Tariq stored this information in his mind but still wanted more.

"So he is obviously very powerful, rich and owns a lot of slaves but what is he actually like? Have you ever met him?"

Akeem, trailing his fingers in the water, thought for a moment.

"Ah! Not quite so easy, that one. Yes, I have met him but Musa, that's his name or rather to give him his full title, Musa ibn Nusayr, doesn't get that familiar with the likes of me. What I can tell you is that, compared with my last master, he's a lot easier to serve under. You see, the last one was a real tyrant and it was he who took me into slavery. Like you I am Berber but from one of the tribes of the country we're going to. When I was taken, that Emir, Hasan, was a real bastard towards us Berbers. He had no respect for our ways and you either took the Faith or you died. This one isn't like that. He converted a lot of us tribes by showing tolerance towards us and having some regard for our traditions and, because he's been so successful in his campaigns, the Caliphate think very highly of him. In fact…" Here he became more conspiratorial, leaning carefully over the girl so that Tariq could hear him. "…rumour has it that he'll very soon be made the Governor of all Ifriquya, although, to be honest, I'm not all that sure what or where that is. You'll have to ask Tala, he knows a lot more about these things than I do."

Deeming that to be more information than he could fairly be expected to deliver, Akeem settled back on the deck and returned his fingers to the gentle currents of the water.

Tariq wanted to know so much more and wished that his upbringing hadn't been quite so parochial. He looked down at the now peaceful Menna, then across to Akeem. The man had just executed one of his own companions and was now washing the stains from his hand as if it were nothing. Would Tariq's slavery mean this degree of indifference to life? Or would it be gardening, or pot-washing or would he, like Tala, be free to make decisions about his own future and that of others? He sighed to himself. Time alone would tell. Whatever, it was outside his control – or was it?

Chapter 5

Tangier, Morocco, 702AD

Musa ibn Nusayr was a big man, in every sense of the word. Now aged well over sixty, a black Arab, his physical presence was impressive, as was his intelligence, his imagination and his tactical ability. If he had a weakness, it was his venality and, when co-Governor of Irak, he had narrowly escaped execution after a scandal involving the misappropriation of huge amounts of tax revenue. The Caliphate, however, decided that a Musa with his head on his shoulders was of greater value to them than a Musa without, and continued to reward his considerable feats of warfare and diplomacy by making him Governor of all Ifriquya. He then continued to expand the Umayyad Empire by conquering the Balearics as well as building a defensive fleet which he deployed successfully against the marauding Byzantine navy.

•

Now he stood on the defensive wall of Tangier and looked towards the distant shape of Monte Anyera and wondered. This had recently become an ever-recurrent theme in his musings and he couldn't get it out of his mind. Behind the shadow of the mountain, nestled the ancient city of Septem and, although physically part of Morocco, it was a tiny jewel on the continent which, as yet, had not been added to the crown of the Caliphate. They had tried in the last century but had been resisted and this tiny colony had retained its independence from Islam and was part of Visgothic Iberia. It was ruled over by an agent of Toletum called Julian who was, himself, not a Visigoth but a Byzantine Christian. Musa and Julian had met, indeed had met on several occasions each enjoying the company of the other. Religions apart, they were pragmatic politicians, sophisticated and well travelled men and it suited both of them to have a source of information about what was going on in Toletum and Damascus. There was one subject though, that had particularly captured Musa's attention and it was this that often led him to this spot, thoughtfully gazing westward. Suddenly his deliberations were interrupted by a respectful cough. His bodyguards were in attendance so he didn't react immediately. When, with some reluctance, he did turn from the direction that had occupied him, the young man who had disturbed him coughed again apologetically, bowed in salutation and held out a rolled-up map.

"You asked for this to be brought to you, Sir."

Musa looked at him, frowned as if trying to remember who he was. Then his brow cleared.

"Of course, it's Tariq isn't it? Sorry I didn't recognise you straight away, my thoughts were completely elsewhere." He took the proffered map.

•

It was seven years since Tariq had been marched into Tangier, not knowing what the future held for him. Inwardly, he had changed little. He still retained an almost abnormal zest for experience and knowledge, but showed no signs of losing the honest simplicity that had characterised him as a youth. His stature was still impressive without carrying any excess weight, his beard was fuller and he was universally popular with almost everybody with whom he came into contact and he had done extremely well for himself, just as Tala had predicted. It was to be over two years before he was to meet Musa but, by applying himself to his religious and military studies and by adapting quickly to the army life into which he'd been immediately conscripted, he had soon come to the attention of his superiors. Then, one day, came the order to attend upon the Emir himself. This was not especially significant, for Musa always required his army commanders to make him aware of talent which was worth nurturing. Fortunately Tariq had a natural chameleon-like quality of fitting into any situation in which he found himself so the sumptuous apartments, and the grand figures gravely making their way through the day's business within them, did nothing to impress a young man who, a few years previously, had been happily tending a flock of sheep and was unaware of a world outside his own environment. Musa had seemed interested in Tariq's background and asked for a first-hand account of the slaying of the lion. Within a year, Tariq had become a very junior member of Musa's military staff. So junior in fact that it was in excess of another two years before he saw him again. If he imagined that this was because the Emir had forgotten him, he was mistaken. Musa never forgot anyone who was likely to serve his interests and, when Tariq appeared with the map, Musa had recognised him straight away; he just didn't want Tariq to know that he had.

•

Musa unrolled the map and, after giving Tariq a second look, turned with it to the direction he had been contemplating earlier. Tariq, assuming his role of messenger was finished, started to descend from the ramparts but was stopped short by Musa.

"Up here Tariq, come up here with me."

Tariq did as ordered and stood at Musa's side while the Emir studied the map and, from time to time, glanced up from it, presumably to identify various landmarks which appeared on it. This went on for long enough for Tariq to feel somewhat redundant. He, after all, had other commitments and he was about to say as much to Musa when the latter turned to him and said, pointing towards the west, "Tell me what you see when you look over there?"

Tariq shaded his eyes and looked long and hard but could see nothing that might be significant or worthy of comment. Musa patiently stood there while Tariq searched the horizon. Eventually Tariq, unable to come up with anything more interesting, shrugged and said, "The sea?"

Musa turned to him and, tapping the rolled up map against his hand said, "More, tell me more."

Then Tariq understood what it was that Musa was after so, without hesitation, he said, "Two seas!"

Musa chuckled and handed the map to him.

"You've looked at this haven't you?"

"Yes my lord." He lowered his eyes. "Before I brought it to you. I am sorry."

Musa gave another chuckle.

"Don't be sorry, it is exactly what I would expect you to do. It occurred to you that, should I want to question you about it, you would have answers for me. Am I not correct?"

This time Tariq looked him straight in the eye and said "Yes, Sir."

Musa rolled up the map again and pointed it at the mount sheltering Septem.

"Can you tell me what is behind that hill?"

"I believe it to be the city of Septem, my lord."

"Believe it to be?"

"I have only noticed it on the map, my lord. I haven't actually been there or physically seen it."

Musa stroked his beard. "Mm. Did you not have sight of it when Tala first brought you here?"

"If I did, my lord, nobody told me what is was."

Musa thought for a moment then, having come to a decision, turned again to Tariq.

"Would you like to see it?"

Tariq's delight was unmistakeable as he gave Musa a spontaneous grin.

"Indeed I would, my lord. I am always happy to experience new places and learn what goes on there. I understand that the people there are not of our race. How is it, my lord, that they have retained their independence? It is a part of Ifriquya is it not?"

Musa nodded.

"Believe me, it is not for want of trying but, as it happens, I think it to our advantage to have a Byzantine outpost on our doorstep. Because of its position, guarding the Strait between us and Hispania Ulterior, it has considerable strategic value but there is more to it than that. I will arrange for us to make a diplomatic visit to the agent there. I think you will find him an interesting man and it will do you no harm to learn how relationships such as these are conducted. But first, I think a little more professional experience in the field might be good for you. I am going to give you the command of a small force, say a hundred men, all mounted, and I want you to retrace the journey you took here nearly seven years ago. We have a problem with a small but resolute group of dissidents, not far from Pomaria. Their original leader, a man called Kusaila, has recently converted to us but some of his people continue to reject the true faith. Does the name Kusaila mean anything to you?"

Tariq shook his head. Musa said,

"I must say, I am surprised; I always assumed that everyone knew everyone else in their territory."

Tariq shook his head again and smiled.

"Not in the part of Pomaria that I came from we didn't. I have to admit, my lord, I scarcely knew a soul on the other side of the river, let alone much further away. We were not exactly isolated from the rest of the world but we kept ourselves very much to ourselves."

Musa thought about this for a moment, then said, "The time that you have been with us, enjoyed yourself have you?" Without waiting for a reply, he went on, "You have matured enormously in that time. You learn quickly and your leadership skills are amazing for one of your background. You have literally outgrown your instructors and, when put to the test, can out-think them. This, your first command, could be the start of a fine career. How you approach it is up to you of course. What about a second in command?"

Without pausing to think, Tariq said, "Tala, and I want Akeem as well."

There was an audible intake of breath from Musa.

"Do you think Tala will be happy to serve under you?"

"Yes, my lord, at least I think he will and Akeem, I know, will be only too happy. He's always asking me if he can be transferred to the division in which I'm serving."

Musa said, not without a degree of irony, "You'd better go and give him the good news then. Oh, by the way, while there, should you wish to revisit your old haunts, you have permission to do so. Just don't drag it out too long."

Tariq bowed. "Thank you my lord, I did promise my grandfather, should he still be living, that I would return one day."

Musa nodded then turned back to the view that had occupied him earlier, while Tariq made his respectful exit, clutching the map, his mind a confused amalgam of excitement, anticipation and apprehension.

As soon as he could, Tariq contacted the two men in question and, to give him his due, Tala accepted with nothing more than a resigned shake of the head and a rueful smile. Akeem's response came in the form of a grumbled "About time." Thereafter it was only a matter of recruiting the rest of the men, most of whom came from Tala's old division, appointing a quartermaster to handle provisioning and a couple of farriers to select and make ready their Berber mounts. Each man was responsible for his own weaponry, principally bows, spears and short, straight swords, and within a week Tariq was prepared for the first military expedition under his command.

•

The people of Tangier were so used to seeing military units riding out on forays or the occasional defensive operation, that nobody took much notice when yet another one was about to depart headquarters. The exception was a tearful Menna who was hanging about the gates hoping to catch the eye of an unresponsive Tariq. Ever since their arrival here, she had made no secret of her feelings towards him and whilst, in many ways, she had settled down and was not unhappy in her role as dressmaker in the household of Musa, she was condemned to disappointment when it came to Tariq's feeling for her. As it was, he actually held up a hand to halt his men, gave her a friendly greeting and promised to remember her to Idir who would be invited to move to Tangier to spend his declining years with his daughter. She smiled a tearful farewell and, with much regret, resigned herself to the fact that it was probably as good as it was ever going to get.

•

Tala trotted up alongside his new commander and asked where they were going to embark, here or further along the coast. Tariq's reply caused a momentary loss of composure.

"We're not, Tala, we are going overland."

Tala looked disapproving and just managed to bite back some comment about inexperienced officers. This didn't escape Tariq who carefully explained that his countrymen were so used to the Emir's men using the marine route into their territory, that lookouts were now posted along the coast and up the rivers to alert those who had an interest in not being taken into slavery or otherwise punished. Tariq went on to say that, when they camped that night, he would be grateful if Tala would spend some time with him, going over maps of the mountain passes that he, Tariq, had thought best suited their purpose. Thus mollified, Tala happily agreed and even went on to admit this might well be a good alternative to previous routes taken under his command. Tariq meticulously kept his counsel.

Chapter 6

Toletum, 702AD

The rays of the early morning sun shone through the horseshoe shaped openings of the east facing wall of the council chamber. The treasures, housed therein, responded as their own brilliance was reflected around the walls in a kaleidoscope of colour. As the solar journey progressed throughout the year, King Solomon's table was moved, with mathematical precision, in order to benefit from this. Of course, the sun did not appear on every single morning but the table was still moved so that, when the sun did reappear, it would be in place for the next benediction. It stood on heavily bejewelled legs with a top fashioned from gold and silver. Although not large, it was extremely heavy, and the stretcher arms, by which two or more strong men moved it, were always left in place. Its value was beyond price but even that could not compare with the spiritual value placed on it by the current custodians of the table, who revered it with a religious passion that was almost idolatrous.

•

By this time in the morning, the vast plains below Toletum were bathed in sunlight, and the hill, on which the city stood like a vast anthill, was alive with the comings and goings of the inhabitants as they scurried about their duties with the kind of relentless energy normally associated with that industrious insect. Seat of whichever ruler clung on to their precarious power and political centre of the Visigoth Empire, Toletum was a busy and important city. Legislation, both local and national, resulted from the councils held there and attended by the temporal and Christian leaders of the state. It was the centre of education for the nobility but, above all, it was a hotbed of intrigue as different factions jostled for position and families fought for control of Hispania.

King Egica and his son stood close to the table, as if enjoying some sort of security from its proximity, and discussed the gossip currently circulating around the court. This had become a ritual for them and for them alone. Councils were all well and good but they had a habit of deposing one king and electing the next. Natural succession to the throne was not feasible in a society whose historic nobility was drawn from so many different tribes and cultures. While Egica could do nothing about this arrangement, by adopting his son as co-ruler he hoped to establish some form of continuity for the throne but it was never easy. The Church was a powerful influence in the State and was, itself, responsible for fermenting insurrection if it felt it was in its interests to do so. In fact it had done just that only a few years earlier, but it was not that event which currently engaged the minds of Egica and his son but the last attack on their authority. That too had failed but there were still conspirators at large to be hunted down and punished. Not the ringleader though, he had been easy to apprehend. Not the first time he had attempted a coup and consequently he was under close surveillance. Egica was making the point that, another time, they should not be so lenient, thus permitting a discontented noble a second chance. A commotion behind one of the heavy, iron-studded doors leading to the hall caused them both to turn around. As it was flung open, their personal guards moved closer. Two burly men entered, supporting between them a third figure, barely conscious, bound, blindfolded, his body twisted with pain. Egica beckoned the trio forward.

•

"So Theudefrid, have we succeeded in slaking your thirst for power? Perhaps you would like to take a tour of the palace you thought to make your own, or even," he dropped his voice to a caressing whisper, "the fabled treasures of which you have heard so much and so unwisely coveted." He called the guards to bring him closer.

The guards roughly dragged the prisoner towards him. He went on:

"This table, for instance. The table of Solomon himself, on which, so it is said, the Holy Scriptures rested. Why don't you take a long look at it and remind yourself what might have been?"

Egica smiled at his son and stepped forward, whipping the bloodied bandage from the man's eyes. He stepped back again.

"Oh dear! I quite forgot, I gave orders for you to be blinded. Perhaps you would like me to describe it to you? No? Oh, very well. By the way Theudefrid, I hear you have a son. What did you have him named, Roderick wasn't it? Yes that's it, Roderick. Growing up to be a fine young man, I hear. What a pity you will not be there to advise him, but then, considering your past actions, your advice might not have been worth giving."

He jerked a thumb towards the door.

"Kill him, slowly."

As Theudefrid was hauled back through the door, Egica turned to his son, who was called Wittiza.

"Remember the name Roderick, my son. He will seek his revenge on our house. You will do well to monitor his activities closely. Although a young man, as you are, once he hears of this day's work he will start plotting our overthrow."

He thought for a moment, resting his hand on the Table, and then continuing:

"He will be looking for allies among our known enemies, such as the Jews who still smart under the severe decrees we have imposed upon them. Mark what I say and beware the son of Theudefrid."

Wittiza nodded gravely and listened for the umpteenth time as his father droned on about the provenance of the Table. He had heard it so many times before but, to please the king, he dutifully ran his fingers over the emeralds and diamonds and asked the questions to which he already knew the answers.

•

Further south, in Cordova, the summer sun was scorching down and the occupants of the villa were doing everything, within their limited means, to escape the heat. Generations of their people might have lived here, in Hispania, but their northern blood could never adapt itself to these temperatures, which was why most of the Visigothic nobles preferred living further north. It had never occurred to them to repair the original wooden shutters covering the windows. Now all that was left were sad fragments of splintered timber, bleached by the sun and useless at keeping the blistering rays from entering the building. The marble mosaic floors, which, with shuttered windows, were designed to keep the rooms cool, were now so hot that it was impossible to venture on them bare-footed. The intervening years had done little to halt the building's decay or the temper of its inhabitants. Riccolo had descended into her own fanciful world in which her Theudefrid, crowned and stately, roamed the peeling corridors, visiting her nightly to plant his ghostly seed into her shrivelled womb. It was unlikely that she even knew of his fate, the apparition being altogether more pleasant to her than the reality had been. She, who was so thrilled at Roderick's birth, did not even recognise her son any more, while he had long since realised the futility of his mother's company.

•

Roderick, against all the laws of probability, had not grown up quite as wild and undisciplined as might have been imagined. Theudefrid, on his infrequent visits to Cordova, had seen to it that the boy had, at least, a good education. The tutors employed for the task had been carefully chosen to instil the basics of leadership, a self-awareness of his nobility and a destiny due to his status. On hearing of his father's death, revenge was an automatic response but not one in which sentiment or emotion played any part. He remained under the tutelage designed for him but now his questions were different; less concerned with the academic niceties of culture than with the practical considerations of prevailing politics and the manipulation of power blocs. Although now twenty-two years old, he had few friends of his own age and background with whom to pass his time. Cordova was too provincial and not the most fertile of regions for prospective allies but he was left in no doubt that any move to the heart of Hispania would, at this time, be too dangerous for him. Accordingly, he had plenty of time to ferment his ambitions and he became known as a serious boy, proud to a fault and not easily given to laughter. If he possessed an obvious weakness, it was for members of the opposite sex. Puberty, for him had produced an explosion of hormonal activity and the women of Cordova, whatever their colour, creed or quality, soon learned to keep clear of dark corners and lonely courtyards when, the then, fifteen year old Master Roderick was on the prowl. His mentors paid little heed to these goings-on since young Visigoth nobles were expected to take advantage of girls of lesser breeding, as, indeed, most of Roderick's victims were, and it was assumed that he would outgrow this predilection. He didn't, and nobody quite realised the extent to which his future was to be determined by it.

Chapter 7

702AD

Camp fires flickered over the area of the encampment, the evening meal was eaten and sentries posted, although the latter was more a case of practice than necessity. They were camped in the foothills of the Rif, and the night air was just starting to chill so woollen blankets were adjusted to shoulders. Muted conversations of one hundred and one men, accompanied by the comforting snuffling and snorting of their tethered mounts, made a counterpoint to the chirruping and buzzing of the insects of the night. All in all, the relaxed, harmonious scene of a troop of fighting men with no one to fight, for this was their first night from Tangier and they were camped above the small village of Tetouan and the sea.

•

Tariq, slightly apart from the rest of his troops, sat watching the reflection of the moon bobbing about on the quiet waters beneath him. There was a movement nearby, a polite warning cough and he looked up to see Tala standing beside him. Tariq motioned him closer and moved over on his sleeping blanket for Tala to join him. For a moment neither said anything but sat looking down on the tranquil scene below them. An owl hooted and they both looked up at the sound. Tariq spoke first.

"We seem to live in a world where something is always hunting something else and I suppose we are no exception."

Tala's rejoinder was succinct.

"Surely that is the natural order of things?"

Tariq looked at him, thought for a second, then said, "I think, or perhaps hope is the better word, that is one thing which sets us apart from the rest of the animal world."

Tala said, but not unkindly and without any sign of rancour, "There is no stopping you is there? Shepherd, slave, soldier, commander and now a philosopher. Me, I'm just a plain soldier. I know nothing else and I'm not sure that I want to but then, that's probably why you're in charge and I'm not.

That said, I know why you didn't want to take the sea route and I concede you might have a point there, but why this route? You realise that we've gone out of our way to travel via Septem and the coast to get here? We could have saved a couple of hours by riding in a straight line."

"Of course I realise that," replied Tariq. "I have my reasons for wanting to get a closer look at Septem, but if you were to ask me what they were I'm not sure I could tell you. It's a feeling I have, that's all. A feeling that somehow that city is very important to us, even though it isn't ours."

Tala shrugged. "Feelings! That's something else I don't understand, but if you tell me Septem is important to us then I suppose it is. Akeem's never tired of telling me how you are always right. Anyway, I just wanted to clear up that little point. I'll see you in the morning." A pause "Sir."

Tariq grinned at him in gloom. "Get away to your bed Tala, we ride at first light."

A friendly wave to each other and Tala walked away. Tariq stood up, turned and looked back towards Septem, in much the same way that Musa had a few days previously.

·

The hazy light of early morning was witness to the usual comings and goings and the soft snickering of the horses recognising their riders who had come to prepare them for the day's ride. The more pious of the troops kneeling, heads bowed towards the sun which was barely perceptible above the distant horizon. Tariq had already been awake for some time in order to check his direction of travel from the still-visible stars. It was one of the disciplines he had most enjoyed from his military training. As a country boy with generations of nomadic blood in his veins, navigation by the night sky was almost second nature, but his instructors were able to re-awaken this dormant interest by employing more sophisticated and detailed star-mapping techniques. This science, together with other mathematical theories, had been discovered some two hundred years previously, when Islam had conquered Egypt but, more particularly Alexandria, the repository of a huge library of ancient Greek texts, including the original writings of philosophers like Pythagoras. Unlike the Western Christian cultures, who regarded these texts as irreligious and pagan, the Islamic attitude towards learning, of whatever origin, was open and welcoming and not only to scholars. New ideas were widely disseminated at all levels of society, and there was no happier recipient of these ideas than Tariq ibn Ziyad.

Tariq looked up to see Akeem walking towards him, leading both their horses. They greeted each other, Tariq asking if all was well with the men.

He had given Akeem the responsibility of making periodic rounds to assess the general mood and morale. Akeem and Tala knew the soldiers much better than Tariq and, although as commander, Tariq was always accessible to anyone who might wish to approach him, he thought some distance was necessary to his authority.

"All's well. Just the usual questions like how long this expedition is likely to take and how many of these dissidents are they going to have to fight."

Tariq squinted at the new-risen sun.

"We should be there in about five days. We're not in any rush so five days more steady riding should do it. There's no need to tell them this yet but there won't be any fighting. At least, I hope there won't."

"No fighting!" Akeem looked and sounded quite indignant. "What's the point of all this then?" He waved an arm around the camp, now packed up with all his men mounted and ready to move. Tariq gave him a conciliatory pat on the shoulder.

"You'll find out soon enough. Send Tala to me will you. I want him to ride with me. You take twenty men and bring up the rear, keeping a reasonable distance between us. Not for a moment do I expect any trouble, but should it creep up behind us, you can deal with it."

Akeem seemed cheered by that prospect and led his horse off to find Tala.

•

Once they had moved off, Tala trotted up to join Tariq at the head of the depleted column, while the dust, raised by the hooves of Akeem's detachment, was just visible to their rear. They rode in silence for a while, taking in the countryside as it unfolded before them. Rugged mountains rose steeply to the right of them, while Tariq's route through the foothills was fertile and green which, as the two colours converged in the distance, contrasted picturesquely with the blue of the sea to their left. At Tala's pre-arranged signal the Berbers would walk, trot and canter in turn, stopping only for water until their evening encampment. At this rate, Tariq was confident that his force would have sight of Pomaria within six, if not the five, days that he had originally forecast. As they rode, he and Tala talked companionably of their early memories as village boys until Tala, quite casually, said, "You don't foresee any action apparently? That being so, what on earth are we doing, riding all this way with a hundred armed men together with all their support equipment? Bit excessive for a prolonged exercise isn't it? Does the Emir know what's in your mind?"

Tariq just gave him a grin and said nothing. They cantered on for a while then, as their mounts resumed walking pace, he turned to Tala and said, "I suspect Lord Musa has guessed my intentions but no, he gave me complete freedom to make whatever tactical decisions I thought necessary." Tariq turned again in the saddle and gave Tala another grin.

"I have to admit, though, that I wasn't entirely honest with him. In fact I lied."

Tala gave an involuntary pull on the reins, causing his horse to swerve. He quickly pulled it back into line and said, "You did what?"

Tariq thought for a moment and went on, "I was asked if I knew Kusaila, the man who led the dissident tribe that we're going to…"

Tala broke in, "Yes, yes, I know all about Kusaila. Do you mean to tell me that you do know him? That being the case, why not tell the Emir that you do?"

Tariq answered, "Because, my dear Tala, representing Kusaila as a complete stranger makes this appear much more difficult than it is going to be. I intend this mission to be a success but I don't want it to look too easy. There's no merit in commanding a walkover. Besides, Musa wasn't totally honest with me."

Tala suppressed a snort of laughter.

"The Emir can afford to do what he likes, you can't. Anyway, as a matter of interest, in what way did he mislead you?"

Tariq's eyes narrowed as he said, "He claimed not to know who I was when I reported to him, just before he handed me this command. He recognised me as soon as he saw me but pretended not to."

Tala considered this, shook his head and responded neutrally.

"I daresay he had his reasons."

Tariq's response was equally bland.

"So have I. For what I did Tala, so have I."

They continued to ride in silence for some time before Tala, unable to contain his curiosity any longer, asked, "Well, what are your plans then, or do you want to keep them a secret?" He gave Tariq a long look then continued, "You can trust me, you know that don't you? I don't give a damn that you've leapfrogged my seniority because I knew, the moment I laid eyes on you, that you were destined to achieve things that I could never aspire to. The Emir knows it too, believe me."

Tariq, turning to meet his gaze, said, "If I didn't trust you, I would hardly have confided in you, would I? Neither would I have risked asking for you to come in the first place. Of course I trust you. So, you'd like me to share my ideas with you? Very well, this is what I intend we should do…"

•

His calculations had been nearly accurate. By the time he halted his column, the river which divided Pomaria was in sight. The river, but not the town. Tariq had brought them to a place up-stream of Pomaria from where their approach could not be seen. They were a day later than intended but the fault lay not in Tariq's mathematics but the time taken to find an encampment sufficiently isolated from any known settlement in the area. This they had now found. A depression in the foothills of the Atlas where, so far as any of the scouting parties could discover, there was no sign of human habitation or even recent occupation by a nomadic source. Neither Tala nor Akeem or, indeed, the rest of the troop, could understand this apparent need for concealment. They were, almost certainly, the only militarily trained body in the region so why hide away when their mission was one of subjugation and their force the instrument with which to accomplish it? Tariq continued to keep his counsel, except to inform Akeem that, this night, he intended riding down to his old village, a journey of perhaps three hours, and he wished Akeem to accompany him. Tala, who was present at the time, started to say something but Tariq shook his head and ordered him to take over command while he was absent. He didn't expect to be long and would, almost certainly, be back to resume command by morning. The thought of having his men restored to his control seemed to cheer up Tala somewhat and he set about organising the encampment with his usual cheerful efficiency. He was always very popular with the men, very strict, as he had shown years ago in Pomaria, but always just. Tariq and Akeem were now mounted and ready to leave but Tariq trotted over to Tala for a final word. He bent down from the saddle to make sure he was heard by nobody except Tala.

"Whatever happens Tala, I don't want any fighting, not under any circumstances."

Tala gave one of his exasperated snorts.

"Oh yes, and what if we're attacked? Do we just lie down and let them walk all over us?"

Tariq gave him an amused, quizzical look.

"Come on Tala, you and I both know there isn't anything within a day's ride of here that'll take on a force this size. All right, say some small band of idiots appear from nowhere and cause trouble, just restrain them. I don't want any killing except as a very last resort but, believe me, you are going to find it so quiet, I shall be very surprised if your sentries manage to stay awake all night. Right, we are on our way now, we'll be back before dawn."

That said, he beckoned to Akeem and the two of them trotted through the lines and down the hill in the direction of Pomaria. As soon as they had left their colleagues, Akeem said to Tariq, "I know where we are heading for, Sir, what I don't know is why."

Tariq's reply was to the point.

"We, Akeem, are going to visit my grandfather, Izem, another lion slayer."

•

As they reined in their horses on the outskirts of Tariq's old village, he asked Akeem if he could remember the first time they had met here. Akeem said that he did indeed and that memory was particularly painful. After that encounter, it was some time before he could sit astride a horse again without feeling discomfort. Tariq said nothing but gestured that they should dismount and quietly lead their horses through the ramshackle collection of poor dwellings which he had once been happy to call home.

It now being late, there was no sign of life as they stopped outside his grandfather's hut. He very quietly motioned Akeem to lead the horses around the side of the hut and to stay with them while he announced himself. He gently knocked on the door which was immediately opened by his grandfather, surprisingly untouched by the years since they had last been together. They embraced and Tariq could sense, rather than feel, the old man's tears on his cheeks. They spoke in whispers and as soon as they had assured each other of their mutual good health, Izem murmured, "He's here, waiting."

Tariq signified his pleasure at the news and followed the old man into the dark interior of the hut. Inside, he could just make out two more figures, standing ready to greet him.

One of them he recognised immediately and, even if he hadn't, the bear hug with which he was enveloped left him in no doubt that Idir too, was pleased to see him. The other hung back in the shadows until Izem brought him forward.

"Tariq, this is Kusaila. He has been my honoured guest since this morning, when Idir brought him to me at your request."

They formally greeted each other, then Tariq turned to Idir.

"Thank you my friend. I wasn't sure if you would receive my messenger after what happened the last time we met. It seems so long ago now." Tariq turned back to Kusaila.

"I am grateful to you for agreeing to meet me. We haven't met before but I think we can be of some service to each other and our people."

Kusaila bowed respectfully and said, "You are aware that I am of the true faith but my erstwhile followers, basically all good men and women, have had their traditions and their purses abused by those who practise it. We are a remote community and change does not come easily. I have tried to explain to them that they cannot remain isolated for ever but I need a stronger voice, and probably a younger one, to persuade them to commit to the word of the

Prophet and join the rest of their brothers. That is why I responded to your call. Perhaps you are the one they will listen to."

Tariq, looking at Kusaila, saw a man of similar years to his grandfather but one whose years had not coped well with the responsibilities of leadership and challenged authority. Tariq smiled at him, gently took him by the arm and led him outside, where Akeem was patiently standing with their horses, loose reined and cropping the meagre foliage at their feet.

"Akeem," called Tariq, "I want you to meet Kusaila."

Akeem's head shot up.

"Kusaila! Isn't that the rebellious bastard that we've come to sort out? What's he doing here?"

Kusaila's head also shot up and, under the bright moon, they could both see his eyes flashing dangerously at the insult. Tariq, restraining the arm that was moving towards his knife, was quick to defuse the moment.

"I asked to meet him here, Akeem. He is here as a guest in my grandfather's house and we will accord him the respect his position deserves."

Akeem frowned in puzzlement.

"But how did you arrange all this, we've only just got here ourselves?"

Tariq answered, "I sent an emissary to arrange it with Idir, you remember Idir?"

Akeem, still frowning said, "Course I remember, big man, father of whatsername. Made a big fuss when we took her with us. Anyway, what's all this about an emissary? What emissary and how did he get here before we did?"

Tariq had to smile at Akeem's obvious puzzlement and bade Kusaila excuse him while he explained his actions to Akeem.

"Menna, Idir's daughter was my emissary. I knew that she was coming here to select leathers suitable for Lord Musa's new wardrobe. She was very excited at the thought of seeing her family again so she told me about it..."

Akeem moved out of the way of one of the horses as it threatened to tread on his feet, and interrupted Tariq, "Hang on a minute, I saw her just as we were leaving headquarters, she didn't look very happy then and, anyway, how did she get here before us?"

Tariq again apologised to Kusaila, who bowed courteously as Akeem once more claimed Tariq's attention. Tariq introduced him to the old man.

"My friend, Akeem. He is forever asking questions," and then, to Akeem, "She arrived here before us because she came by sea. As for her tears," he shrugged, "there I cannot help you."

Akeem, having nodded his existence to Kusaila, turned back to Tariq and asked him if Tariq had told Menna that there would not be time for him and Menna to meet in their old haunts.

Tariq frowned, thought for a moment then said that, yes, he probably had said something of the sort. Akeem then turned to Kusaila.

"You see, Sir, my master is one of the cleverest men in Tangier but some things just don't seem to…"

Tariq cut him off short.

"Yes, all right. We don't have much time." He turned to Kusaila.

"I understand that you and your people still practise a nomadic lifestyle?"

Kusaila nodded a covered head.

"A few, like me, have settled and follow the teaching of the Prophet but most are still intent on preserving their old lifestyle and their even older beliefs."

The old man thought for a moment before continuing. He did not flinch from Tariq's intense gaze and Tariq instinctively liked and trusted him. He was aware, though, that Kusaila had probably forfeited his authority over his people by embracing Islam, a fact that Kusaila went on to acknowledge.

"You see," Kusaila said, "those who enforced the new code did so unjustly, my people were treated with contempt and taxed unfairly. You are one of us, a Berber albeit from a different tribe, one that has been settled for some time. We are still traditionally nomadic. If we feel oppressed, we either fight or disappear into the desert. Fighting is out of the question, the forces of Islam are too vast so the majority of our people chose the second option. Old as I am, I have long sensed the inevitability of these changes but, thus far, have been unable to persuade most of my people that conversion is the only way forward. Perhaps you will be more successful." He bowed again at the end of his little speech but Tariq waved aside the courtesy, he needed to know more.

"How many of your people are there, where are they and how long will it take us to get to them?"

Kusaila looked from Tariq, to Akeem and back to Tariq, before answering.

"When I received your message, I sent out a call for as many as could be reached to assemble in a small plain before the foothills and a day's ride from here. I don't have exact numbers but I would estimate some two hundred men. Their families would have remained in their encampments."

Akeem let out a low whistle, dropping the horses' reins which he trapped with his foot, while he rubbed his freed hands together.

"Two hundred! That'll give us something to play with."

Tariq frowned at him. "No fighting, we talk. You and me, we talk to them."

Akeem appeared to be momentarily deprived of comment, pithy or otherwise. Tariq continued, "I am going to take my farewells from my grandfather and Idir. We will then re-join our troops and I'll explain. So, get mounted and wait for me, both of you. I will not be long."

Tariq disappeared back into his grandfather's dwelling and, true to his word, said his goodbyes and, within minutes, was back in his saddle riding with Akeem back the way they had come. Akeem led the way while Tariq bombarded Kusaila with questions as they rode a few paces behind. By this time the moon was high and Izem and Idir watched them until they were out of sight. Idir turned to Izem and said, "Don't suppose you ever thought you'd live to see young Tariq turn out to be as important and grand as he has?"

Izem chuckled. "Important,yes. Grand, never and I wouldn't expect anything else."

•

The three riders reached their camp well before dawn. After being challenged by a yawning sentry, they handed over their horses to be looked after while Tariq ordered his companions to get a couple of hours' rest before they advanced in the direction of Kusaila's tribe. As Tariq explained, "It'll be useful to get there as soon as possible, do what we have to do and then we can spend the evening relaxing in their company."

Akeem retorted that "relaxing in their company" was a really funny way of saying "getting your throat cut" but he supposed that Tariq knew what he was doing.

As soon as morning prayers had been made and breakfast taken, the order was given for them to move out. Surprisingly, Kusaila was leading them back in the direction from which they had first travelled, that is towards Morocco but they then turned a few degrees to the north. They rode throughout the morning, stopped when the sun was at its zenith for water and to rest the horses, set off again and, by mid-afternoon, Kusaila held up a hand to stop the column. He told Tariq that they were almost at their destination and that their arrival would already have been spotted by scouts. Tariq beckoned for Tala to join him and they conferred quietly out of earshot from the rest of the company. He then rejoined Kusaila and Akeem and told them to ride forward, with him, to the encampment. Akeem, turning in his saddle, noticed that the rest of the force was stationary, with Tala at its head. Tala gave a perfunctory wave and started to lead the body of soldiers over a large hill on his right. Akeem watched them until they were out of sight. He started to ask what, to him, were some fairly obvious questions but Tariq waved him into silence as three formidable Berber warriors, mounted on quality camels, loped out of the sun-scorching haze towards them.

Chapter 8

The Rif

The three riders stopped and waited for the strangers to come to meet them. As they approached, Kusaila lifted a hand in greeting while Tariq gently indicated to Akeem that the two of them leave their hands in sight, resting on their horses' necks and well away from the hilts of their swords. One at a time the camel-mounted tribesmen stopped next to Kusaila, bent down from their taller mounts and solemnly accepted a blessing from the old man's hand. Kusaila turned to his two companions and said, with a degree of pride, "My sons." The small group then continued towards the encampment, and the noises indicating intense social activity ceased immediately on their entry.

•

Having already made inquiries of Kusaila, Tariq was not surprised at the sight which greeted him but it did seem an unusual choice for nomadic tribesmen.

In fact the camels, of which there were fewer than he imagined, looked slightly bemused as if they found themselves in an unaccustomed environment. The encampment had been struck in a natural saucer. To the south were gently sloping hills, heavily wooded in parts. The hills folded around them on two sides while, to the west, they gave way to a much more rocky and mountainous backdrop. It was in this direction that Tariq cast a wary eye, hoping that Kusaila's description had been accurate enough for his plan to work as he intended.

They continued into the centre of the camp and Tariq wondered how their Berber tents had been constructed without the usual desert thorns with which to pin the canopies together. It did not take him long to realise that this tribe was out of its natural habitat and had been forced to settle for it rather than somewhere more in keeping with their traditional landscape. It also did not take him long to appreciate that this fact would work in his favour.

•

Kusaila was greeted kindly by his tribe who also extended a more cautious welcome to the two strangers. Whatever the differences between him and his people, Kusaila was still respected by them, and his sons, in particular, seemed anxious that the proper courtesies be extended towards their father's guests. So much so, in fact, that even Akeem relaxed his guarded manner and returned the greeting with a friendly nod while, at the same time, checking on Tariq to follow whatever move might be expected of him next. He just wished that he'd been able to share in his master's thinking. It was all very well indulging in these social pleasantries but they had come here to achieve something, not just to chat to Berber tribesmen; they could have done that back in Tangier. Eventually, the important introductions seemed to have been concluded, and Tariq started to manoeuvre the group towards a small hillock, which provided a natural platform on the eastern edge of the encampment. Once there, he conferred with Kusaila, who nodded in agreement. Kusaila's sons stayed at the foot of the platform while Kusaila, together with Tariq and Akeem, climbed to the top of the mound where they found themselves confronting an audience of a couple of hundred. Tariq scanned the crowd carefully and tried to sense what it was that didn't feel quite right. They were all male, of various ages, the size of their beards giving some indication of the age of the men who sported them. They seemed friendly enough but there was something that he couldn't quite identify. It was more an atmosphere of unease, of discomfort. He didn't feel threatened. It had more to do with their feelings than with his. Then it struck him. The camels! They were like their camels, uncomfortable in this region of rocks and trees, hills and mountains. Kusaila raised his arms for quiet and, as soon as he was granted it, he started to speak. His voice, surprising for a man of his years, was strong enough to be heard clearly by all.

He started by saying that although, for reasons of faith, he had elected to follow a different path from his people, he still regarded them as his children and they should always be aware that he had their best interests at heart. This elicited a murmur of approval, led by his sons who, in his absence, had obviously assumed leadership of the tribe. (Tariq made a mental note of this). Kusaila went on to say that their guests were emissaries of the Emir in far off Tangier but they were not here to threaten or to impose any kind of punishment for the tribe's rejection of the Faith. They were here to talk and to reason with them. On the mention of the words "threaten" and "punishment," Tariq tapped the shoulder of Kusaila's eldest son and, with a broad smile, indicated Akeem and himself, as much as to say, just how were two men, against so many, in the position to threaten or punish. For a moment there was silence and Kusaila clasped his hands, as if in prayer. Then his son gave a chuckle which was echoed by the second and finally by the third, by which time the chuckle had developed into full blown guffaws of laughter which spread like fire through the entire camp. So much so that Kusaila's introduction was suspended for several moments. When the crowd had settled down again, he continued, going on to say that he had personally met with Tariq's grandfather and could assure everybody that Tariq was one of their own, a Berber, albeit a settled one, whose background was not so very different from theirs. Tariq, meanwhile was keeping an eye on the sun. If the old man went on for much longer, his own oration would have to be curtailed, and it was important that he had time to say what he felt was necessary. He need not have worried for Kusaila finally concluded his speech, closing it by formally embracing Tariq before presenting him to the assembly. Sensing a need for more solidarity, Akeem moved closer to Tariq and it was obvious, to those close enough, that it would take a brave man, if not a strong one, to prise Akeem's hand from the hilt of his sword.

●

Tariq bowed to Kusaila, thanked him for his words and took another glance at the sky. If he timed his speech correctly everything, including the sun, should be in place. The eyes of Kusaila's three sons were fixed intently on him and it was important that he make contact with them, as well as the wider audience. He started by thanking Kusaila for his introduction, then continued to make the points that would constitute the first, if not the most important, public address of his life.

"It is true that I am one of you and it has not been that long since I was tending my grandfather's flock. I was then taken as a slave by the master I now serve. This man standing beside me, Akeem, another Berber just like us, was my captor. Now I stand beside him as his captain. You see, although I might have been taken as a slave I was not taken into slavery. As Akeem will testify, I volunteered to accompany my captors and do you know why I did that? I went willingly because I knew there was more to learn, to experience and to enjoy, yes enjoy, beyond the narrow boundaries that confined me. As you can see, my hopes, my expectations were justified and not for one moment do I regret the day those soldiers appeared in my village. This man," again he indicated Akeem, "This man, as I have told you, was one of those soldiers. Ask him, he will tell you that although I was not unhappy being what I was then, I am much happier being what I am now."

He paused for a moment for his words to sink in, then continued,

"Our world is changing and, while you might wish to continue fighting your local tribal wars, you cannot fight change. Change is inevitable and it is how you adapt to change that will define your future and that of your children.

Now, I understand totally your reluctance to change. You have your traditions and they represent continuity to you and there is, in your minds, safety in continuity. When the new authority of the Caliphate attempted to convert you, they treated you as inferior beings, they taxed you disproportionately because of what you are. Of course you rebelled against this injustice and, of course, I can understand why you did so, but things are different now. Attitudes have changed along with everything else. Our people are no longer considered inferior, the taxation laws have been re-written. Again, changes. The world has changed.

Your world has changed but you have not."

Again a pause as he allowed his first real point to be absorbed by a crowd who were beginning to sense a change in the rhetoric. He went on, "If you are honest with me, your traditions, the occasional raids on neighbouring tribes, the constant movement of communities are no longer viable. You are rapidly becoming a minority people and the regions in which you travelled, fought over and traded with have become depopulated. Those who now believe in the true Faith are building towns and cities and becoming one people from whom you are excluding yourselves."

He waved an arm to encompass the area in which the crowd was gathered.

"This is not your natural environment, is it? Admit it, you are not happy here. You feel uncomfortable because there are too many trees, too many rocks, too many mountains.

Why not join the rest of your race and once more feel part of a community that is empowered by its strength and its numbers? This time, I promise, you will not be looked down upon, victimised or persecuted because now it is different. Now we have a new Caliphate, new laws and a new inclusive society of which *you* will be a part."

He drew breath and looked up. The time had come. He spread his arms wide, motioning the crowd to turn away from him and towards the west. The crowd turned and, as one, audibly gasped. The vivid sunset provided a backdrop of dramatic intensity for Tariq's small army. Only it didn't look that small. Tala, as instructed, had silently positioned each mounted soldier at different levels on the foothills, some half hidden behind outcrops and some standing slightly forward on each wing. They were motionless and with the bright red glow reflecting from armour and weapons, they looked like warriors from another world.

"That is the army of the true Faith."

Tariq's voice now rang out with authority and intensity.

"They have come, not to fight with you, but to embrace you, to talk with you and, above all, to welcome you to our sacred cause. I now call upon you to welcome them for they are your future and the guarantee of your survival."

One by one, with Tala at their head, the men now dismounted and slowly walked their horses towards the camp.

•

Akeem, knuckles whitening as he gripped his sword even more tightly, muttered, "This could be interesting!" while Tariq held his breath. Seconds later he felt Kusaila's sinewy arms around him, then Kusaila's sons, as, in turn, they clasped their father's hands before grasping those of Tariq. They then turned their attentions to Akeem who couldn't quite make up his mind to release the hilt of his precious sword but found himself literally disarmed by the eldest son who wrenched free the reluctant sword hand and shook it enthusiastically. Tariq's men, having tethered their horses on entering the arena, ostentatiously laid down their weapons before proceeding into the heart of the encampment, greeting individuals as they went, engaging them in conversation, answering their questions and, in their own way, confirming everything of which their commander had spoken. The noise of excited voices rang around the hills and continued as the sun disappeared behind the ridge and the fires were lit. It carried on during supper and on into the night.

As soon as Tariq could separate himself from the throng, for it seemed the whole world wanted to shake his hand, he sought out Tala and warmly thanked him for his part in the plan. Tala shrugged in his usual self-deprecatory manner and replied that mounting his tableau had probably been one of the most difficult assignments in his military career, but it would not have been possible if Tariq's eloquence had not held the attention of his audience. It only needed one tribesman to look over his shoulder at the wrong time and the whole effect would have been destroyed. This time it was Tariq's turn to shrug but he was secretly pleased when Tala added, "Well done Sir, that was masterly." It had been a long two days and both men were tired. However sleep was to be denied them for some time yet, for they and Akeem were being approached from all sides by tribesmen wishing to join their ranks. Eventually Tariq, with the help of Kusaila and his sons, made it known that no married man, no man shortly to be married and no widower with dependent children would be able to accompany the force back to Tangier. Even then, not all the remaining men were chosen, since Kusaila decided that some of marriageable age and some of the older men be exempted, thus leaving a reasonable number to ensure the community was still a viable unit. He almost insisted, though, that two of his sons return with Tariq, the other being married, and he promised that instruction in the true Faith would be his first priority.

Tariq had always known that, powerful as he was, Musa was still subject to the authority of the Umayyad Caliphate in Damascus for whom Islamisation was a central tenet. When debriefed therefore, Kusaila's promise was the first item on his report and Musa was, accordingly, pleased to hear of the tribal conversion. When he asked for details of a military nature, casualties, and so on, Tariq, respectfully invited him on to the balcony. From there, Tariq pointed out not only his hundred men, all intact and headed by an immaculate Tala, sword raised in a salute to the supreme commander of the Umayyad army, but fifty more Berber tribesman being given rudimentary drill exercises by a somewhat less immaculate Akeem. This involved much shouting on the part of Akeem and some confusion on the part of the virgin soldiers. Musa shook his head and smiled.

"You have done well, Tariq. I admit that you have exceeded my expectations. Your tactical competence was never in doubt but to combine it with a skill in diplomacy is a rare combination and one, I like to think, I possess myself. Possibly time for you to meet our fascinating neighbour, don't you think?"

Chapter 9

Septem, 708AD

Count Julian, Exarch of Septem and one of the last Byzantine Christians to have any power in Ifriquya, was by no means unhappy in his cultural isolation. Quite the opposite. On this bright May morning he was seated under a vine covered terrace overlooking the sea and the great rocky outcrop which stood between him and the coast of Hispania Ulterior. Beside him stood a servant, peeling a succulent orange with a fine silver blade and opposite, her own servant performing the same service, sat a beautiful girl of some sixteen summers. Having eaten the last segment of orange, Julian wiped his hands carefully, for he was a fastidious man, on a fine Egyptian linen napkin and looked fondly on his daughter, Florinda, who was still eating. He smiled, for orange juice was dripping down her chin and her maidservant was continually swooping in with a dampened towel to mop up her face and her clothing. He chuckled and she, a mouthful of extremely juicy orange, attempted a smile in return without dribbling any. She failed and he laughed again and said, "Do you realise, my dear, you have been feasting off oranges since you were weaned from your mother's breast and you still haven't mastered the art." He added, "It costs me a fortune in clothes."

With as much dignity as she could muster, which, it has to be said, was very little, she took the towel from her attendant and wiped her own face with it before smiling back at him and saying, "Perhaps, Sir, when I am as old as you I might have had practice enough to consume an orange with your expertise." She smiled at him again, a fond, laughing smile and Julian could not help thinking, for the umpteenth time, how he was going to miss her when the time came for her to leave him for the more sophisticated education she was expected to receive at the court in Toletum. Not yet though. Not for another twelve months perhaps. For the moment he had to concentrate on his duties here in Septem. Duties for which he was particularly suited.

•

Julian was quite aware that this tiny Christian outpost was becoming more and more isolated by the ever acquisitive forces of the Umayyad Caliphate. Early in his career an attempt had been made on Septem but it was half-hearted, probably because it was not thought worth the trouble, and Julian's Christianised Berbers, well trained in the old Roman tradition, had little problem in repelling the attack. Since then, and the appearance of Musa ibn Nusayr, there had existed an easy relationship between these close neighbours of differing beliefs. They worked well together, not that they spent a great deal of time in each other's company, for while their administrative duties left little time for socialising, each could see the advantage of fostering a genuinely friendly association. That way, although neither would dream of divulging information of a tactical nature, each could see the benefits accruing from the exchanges of information, and their interest in each other's cultures was not assumed. Both men were well educated and intellectually drawn to the other's experiences and lifestyle. Musa, on his part, was fascinated by Julian's stories of court politics in Toletum, the history of Imperial Rome and its current legacy down to the last remnants of the Byzantine Empire, while Julian was eager for explanations for the explosive rise of Islam in Ifriquya.

•

Mid-morning now and, despite the cover of vine leaves, the day was heating up and Julian beckoned to his slave to fetch the huge ostrich fans resting in the corner and they, together with the soft breeze blowing from sea, kept them comfortable while they talked.

Florinda read his thoughts, not difficult because they spent so much time in each other's company and this was a subject that was frequently raised between them, the subject of her move to Toletum. She was impatient for a change in her lifestyle. Much as she loved her father, they actually doted on each other, there was little to occupy her socially within the restricted, fortified boundaries of Septem. From time to time, Julian had taken her with him when he visited the region of Hispania, just visible beyond the huge rock which served as a staging post between the continents. Trade was one of the things that made Septem, tiny as it was, a wealthy outpost of the Visigothic Empire which, in turn, made Julian a very wealthy and influential man. While, for Florinda, these excursions represented a welcome change from Septem which offered little opportunity for associating with others of her age and station, what she really wanted more than anything was to visit the fabled court of Toletum. Her father had promised her, since she was a small girl, that a position of handmaiden to the consort of the ruling king would be hers as soon as she was old enough. Florinda, for years now, had protested that she was ready and her father had argued that the time was not yet ripe. He now repeated his objection and, before she could say anything, he went on, "Believe me, my angel, the time is not right. There is much unrest in Toletum and until things calm down and there is a settled succession to the throne, you are much safer here. I am not prepared to take any risks with you because, as you know only too well, since the death of your mother you are all that really matters to me."

She was about to make the expected protest but changed her mind, jumped up, nearly knocked over the servant, a small woman already having trouble managing a fan as big as she was, ran around to her father and kissed him on the cheek.

"I know I am but you will promise me that I can go soon, before I am too old to enjoy it? Even if you took me with you, just for a visit, I would love that."

Julian turned in his chair and took both her hands.

"You would not want to go with me because what I do there is exactly the same as I do when I trade locally. I take Berber horses, hunting hawks and I bring back cultivated crops that I sell to the Umayyad. You would be just as bored. When you go, it will be because I think that you and Toletum society are ready for each other." He forestalled the inevitable pout. "But, I do have one piece of news for you. Your friend Musa ibn Nusayr is coming to visit us and he is not coming alone."

Florinda twirled away from him, clapping her hands.

"I love it when Musa comes to see us. He makes me laugh and tells me stories of far- away places that sound even more exciting than Toletum. Who is it that is coming with him?"

Julian waited until she had moved back to her chair and, chin resting in her hands, eyes fixed firmly on his, was eagerly awaiting his reply.

"Well," he paused for a tantalising moment, "I don't know exactly who he is but he must be someone quite special because, up until a few years ago, as I understand it, he was a slave, and now it appears he is not only one of Musa's most trusted military commanders but could even be destined for the Governorship of Tangier."

He waved an arm in the vague direction of the Umayyad's northernmost citadel.

"Mind you," he went on thoughtfully, "Musa having now assumed control of all Ifriquya, he isn't going to have the time to devote himself to running a single settlement, important as it is. Still, I shall be interested to meet this young man of his. Islam, religion aside, is fast becoming a multi-disciplined culture and has not been slow to adapt to the sciences and philosophies of our own ancestors." He gave a rueful smile, "I only wish that I could say the same of our people now, the descendants of that particularly golden age."

Catching sight of Florinda's frown he gave a self-deprecating laugh and apologised to her for becoming serious, as it was clear that she was more interested in people than in what they represented.

"But Papa, is he handsome, is he married? I mean, how romantic. From slave to Provincial Governor in a few years. That is incredible. When are they coming, is it soon?"

The curtain to the terrace was disturbed by the entrance of an earnest looking young man, Julian's secretary and hopeless admirer of Florinda. She, apart from the social disparity of their positions, found his devotion to her and to his duties extremely boring. Catching sight of her, he blushed as he inevitably did in her company, hurried over to Julian, bent down and whispered in his ear. Julian nodded and the young man made an unfortunate exit, tripping over the lowered ostrich fan as he rushed out. Florinda giggled and her father waved an admonitory finger at her.

"My dear, you must learn to show respect to those who are not of your station. Maysara is an extremely competent secretary and, although a Berber, he is of our faith and the recipient of an excellent education. Better, I might add, than yours so you mustn't make him feel uncomfortable. You have always pleased me by being politeness itself to Musa and the other emissaries of the Umayyad. Quite the little diplomat, in fact and I would urge you to extend the same courtesies to our own servants."

This was not the first time that Julian had delivered this lecture to his daughter and he assumed it probably wouldn't be the last because, as if he hadn't spoken, and bursting with impatience, she said, "Did he come in to tell you that Musa and this other man are here?"

"No." Her father replied. "They are not here."

"Well, what did he… then when are they coming?"

Julian said nothing but his mouth twitched as he watched Florinda frowning and tapping her fingers impatiently on the table top. Then she gave a resigned shrug and pretended to study the tracery of the vine over their heads. Deciding that she had been left in suspense for long enough, he leaned over the table and said quietly, "They will be here tomorrow and before you ask, yes, they will stay as our guests until the morning after and, yes again, before you ask, you will be invited to join us at our feast."

He smiled indulgently as she gave a shriek of delight, jumped to her feet and, in her haste, again bumped into her servant. She was about to run around to her father when, seeing the disapproval in his face, she stopped, turned and made a gracious apology for her clumsiness, gave the maid, of whom she was genuinely fond, a quick peck on the cheek and continued to her father and flung her arms around his neck. Julian disentangled himself from her embrace and steered her to the seat beside him. When he spoke it was as much to himself as sharing his thoughts with his daughter.

"I imagine this is nothing more than a social visit with both Musa and myself having a gentle probe as to intentions on both our sides but the fact that he is bringing Tariq ibn Ziyad with him on this occasion might also indicate that Tariq is going to be my main intermediary with the Umayyad in the future."

Florinda clapped her hands gleefully.

"That would be wonderful! I mean," she went on, "I like Musa, of course I do, he is a most interesting man but he is getting on a bit. Having someone young like this Tariq ibn... whatever his name is, will make our life here so much more interesting and, who knows, Papa, perhaps I won't mind quite so much having to wait to go to Toletum."

Julian laughed and patted her hands.

"You may well feel like that but I shall miss Musa's company if he does disappear back to Damascus, or wherever it is he's going. When I talk to him about Toletum it's just like talking to you about it, he gets as enthusiastic as you do, although I have no doubt that some of his interest is of a military nature, although he doesn't talk much about that side of things. He seems much more interested in the culture of my masters and the politics which drive the Visigothic Empire. Oh, and their ancient treasures, mustn't forget those. I've lost count of the number of times that I have had to describe that wretched table to him. You listen tomorrow. I'll wager he brings it up in conversation during our meal."

Florinda laughed. "That is another of the reasons why I can't wait to go to Toletum, to get a glimpse of those fabled artefacts. So, if Musa mentions it tomorrow, does that mean you win your wager or does it mean I get a new robe?"

"Ah!" said Julian, "That's how your devious little mind is working is it? And if he doesn't mention it, what do I get?"

Florinda wrinkled her nose, grinned at her father and said, "I'll be nice to Maysara for a whole week, well, perhaps not a *whole* week."

"Go and look to your wardrobe, my girl. Knowing you it will take you the rest of the day to prepare yourself for our guests. Go on, off you go and leave me to get on with my work."

Another grin from Florinda, and Julian, smiling indulgently, watched his daughter make her exit.

•

Musa, Tariq and their entourage were halfway to their destination. While the soldiers remained alert and the grooms were attending the horses, the two principals were taking their ease on a grassy knoll overlooking the sea. Indeed, the sea had been within sight throughout their journey which, as Musa explained, was but an easy two day ride. Tariq reminded him that it was but six years ago that he and his force of one hundred men had taken a similar direction although, as he now explained, waving a hand towards the south, they were camped further back from the sea in the foothills of the mountains. He had, however, made a detour so that he could take a distant look at Septem. Musa, who was doing exactly that from their current position, turned sharply.

"Why would you do that?"

Tariq, by now feeling secure enough in his relationship with his Emir, replied, "Well, my Lord, I have noticed that you spend a lot of your time looking in the direction of Septem so I imagined that there must be something quite special about it. If you remember, you did tell me of your fascination for the place, what a remarkable territory it is and how important it is strategically. That it is the one remaining Visigothic outpost in our lands and how we, powerful as we are, have failed to make it our own." He grinned.

"If you must know my Lord, you succeeded in capturing my interest and I can't wait to see it – or the man who controls it."

Musa ran his fingers through his beard with one hand and idly plucked at blades of grass with the other.

"Mm," he pondered his answer. "Not that easy to pin him down. I think I told you his name is Julian and I also think I told you that he is Agent for the Visigothic kingdom and, as such, is answerable to Toletum. Actually it's not quite as simple as that. He has, or at least he practises, some autonomy and he independently trades with Hispania. He is militarily skilled and trains his own army in the old Roman ways. They are highly disciplined and, as you can judge from the fact that my predecessor failed to defeat him, highly effective. He is very shrewd and not to be underestimated."

Musa shaded his eyes and looked towards Septem, as if trying to conjure up a vision of the man he was talking about.

"I won't tell you anymore because I would like you to form your own opinions. We'll be there tomorrow and we can compare notes on our way home. Oh! There is one more thing. He has very beautiful daughter, named Florinda. I do appreciate that your accelerated climb up the ladder of ambition has left you with little time to enjoy the company of women but the fair Florinda might cause you to adjust your priorities."

He smiled, "Right; I'm going to my bed. A gentle ride over these pleasant hills tomorrow and we'll be there in time to enjoy Julian's excellent hospitality. Good night."

Tariq didn't even turn to watch Musa's departure. He offered a mumbled "Good night" in reply and continued to concentrate on the mystical distant city and its enigmatic ruler.

•

The next day, as soon as the outline of the city wall was sighted, the small party was met by a group of guards who, mounted on impressively matched greys, greeted them with great civility and escorted them to the imposing gates of the palace. A welcoming committee was waiting for them, one of whom stood out from all the rest. Taller, of a different complexion and radiating authority, this, Tariq assumed, must be Julian himself. It was immediately obvious that Musa and Julian were genuinely pleased to see each other. There was nothing of the ceremony or paraphernalia that Tariq had expected. Rather they embraced and talked over each other in the enthusiasm of their meeting. They appeared to understand each other perfectly, although the mixture of Arabic, Latin and Greek sounded almost incomprehensible to Tariq who, apart from his native Berber, had some classical Arabic although his Latin, which he was still working hard to master, was more than adequate. This was no barrier to Julian who, living up to his reputation as an all-round genius, warmly clasped Tariq's hand and spoke to him in perfect Berber, before having them ushered into the cool and serene interior of the palace.

•

As Tariq's influence grew, so did his standard of living and now, in Tangier, his apartments were hardly any less luxurious than those of Musa who always declared that one's position in life should be reflected by a high degree of material comfort. Tariq, something of an aesthete by nature, submitted to all this outward show although he would have felt far more at home pitching a tent on the edge of the parade ground. For this visit, Musa had decreed that any sort of military uniform was not to be worn and even their escort was dressed in standard desert robes, the escort's weapons concealed and handed over as soon as they arrived at the gates of Septem.

Although he had, for some time now, assumed more administrative duties, Tariq always felt more comfortable dressed in his military kit but for this occasion he had been dressed, more lovingly than he had ever suspected, by Menna who had become one of Musa's more valuable slaves and keeper of the Emir's wardrobe. She had gone to a lot of trouble to acquire cloth of the exact quality and colour likely to show off Tariq to his best advantage and Musa, who assumed the finished robes were to be his, was quite put out to discover that they were far too small for him and destined to be worn by his deputy. In the event, poor Tariq felt somewhat overdressed when he saw that his host dressed well, but simply, in the style of old Rome while Musa, although in his best regalia, could not compete. All, however, was forgotten, when they entered the hall which was completely open to the ocean on one side, an ingenious arrangement of shutters having been opened to allow the room to be cooled by the breezes from the sea, while still providing shelter from the overhead sun. There they were met by Florinda who had plundered her own clothes presses to great effect and looked stunningly beautiful in a white stola, figured in green and segmented in black and white, while her white cloak was edged in gold. She, on her part, could not take her eyes off Tariq, who remained completely unconscious of the fact.

•

By this time Tariq, as the effective deputy to the Emir, had attended a number of social and diplomatic events, and he expected this one to differ little from the others. He had even accompanied Musa to Damascus, had met and been interrogated by the Caliph, Al Walid, himself. Even Musa could not elevate his protégé to high office without the approval of the Caliphate. Tariq was later told that he had acquitted himself well and that the supreme power had been impressed by his intelligence, his transparent honesty and his adherence to the Faith. Sitting here, in the infinitely more relaxed atmosphere of the Palace of Septem, he felt himself looking forward to the occasion and learning something of yet another culture. He had been introduced as Musa's commander in chief and deputy but Musa had also chosen the occasion to make the formal announcement of Tariq's appointment as Governor of Tangier, the position Musa was relinquishing in the light of his increased responsibility for the whole of Ifriquya. A happy, if embarrassed Tariq, then had to accept the congratulations of an effusive Julian although, as Tariq rightly suspected, Julian was already aware of the promotion. Musa, unnecessarily, in Tariq's view, went on to say that Tariq's exquisite costume no doubt reflected the distinction of his new office. Florinda giggled and Julian frowned at her.

•

As the day drew on, and each dish brought to the board was more succulent than the last, Tariq found himself talking openly to his host about the differences that existed between their two peoples and Julian quickly assessed that here was a mind receptive to anything new and interesting. His dealings with Musa had always been similar but he was quite aware that many of the Islamic hierarchy could be insular and dogmatic in their beliefs. He instinctively took to this young man and was relieved to find that his future dealings with Tangier were likely to remain agreeable. Tariq was in the middle of asking his host a question that had occurred to him the moment he had arrived.

"My Lord, I can't help noticing that, with the exception of yourself and your daughter," he bowed to Florinda, who blushed, "the inhabitants of Septem are local, indigenous people. Does it not worry you that, as you are surrounded by the might of Islam, your own Berbers might not prove an internal threat to your security?"

Julian caught Musa's eye and they both smiled. Julian turned back to Tariq.

"Your question is actually a very good one. However, I trust my own people, who as you say, are Berber like yourself, as much as you can trust your followers in Tangier or anywhere else on this continent. You must understand that my people, the people of Septem, are committed Christians and have been so for many centuries. It is thanks to their faith that we have repulsed attacks on our sovereignty by those of your faith. They make excellent soldiers, are disciplined and brave but, above all, they regard themselves as different from their brothers who live outside our territories."

Tariq nodded gravely. "I see, that explains it. You educate them as well?"

Before he could reply, Musa, who had been talking with Florinda, turned to Julian and asked him to tell Tariq about Hispania and, in particular, Toletum.

Julian sighed audibly and asked Tariq if he really wanted to hear about that country over there. He gestured over the sea, where the land mass, partly sheltered by the enormous rock, was clearly visible.

"Well," Julian started. "I serve the people, the Visigothic kings who rule over that vast area that you can see from here. Mind you, you can't even see a fraction of it. To travel from one end to the other would take you a very, very long time indeed." He turned back to Musa. "Are you sure you want me to go on with this? I can't believe that you haven't already told him all about Hispania?"

Musa only shook his head and said, "Toletum, tell him about that."

Another sigh from Julian and another muffled giggle from Florinda as he continued.

"Toletum, if you haven't already guessed, is the principal city of Hispania. It is situated almost exactly in the middle of the country, is the seat of government and the seat of the ruling monarch. It is huge, filthy, and a political quagmire. I am forced to visit it from time to time and whenever I do, I can't wait to get back home. I can't believe that this one," he gestured to Florinda, "is desperate to get there. I keep telling her how dreadful the place is yet she keeps pestering me. Still, I suppose it can be rather dull here for someone of her age and education."

Musa broke in again, "Oh come on Julian, Florinda is not a child. She is very clever and it will do her good to see something of the world and," here he and Florinda exchanged a conspiratorial look, "she can see all those wonderful treasures for herself instead of hearing all about them from her over-protective father."

"You go too far, my friend, I am not over-prot…Ah, just a minute, it was my daughter who put you up to this wasn't it? She told you that I made a wager that, if you mentioned the treasures… You do realise you've just cost me a new wardrobe for the young schemer don't you?"

Musa winked at Tariq. "Come on Julian, you know well that you can afford it. Anyway, I want Tariq to learn all about these wonderful things that you have been privileged to see. He will be curious, we have nothing like them in his country although, when visiting Damascus, I was able to point out that we, or the Caliphate that is, are not without our own treasures. Is that not so Tariq?"

Tariq nodded enthusiastically. "Indeed it is my Lord. The libraries in particular are wonderful to behold."

Julian banged a hand on the table. "There you are Musa, the young man is more interested in learning than he is in artefacts and I applaud him for it." He turned to Tariq. "Am I not right in saying that your own religion decrees that education is important and central to your faith."

Tariq nodded again. "You are quite right my Lord. The Prophet himself, writes that it is a most liberating factor in our lives, both for men and women." He gravely nodded in the direction of Florinda, who held his eyes for just a moment too long for his personal comfort.

Musa laughed. "We are becoming much too serious. Come along, even if Tariq is not interested, you know full well that I love to hear about these things. If nothing else, tell us about that fabulous table. Such is the fame of the piece, even our masters in Damascus are aware of its existence."

Suppressing yet another sigh, Julian started to describe the Table of Solomon and, as he did so, Musa closed his eyes, as though to impose the image onto his imagination, Florinda sat rapt, as she always did when hearing about it, while Tariq, absorbed as he was by the description, was much more interested in hearing about its provenance and history. When he had concluded his performance, Julian firmly intimated that he would talk no more about the fabled treasure. Enough, he declared, was enough. Once Florinda had made her pilgrimage to the "holy city", as he alluded to it, the responsibility for describing its wonders could fall on her slender shoulders. He was done with it.

As the afternoon wore on and the day cooled, they moved to one of the many tree-dappled courtyards where they could recline in comfort in or out of the sun, as they wished. All the while, servants noiselessly moved between them, offering sweetmeats or other delicacies. All in all, the mood was one of contentment and relaxation, and Tariq, who had never quite experienced anything like it before, found himself beginning to be seduced by the experience. Just as his eyes were closing he was alerted by Musa's voice, the tone not quite as neutral as before, saying to Julian, "You speak and we hear of the treasures of Toletum and, yes, before you tell me so, that was at my behest but what of the current political situation. Any changes since last we met? Never seems to me to be a regime at peace with itself."

This time Julian's sigh was one of real exasperation.

"Even I have difficulty in keeping up with events there. From what I can make out, Wittiza is not in good health and, as ever in these circumstances, there appears to be a certain amount of jostling for power. One or two contenders for the role of sovereign, so nothing new there either. The Church is flexing its muscles and, apparently, much will depend on its choice. One hears things, one hears names. Achila and Ardo, Wittiza's sons, can't be ignored but my guess is that the Church will have the final say. If it does, then Roderick, Duke of Beatica, might be in with a chance. I don't know much about him. Of royal descent, good brain but a bit wild so I hear. As I say, Wittiza is still in power and just about holding it all together but if he really is as ill as he is rumoured to be, then anything could happen. Anyway, why are you interested? Now you have a whole continent to govern, I would have thought you had enough to occupy yourself."

Musa carefully put his cup back on the small table a servant had thoughtfully placed beside his couch. He waved his hand.

"Making conversation, that's all. Although I must admit to being fascinated by what goes on in this Empire of yours. Just as, I imagine, you are with developments in my world. What about you Tariq, are you not curious about what life is like over there?"

He airily indicated the world that lay over the ocean.

Tariq was, as ever, thoughtful.

"At this moment, my Lord, I am more interested in our present location. To be at the junction of two oceans *and* the Pillars of Hercules is, for now, wonder enough. Now that you have mentioned it though," he raised himself on one arm and looked over towards the land mass on the other side of the great rock which constituted one of the 'Pillars' "it is another world over there and the thought of something new, different and unknown, is something that always draws me."

Florinda also raised herself up on one arm and piped up, "It draws me too Sir. You ask my father. He might not like it, but to me it all sounds wonderful and yet I am denied the opportunity to find out for myself."

Tariq was about to make his reply as non-committal as good manners would allow when he was saved by Julian, who put an end to the discussion by saying, "All right, all right, Florinda. I will promise you this. As soon as the succession in Toletum is resolved, I will make representations to have you serve whichever luckless woman takes on the role of consort. There now, I have said it and you have witnesses."Upon which, Florinda leaped up, rushed over to her father and threw her arms around his neck, embarrassing him totally and confusing their guests who did not imagine that young ladies of whatever religion, or station, behaved in such an unseemly manner.

·

While Musa and Tariq were being shown to their quarters, Julian gently chided his daughter for her lack of restraint. If she heard him, she didn't exhibit the slightest show of contrition but started walking around the patio, touching each vacant couch as she passed and enthusing about the recently departed occupants.

"Lord Musa is such an interesting man, so amusing and worldly and, as for the new Governor of Tangier.. Why, Papa, isn't he just so handsome and ..."

She continued in this vein until Julian stopped her.

"Yes, my dear, two very interesting, one might even say formidable gentlemen. On the whole, apart from that last regrettable show of emotion, I thought you behaved in a very responsible and adult manner."

She turned to him, beaming with pleasure, "You really think so Papa?"

"Why, yes," her father replied. "It is just such a pity that you have that unfortunate smear of orange pulp on your chin."

She shrieked "Oh no!" and vigorously rubbed at her face with a napkin.

Julian smiled at her and said, "Only joking."

Chapter 10

Toletum, 708AD

This time it was not the blinding brilliance of the sun that was illuminating the Great Hall of the palace in Toletum. It was now the middle of the night and the treasures were bathed in the cold blue of moonlight. The Table of Solomon had been transformed from burnished gold to glittering ice. Even so, the attraction of the artefact was no less compelling to the present incumbent of the Visigothic throne who stood, just as his predecessors had through the years, with his hand caressing the cold gems which decorated the surface.

As a child, Wittiza had grown tired of his father Egica's obsession with this over-weight, ugly but undoubtedly priceless, piece of furniture but now, the old king dead and he, Wittiza on the throne, the talismanic value of the object was beginning to exercise the same fascination for him but not for the same reason. Wittiza had problems, which were not so very different from the problems experienced by every Visigothic monarch before him. The Crown was an elected, not hereditary, gift; therefore whoever assumed the title was beset by a number of discontented nobles who had not voted for him in Council. These nobles, who had their own preferred candidate, would then devote themselves to plotting the downfall of the one currently in control. King Egica's remedy for this was to impound the estates of his predecessor and send all his followers into exile - or arrange a more permanent disappearance of which Roderick's father, Theudefrid, was one example. Theudefrid's fate, however, did little to dampen his associates' enthusiasm for treason so Wittiza, in an effort to minimise the threat, pardoned his father's enemies and restored their lands to them. Unfortunately for him, this meant that the restored estates had to be relinquished by those who had benefited from them under Egica, and murmurings of revolt hung heavy in the alleys of Toletum. Rather more sceptical than his father, Wittiza reasoned that, had this iconic table the power to bestow inspiration, or luck on its current guardian, it hadn't, thus far, been spectacularly influential. In fact, he mused, might it not be better stored in another location where, whatever its powers, benign or malign (he suspected the latter) it could be kept well away from the throne in general, and him in particular.

•

King Wittiza had every reason to be concerned. The expected group of nobles were, indeed, planning insurrection but were themselves divided and could not agree on how to go about it or who would lead them. One of these, although at the moment in a minor capacity, was Roderick who, as a result of King Wittiza's amnesty, now felt safe to return to Toletum. This he did in the company of his former tutors, now elevated to the role of advisors, and they advised him to keep out of trouble, politics, the centres of intrigue and the bed of anyone favoured by the king – for the immediate future. Time was on Roderick's side and he could afford to spend it cultivating those who were likely to be of most use to him when the time was right, be they secular or church.

•

Roderick was enjoying himself in Toletum. After the comparative back-water of Cordova, Toletum was busier, cooler and much more entertaining. There were plenty of young men of his age, scions of important Visigothic families, with whom to carouse and scheme. Entertainment was freely available for those who could afford it and, since the restitution of his father's properties, Roderick could. There were girls of every class and race eager to form a liaison with a young aristocrat who was still in possession of his lands and his head, and Roderick was, as ever, more than ready to oblige them. The one currently being obliged was the daughter of an aristocrat, so impecunious and long out of favour that she was encouraged by her family to ensnare anybody with influence or money. As she faked yet another orgasm, she was beginning to wonder if it was worth the effort. As it happened, as soon as Roderick learned of her family's inability to provide useful support in the event of a coup, she was politely, but firmly, excused and Roderick, satisfied in one sense, continued his quest for political allies with real power that might help him satisfy his other lust.

The young Duke of Beatica, as Roderick now was, his titles having been restored to him, actually worked assiduously to cultivate those members of the Council in whom he could detect a spark of sympathy. This was not too difficult, especially as far as the powerful clergy were concerned. Wittiza might have shown himself to be a lenient and inclusive monarch but, in doing so and particularly with his clement attitude towards the Jewish population, he made many enemies within the Church. Roderick, patiently over the next few years, made himself a favourite of this particular faction and knew that he could count on their support when the time was right. In the meantime, he plotted by day and caroused by night.

Chapter 11

Toletum, 709AD

King Wittiza shivered. He shivered quite a lot these days. Although still young, his face was grey, his eyes sunken. More often than not the pains in his stomach caused him to double up in agony, even when receiving important dignitaries or when addressing the Senate. The senators would exchange looks of pity, if they were loyal, or of contempt if their allegiance was elsewhere. A faction, or factions, for there was more than one contender waiting in the wings, were multiplying inexorably.

Now there was nobody to witness the ailing King's discomfort. Well, nobody of any importance. Just his personal guards, six of them, four of whom were carrying the iconic table, the other two leading the way with flaming brands, for the night was pitch black and the way underfoot uneven. They halted to gather their breath. The table was absurdly heavy and Wittiza's condition forced him to stop frequently anyway. On the distant plains though, light was clearly visible. Not moonlight, for no moon was ever going to emerge from behind the heavy black clouds that covered the sky that night, but a powerful intermittent glow that illuminated the horizon. One of the guards, wiping his brow, grunted, "It's a storm."

Wittiza watched the eerie light as if it were an omen of some sort. Perhaps the table should have been left where it had been on display for centuries, and here he was, about to hide it away. He shivered again and muttered, "If it's a storm, why can we not hear it?"

The guard, a grizzled thick-set man who had served Wittiza's father, growled, "I've seen it before, Lord. You get the lightning but not the banging that usually goes with it. It's coming this way. We'd better get a move on, my Lord. Just because you can't hear the rumbling and the banging, doesn't mean to say you can't get struck by the lightning."

•

They struggled on until they reached their destination. A dark, bleak-looking group of buildings on the edge of the city, which, as the storm came closer, was starkly illuminated by sheets of white lightning. A door was opened and a cowled figure hurried towards them, picked out Wittiza and bowed before him. At the same time Wittiza was struck by one of his spasms and it looked, ludicrously, as if the two men were bowing to each other as Wittiza doubled up in pain. The guards exchanged sardonic grins while the newcomer, realising the plight of his King, supported Wittiza on his arm and led him into the main building. The guards were ordered to remain outside with the table. Once in the refectory of what appeared to be a deserted monastery, Wittiza turned to the priest and asked him, "Did Gunderic tell you what I wanted you to do?"

"Yes, my Lord," was the reply. "The Archbishop commanded me to meet you here and to help you hide a most precious relic. He told me that it had great significance but that you suspected it of possessing an idolatrous, and therefore un-Christian influence."

Wittiza nodded wearily.

"The truth is, Father, I don't know. All I do know is that my reign, my health, my security is constantly threatened and, quite illogically, I feel that infernal object to be somehow unhealthy. My father, and his father before him, virtually worshipped it. There is no way that I could destroy it but if I could only keep it safe and out of my sight, out of the palace. You, so Archbishop Gunderic tells me, know of such a place."

"Yes, my Lord, I do and I am the only one who does. I am the last of this order to live here; the rest, responding to evangelical fervour, have gone out into the world to preach the message. "

Wittiza nodded. "Show me the place."

The priest did and after having done so, the two of them made their way back outside to where the six guards stood waiting around the table, a couple of them running speculative fingers over it, perhaps wondering how easy it would be to prise out a jewel or two. Upon sighting the King and the priest they sprang away from it and made a show of looking up at the storm which, by now, was almost overhead. Still no sound, only the dramatic flashes of brilliance that momentarily lit up this bizarre scene.

Wittiza ordered two of the guards to see that nobody approached the monastery, while he beckoned the other four to him. He turned to the priest and asked, "Do you have them?"

The priest nodded, thrust a hand into his habit and pulled out four lengths of cloth.

Wittiza turned back to the four guards.

"You are to be blindfolded. You must understand that this is for your protection, you will not be hurt so do not resist."

He beckoned the priest forward.

"Make sure you tie them tightly, leaving not the least gap through which they might see."

The priest nodded again and proceeded to blindfold the four guards, Wittiza checking each one as he did so. Then the four, one at a time, were led by Wittiza to the four corners of the table. Once again ordering the remaining two to stay where they were, Wittiza and the priest took the two front bearers by their free arms and led them back inside the monastery. The men were ordered to put down the table while Wittiza closed the door and locked it. Lifting the table, the odd little procession moved into the refectory where they were ordered to halt before the huge open fireplace. The priest then went to the fireplace and pulled on one of the meat curing hooks that hung from the rear. There was the grinding of stone rubbing on stone and the floor of the fireplace slid back into the rear wall. Wittiza peered down into what he imagined would be a cavernous hole but was surprised to see, a hand's breadth below ground level, what appeared to be yet another solid floor. The priest motioned for them to guide the table-bearers onto this platform and he then indicated that they all step back. Once they were out of the way, the priest pulled another of the hanging hooks and the platform, with the table on it, slowly descended out of sight. He then returned to the first hook, pulled on it again and the original floor slid, not without some protest, back into its place. Wittiza let out a sigh, almost a sob, and gave thanks that the sacred table was safe but not the distraction for him that it had been previously. The guards, still blindfolded, were then led back outside to rejoin their two comrades and the cloths were removed from their eyes.

•

Wittiza stood apart from them for a while, then called the senior man, the one he had talked to about the storm, over to him. He made it clear that, while the absence of the table from the palace would obviously be remarked upon, none of them were to give the location of where they had last seen it. They could only give an assurance that it was still a treasured possession of the kingdom and had been removed for its greater safety.

He then beckoned the priest to join them. He put a hand on his shoulder and said to him, "You swear that you are the only one, myself apart, who knows where the table is hidden?" The man nodded earnestly.

"Yes, my Lord, I swear that we are the only two."

Wittiza nodded, removed his hand from the man's shoulder, turned to the guard and said, "Kill him!"

•

Roderick was getting married. Her name was Egolina and she was the daughter of lesser nobility. She was not, however, the daughter of lesser nobility who had to resort to faking multiple orgasms. That was something that Egolina never had to do and, in that respect, she and Roderick were particularly suited. It was also a match which brought advantages to both houses. For her family, the opportunity to ally their failing fortunes with a young, ambitious man who could claim royal antecedents and, as such, could prove a future contender for the highest office. And from Roderick's viewpoint, while Egolina's family might be lacking liquidity, they did have important connections to the Clergy and it was the Bishops in the Senate who were central to Roderick's strategy.

While it was known that the Archbishop of Toletum, Gunderic, was a champion of the ailing Wittiza, other Episcopal representatives on the Senate were much less tolerant of Wittiza's decrees carried at the last synod. These stated that many of the harsh anti-Jewish laws, which had been in force for a couple of hundred years, be repealed. Roderick sensed, quite rightly, that if and when it came to a usurpation of the throne, many of the ecclesiastical senators would back anyone sympathetic to the old, tyrannical, statutes, which included forced conversion or banishment and crippling taxation. In his time in Toletum, Roderick had carefully fostered the more extreme elements of the church and the aristocracy (nobody else mattered, anyway) and was starting to garner a useful harvest of influence. Enough, he thought, to make his move, and that quite soon.

•

Roderick stood on the terrace outside his ground floor bedroom, and watched the electric storm approaching from the plains below. The villa, like that of his birthplace in Cordova, was Roman in origin but, unlike that derelict old ruin, had been restored. Certain features, such as the upside-down horseshoe-shaped windows and door frames showed the Visigothic influence of the rebuilding and, while not as luxurious as it would have been when home to a Roman, it was a distinct improvement on anything Roderick had occupied previously. The mosaics, on which he now stood, were original and, as with many of his race, Roderick marvelled that so much time and skill had been spent on decorating something as uninteresting as a floor. The villa had formed part of the restoration of his family assets, but Roderick, who scorned the delicacy of mosaic tiles, would probably have been still living, just as happily, in cheap lodgings in the town. Another sheet of lightning silently hurled itself across the night sky, lighting up his long, fair Germanic hair, and Egolina, temporarily satisfied and propped up in bed, watched Roderick's silhouette flash across her vision and wondered if the hoped-for future of her betrothed was likely to be just as fleeting. He came back into the bedroom and slipped off the simple tunic he had thrown on against the night air. She looked at his body. He knew she was looking and responded. She threw back the cover and substituted an uncertain future for an absolutely predictable here and now.

Chapter 12

Tangier, 709AD

Tangier was beginning to bustle. Essentially a garrison town, the northernmost post of the rapidly expanding Umayyad Empire, the settlement was now growing in size and importance and urbanising rapidly. Daily, new slaves, new fighting men and families were being absorbed into the melting pot. The slaves, apart from performing the more mundane domestic tasks, which inevitably fell to their lot, were also being put to work in new industries needed to support a growing city. Weapons, buildings, furniture, rugs and other household necessities were now being produced there, while the original small street markets were gradually turning their stalls into more permanent small shops. The masculine smells of sweat, horses and constant burnishing of weaponry were still present but now intermingled with the more heady aromas of perfumes and spices. The shouting of drill masters and army training now competed with the laughter of women, the shrill giggles of girls and children and the thumps of beaten rugs. As a coastal settlement it was also one of the Umayyad naval ports. Once more of a defensive arm against marauding Byzantine ships, Musa developed it into a legitimate offensive base and it was from here that he conquered the islands of Majorca, Ibiza and Sardinia.

As a rural Berber, Tariq had marvelled at what he saw on his arrival. Now there was so much more to see and, except for being ultimately answerable to his Umayyad masters in Damascus, it all came under his jurisdiction.

He was proving, just as Musa had suspected, an able Governor. Always fair in his dealings with other people he, nevertheless, radiated a natural authority which was always respected. There were though, some things on which he was immovable. One was a strict adherence to the Faith, and others such as discipline and loyalty from his army. This latter was never a problem because of the regard in which he was held by the soldiers, who saw him as one of themselves. The former was not quite so straightforward as there were still a few new recruits who resented a religion which was not only alien to them, but one which had resulted in them being forcibly removed from their tribal homelands. In the company of more seasoned comrades-in-arms, however, it did not take them long to realise that they were a part of an interesting, even exciting, new adventure.

•

In spite of the dizzying ascent to his present position, Tariq felt himself, at heart, still a Berber tribesman but now his duties allowed him little time to speculate on what might have been. His grandfather, frail but still quite active, had been brought to live with him and, although immensely proud of what Tariq had achieved, Tariq could see that Izem felt a little out of place in his new home and was never comfortable asking a slave to do what he could easily have done for himself. This sort of inhibition had never troubled Tariq, although his treatment of those who served him was ever exemplary. Not only Governor of one of the most important cities, Tariq was now an established General in the army and, as throughout his life so far, he accepted the challenge and worked at it until he had mastered what had to be done in order to fulfil the role satisfactorily. Life, to Tariq, was something of a jigsaw puzzle. He always found the right piece to fit the right hole and, having done so, moved effortlessly to the next test. There was, however, one piece which consistently eluded him although, to be fair, he remained unaware of its existence. That was his personal life which, thus far, lacked any relationship of an emotional or intimate character. It wasn't that he didn't like people, quite the contrary; he enjoyed the company of both sexes and was liked by everybody in return. It could be argued that his mercurial rise to power left him with little time to devote to an affair of this nature. It certainly wasn't that he deliberately avoided any such relationship; it was more as if it had never occurred to him. His closest associates continued to be Tala and Akeem. Tala, now getting on in years and too old for active service, had been given the task of overseeing the training and integration of new recruits. He was still an understanding, hard but fair, man who always enjoyed the loyalty and trust of his charges and, even if he lacked imagination, it didn't stop him carrying out his duties efficiently. As for Akeem, his already imposing figure now expanding outwardly, he seemed to have appointed himself Tariq's personal bodyguard. It had never been suggested that Tariq needed any protection but wherever Tariq went, Akeem was not far away and, if Tariq had a confidant, Akeem was probably as close as anyone was likely to get. Never the most subtle of beings, Akeem had more than once made the point that it was time Tariq found himself someone with whom to settle down, but Tariq had just laughed and told Akeem to stop acting like a bossy mother. Akeem would mumble something uncomplimentary and amble off while Tariq would laugh at him and the subject would be forgotten until Akeem, never a man to accept defeat, tried again a few weeks later. At the moment though, it was certainly the last thing on Tariq's mind as he concentrated on the large pile of vellum messages that his secretary had just placed before him.

•

The curtains over the doorway parted momentarily as the door at the end of the corridor was opened and the hot Saharan wind entered the building. It was the middle of a November day and all openings to the building were shuttered against the scorching wind and the fine sand that, invariably, accompanied it. The sand found its way into everything and Tariq frowned with annoyance at having to cover his mouth and nose against the sudden onslaught of desert detritus. Then the door was closed, the wind was halted and the curtain fell back into place, only to be disturbed again as his glass of mint tea was brought in. He continued to concentrate on the vellum pages that had so absorbed his attention before the distraction of the sirocco-borne sand and he barely acknowledged the tea-bearing servant until a low cough caused him to look up from his work. He failed to stifle a groan, managed a friendly smile and said, "Menna, Menna, what are you doing?" He pointed to the glass. "I have servants to bring this for me. You have far more important things to do."

Menna was still a slave, albeit one who had earned herself, by her own industry and intelligence, a position of some influence in Musa's household. When Tariq had been granted the Governorship, she had begged to be allowed to move to his service. Musa had regretfully agreed, for not only was Menna a superb seamstress, she had become an astute procurement agent for materials and leather. It was widely known in the garrison that she doted on her former childhood friend and her hopeless infatuation had become something of a sad joke among the inhabitants, for she was attractive and popular and, had she so wished and permission been granted to one of her status, she could have had the pick of a number of highly eligible young officers. She now loosened her headdress from her face, where it had protected her from the sand.

"Don't worry, my lord. I just happened to meet your servant as I was coming to see you so I saved her the trouble of bringing it. The fact is I wanted to show you this."

She searched in the large bag that was belted to her waist and withdrew a piece of vellum and handed it to Tariq, who shook his head as he took it.

"When we are alone, Menna, please don't call me "lord", it makes me feel more important than I am."

Menna smiled, to herself rather than to him.

"You are important, lord. You are the most important man in this territory and I am still a slave."

Tariq frowned. " Menna, you are still a slave because you refuse to accept the Faith. Do that and I will see that you are freed. Then you can marry who you like and go where you like."

Menna put her head on one side and looked at him for a moment then said, "Can I really, lord? Perhaps I should think about it then. Are you not going to look at those drawings?"

Tariq picked up the sheet and saw a series of rough sketches and then looked at her.

"Shields and what looks like upper body protection! Why show them to me?"

"Because, lord," Menna replied, "I have located a plentiful supply of cattle and camel skins. You probably don't know this but there is a new tannery on the outskirts of the town. I have been talking to them about processing skins and they tell me that they have developed a technique which will harden the leather, making it suitable for shields and body armour, without compromising its strength."

Tariq stared back down at the drawings, then back up at Menna.

"Do you remember, when we were children, I used to make you cross by not pronouncing your name properly?"

Menna giggled, then said, "Of course I remember. You used to call me Um Um and pretend you had a stammer but I wasn't cross, it made me laugh instead."

Tariq frowned. "You laughed? Oh yes, so you did. Anyway, the point I was going to make, what is a girl with a name like Um Um doing with things like this?"

He waved the vellum at her.

"What do you know about shields and armour?" He held out the drawings and she took them back from him.

"Well," she said, "some time ago, lord Musa asked me if it would be possible to sew some sort of metal, rings or plates, to fabrics which had been stiffened to take them. I experimented but found that it was very costly, which he didn't like much, and it also made the garments very heavy and difficult to move around in. Living amongst soldiers, of course I knew about leather as protection but I learned that it tended to get brittle after a time and was likely to split or crack when struck by a weapon. Then I.."

Tariq broke in, "Exactly, and that is the result of processing the leather to make armour, so why are those," he pointed to the drawings, "any different?"

Menna gave a sad smile and said, "Do you realise that this is the longest conversation we've had in years and it's all about armour?"

Tariq shook his head impatiently. "Menna, please, I am very busy."

"Of course, lord, I'm sorry. Well, I have talked to the tannery master and he said that the final strength of the armour depends on the exact time the leather is dipped in boiling water. Not only that, but I have designed these," she put the drawings back in front of Tariq so that he could see them, "so that the curvature on the shield provides extra strength, and the same with the plates for the body armour. The leather can be moulded while it is still wet. It's much cheaper than using metal and very much lighter for your soldiers to fight in. I know you already use leather for battle protection; wherever I go in this place I'm falling over battered wicker shields and old leather shields." She waved the drawings at him. "These, I think, will be more durable and cheaper in the long run."

Tariq picked up the drawings again, studied them more carefully this time, then lifted his head and beamed at Menna.

"You've done well, Menna," he said. "Now this is what you do. You take these to Tala, tell him what you've told me, have some pieces made up and have him test them and report back to me. All right?"

"Yes, lord, thank you." She took the vellum from him, looked as if she was going to say something else, but turned and almost skipped to the curtain, remembering to cover her face against the searing wind before she went out.

•

Tariq ran his fingers through his beard, a beard which was just beginning to show a few grey hairs, and returned to his work. Possibly it was the insistent wind which, despite shuttered windows, was causing the oil lamps to flicker but he was finding it difficult to concentrate and his concentration certainly wasn't helped by another blast of hot air and sand as the door was re-opened and shut with a bang. This time the curtains were swept aside as Akeem blundered into the room, giving a perfunctory salaam, brushing the sand from his robes and cursing the sirocco.

"I hate this damned time of year," he boomed. "Gritty eyes and gritty teeth, I'll be glad when it's finished and we can get back to normal. Just seen young Menna leave the building; what's she been up to then?"

Tariq explained and then went on to say that he'd handed her over to Tala for his opinion and couldn't really understand, as Tala was more directly concerned with such matters, why she hadn't taken her ideas to him in the first place.

Akeem looked up at the ceiling, then just said, "Really? Did it never occur to you that…? No, I don't suppose it did! Anyway, the reason I'm here is that you've one very storm- battered messenger waiting to see you."

Tariq looked up. "Oh yes, what does he want?"

"He is from Lord Musa, who commands that you join him, in Damascus."

Tariq groaned. "Damascus! It will take months to get there and back. All right Akeem, send up one of our Boat Masters and, whatever you do, make sure you pick the one with the fastest vessel. You know them all better than I do. And tell Malik I want to see him."

Tarif ibn Malik was Tariq's second in command but, because of the similarity of their names and to avoid any confusion, especially in battle, Tarif ibn Malik was always referred to as Malik. He too was a Berber who, just like Tariq, had achieved freedom and status through his natural intelligence and ability, but Tariq's tactical perception was, by far, superior. However, during Tariq's absence from his post, Malik assumed military command while the administrative duties of Governor were in the capable hands of Tariq's clerical and secretarial staff. Akeem acknowledged the orders but, just before he left the room, Tariq called him back to tell him to make sure to arrange a berth on the boat for himself. Akeem said that he would and left grumbling that if there was one thing he hated more than a sand storm, it was a sea storm.

•

Akeem had scarcely signalled his exit from the building by letting in another blast of air and sand and slamming the door when it was opened again, this time to admit Tarif ibn Malik who, it appeared, had been coming to see Tariq anyway. Malik was roughly Tariq's age but Moroccan born and from a rather more sophisticated background. His slavery was the result of some misdemeanour as a young teenager but, like Tariq, he adapted so well to the discipline of military life that he earned an accelerated promotion to the rank of Junior General of the Umayyad Army. He was an excellent field officer, brave and resourceful, but could be impulsive in his decisions and there he differed from Tariq who, as ever, considered his options carefully before committing himself. Malik also lacked Tariq's inquiring nature and was usually happy to accept the status quo. He was sensual, while Tariq tended towards the ascetic but the respect between them was mutual, they got on well together and made a formidable team. As Julian once remarked to Florinda, "Musa Ibn Nusayr may have some faults, I detect veins of avarice and overweening ambition within the man, but his ability to find and develop individuals of real quality from the most unlikely sources is quite uncanny."

•

Tariq gave a casual greeting to his visitor, they had already met earlier in the morning, and informed him that he had been summoned by the very highest authority and therefore the garrison was Malik's to command until such time as he returned. Many of the duties involved were administrative and carried out on a routine basis by junior staff anyway but the prime responsibility of the Governor was to defend the region against Visigothic raids. These took place from time to time and, as much as anything, were of an exploratory nature but, as Tangier grew in size and prosperity, so did its attraction as a target for attack. This was one of the reasons that Musa had established a small but highly trained naval fleet. This had proved to be an effective weapon in Musa's conquest of the Balearics and other outposts of the late Byzantine Empire. Now, however, its role was more that of a defensive arm and to provide troop transports to other coastal destinations. As both generals were aware of their responsibilities, the projected hand-over was brief but, as Malik salaamed his exit, Tariq called him back and said, "One more thing, just before you go. There is some newly designed body armour which I'd like you to have a look at, if the new samples are here before I get back. Naturally, I've arranged for Tala to take over the project but if you and he could liaise and mock up some combat situations it might prove interesting. I'm not sure why exactly but I've a feeling that any equipment designed to increase the mobility of our troops might prove a decisive factor in certain situations."

The door banged again and another gritty blast swept through the room. Tariq said, "That'll be the shipmaster, although I'm not going anywhere near a ship until this wind drops. All right, Malik, make sure you close the door when you go out."

Malik edged out through the curtains which opened a few moments later to admit a squat, hairy figure who planted his big feet carefully as if unsure that the floor wasn't going to move underneath him. He was an Arab, as were most of the ships' crews. Berbers seldom made natural mariners and, although he would never admit it, Tariq was dreading the impending voyage as much as Akeem. He welcomed the man, who he recognised from his last journey to Damascus. His name was Asif and when on board his vessel he took orders from nobody. He was, however, acknowledged to be the best sailor and navigator in the fleet and Tariq, on the last voyage, was most interested in comparing Asif's navigational skills with those he himself used when making journeys across land. On this occasion he was relieved to learn that Asif was also opposed to setting out to sea until the sirocco had abated somewhat but, by the master's reckoning, the worst would be over within three days and, as soon as considered safe, they'd set sail. Asif also said that, for the intended voyage, even a reduced wind would be favourable although it was too soon to predict what it would be like for the return journey. Tariq asked if they would be taking the same course as last time and was told yes, the identical course taken by Musa on his expedition to capture Majorca then, winds being favourable, straight for Berytus. From there, Tariq and Akeem, together with their escort, would have a couple of days' ride to Damascus. Tariq thanked Asif for coming and ordered him to prepare for sea at the earliest opportunity. Asif retorted, somewhat acidly, that his ships were always ready for sea but he would be in a position to give Tariq a day's notice of sailing.

•

Three days later, Tariq learned that he would be sailing on the following day. He instructed that Akeem be informed and made last minute checks on all the things on which he expected to be questioned, such as revenues, the latest population estimates, commercial newcomers to the city and steps taken to educate non-believers into the Faith. Being a scrupulous administrator, these statistics were soon noted, and the following morning he and a scribe made their way to the port. Behind them, grumbling to himself about how he was a soldier and not a sailor, ambled Akeem, enveloped in heavy robes against the sea rather more comprehensively than he had been against the sirocco.

Asif met them on the quay and ushered them on board and out of his way, while he made ready for sea. Despite Akeem's claim that a soldier's place was on dry land, the shalandi, or galley onto which they embarked, was crewed by fighting men who also manned the oars. Asif explained to an attentive Tariq that the essence of this voyage was speed and not attack. Therefore the vessel he had chosen was smaller and lighter and, with banks of fifty oars, should make good time to Berytus. He would hope to be faster on the return because the winds should be in their favour, they could set the square sail and be back in half the time. He then went on to explain that the most dangerous section of the journey was at the beginning, when they would be passing within sight of Visigothic Hispania. Thereafter the vessel should bear them across the Tyrrhenian Sea toward the ancient land of Greece, then down to Berytus. He reckoned under three weeks outward and could be two weeks on the return. The voyage proved uneventful and, as it went on, boring for Tariq and purgatory for Akeem, who spent most of his time with his head over the side. He did not appear to be cheered by Tariq's observation that the subsequent loss of excess weight would be to Akeem's advantage. At the port of Berytus, they were met, with great civility, by a detachment of Al Walid's personal guard and within two further days were entering the impressive gates of Damascus.

•

Damascus had not long been the headquarters of the Caliphate and the grand mosque, the building of which had been initiated by Al Walid only a couple of years earlier, was still in the first stages of its construction. Even so, as the visitors passed beneath its already imposing shadow, it was easy to visualise what an impressive building it would become. Tariq was looking forward to meeting Al Walid again and, although Tariq was unaware of it, the Caliph was, in his turn, looking forward to renewing his acquaintance with the young Umayyad general that had so impressed him on his first visit. With due ceremony, Tariq was ushered into Al Walid's presence and invited to join Musa on an ornate sofa, inlaid with mother of pearl, which was situated in front of, and slightly lower than, the platform on which the Caliph reposed on a throne of sumptuous cushions. Tariq was warmly welcomed by both his overlords and, when asked, was able to tell them that his journey had been free of incident. Mint tea was brought in, and Tariq was asked to give an account of his stewardship, which he performed concisely and confidently, at the conclusion of which Al Walid leaned forward and started to tell his eager audience of the reason for their summons.

•

"Musa," Al Walid politely indicated his guest, "has come to me with an intriguing suggestion which I would like to share with you."

This time it was Tariq who was the recipient of a gracious nod. Al Walid continued, "What would be your response if we were to ask you to mount a military offensive against the forces of Southern Europe? By that, of course, I mean Hispania Ulterior. Musa contends that it is the next logical step in our ambitious expansion. At this moment in time, all I am looking for from you is an instinctive reaction, anything more would be unrealistic. So, what is your instinctive reaction?"

Without any hesitation whatsoever, Tariq shook his head. He glanced at Musa and thought he detected a flash of disappointment. He took a deep breath.

"No, my lord. At this moment in time I would consider it to be complete folly and the inevitable sacrifice of most of my army. I'm sorry, my lord, I mean your army, in the north."

Musa frowned and said shortly, "Your reasons?"

Tariq turned to him and then to Al Walid.

"We don't know enough about the enemy. I grant that we have successfully mounted exploratory raids into their territory but that was with small forces, in and out again before anyone knew they were there. What you are proposing is an invasion against a power we know nothing about. Without more information, I think it would be madness."

Musa frowned again. "What about the information we have from Count Julian? According to him, the entire country is in a constant state of flux. The King is sick and the nobility is divided. Surely, now is the time to take advantage of a nation as divided as that one."

Tariq shook his head again. "Count Julian only tells us as much as he wants us to hear. Believe me, I like and respect the man as much as you do, my lord, but to commit an army to an enterprise of this magnitude, without further intelligence, is most unwise."

From the look on his former mentor's face he feared he had gone too far but Al Walid held up a conciliatory hand.

"Thank you Tariq, that was what I expected you to say and," he turned to Musa, "that is also my position. I do not say that it will not happen in the future because it might, and you have our thanks, Musa, for promoting so interesting an idea. Meanwhile, I hope that you are not going to hold it against your gifted young protégé for expressing a view different from your own."

Musa smiled. "Of course I won't, my lord. Had I thought Tariq's not worthy of his position, I would hardly have recommended him for it. He is probably right, although I stand by my argument that, if we are going to invade, now is probably as good a time as any."

Al Walid said, gently but firmly, "I prefer certainties to probabilities, Musa. Now, while we are here together, is there anything else the three of us need to discuss? No! Very well then. Musa, I understand that you have other pressing engagements with some of my advisors. You have permission to leave us. Before you leave Damascus though, perhaps you could spare us some more of your valuable time? Thank you."

Musa bowed, first to Al Walid, then to Tariq and left the room.

Tariq, having stood up when Musa left the room, sat down again at Al Walid's invitation and waited to hear what the Caliph had to say next. Al Walid asked him searching but fair questions about Tangier and seemed particularly pleased with the numbers who had converted to the Faith on, or soon after, their arrival in the growing town. He also appeared to be happy with Tariq's admitted policy of inclusivity. Those who did not wish to convert were not forced to do so and were able to live harmoniously with the rest of the community. The only penalty they were expected to pay for their independent beliefs was levied in the form of reasonably higher taxes. Al Walid, despite his piety and gentle manner ruled his Empire firmly and shrewdly but his next question came as something of a shock to Tariq, for he was asked, "The lord Musa, do you trust him?"

Tariq blinked, "Trust him, my lord?" The briefest of pauses, then, "Yes, my lord. Of course I trust him. Why, without him I would still be tending my grandfather's flock. Without his patronage, I would not be here today. Without him, I..."

"Yes, yes, I know Tariq, had lord Musa not taken an interest in you, you would be still killing lions instead of my enemies. Oh yes, Tariq, I know all about that too. As we rule more and more of the world, it might be getting more difficult for me but I think I can say that I am aware of everything that goes on in this great movement of ours. I ask the question, not because I suspect any disloyalty on his part, or yours towards him, but I thought his suggestion that our armies take on the might of Hispania was surprising for one of his tactical acumen. You thought so too, didn't you?"

This time, there was no hint of a pause as Tariq answered, "I did, my lord. As you are aware, we have very good relations with Septem and, never to my knowledge, has Count Julian indicated that the resources of Toletum were weakened to the extent that they could be overthrown without a huge sacrifice on our part. I believe there to be enormous spoils to be gained from such a conflict but that is assuming a successful outcome and, as I have already said, I do not think that possible."

He thought for a moment, then, smiling said, "My lord Musa is never tired of hearing Count Julian tell of artefacts and treasures beyond price that are to be found in the palace in Toletum. Perhaps he is imagining how much more they would be appreciated here, in Damascus, because, as I understand it, some have great spiritual value."

Al Walid nodded gravely. "I too have heard of these wonderful objects, and not only from the lord Musa, who I think is a more worldly man than you or I. I don't have to tell you that he is invaluable to our cause, no one more so, but he sometimes regards the acquisition of territory and riches equally as important as the acquisition of new followers to the Faith. Without his service though, it is unlikely that we would be where we are today so perhaps it is just as well that we are not all from the same mould."

He rose from his cushions, Tariq rising from the couch at the same time. Al Walid gave one of his gentle smiles.

"I hope you don't mind, Tariq. Being brought all the way here to answer one simple question but I thought it important to hear what you had to say, rather than read a carefully considered message. You are, of course, welcome to extend your stay here, should you so wish but, I have no doubt, you will feel an early resumption of your duties to be more important."

"Thank you, my lord," Tariq replied, "With your permission, I will take my leave immediately."

Another smile, this time of dismissal, from Al Walid and Tariq left the room. Outside, in a courtyard, he met up with Akeem, just recovered from his sea-sickness and eager to know the reason for Tariq's summons. Tariq wondered how much he should say then decided that, if he couldn't trust Akeem, he couldn't trust anybody.

"The lord Musa thinks we should conquer Hispania." Akeem stopped short, let out a whistle of incredulity and said, "Does he now?"

Tariq grinned at him, took him by the arm and hurried him along."But we're not and, before you ask, we're not staying here, we're going straight home."Akeem groaned. "Home! I've only just…"Another grin from Tariq. "Don't start moaning, just go and find our horses."

Chapter 13

Septem, 710AD

August, very hot, and an early morning sea fret was just beginning to clear from the port. The look-out, at his post on the corner tower of the fortress, was just able to make out the skiff as it skimmed into the mouth of the harbour, its crew of ten muscular oars and the man standing in the prow poised to leap onto the quay as soon as the vessel was close enough. When he did and started to run towards him, the look-out recognised him and shouted down to the guard at the gate to open it. Minutes later, Count Julian held out a hand for the scrolled message carried by the breathless messenger. He ordered his servant to see the messenger rewarded for his service and given refreshment. When they had left, Julian ran a speculative hand along the length of the scroll but still didn't open it. Florinda looked at him and raised an eyebrow but said nothing. Even their personal servants seemed to be holding their breath while they waited for the sight and sound of two hands spreading open the vellum. When the expected crackling of cured calfskin had ceased, the silence appeared to be even more intense, while Julian scanned the document. It was, predictably, Florinda who broke the silence when she jumped up and stamped her foot impatiently on the floor.

"Papa, please don't keep us waiting any longer. The messenger came from Toletum, I recognised him immediately and I know it's something important because of that look on your face. What has happened there, was it what you have been expecting? Papa, please," she stamped her foot again, "please tell me."

Julian looked at her and shook his head.

"Florinda, my dear, you really must learn to curb your impetuosity. It is not seemly in one of your age and position. While we are here, together, it doesn't matter that much, but when you are in company it will make you appear provincial and one unused to good society."

Florinda only grinned at him and said, "Well, whose fault is that Papa? For as long as I can remember, I have been begging you to allow me to take my place at the court in Toletum, and what happens? Nothing! Anyway, you always say how well behaved I am when important people, like Musa and now, Tariq, come to visit us. By the way, when can we see Tariq again? I like him, he's different."

Julian regarded his daughter affectionately, pleased that, for the moment, she had been diverted from the document that he held in his hands.

"In what way is he different?"

Florinda thought for a moment then lifted a more serious face to her father.

"Well, he's different because he…because…"

"Because of what, exactly?" interjected Julian.

"Because he doesn't take any notice of me!" Florinda blurted out, then went on, "He is so serious and yet he's so attractive. Other guests, even Musa, and I know he's ancient, but even Musa flirts with me a little. Tariq is polite, attentive, but doesn't seem to notice me as a.., as a woman. I'm not that repulsive am I?"

Julian laughed at this question, which was delivered so guilelessly.

"Of course you are not repulsive and, what is more, you know very well that you are not. No, I agree with you, Tariq is an extremely interesting man and I have heard or seen nothing to suggest that his preferences are other than normal, but I do know what you mean. There is almost something other-worldly about him. He is not ambitious, so far as I can tell, and yet he treats his quite extraordinary advancement as though it is the most natural thing in the world. I know he is devout without being strident about his beliefs, and his capacity for the acquisition of knowledge appears to be limitless. I must confess I like him but, believe me, my dear, his apparent lack of interest in you, as a woman, is not due to any fault on your part." He smiled and took one of her hands in both of his but, in doing so, had to place the scroll on the table beside him. This immediately drew her attention to it and she snatched her hand away.

"You did that purposely didn't you?" she said accusingly. "You deliberately had me talking about something else so that I'd forget about that important message you're hiding from me."

He retorted, "No I did not. It was you that started talking about Tariq, not me. Anyway, I'm not hiding it am I? It's there, in full view, in front of you."

She went to snatch it from the table but he caught her wrist and said, "I will read it to you but, before I do, you should know that I have good reason not to make you aware of its contents. The fact is," he went on, "that the succession in Toletum has been agreed."

Florinda gave a shriek of excitement and twirled around, clapping her hands.

"That means I can go to Toletum? You promised me, as soon as things were settled and it was secure, you would let me go."

Julian grimaced and the two servants present looked at each other and frowned, Florinda's attendant, hand to her mouth, stifled a sob and was immediately consoled by the briefest of hugs from her mistress who, having administered consolation, flew back to her father and bombarded him with questions.

"Papa, when can we start, can it be this week? *Please*. Please can it be soon? Next week then but no later, please…"

Julian disengaged himself from his daughter and held her at arm's length so that he could focus on her properly and she could see, from his expression, that he was being serious.

"Look, my angel," he said, "you must understand that, while Roderick has been granted the title of 'King', the situation is far from settled. Wittiza's sons still live and, as far as I can judge from this," he indicated the scroll, "they have taken control of some of the more northern territories of Hispania where, I have no doubt, they will be busy plotting their revenge but…" he placed a finger on Florinda's mouth to stem the inevitable wail of protest, "I promise you this. If, in one month from today, the situation in Toletum appears to be peaceful, I will take you there and find you a suitable position at the court. You have my word on that, so no more questions."

Florinda pushed herself away from him but her pout of disappointment lasted no longer than a second and she danced round behind his chair, gave him a sloppy kiss on the top of his head, thought for a moment, then rushed over to her, still tearful, attendant and dragged her off to talk about what clothes they should pack ready for her entry into the Visigothic court.

Julian sighed heavily as he picked up the scroll and studied it anew. Then he instructed his servant to find the messenger and bring the man to him. There were questions he needed to ask.

•

Meanwhile, in Toletum, Roderick was asking questions of his own, one of which was, what had become of the table of Solomon. It certainly wasn't where he expected it to be, and the most likely explanation for its disappearance was that Wittiza's sons, both minors but supported by those nobles opposed to Roderick, had taken the table to the north-east of Hispania, where they had fled following their father's death and Roderick's accession to the throne in Toletum. There did not appear to be anybody in Toletum that knew of the table's present whereabouts or, indeed, the exact timing of its disappearance. Roderick was no fool and had been schooled well in the machinations of power, and his most immediate concern was to consolidate his precarious hold on the crown so, for the moment, the whereabouts of the table was not important. What was important was identifying and isolating those factions opposed to him. These, quite naturally, were parties who either had expectations of attaining the highest office themselves, or those who supported the succession of the former monarch by one or both of his children. Other potential threats came from fragmented religious groups, such as pockets of Aryanists, still adhering to the old Visigothic Christian principles, and nobles in the south, still swearing loyalty to the houses of previous kings.

It soon became clear to Roderick that the throne of Toletum was something of a poisoned chalice and he was going to have his work cut out to keep the crown on his head. At the same time, the sensual side of his character was not to be denied all the trappings associated with kingship. He, his consort and his court dressed extravagantly in materials imported from the outermost reaches of the old Roman Empire and these were further embellished with embroidery and jewels. This was in some contrast to the court of Wittiza and paid for by punitive taxes levied on Jews, non-believers and former enemies. A network of spies was employed to keep Roderick informed about dissenters occupying those regions in the north and south of the peninsular, and he was left in no doubt that at some time, in the not too distant future, he was going to have to mobilise a force to put down insurrection.

•

Although unaware of what was happening across the Strait, back at his headquarters in Tangier Tariq was having a sleepless night. Not the first, as it happened, since his visit to Damascus where Musa had proposed an expeditionary assault upon Hispania. Had Musa really intended that he should be taken seriously? This was the problem that Tariq was trying to resolve as he sat in his room. Musa, after all, was an enormously experienced commander, eminently sensible and unlikely to come up with any hare-brained scheme that was not based on good intelligence.

Why then had he, Tariq, not embraced the idea with the same sort of enthusiasm? As he turned these questions over and over in his head, the answer consistently eluded him. There was, of course, the fact that Al Walid's response was the same as his own: "Now was not the time!" Eventually, he resolved that he must seek an audience with Count Julian. By now they had met on quite a few occasions and, each time, Tariq had been impressed by Julian's common sense, his courtesy and his pragmatic attitude to their relationship. More than anything, Tariq was intrigued by the descriptions of Hispania. Fertile, picturesque and peopled by so many different races and religions, it stimulated Tariq's imagination, as did anything that was new and yet to be experienced. He would also speak to Malik who had actually landed on Iberian soil on several occasions. These were not full-scale offensives, little more than piratical raids and, naturally, Tariq had debriefed Malik on his return but never with the intention of planning an invasion, calculated to overthrow the ruling power. He summoned a messenger, one of whom was constantly on call outside his room, and ordered him to ride to Septem and seek a meeting with Count Julian. He then ordered that, as soon as Malik was awake, he was to report to Tariq. By now wide awake himself, he also arranged that Tala be sent to him. The new armour! He hadn't yet had the chance to hear his report on that. Satisfied that there was nothing else to do until morning, he settled for the few remaining hours before dawn but sleep still didn't come and, although there was something keeping him awake, he had no idea what that 'something' was, and that was the problem.

•

Musa's apartments in Damascus were much more palatial than those of Tariq but Musa couldn't sleep either. He, too, was occupied by thoughts, not dissimilar to those of Tariq, in that Iberia was central to them but, whereas Tariq was captivated by the idea of different landscapes, languages and cultures, Musa thought of booty, of wealth and fortune.

•

Count Julian hadn't even attempted to go to his bed. He stood, in the now chill before dawn, looking over to the Rock and dreading his next journey across to the land beyond it. Next time he would not be alone; he would be accompanied by his only daughter and something, he was not sure what, was weighing heavily on his mind.

•

Roderick, the most sumptuously accommodated of them all, rolled away from Egolina and into the welcoming arms of her maid. He grinned; it had been a good night.

He had watched his wife and her maid pleasure each other before Egolina had claimed her husband's eager attention. Now it was the maid's turn. A restless night for everybody, or so it would seem!

Chapter 14

Tangier, 710AD

The following morning, before Malik and Tala were announced, Tariq made sure that he was ready to receive them. Tariq's boundless energy, both mental and physical, was legendary among his followers and he felt it important to disguise any evidence of his sleepless night. Tala, however, who by now knew Tariq as well as anyone, Akeem excluded, noticed immediately he entered the room that the Governor had something on his mind. Malik, on the other hand, who enjoyed a rather complicated social existence and the late nights that this entailed, noticed nothing amiss and breezed into the room in his habitual swashbuckling manner. Tala started to ask if all was well but, on catching Tariq's shake of the head, subsided back into silence. Tariq cleared his throat and opened the meeting.

"Thank you both for coming so promptly. You can probably guess why I've asked to see you since, while I was in Damascus, you were both involved in testing the new armour that Menna, of all people, thought might be an improvement on what we've been using. I must say that she appeared to know what she was talking about and, as you know, I'm a great believer in giving anybody, regardless of gender, an opportunity to contribute to our great movement. I hear she wasted no time and that you were provided with prototypes within a couple of weeks. So, what's your verdict? Waste of time or worth pursuing? You first Tala, what were your findings?"

Tala's lined features broke into a smile and Tariq reflected how much Tala had aged since first they'd met.

"Well, Sir, I have to say that I was pleasantly surprised. When young Menna came to me and told me of her conversation with you, I was quite sceptical but, as you say, she'd looked into it thoroughly and, although I never asked her, it would have surprised me if she hadn't done a bit of experimenting herself first. You know, had some shields made up and thrown rocks at them or something like that. Anyway, it works quite well and in certain situations, extremely well. There is no doubt that the protection is stronger than we have been using but I wouldn't say that it comes anywhere near as effective as metal plates…"

Malik now stepped forward and broke in.

"Tala's correct, Sir but, for my money, the big advantage is the lightness compared with metal, especially for mounted men. They can manoeuvre more easily which would give them an advantage both in attack and defence. As for infantry, much would depend on the combat situation. Close quarters, there is no doubt that linked plates offer better protection but, again, there are advantages to be had in terms of speed of movement, flexibility and so on. The curved shields are much stronger, no doubt about it and, again lighter, allowing for quicker reactions and…"

This time, Tala interrupted.

"I agree, but only up to a point. In order for our soldiers to maximise this manoeuvrability, they need training. These new shields, although lighter and stronger and cheaper to replace, would be of little use in a defensive wall situation for example. Perhaps we should look more closely at the tactical advantages and instruct recruits accordingly."

Tariq nodded his approval, and asked Tala to let him have a proposed training programme involving the most efficient use of the new equipment. He added, "Of course, the tactics of the enemy force might or might not be responsive to our own battle plan so I would like to see a degree of adaptability built into your programme. I have to say though; anything which gives us increased mobility has to be in our favour. You agree Malik?"

"Absolutely my lord," was Malik's immediate response. "Was there anything else you needed me for? Taking over some of your duties in your absence meant that I had to neglect my own and I ought to do some catching up."

Tariq said nothing to this and, for a moment seemed deep in thought until he held up a hand to stop Malik before he took his leave.

"Just one moment," he said, "I would like another quick word before you go." He then turned to Tala. "Thank you Tala, if you would let me have your ideas on what we have just been discussing. Outline will do, so no need to be too specific at this stage. Now, if you don't mind, I'd just like a few words with Malik about something else I've got on my mind."

Tala made his obeisance to Tariq and, with a less formal acknowledgment to Malik, left the two generals together.

•

"Have you brought it?" Tariq asked.

"Of course," said Malik and he foraged in his robes for a satchel slung around his waist which was not dissimilar to the one from which Menna had produced her designs. In fact it was exactly the same. Several notables in Tangier had similar bags and it was Menna who had first thought up the idea, and she had developed quite a lucrative sideline in making and selling them. Opening the bag, Malik also produced a sheet of vellum, which he passed to Tariq, who studied it carefully before asking, "How large an area does this cover?"

"Only half a day's ride," was the reply. "That's only as long as you have allowed me to stay there. Mind you, Sir, I think that you are right. With such a small detachment, any further might have been unwise." Malik came over and joined Tariq at the table on which the document rested, before he continued. "As you can see, there is very little here in the way of defensive fortifications although we did meet a token resistance but it wasn't big enough to present us with any real problems. We lost no men and neither did they. To be honest with you, I think we frightened them rather than inflicting any real harm. If you look just here," he pointed to a mark on the rough map, "you can see this is where they were stationed, little more than a rustic building surrounded by a ditch. Obviously, there are substantial defences elsewhere and in this direction," here he moved his finger towards the east, "it was possible to make out a hilltop town in the distance which looked quite large and, I have no doubt, is quite well defended. I was tempted to take a closer look but we were already at the limits of your orders so we came back. As you know, we did manage to bring back a couple of captives from the force that attacked us but that was about all that we had to show for the raid."

Tariq stared down at Malik's rough map and ran a tentative finger both east and west along the coastline, tantalisingly in view across the Strait yet so far away in every other respect but his imagination. He stroked his beard as he thought, then turned again to Malik.

"What is it like there? I mean compared with here? Are there roads, is it cultivated and if so, with what? Those two prisoners you brought back seemed very ordinary and could almost have come from a Berber background like you and me. I couldn't understand them of course. They talked in some strange tongue I've never come across before and they obviously weren't educated. I'm not surprised they didn't put up much of a fight. So, tell me, what is it like over there?"

Malik shrugged, and then thought for a moment before replying, "Well, the fragment that we saw was quite hilly to the north but we rode through country that was green and looked fertile. Quite pleasant actually although, as I say, that was just a tiny part of what I would imagine is part of a large land mass. Why the interest? Are we planning another raid? "

Tariq didn't answer directly but continued running an exploratory finger over the map, as if hoping that, by doing so, the action would illuminate something the map was not telling him. Eventually he turned to an expectant Malik who, for one for whom patience was never exactly a virtue, was standing still and silently at his side.

"To be honest with you Malik, I don't know. Perhaps another raid, perhaps something more ambitious, perhaps nothing at all. I just don't know but, what I can tell you is that this place," he jabbed the finger into the map, "this land is keeping me awake at night. I can't tell you just what it is that makes it special but whatever it is, it's bedevilling me and I need to know more about it than this." Again the finger jabbed into the vellum.

Malik shrugged again, perhaps with more nonchalance than the last time.

"Look, Sir, if it's playing on your mind that much, why don't I take another look at it and try and come up with something more detailed than this? It's not a big operation so far as I am concerned. Another small force, well mounted and lightly equipped, should be able to cover quite a lot of ground in, say, two days. If we're unlucky enough to encounter any real resistance we should be able to outride it and be safely back here without any difficulty."

Tariq's answer, in contrast to his hitherto thoughtful mood, was immediate and decisive.

"No! Sorry. Malik, I know that you would look forward to a little adventure such as that but no; if we do mount another raid on Hispania I would like it to be something more than what you have just proposed. You are right in one thing though. I do need to know more about conditions over there but, if we do as you suggest, it might be regarded as what it is, an intelligence gathering expedition. That being so, the Christians will be on their guard against a more serious assault and..."

Malik, his eyes alight with interest interrupted.

"Excuse me, Sir but is that what's on your mind, a full-scale invasion of Hispania? But do we know enough about their resources, their tactical methods, their...?"

This time Tariq interrupted, with a laugh. "No Malik, we know nothing about them, or rather, not nearly enough to contemplate a total war but, and this is my point, should that situation ever arise, and I'm not saying it will but should it, we lose any element of surprise by giving them warning. Believe me, that is exactly what your proposal would amount to, a warning."

Malik looked puzzled. "I don't understand, Sir. You say that we need intelligence if we are to ever consider an all-out assault but then you tell me that, by gathering that intelligence, we are announcing our intentions, thereby losing that element of surprise which, as you quite rightly say, would be a contributory factor to the success of any invasion. So how are we supposed to reconcile the two?"

Tariq laughed again. "The short answer, Malik, is that I am not sure but I do have an idea."

"Which is, Sir?" Malik asked eagerly.

Tariq laid a friendly hand on Malik's shoulder. "I'll tell you later, Malik, but first I have to travel to Septem. There are a few questions I need to ask for myself. I only hope that Count Julian will be more generous with his answers than I am with you."

Malik nodded, and then frowned. "Ah! Septem. We all know that you and the Emir are made welcome in that city fortress but, even so, surely Count Julian would not contemplate discussing anything that might jeopardise his alliance with Toletum? Talking of which, Sir, I heard rumours the other day that Count Julian was even distantly related to the new ruler there. Roderick, I think his name is."

Tariq dropped his hand from Malik's shoulder and his eyes narrowed.

"Is he now? At what particular social function did you hear that interesting piece of gossip?"

Malik thought for a moment then, remembering, said, "Actually, Sir, it wasn't like that at all. It was from one of the trading ship skippers on the Rock. We commandeered a few of them to carry us back across the Strait. It might even have been one of the fleet owned by Count Julian himself."

Tariq replied, "Oh dear! I hope we haven't upset him. Count Julian, that is. That wouldn't do at all."

Malik shook his head. "Don't worry, Sir. We paid for our passage and they were coming back over here anyway."

Letting out a sigh of relief, Tariq indicated that their meeting was over and the two generals agreed to meet as soon as Tariq had returned from his meeting in Septem.

•

Three days later, the messenger returned, hot and breathless from his dash from Septem, and was ushered into Tariq's presence, where he reported that the Count Julian would be pleased to welcome the Governor. It would, though, have to be within the next few days as he, Count Julian, had been summoned to Toletum. Not waiting to reply by further messenger, Tariq promptly called on Akeem to assemble his personal guard and to be ready to ride to Septem within the hour. A change of horses was made available at a halfway point and by sunrise the next morning, Tariq and his troop were being admitted through the great gates into the city.

•

As soon as his party had deposited their weapons at the gate, as protocol dictated, Tariq was aware of a change of atmosphere from his last visit. Normally Septem was alive with activity and, although busy, the feeling was one of a relaxed and happy community. This time, although there was still plenty going on, it was lacking the customary high spirits which had previously marked out Julian's domain as a happy and efficient one. Soldiers and domestics alike were unsmiling and voices were subdued. The one element that wasn't lacking was the courtesy and politeness with which the arrivals were greeted. Akeem and his men were led away to quarters where they were invited to take advantage of the baths after their journey, and thence to the mess hall, where good fresh food, prepared in accordance with their religious practices, awaited them in abundance. Tariq was invited to avail himself of Count Julian's guest suite but, for the present, he declined, stating that he was aware of Julian's imminent journey and was anxious not to delay his host's departure longer than was necessary. He was, therefore, straightaway ushered into Julian's elegant office, where Julian sat, surrounded by scrolls of vellum and a small army of clerks, scribes and their assistants. On Tariq's entry, Julian immediately stopped what he was doing, ordered all but his personal servant to leave the room and quickly walked over to where a somewhat mesmerised Tariq waited. He embraced him warmly.

"My dear Governor," he began, "I must apologise for not meeting you in person at the gates but, as you can see, my attention, quite inexcusably, has been on other things. Come, let us sit." He led Tariq over to a luxurious ottoman, positioned next to one of the large windows overlooking the sea. "Now, to what do I owe the honour of this visit?"

Tariq was about to apologise for his travel-stained condition, but one look at Julian told him that it was unnecessary. The man appeared more careworn than when Tariq had last seen him. He looked tired and stressed and, in spite of observing the social niceties himself, he had more on his mind than Tariq's dusty robes. Tariq accepted the offer of tea and said he hoped that this intrusion wasn't too inconvenient but he had heard of King Roderick's accession in Toletum and, since it was also rumoured that Count Julian was related to new king, he wanted to congratulate Julian in person before he left for that city.

The tea was brought in and served with due ceremony, while neither man spoke. Eventually, Julian said, smiling sadly as he did so,

"Come now, Tariq, you haven't rushed over here just to congratulate me on the good fortune of a distant relative. Incidentally, how did you hear about that? You're very well informed."

Tariq had the good grace to blush and decided that, as ever with Julian, truth was important. Both men were too fundamentally honest to profit from the usual diplomatic double-talk.

"You are absolutely right, my lord. I am sorry but, as a senior general in the Umayyad army, the accession of a new King in a neighbouring territory is significant. Might he, unlike his predecessor, have thoughts of enlarging his kingdom at our expense? Not that I would expect you to tell me if he had but you might just be able to give me some indication of his character, what sort of man he is."

This time Julian actually laughed and, for the first time, looked more like his old self.

"This time it is I who am sorry but that is one question I cannot answer. The reason being that I have yet to meet him. I take it your information on Roderick was derived from those two natives that your General Malik captured during his recent raid on Hispania, or was it from one of my trading boat crews? They mentioned transporting your Berbers back across the Strait, a passage for which I believe your people were generous enough to pay."

This time it was Tariq's turn to laugh. "We wouldn't like you to be out of pocket, my lord and, if I might remind you, your people have mounted many a raid on our shores. Is it true though, are you related to the new ruler in Toletum?

Julian nodded. "Apparently so, although I have never met him. As you must know by now, I like to keep a little distance between myself and my masters. That said," he went on, "that is where I am bound for in the next few days and I am not looking forward to the experience."

Tariq waved a hand towards the sea and the Rock that stood sentinel over the land that so excited his curiosity. "I can understand why you are reluctant to leave your own citadel, it is beautifully situated."

Julian shook his head. "It's not that, my friend. It's my daughter! You have been in our company when she has, somewhat forcibly I must confess, expressed a wish to complete her education in Toletum. She is in thrall with the idea of the place and I made her a promise that when a succession to the Visigothic throne had been agreed and all seemed calm in the city, I would take her there and leave her to enjoy the sophistication of life at court."

Tariq placed a comforting hand on the older man's shoulder. "Now I understand," he said. "When I arrived here, I noticed that your household seemed different. Not as happy as on other occasions. Your daughter is well loved I think and will be much missed."

"Indeed she will," retorted a miserable looking Julian. "That girl is the centre of my life and, I might add, that of most of my people here. I know she can be headstrong and wilful but she just lights up this whole city. I am going to miss her but it's not only that…"

Seeing how upset Julian was, Tariq allowed him a moment to gather his composure before saying gently, "I do not, of course, know her well but she is probably one of the most beautiful women I have ever seen and I would think her kindly as well. But you were going to say something else, what was it?"

"Nothing important, I suppose but, as you say, I am related to this Roderick, albeit distantly which is one reason why we have never met, but I have heard things about him which…" Julian suddenly laughed, his melancholy forgotten for the moment, and went on.. "I wish Florinda had heard what you just said about her, it would have delighted her beyond measure. I could have her called so that you could repeat those words to her yourself but I dare not interrupt her travel arrangements. I am not sure that her maids regard her with quite the affection they once did; I understand she has had them re-pack at least ten times."

"Really?" said Tariq. "Why on earth would she do that?"

"Ah!" sighed Julian. "That is a question that has long eluded greater men than us. So," he went on, "your only purpose in galloping over here was to congratulate me on our new king? While one appreciates the gesture, it does seem a little extravagant on your part," he regarded Tariq shrewdly, "or did you have another purpose?"

Tariq met Julian's gaze squarely. "My purpose was twofold, my lord. As I have already said, I am responsible for the security of my territory and any change that might affect that security has to be of interest to me. Having learned that you are related to the new ruler in Toletum, I also wished, quite naturally, to extend my good wishes to you. My role as a military governor in no way detracts from the sincerity of those good wishes. Was the succession trouble-free or was it more in the nature of a coup – or would you rather I didn't know?"

Julian laughed again, and ordered more tea for his guest. "It is good that you came to see me, Governor. For, whatever your reasons, your visit has raised my spirits but as to your last question, however innocently framed, the answer is easy. The previous incumbent, King Wittiza, never a robust man, died of natural causes and Roderick was elected, by the Council, to succeed him. Since you seem to follow matters in Toletum, you will be aware that our heads of state are elected, the title is not hereditary. As I have already told you, my relationship with Roderick is not a close one, and until I meet him, I probably know little more about him than you do."

Tariq, who never expected to learn anything of strategic importance, nodded gravely and started to express his apologies for interrupting Julian's preparations but Julian would have none of it and insisted that Tariq stay the night and leave, refreshed, the following day. Florinda did not put in an appearance, but when told by her father that she had missed Tariq's visit, she upbraided him severely for not informing her. So severely, in fact, that Julian omitted to relay Tariq's complimentary words of the previous day.

•

On their return journey, Tariq remained quiet and thoughtful and Akeem, sensing his master's wish for space, rode several lengths behind him and restricted conversation to reprimanding his men for not looking smart enough or losing formation. Eventually, Tariq began to feel quite sorry for them and ordered Akeem to ride at his side so that they could discuss their visit to Septem. In fact, Tariq was not sure that there was anything of real import to discuss, so he was surprised when Akeem launched into a full and detailed account of his experience in the company of the lesser mortals of the community of Septem. Most of it concerned the quality of the food and the service and other tiresome details which Tariq would happily have missed hearing about, but the boring nature of Akeem's narrative was suddenly interrupted when Tariq heard the name 'Roderick'. He pulled up his horse so abruptly that Akeem, immersed in his anecdote, had ridden on for several paces before realising that he was talking to thin air. He reined in his mount and rode back to Tariq who leaned towards him and said, "Roderick! What about him?"

Akeem gave a shrug and replied, "Well, I was talking to one of Count Julian's junior officers and he just mentioned that this Roderick was the new ruler of Hispania." He frowned. "Why, is it important? I thought you already knew that."

Tariq shook his head impatiently. "Yes, of course I knew of his existence but what of the man himself? Was anything said about him?"

Akeem gave another shrug. "Nothing much, that I can recall. Apparently he's quite bright, comes from old nobility and throws his weight about a bit, but apart from that he…" He gave a short guffaw. "Oh yes! Apparently he likes to get his leg over."

Tariq, not immediately understanding, said, "He likes to what? Ah, I see what you mean. Now that is interesting."

Akeem looked at him uncomprehendingly. "Is it? From what I hear of that lot over there, they all like…"

"No, Akeem, that's not what I meant. It does, however, go some way to explain why Julian is so reluctant to introduce his daughter to Roderick's household. I don't suppose you found out anything else about the man? No weaknesses, apart from the one you've just mentioned? Nothing about his military experience or prowess for example?"

Akeem replied that, no, he had learned nothing more about the man than he'd just reported and, for the rest of their journey, Tariq relapsed into his reverie, while Akeem rode alongside him in silence.

•

In Toletum, King Roderick sat in his chair of state and looked at the man standing in front of him. The man's name was Lucius and he was one of Roderick's informers. Roderick only ever received one spy at a time because, in a country rife with potential insurrection, it was as well to trust nobody. Lucius was responsible for knowing what was going on in the south eastern corner of the kingdom, the part of Hispania that was overlooked by Septem and the Pillars of Hercules. Roderick spoke. His voice was a pleasing baritone, invested with newly assumed authority.

"This Berber raid; can we be sure that is all it was? Not an intelligence mission?"

Lucius' reply was confident. "No, my lord. It happens all the time. We raid their shores and they raid ours. They were only ashore for a day, took a couple of prisoners, a few items of booty and they went home. Just like we do."

Roderick tapped his fingers on the arm of the chair. "Just be vigilant. I know we have some strength in the region but we must remain alert. My kinsman, Count Julian of Septem, he knows that area well doesn't he? I understand that I am to receive him in the near future so I shall recommend him to keep his garrison prepared for any problems that might arise there. You may go." He waved a hand in dismissal and Lucius bowed himself out of the room. Roderick sat thinking for while before summoning his next agent. This one covered a territory at the other end of Hispania and he entered from a different anteroom from that from which Lucius had made his exit.

Chapter 15

Toletum, 710AD

The building had become home to dozens of feral cats. Empty for some time and, apart from a brief, if busy, human visitation some months earlier, nobody had set foot in the place for years. Since vermin took up residence in any building, occupied or otherwise, this one was no exception and its remoteness, together with the plentiful supply of rats and mice, made it an ideal refuge for feline squatters. Until, that is, the sound of a key turning in the lock put an instant stop to their activities. As one, their backs arched and they hissed their displeasure at this unexpected threat. The door opened slowly, cautiously and surprisingly quietly, causing a flurry of fur and yowls as the cats scurried into the darker corners of the cavernous space, away from the beams of moonlight falling through the open door. The figure standing there, in the doorway, sniffed and wrinkled his nose. The smell was nauseating and he set about herding the cats out into the night. He then reasoned that, since the door had been locked shut, they must have found another way to get into the building so he set down the bag he'd been carrying over his shoulder and started to look around for places where they might have gained entry. It was too dark to see very much and, suddenly, he felt overcome by fatigue. He slid the cowl from the back of his head and yawned. It had been a long journey. He was very old and desperate to rest his aching legs. The cats would have to wait until morning. After all, he had nothing else to do. Tomorrow would be soon enough to deal with them. Moving gingerly, with the door shut there was now no light to guide him, he felt his way around the walls of the room until he encountered a stone settle. He had no brush so he swept the seat with an old piece of cloth from his bag, which then served as a pillow as he lowered his body on to the cold stone bed.

•

Not too far away, in the city itself, the scene was very different. Although night, flickering lights could be seen throughout Toletum as wall sconces illuminated social gatherings in villas, and a host of moving torches lit meandering alleyways for late-night revellers following their servants home or to another party. While the more pious Wittiza ruled, the social energy of Toletum had suffered but now that Roderick was in power, the nobility were beginning to rediscover their taste, and opportunity, for having a good time. Thanks to his newly elevated position, Roderick's social activities were now largely limited to more formal gatherings involving statecraft and political manoeuvrings. In contrast with the previous court, these were now lavish affairs that served a dual purpose of introducing Roderick to foreign emissaries and cementing some tenuous ties with more local activists. The next day, preparations were to begin for the visit of one who was an important keystone in the security of the Visigothic state. He was also a vassal of Roderick but, because of his strategic location, known to be a man of independent means and mind. He was also a distant relative of Roderick, a fact which intrigued Egolina who said, "You keep telling me that he is kin but what sort of kin? First cousin, second, third cousin? Mother's side or father's side? What exactly? And he is bringing this daughter of his, this Flora…whatsername, and leaving her with us? Can you imagine having a provincial frump mooning around the palace? Think how depressing that is likely to be."

Roderick laughed and dismissed his secretary with whom he'd been working. He rose and took his wife's hands, turned them over and implanted light kisses on the palms.

She snatched them away. "Not now Roderick. I want to know more about Count Julian if I am to prepare for his visit. If he is your Exarch, why go to a lot of trouble, why can't you receive him as just another supplicant?"

Roderick sighed. "Because, Egolina, he has power and he is the last bastion between ourselves and the pagan hordes. If what I hear is true, they are becoming stronger by the day and moving westwards. Count Julian's stronghold, Septem, is in the middle of their northern territories and, by a combination of diplomacy and military strength, he has maintained a balance in the region. We need him and, because of that, he has to be given the status of an honoured guest. Already the Berbers have mounted raids on our mainland. Nothing serious and only small scale, but I must have good friends in that part of Hispania because you never know what could happen there." He kissed her forehead and gave a chuckle.

"As for the girl, the daughter; well she might not be so ugly." He bent over Egolina and, drawing her to him, crushed her mouth to his. "In fact," he went on, having caught his breath, "she might even…" He stopped there, winked at his wife then waved an admonitory finger at her. "I was joking, Egolina. You really must not entertain the idea. Now, I must get about my business and leave you to prepare for our guests. I understand that they are leaving Septem this day and should be with us in, say, ten days' time."

As he turned to leave the room, he brushed against her and she reached after him to pull him back but he had gone. She shivered and ran to her apartments.

•

The small fleet of trading vessels sailed serenely into the port at the base of the Rock. As always it was a scene of fevered activity and hardly had Count Julian set foot on land, than he was busily engaged in conversations with other ships' captains, traders and like men of business. Florinda, assisted by a huge Berber, carefully descended to the dock and impatiently shook her head. It was always the same. As soon as her father smelled a likely source of commerce he was off, and everything else, herself included, was sometimes forgotten. Since he wasn't there to do it, she took over her father's duties and started organising the careful unloading of her personal baggage. The unloading was in the capable and surprisingly gentle hands of the giant who had assisted her disembarkation. His name was Tamegrant, he was a eunuch, he was deaf, he was dumb and he adored Florinda who, since a small child, had established a process of communication with him, using hand and mouth signs that only they could understand.

It had long been a mystery to Julian who, although he knew and understood his daughter better than anyone, had never been able to decipher this coded language between her and Tamegrant. What he did know, and appreciate, was that Tamegrant's unswerving affection for Florinda made him an ideal bodyguard and servant. Being the headstrong girl that she was, from an early age she had railed against the confinement of the fortress at Septem and when he gave in to her demands, as he usually did, and permitted her to ride outside the protective walls, she was always accompanied, and dwarfed, by Tamegrant, mounted on the biggest and most powerful horse in the stable.

Now she watched as her baggage was being loaded onto one of the carts that were to form their train on the way to Toletum. That done, she thanked Tamegrant for his efforts and made off, with him at her heels, to find her father. Eventually she ran him to ground in a warehouse. He was in deep discussion, just as she had suspected, with a trader who appeared to be reluctant to agree to the terms that Julian had just offered. Florinda gently touched Tamegrant's sleeve and communicated something to him. Tamegrant left her side, marched up to the trader, planted two enormous hands on the man's shoulders and just looked at him. The trader looked up at Tamegrant's expressionless face, then at Julian and immediately agreed to Julian's terms. Florinda nodded to her colossus, who returned her nod, removed his hands and ambled back to her side. When they were walking back along the quay,

Julian gave Florinda an admiring look and said, "Do you know, I've never thought of doing that, it was clever of you. How did you know it would work?"

"I didn't Papa," came the reply. "And I don't care. All I want to do is to start making our way to Toletum. How long are we going to be on the road?"

Julian squinted up at the sun. "Probably between eight and ten days. It depends on how often you need to stop and change." He nodded at her luggage which just about fitted into a single large cart. Everybody else's personal effects, gifts, bodyguards' spare equipment and food fitted easily into the second cart.

She pouted. "Don't worry, Papa. I shan't get in your way. So long as we can stay just outside the city long enough for me to have a good rest and plenty of time to prepare myself for my entrance to the Court."

Julian grinned. "Let's say ten days then, shall we? For a start, though, we have a long and difficult ride to our first stop." He looked up at the sun again. "If we're to get to the gorge we will have to get a move on." That said, he spurred his horse and, with the carts rumbling behind them, they set their faces to the north.

•

It was, indeed, quite a long ride to Arunda, and darkness had set in by the time they gratefully slid off their horses. Julian had not exaggerated the difficulty of the journey. Not only was it long but quite arduous, involving ascents and descents through mountain passes. At first, Florinda kept up a ceaseless commentary on the changing countryside, the hamlets through which they passed and the abject state of the inhabitants who displayed a degree of poverty quite foreign to her and, as they progressed, Julian could not help but notice that her enthusiasm for the adventure was becoming more subdued by the mile. At first he assumed it was fatigue that was the cause of this drop in her naturally high spirits but, as time went on, he deduced that it was something more than mere tiredness, but he knew his daughter better than to question her when she was surrounded by their escort and servants. As it was, the group was being continually broken up as they took their turn in helping push the carts up the steeper gradients. Drawn by teams of six horses, there was normally no problem for them to keep up with the rest of the party but these mountain roads, although reasonably maintained – they had, after all, been originally laid by Roman engineers – took their toll and a helpful push was always welcome to the waggoners and their charges. Thankfully, the more hazardous stretches were behind them when they started to lose the light, and those familiar with the route breathed a sigh of relief as soon as the distant lights of the city came into view.

It was known well to Julian, who had not only made this journey on several previous occasions but also because the villa, in which they were spending the night, was in shared ownership between himself and a Visigoth aristocrat. This noble had fallen out of favour with King Wittiza and had yet to make his peace with the new king who, he was hoping, would restore some of his former fortune in exchange for an oath of allegiance. The current arrangement suited Julian who, although not meeting frequently with the man, used him as an agent for business in the region and as a useful source of information concerning the power struggles that characterised the Visigothic regime. Having arrived safely, Florinda appeared to regain some of her former animation and instructed the long suffering Tamegrant to deal with the packages that she wanted unloading. When her father intervened by saying that she shouldn't go to too much trouble because they would only be stopping long enough to rest the horses and themselves, perhaps two days would suffice, she looked horrified.

"Two days! We'll never get to Toletum if we keep stopping for two days."

He managed to calm her down by telling her that Arunda was different because, for one thing, it was the hardest leg of the journey and, for another, he wanted some extra time to conclude a trading agreement that he and his friend had been working on for some time. The resulting pout was soon replaced by her customary good humour and a rejuvenated Florinda was soon bustling around, meeting the villa's residents and supervising the next day's activities, until the rigours of the journey finally overcame her and she was led away to her apartment by one of the local servants.

•

The next morning dawned beautifully clear and the household was woken by the excited shouts of Florinda as she stood at her window and looked down on to the drama of the deep gorge which, because of their late arrival the night before, had not been visible to them. For once she didn't take too much care with her dress but donned the first things available to her, which happened to be the travelling clothes she'd worn, ran down the stairs and out onto the balcony overlooking the gorge. She heard a noise behind her and turned to see her father, a slightly smug smile on his face, standing in the doorway.

"I have arranged for a guide to take you to see some interesting sights. I do realise, my dear, that this isn't the city of your dreams but it's time you learned that there are places other than Toletum which are worthy of your attention. I wouldn't bother to think about changing because the terrain, as you can see, is extremely rugged and mules have been organised for transport. Tamegrant will, naturally, accompany you and see that you are not subjected to any danger. In particular, there are a number of artefacts and ruins which go back to our Roman ancestors." He smiled at the face she was pulling.

"Florinda, when we arrive at Toletum, you will be expected to have some knowledge of your history. Yes, I know," he went on, holding up his hand to halt the expected objection, " you have already been schooled but there is no limit to knowledge and you will make a much better impression on the Court if, for example, you could say that you'd taken the trouble to visit the remains of Scipio's original fortress."

She frowned. "Scipio?"

"Yes, my dear," Julian replied, "Scipio, the Roman general who conquered much of Ifriquya. Our hosts in Toletum are great admirers of our ancestors, which is why, I imagine, they go to such great pains to copy their dress and customs." He broke off and, as if muttering to himself, said, "With them, though, it's all show and affectation, the barbarian is not very far beneath the surface."

"Papa?" said a bemused Florinda, "What are you talking about?"

"Nothing, my dear. Nothing at all. Now, you've just time to break your fast and then you can be off on your sightseeing adventure. I will meet with you later." Which said, he turned on his heel and Florinda hardly had time to renew her acquaintance with the impressive view when there was a knock, and she turned to see the doorway filled by the massive figure of Tamegrant.

This pattern was more or less continued as they travelled north. Cordova, Julian explained, was reputedly where the present king had been born but the town held little other interest for Florinda and she announced that a single overnight stop would be more than enough. Thereafter, through the flat plains, their progress was much faster and it was only a few days before Julian was able to point out to his daughter the outline of Toletum, silhouetted against a creamy early evening sky. She immediately insisted they stop at the nearest available and suitable residence so that, the following morning, she could prepare herself for what she saw as her triumphal entry into the magical city.

It was against the better judgement of Julian, but she was not to be moved on this point so Julian directed the party to the home of yet another old business friend of his and it was in a comfortable bed, provided by their kind host, that Florinda spent the most sleepless night of her uneventful life.

•

For the inhabitants of Tangier, it was also to prove a sleepless night. The early evening had resounded to the sound of horns blowing, much shouting and the sort of activity that denoted the arrival of someone important. So important, in fact, that Tariq's servant, under strict orders not to disturb his busy master, felt himself with no alternative but to do just that. Already alerted by the commotion, Tariq was prepared for an interruption and, on being told what it was about, instructed his man to waste no time in passing an order to Malik and the other commanders to assemble their troops in the best order that time allowed. A visit by Musa ibn Nusayr, no matter the time of day or the inconvenience, had to be given due attention and ceremony and, after his last encounter with the Emir, Tariq was determined not to be found wanting. He hurriedly changed from his informal working attire into something more suitable. At least he hoped it would be more suitable because he chose the robe that Menna had made, ostensibly for Musa who was far too big for it, whereas it suited Tariq perfectly. He had last worn it when he and Musa had visited Septem together and he rather hoped that Musa might have forgotten the occasion. As he made his exit from his apartments, he noticed Malik, Tala and others were getting together as many of those soldiers who were available into some sort of presentable shape. Malik nodded to him and Tariq ordered the gates to be opened. Musa seemed to have put on a great deal of weight since Tariq had last seen him in Damascus, and he was mounted on one of the biggest horses Tariq had ever clapped eyes on. Musa raised a hand in greeting and waited to be assisted from his saddle. An attendant ran up with a mounting block and Musa, breathing heavily from the effort, dismounted carefully, walked the few paces to Tariq and embraced him warmly. Tariq was surprised; he hadn't known what to expect but it had entered his head that, as a result of his rejection of Musa's plan, in front of Al Walid, he might have lost favour with his mentor but, apparently, it was not the case. Musa must have sensed Tariq's hesitancy in returning the greeting for he laughed one of his deep barrel laughs, clapped Tariq on the shoulder and said, "I don't hold grudges, my friend. Just because we disagreed, it doesn't mean that we have to become estranged. Let us walk awhile, I had forgotten just how pleasant it is here and the evening is cool. What do you say we take a stroll on the upper walls?"

He gestured to the spot which overlooked Septem and the Strait.

"Oh! And tell your men to stand down, this is an informal visit." He ran his eyes slowly over the ranks of men, standing smartly, spears and swords glinting in the last of the sunlight.

As the two men walked towards the stone stairs leading to the parapet, he turned to Tariq.

"They look in good shape, Tariq. You are doing an excellent job here, but then, I knew you would."

They reached the top and Musa leaned on the waist high wall, looking out to sea and Tariq remembered the first time they had been together on this spot. The relationship had changed more than he could have thought possible at the time. He asked Musa if he too remembered the meeting, when Musa had pretended not to know who he was, although he kept this last thought to himself. Musa, his eyes firmly fixed on the sea and the blurred, scarcely visible shape of the Rock and the outline of land beyond, said, "Yes, of course I remember. I remember when you were first marched into the compound here. I asked Tala who you were, your name, and do you know what he said to me?"

Tariq shook his head.

"He said 'That boy, that Berber slave, is going to be giving me orders before too long.' And you have done, haven't you? Excellent judge of character is Tala and an even better judge of a good soldier."

Embarrassed, Tariq tried to change the subject.

"Not a good enough soldier to want to conquer whatever it is over there though."

Musa laughed again. "So we disagree! As I said, I harbour no bad feelings but, I tell you now, we will invade Hispania and I have no doubt that you will be part of it."

For the first time he took his eyes from the far horizon and looked at Tariq who said nothing. Musa continued, "You know it too, don't you? You've changed your mind haven't you? I don't suppose you'd like to tell me why?"

Still Tariq was silent until, eventually, he replied thoughtfully, "Yes and no. Ever since that meeting with the Caliph, I have thought of little else. My lord, I need to have more information and I need to know that we will succeed. I still feel that the time is not quite right. The disposition and strength of the Visigoth army is still too much of an unknown quantity and the risk is too great. I do, however, have an idea that I would like to discuss with you and, of course, with the Caliph. We can do nothing without his approval."

Musa returned his gaze to the horizon before saying, not without a hint of exasperation, "Naturally we would need his agreement before we embark on anything as important but does that preclude you from sharing your idea with me first?"

Tariq waited until Musa turned to face him again before replying, "No, lord, I am interested to have your opinion. You see, I don't think that the Caliph will countenance any project that is not assured of success and it is my opinion, as well you know, that success is not assured unless we have better intelligence. This will not be obtained by sending small raiding parties to test their defences. They are regarded as little more than a minor irritant and those we have sent thus far have yielded little in the way of useful information. No,

I think we should send over an army. If they are lightly armed and equipped for speed, there should not be too much risk involved. If they are confronted by serious enemy numbers, they should be able to out-run them back to where our transport fleet will be moored, ready to sail them back here to safety."

Musa shook his head.

"I am sorry. Tariq, but I don't understand your strategy. If we are going to send an invasion force, as you suggest, then why bother to let them run back here at the first sign of trouble. What is the point?"

"The point, my lord, is that we land, say, a thousand soldiers. Something big enough to lead the Visigoth to believe that it IS an invasion force. The Visigoth will assume that we attempted an invasion and that, in the event, their security was not seriously threatened. That way, we learn something of their response to a large scale attack, but without any great risk to Umayyad troops. Should the time come when we *are* ready to invade, then we send in a much more substantial force which they won't be expecting because, having seen us off once, and comfortably at that, they will think that we are unlikely to suffer further ignominy by attempting another invasion. This would give us two advantages. One, we have more knowledge of the enemy and two, that of surprise. What do you think of it, my lord?"

Musa, slapped the top of the wall with his meaty hand. "I think it interesting, Tariq. Let us discuss the detail of the tactics and we will then seek the blessing of Al Walid."

So saying, he turned his back on Tariq and held both his hands out to the distant horizon as if ready to embrace the lands of Hispania Ulterior.

Chapter 16

Damascus, 710AD

Busy at the best of times, Tangier was now buzzing with heightened activity. Military training was intensified and tactics refined. Intelligence sources were being asked to step up their efforts, and messengers arrived and departed almost hourly, or so it seemed. Musa had returned to Damascus where, as he and Tariq had agreed, he was to put Tariq's plan before Al Walid, without whose approval it was not possible to mount a significant military operation. Although the Caliph might be lacking direct experience in the field, such as Musa, and might err on the side of caution, his grasp of military matters was exemplary and it was under his rule that much of central Asia had fallen to Islamic forces. Accordingly, Musa knew that he was going to have to put the case for a large scale attack on territory about which relatively little was known, both in terms of defence or culture, with care and diplomacy. He was also aware that Tariq and Al Walid shared a spirituality of which he had no part. Musa's military success, particularly as a naval commander, ensured his place as a valued player in the Umayyad Caliphate but he was under no illusions that his worldly views were considered to be out of step with the spiritual values of his master.

As he walked from his apartment, set in one of the palace towers and reserved for his use when he visited Damascus, he turned over in his mind the approach most likely to succeed in his embassy. From an orangery, he entered the main palace through one of the horseshoe arched doorways, now one of the distinguishing features of Islamic architecture, passed the bathhouse and started to mount the stairs to the first floor which housed the executive suites and meeting rooms. It was a journey he'd made several times in the past and, since he was known to most of the important occupants of the palace, his thoughts were constantly interrupted by greetings from scholars, clerics and administrators brushing past him as they went about their business. At the head of the staircase he halted, nodded to another guard and then another cleric, before turning his face to the wall and pretending to study the detail of an ornate mosaic while he marshalled his final thoughts. Musa Ibn Nusayr was not normally this cautious. In fact, he was probably one of the most self-confident men of his time but Al Walid inspired enormous respect in everyone and Musa was no exception. His narrow escape from capital punishment, at the hands of Al Walid's father, for diverting Umayyad revenue into his own pockets during his stewardship of Irak, was a constant reminder, when in the company of the Caliph, that he was answerable to a higher authority. It therefore seemed politic to present Tariq's plan as something for which he, Musa, was little more than an emissary. This was, of course, true. The plan was Tariq's but Musa would dearly have liked to have taken credit for it. The problem was that, at their previous meeting, Tariq appeared to have gained the confidence of Al Walid to the extent that he, Musa, was excluded from part of their conference so he resolved that pride would have to be swallowed on this occasion. In any case, when the Umayyad forces attacked those of the Visigoth – and conquered them - the plunder would be more than adequate compensation. The Table of Solomon for example! Why, even if he couldn't profit from it directly, its value to him, as a gift to the Umayyad, would be beyond price and surely involve a return to unquestioned favour and all that that would represent.

He moved to the door leading to Al Walid's suite. His fingers ceased tracing their way around the intricate relief carved on the door before they folded into a fist and tapped on the heavy portal, through which he had to strain to hear the gentle voice within, bidding him enter.

•

In Tangier, Tariq surveyed the battlefield and stroked his bearded chin, thinking what to do next. He had run out of ideas and was reduced to seeking inspiration from the doubtful source of his imagination. It was the same old problem; not knowing the opposition well enough to be able to keep ahead of the game. He leant over the table and speculatively moved another block. The table was covered in different shaped wooden blocks. The black ones were the army of the Umayyad and the white ones that of the enemy. The different shapes designated the role of the different units such as cavalry, infantry and archers.

He assumed that the Visigothic forces comprised the same elements but, again, he couldn't be certain. Should permission be granted for a pseudo invasion, he might know more from the intelligence that it provided but, for the time being he had to assume that, thanks to Count Julian, the Visigoth probably knew much more about Umayyad strategy than he knew about theirs. That being the case, he picked up a battalion of infantry and tapped it on the table while he thought out his next move. If his assumption was correct, and the Visigoth knew what to expect from the Islamic forces, then he needed to think through, and change, what until then, had become an established pattern of warfare for Islamic armies. Generally, this entailed a strong phalanx of spear carrying infantry, smaller battalions of archers stationed towards the rear, and even smaller bodies of mounted soldiers engaging the flanks of the opposing forces. If this is what Roderick would be expecting, then why not revise the tactics? So involved was he with this question that he didn't hear the door open and slippered feet enter the room. Menna's voice, apologetically subdued, took a moment to register with him. When it did, he turned to face her and was about to rebuke her for the interruption when he saw the look on her face as she surveyed his table-top battleground. At first she frowned, as if she wasn't quite sure what it was supposed to be all about; then the frown dissolved into a smile as the realisation hit her. She put a hand to her mouth and looked at him, he looked back at her and they both burst into gales of laughter. Once they recovered, she dabbed at her eyes, sniffed and picked up a cavalry battalion.

"Really, my lord," she said, "I never thought I'd see you playing at soldiers. At least, not now, when you have so many of the real ones to play with, or am I not taking it seriously enough?"

"No, you are not," he said, taking the block from her and placing it back exactly from where she had taken it. "Not if you realise that making decisions at this table are not likely to put real lives at risk. Not like they would be in a battle. You probably don't understand this but, for me, fighting is not only about winning battles. It is equally about winning them with the least number of casualties. Those men out there," he held up his hands to indicate the whole garrison, their lives are in my hands and that, believe me, is an enormous responsibility so I do everything within my power, including playing games if necessary, to win a campaign without sacrificing more lives than I have to."

She looked at him for so long that he felt compelled to drop his eyes from hers. She saw that he was looking tired and asked if he were completely well. He sighed, then laughed and said,

"Yes, thank you Menna. You don't have to worry about me. It's high time you married and had children. Someone of your own to worry about."

Her smile was bright. "So you keep telling me Tariq. Embrace the Faith, then a follower of it. Perhaps, when I am ready." Her smile faded as quickly as it had appeared. "Anyway, I can quite understand that you are tired. From what I hear, you have been in and out of meetings, debriefing couriers and running a garrison that is expanding by the day. Akeem is worried about you, he thinks that you are .." Tariq broke in, the surprise in his voice quite genuine.

"Akeem! If anything, he's the one who has been overworking. I'm always giving him jobs to do. For the last two days he has had a battalion of cavalry practise embarkation and disembarkation from our transport fleet. It not only takes a lot of patience but, physically, it's very demanding, manhandling horses that aren't used to it. And, don't forget, Akeem's not exactly young now. If you want to worry about anyone, worry about him and, while we're on the subject of fatigue, you look as though a rest wouldn't do you any harm."

Menna reddened, started to say something then swallowed it back. Before she could regain her composure, Tariq moved to her side and took both her hands in his.

"I'm sorry Menna, I didn't mean it to sound like that. The problem is that we are all under strain at the moment. I am awaiting a very important emissary from Damascus, possibly even Musa himself, and before it arrives I need to be as well prepared as I possibly can be." He attempted to release Menna's hands and move away but she held on to him.

"I have been working quite hard too, you know," she said. He smiled at her. A neutral smile which made her grip his hands even more tightly. She continued, " My team and I have been working non-stop for weeks now." Tariq's smile turned to puzzlement.

"You have? Doing what?"

She let go of his hands and held hers out for his inspection. He could see that they were criss-crossed with a web of tiny cuts and scars.

"Sewing together the leather plates for the body armour that your cavalry are wearing while they practise getting their horses on and off the transports. It's very hard work and, after a time, quite painful too, as you can see. How are they getting on with the new armour, or haven't you had Tala's report yet?"

Tariq nodded. "Yes, I have and it's very…Menna, please forgive me. I am so very sorry not to have registered how hard you have been working. I have been so pre-occupied with..well, with other matters, political as well as military, that I just take the supply element for granted. I should have spoken with you before about how pleased we are with your new designs and the increased flexibility they will give our troops. In fact…" He stopped short, his eyes narrowed in thought, then turned away from Menna and started to move the black blocks around the table.

"Of course!" He muttered to himself. "This might allow them to…" He turned round.

"I'm sorry, Menna, but I'm going to have to ask you to leave me while I…"

Menna biting her lip, whispered, "Yes, of course Tar…, my lord,"turned and ran out of the room. Without looking, Tariq called out, "Send Malik and Tala up to me, please." But she had already gone.

Down at the waterfront, Akeem was, as Tariq said, organising the best way of getting five hundred troops, together with their horses, on board the transport barges used by the Umayyad navy. This had been done often enough but, in the event of a couple of battalions making a landing on the other side of the Strait, Tariq had emphasised that speed was of the essence and the risk of casualties resulting from a laborious and slow boarding had to be minimised. Actually, Akeem was not totally aware that any such military expedition would be taking place since the proposed "invasion" was, at this stage, known only to Tariq and Musa. True, Malik was aware that something was afoot but even he did not know the exact nature of it. The fact was, Tariq always kept his army on alert and was constantly changing their training routines because, as he argued with his staff, it kept the men interested and their officers on their toes. It also gave Tariq the opportunity to exercise his imagination and further his study into the tactics of other, often historical, cultures from which he always found something to learn. This apparent fascination with the theoretical science of warfare was currently lost on Akeem who was getting heartily fed up with loading unwilling horses and their riders onto ships and unloading them again. The horses weren't appreciating it much either and by the time that a couple of them had sustained injury through panicking, Akeem deemed sensible to call a halt to proceedings. He ordered the troop commanders to stand their men down while he hurried back to the fortress, where he waited impatiently for a free moment of his master's time. As it happened, he didn't have to wait long as Tariq had just finished debriefing a messenger from Damascus and as the man slipped out of the door, Akeem slipped in, if the word might correctly be ascribed to one of Akeem's bulk, and presented himself before Tariq had a chance to deny him entry. If Tariq was put out by the interruption, he had the good grace not to show it and he listened carefully to Akeem who quickly reduced his problem to two things, time and numbers.

If speed were essential, as Tariq had insisted it was, there was no way that five hundred horses could be embarked. Fewer horses, more time, and Akeem thought he could make it work with blindfolds or slings for getting horses on board but the way it had been done in the past, where time and numbers weren't important, just didn't add up and he was out of ideas so…Tariq, who had, more or less, anticipated this conversation, broke in.

"I understand what you are saying, old friend, but if the horses can't or won't adapt, then we will have to view the problem from another angle. Horses and ships are not designed for each other so, as we cannot redesign the horse perhaps we ought to look at redesigning the ship. Who do we know in the shipyards? We need someone who is not afraid to break away from tradition because, believe me Akeem, before Lord Musa returns here, I need answers to these problems."

Akeem thought for a moment then beamed at Tariq.

"I know someone, he's a cousin of mine and when we were kids he was always making toy boats for us to play with." He noticed Tariq's look and went on.

"No my lord, not just toys like you're thinking of. Obviously, these were only miniature vessels but each one was designed for something different and, I'll tell you this, they all floated nice and trim. Amayuu's his name. Haven't seen him for years but I'd heard that he'd moved up here for the ship building. I'll go and see if I can find him."

Tariq grinned at this show of enthusiasm, Akeem was seldom as animated unless he was angry about something. He called Akeem back.

"Look," he said, "don't just bring him straight back here without explaining what it is you want from him. I haven't the time to go over it all again, but you have. If you think he has something to offer us and can come up with some practical solutions, then bring him to see me. A rough model might be useful, quicker for me to understand."

Akeem nodded and took himself off to search for this cousin who, Tariq thought quietly, was probably a figment of Akeem's imagination or working elsewhere in the Empire.

It took nearly half the day to prove Tariq wrong, but wrong he was. An excited Akeem appeared in the doorway to Tariq's office, dragging behind him an individual who could not have been more dissimilar to his escort. Scrawny, almost, with a lugubrious face, a high forehead and a workman's pouched apron tied around his skinny waist. More interestingly, he was carrying a small, rough model of a ship. Introductions having been made Amayuu, who turned out to be a great deal more interesting than he looked, lost no time in presenting his idea to Tariq. He apologised for the crude model, saying that had he been given more time it would, of course, have been better crafted but Tariq said that it didn't matter, it was the principle he needed to grasp and, as it turned out the principle couldn't have been easier. So easy, in fact, that Tariq couldn't understand why such vessels hadn't been designed like this before. Amayuu explained.

"It could be, my lord, that for long sea journeys, this design would not be practical, taking into account sudden changes in sea conditions that a long voyage might entail."

Tariq immediately interrupted. "How do you know that I'm not talking about a long voyage?"

"Well, my lord," Amayuu said, "Everyone knows that we are planning to sail an army across the Strait here."

Tariq looked surprised, "Do they?" he said, "How do they know that?"

Amayuu and Akeem looked at each other, as if to say "shall you tell him or will I?"In the end it was Akeem, Tariq's confidant, who replied.

"We have recruits arriving here by the hundred, new armour has been tested and passed fit for use, training programmes have been intensified, Lord Musa makes a hurried visit, envoys keep appearing out of nowhere and we are now practising getting on and off boats. Doesn't take much to figure it out, does it, Sir?"

Tariq regarded the pair of them with a mixture of authority tinged with amusement.

"I suppose it does seem obvious that something is being planned but," he wagged a finger at them, "*Nothing* has been decided yet so don't let these rumours get out of hand. Now then, let's have a look at your idea, Amayuu."

Amayuu put the model on the table.

"It's simple," he said. "So long as the voyage is short and the sea's relatively calm. Swell and light waves are all right but you wouldn't want anything bigger. We can easily adapt our existing fleet and, if we do so, we have another advantage, which is that we could affect beach as well as port landings." He took a deep breath and stood back.

Tariq turned the model over in his hands and then noticed that the bow stood proud of the superstructure and the angles to the superstructure were far less pronounced than he was used to seeing. Amayuu put out a hand, "If you will allow me, my lord."

Tariq handed over the model which Amayuu laid on the table. He then took hold of the strange bow end, pulled gently at the top which he then lowered, forming a ramp between the table top and the deck of the boat. Tariq and Akeem looked at each other, instantly realising the implication of this simple demonstration. Akeem was the first to raise an objection.

"It's all very well and, from the point of view of loading and unloading, could answer a lot of problems but how watertight can you make that?" He pointed to the bow. "Once it's pulled up again, and that's not going to be easy, how'd you stop the sea from getting in?"

Amayuu flicked the bow back up and pointed out that it not only fitted back into the cut-out box section at the front of the hull, but he also drew attention to the rectangular derrick standing mid-way along the deck. "I didn't have time to build it into this model but the ramp can be lowered and raised by means of pulleys running from this. As for being watertight? The short answer is, we can't be sure until we test one at sea but I'm almost sure it won't take on water."

Akeem snorted and pointed out that being 'almost sure' was of little comfort to the human and equine cargo it was designed to carry. Amayuu only shrugged and said that if Akeem knew of a better way to test a new design, then he, Amayuu, would be happy to learn from him. Tariq, seeing that Akeem was bristling visibly at this rebuff, asked how long it would take to adapt an existing vessel and Amayuu answered that it would depend on manpower and resources, then he paused, thought for a moment and said, "Rather than adapting one of our naval vessels, why not use something like a trading barge?"

Tariq smiled and clapped him on the shoulder. "Exactly what I hoped you were going to say. Similar to the ones that sail from Septem. Not something that we could ask Count Julian about, obviously, but are they difficult to build, or perhaps they can be bought?"

Amayuu looked from Tariq to Akeem and then back to Tariq, his eyes sparkling with amusement.

"No need, my lord, we already have some."

"Really, how is that?"

"Well, my lord, some we have captured, as booty, during raids and some we have purchased from disaffected traders from Hispania who, for whatever reason, needed the money." He gave a wry smile. "As you can imagine, my lord, we don't pay very much for them."

Tariq looked at Akeem. "How come I knew nothing of this?" and this time it was Akeem's turn to shrug and direct the question to Amayuu who looked embarrassed momentarily, before replying.

"The thing is, my lord, that Lord Musa was more concerned with naval matters since many of his great victories were gained at sea. If I might say so, my lord, I cannot remember seeing you at the yards, not that that was expected of you," he went on hastily, "and I am sorry if I have given the impression that…" Tariq waved away the apology.

"No, you are quite right, Amayuu. That has been a dereliction on my part and one that I will rectify in the future but, for the present, I need to know how long it will take you to prepare a transport fleet from your.. your acquired collection."

Amayuu used his fingers to calculate and came up with a tentative date, providing that funds and manpower were assured. Tariq gave him that assurance, thanked them for their help and dismissed them. As they left, Akeem ushered Amayuu through the door, turned, winked at Tariq and said, "Told you he was good, didn't I?"

Chapter 17

Toletum, 710AD

The palace was ablaze with light, laughter and music and Florinda was enjoying herself. This was what she had always dreamed about, being a vibrant young woman, enjoying all the pleasures of a vibrant young society here in the city. Her hosts had been more than kind, had introduced her to several noblewomen in the area, all of whom had promised Count Julian that his precious daughter was safe in their maternal hands. These assurances had either not been communicated to Tamegrant by Florinda, or he had chosen to ignore them, for he was seldom from her side, slept outside her bedroom door and kept a watchful and, to her, a somewhat irritating attendance upon her. At this moment, while she sat with a gathering of her new-found friends, watching a local native troupe performing some of their exotic dances as part of the celebrations, she could see her guardian slave, arms folded across his massive chest, his eyes firmly fixed on her every gesture. She frowned, then deliberately turned away and tried to pretend he wasn't there.

Really, she could not complain. It was one of her father's stipulations that, yes, she could remain at the court after he had left, but only if she agreed toTamegrant's constant protective presence. Since she had no intention of returning to her mundane life in Septem, she had little choice but to agree and although she tried every ruse within her power to evade his surveillance, he was never far away and, although she knew he was outside her door at night, it was only there that she could feel total privacy. If the truth were known, Florinda's feelings were more complex than she would have been prepared to admit. True, she relished her new life here in Toletum but, much as she enjoyed her new friends and the stimulation they provided, there were times when she felt homesick and would have given anything just to have spent an hour in the company of her beloved father, back in the serenity of Septem. These moments were, however, fleeting and few. Here, her time was taken up by so many activities that brooding had no part in her life. For one thing, she was being schooled, her continuing education being another of her father's preconditions for her to remain. Before leaving, he had interviewed and engaged a tutor and every day, for two hours, she was subjected to the discipline of learning the history of her forefathers and the ancient languages. Ever an imaginative girl with an inquiring mind, she had always enjoyed her lessons, mainly delivered by her father but occasionally by a scribe or priest, so this was not regarded as an imposition, and even the vast presence of her protector, sitting in the same room, his eyes never leaving her, managed to be forgotten as she concentrated on her lessons. Court etiquette was another of her duties and this she did sometimes find rather tiresome. Sometimes she was instructed, or perhaps advised might be a better word, by one or other of the women of the court who attended upon the queen herself, and on one particularly auspicious occasion, even by Queen Egolina.

The queen was very gracious and flattered Florinda on her beauty, running her hands through the girl's luxuriant hair and telling her how it should best be dressed and what colours she should wear to complement her complexion which, she chided, had spent too much time enjoying the warmth of the sun. Egolina's personal maid was also invited to add her own observations on the subject and she, too, had spoken admiringly about Florinda's hair, again combing it out with her fingers and laughing with her mistress as they talked about the other ladies of the court, not always in the most flattering terms. In fact, Florinda was just starting to feel slightly uncomfortable, both with the attentions of the maid, whose fingers seemed to be caressing rather than combing, and the comments being passed between the maid and her mistress. Florinda couldn't help but wonder what was said about her when she was not present in the same room. Now, though, she had nothing like that on her mind for she was enjoying herself, giggling with her friends and even managing to blank out Tamegrant's disapproving stare. Whether she would have been quite so happy had she been privy to the conversation taking place between Roderick and Egolina, as they sat together on the small raised dais appropriate to their station, would have been debatable. Actually Egolina was not looking at Florinda but at her giant guardian, brooding in the background. She nudged Roderick.

"Just look at him, he is huge and not unhandsome. Do you think that his…?" Roderick grinned at her, "Don't be silly, my dear, you know as well as I do that the man is a eunuch but I will grant you that he has a fine, if savage, appeal. I can, however assure you that, even your legendary appetite would fail to stimulate anyone possessing an unfortunate condition such as his."

Her eyes fixed on Tamegrant, she covertly stroked her husband's thigh and said, "I wouldn't mind trying though."

He moved her hand. "What about his charge then? I have to confess, I find her quite bewitching. All that rural innocence, wrapped up in a body like a goddess."

Egolina's breath quickened. "Oh yes; and to think that, before she graced our presence, I imagined we were going to have to put up with some provincial drab. I could not have been more wrong, could I?"

"Indeed, you could not, my angel," was his reply. "But, and we must not forget this, her father dotes on her and he is a valuable ally, something of which I have only too few at the moment. No, Egolina, we must be careful." She replaced her hand and his eyes closed for a moment, before he went on, "But I will think of something. Yes, be patient, I will think of something."

The group of dancers, having finished their routine, left the centre of the floor and were replaced by another group, this time jugglers and fire-eaters who swirled around in circles breathing out great spouts of flame, making the women guests shriek, gather up their robes and stand further back. So captivated was the audience by this spectacular exhibition of bravado that nobody noticed the quietly dressed little man pushing his way through the crowds towards the dais. Having reached it, he swiftly moved up behind Roderick and leaned over his shoulder, whispering in his ear. All this was done so unobtrusively that even Egolina was not immediately aware of his presence but, like everyone else, was riveted by the entertainment going on in front of her. When Roderick, for the second time, moved her hand from his thigh, she gave a mew of disappointment and turned to get his attention. Then she noticed the stranger and, whatever he was saying to her husband, it was obviously commanding his total concentration.

•

A long way distant from Toletum, back in Tangier, Tariq was also giving his undivided attention to his visitor. There were just the two of them and strict instructions had been given that they were not to be disturbed. Even Akeem, who always assumed that he had the run of the city and everything within it, would not have gained admittance. Certainly Musa would have just strolled in, had he been so inclined, but Musa was not here in Tangier, he was still in Damascus where his meetings with Al Walid had become almost a daily occurrence. So, it was just Tariq, leaning expectantly over the table and listening to Malik's account of the 'expedition', as they had decided to term it, into Hispania. Had he learned anything that would be useful, should a more ambitious expedition be attempted? He waited patiently for Malik to assemble his thoughts and his sheets of illustrations and maps, then...

"Well, my lord, as you can see, we are back."

"And very good it is to see you," replied Tariq warmly. "First things first, casualties?"

Malik smiled. "None, my lord."

"Not one?"

"No, my lord, not one. Not a man or a horse was lost. To tell you the truth, we saw very little in the way of action, but then your orders were to test the difficulties of moving a small army by sea and not to engage the enemy unless forced to."

Tariq sat back in his chair and nodded.

"That must have been something of a disappointment to you, my friend, but congratulations on getting in and out of the territory without losing anyone. So, tell me, what have you learned?"

"Well, to start at the beginning, you were watching, my lord, when we embarked here, at Tangier, so you could see the problems we had?"

Tariq gave a wry smile. "Indeed I could, Malik, and it wasn't until Akeem had the bright idea of blindfolding the horses and throwing straw on the ramps that the problem started to resolve itself. So, that was the first thing we learned. And then?"

"Then we set sail, as you ordered, for the closest point on the enemy shores. The sea was not unfriendly, nor the wind and we landed at Melloria, where the beaches were ideal for our purposes, gently sloping and few rocks to impede a smooth and, I have to say, rapid, landing. That's the second thing to bear in mind. Horses are happier getting off boats than getting on them so we had no troubles there. As for coming back…"

Tariq interrupted, "In sequence please, Malik, so that I can follow events more clearly. So, you landed satisfactorily, no opposition? Nothing at all?"

"Nothing to speak of," Malik said, with a hint of irony. "We landed well away from the settlement and were ashore, mounted in formation and riding towards the place before anyone noticed us. I have to say it's a sleepy part of the world but very pleasant. By the way, Sir, I meant to ask, why did you want me to ride west, and not east where there seems to be a lot more going on and richer pickings to be had?"

"Because, Malik, that is where the enemy would expect you to land. Should we later consider a more serious expedition, they can't be too certain of our intentions. Also, from the viewpoint of our Caliph, it was important that we suffer few casualties and, in that regard, you have done better than we could have hoped. Consequently, his blessing on a more ambitious project is more likely to be forthcoming. Anyway, please continue. You are advancing on Melloria unopposed."

"Almost unopposed, my lord. As we neared the settlement, a small force of, I would estimate, no more than three or four hundred men came out of the gates and moved towards us…"

"On foot or mounted, or both?"

"On foot, my lord. Ill-armed and ill-disciplined. We approached them at walking pace, they formed a ragged shield-wall but before we had unsheathed a sword, they broke up and ran back inside their fortress, such as it was. One of my officers galloped after them and managed to capture a couple of stragglers and hold them for a brief questioning."

Tariq raised an eyebrow, "And…"

"Nothing, my lord. Well, nothing that we could understand. I tried Latin but that was no good. Anyway, the next thing we knew, they'd opened their gates and welcomed us inside. Perhaps 'welcomed' might be rather overstating it but the impression was that the town, village, or settlement whatever it is, was ours."

Tariq's next question seemed to surprise Malik. "The men, our men, they behaved? No plunder or worse?"

Malik frowned. "My men behaved in an exemplary fashion. Just as you would expect, my Lord. All we took were some rude refreshments that were offered to us. As you know, we were riding light and the offer of a cooling drink and fruit was most welcome."

Tariq grinned at Malik's response and assured him that he would, of course, have expected no less. He then asked him to continue.

Malik took a reflective sip of his drink. "The next thing I had to bear in mind, before exploring further, was where and how to retreat quickly if necessary keeping in mind the problem with the horses. We continued west towards a village, Baelo Claudia, I think it is called. Too small to bother us but a very well preserved Roman settlement, which would provide some solid protection should we be forced to fight. Just as importantly, the coast around there looked ideal for an evacuation. Again, gentle sloping beaches so I ordered two of my men to gallop back to Melloria and call up our makeshift fleet to sail up the coast to Baelo Claudia where they could stand ready behind the ruins. I then appointed two of my best men to scout ahead and warn us of any impending trouble."

Tariq nodded his approval and motioned Malik to continue.

"We made our camp at Baelo Claudia. As you would expect, no fires, no lamps and enough sentries to keep watch and fuss around the horses to keep them quiet." He took another glass of coffee from the brass tray, the only item on the table apart from primitive drawings on scraps of vellum that, for Malik, passed as maps.

Again Tariq signified his approval and asked. "No trouble during the night?

Malik shrugged, "None, and to be frank with you we really didn't expect any. Not if the day before had been anything to go by. The next morning, we mounted just before dawn and continued along the coast until we saw it."

Tariq sat up straight. "Saw what?"

"Well, my lord, those of us blessed with keen sight scanned the coast running away from us until it seemed to end in a peninsular of some sort. Then, the closer we came to it; we could make out what appeared to be a very large city."

Tariq said "Ah! Gades."

"My lord?"

"Gades, Malik. Roman, and before that, Carthaginian. Before that, I couldn't tell you but there would have been an earlier civilisation. I think it is reputed to be one of the oldest cities on that continent. How close did you get?"

"We didn't, my lord. My scouts came galloping back to warn us, but not before we saw the huge cloud of dust meaning a large number of men had been mobilised. Following your orders, we turned and retreated." The bitterness with which Malik spoke that last word brought a smile to Tariq's face. He quickly hid it and hastened to placate his lieutenant.

"It wasn't a retreat, Malik, it was a tactical withdrawal. There is an enormous difference between the two and you know it as well as I do. So, what happened next?"

"What happened next, my lord, was that we galloped back to Baelo Claudia, hoping that our transports would be…"

Tariq raised a hand to interrupt him. "This force that came out to meet you from Gades, how was it made up? How close did they get to you?"

"Not at all close, sir. In fact, the distance was such that we had no means of identifying the composition of their army, anymore than they could ours. I mean, for all they knew we could have constituted a sizeable invasion. A battalion of cavalry creates a lot of dust, just as we saw created by their force, but my men scouting ahead did get a reasonable look at them before they turned and…" Malik stopped in mid-sentence.

"And..?" Tariq prompted.

"Before my scouts turned and ran, they saw enough to determine that it was a full scale army confronting them. At least five or six battalions, although they weren't close enough for an accurate tally, but it appeared to be mainly composed of infantrymen. There was some cavalry but it was very heavily armoured and slow. It was so slow that my scouts could have trotted back to join us without fear of capture. As it was, I had already given the order to retre..Sorry, sir, withdraw, and by the time we'd galloped back to Baelo Claudia, there was not a sign of anyone."

"I see," said Tariq, "so they did not pursue you? Your fleet of barges awaited you, so far as you are aware, undetected and you were then faced with the ordeal of reloading your animals and men?"

"Precisely so," replied Malik, "only this time it was a great deal easier. Whether or not it was because the horses were now accustomed to the experience or the more gradual slope of the sands, thereby enabling the ramps to level out, I couldn't say. All I do know is that we were virtually all on board by the time my scouts had caught up with us."

Tariq raised himself from his chair and paced the room, thinking and talking as he did so. "To sum up then! We have achieved what exactly? We have learned something of how best to transport cavalry, not with warships but with trading barges, we now know that the western region of southern Hispania is not that well defended, at least as far as Gades, and we have learned that there, at least, they possess a military capability that is powerful but slow and cumbersome. Well done, Malik. Your adventure was a success, and to return without losing a man or a horse, either in an engagement or by drowning, is going to go a long way to pleading our cause with the Caliph. That is, of course, on the understanding that we are going to plead this particular cause to begin with."

Malik, knowing the debriefing was at an end, stood up. They embraced and, before Malik left the room, Tariq asked him to convey his personal thanks to all officers and men who had taken part.

•

Left to himself, Tariq went to a press in the corner of the room and took out the different coloured blocks that represented the elements of his army. He placed them on the table and started to move them about.

•

Back in Toletum the festivities continued unabated. Egolina tried to overhear what the man was saying to Roderick but the noise was too intense. Eventually the fellow withdrew, vanishing into the crowd as anonymously as he had arrived. Roderick spoke to his ever present chamberlain and the man rapped his staff on the floor. Because of the surrounding noise nothing happened, and it wasn't until he had moved to the front of the dais and repeated the action, even louder this time, that the social buzz dwindled to a halt and the performers fled the centre stage. Roderick stood up and Florinda could not help but notice what a fine figure of a man he made, tall, handsome and dressed in his celebratory regalia. The court turned, as one, to hear what he had to say.

"My friends," he began, "it is only fitting that, on this day of national celebration, we are able to announce that we have achieved a significant victory over the Infidel, who attempted to invade the southernmost region of our Empire. The cowardly heathens did not even engage in battle but fled in confusion when confronted by our glorious army from Gades, which city they were doubtless intent on assaulting. I must confess that it has sometimes concerned me that our lands are so vast that defending the more remote of them might prove a problem for us. We have ever been vigilant concerning our provinces to the north, where the renegade sons of your former king are a constant threat, so it is a comfort to know that in the south, at least, we now have nothing to fear from the Berber hordes. With that knowledge, we can now concentrate our efforts on subduing the rebellious north. It is, therefore, my intention to lead our armies to the mountains of the north and deal with these insurgents once and for all. Because of the treacherous weather and terrain that will confront us in that region, such a march will not be undertaken until the end of winter, after which the security of our kingdom will be beyond doubt." He paused as the gathering started applauding. He held up both hands to stem the applause and, even from where she was seated, Florinda could see a twinkle in his eye when he went on to say, "And should there be, amongst us here, anyone sympathetic to the northern rebel cause, or even an agent for it, please feel free to pass this information to Wittiza's whelps so that they may be better prepared, because the harder the battle the more will I relish it."

More applause followed this announcement and Florinda joined in but her clapping lacked enthusiasm. She thought of Tariq and the shame he must feel at the ignominy of such a defeat. Her compassion did not last long, however, as she soon re-engaged with the laughter and chatter of her new-found friends.

•

Not far from the palace and the scenes of revelry, an old man was doing his best not to die from the cold. He had got used to the cats and didn't notice the smell anymore. Although they were far too wild to be petted, he'd actually come to welcome their company and managed to establish a distant rapport with a few that had known him when they were kittens. These he cultivated as best he could with scraps of food left over from his trapped meat and the promise of the fire which had become a necessity during the long, cold hours of the night. It was the fire, though, which was proving difficult for him. Collecting the materials, the tinder, the kindling had never been a problem until now, but the effort of opening the door, the creaking of which harmonised with that of his wasted muscles, the bending, the picking up and carrying, was almost more than he could stand. If only he had blankets, warmer clothing, something to keep out the night chills. He had explored every press, every room in the place, but his former companions had left nothing and even if they had, after all this time materials, especially wool, would have been eaten by moths or mice or maggots. Except! No, surely not there? He'd forgotten about it until now, when necessity had sharpened his memory. But it was most unlikely that anything of that nature would have been left in that place. That place was reserved for the valuables. Their plate, the few priceless relics possessed by the brothers, not coverings, unless...He tottered over to the fireplace and brushed aside a curtain of webs. The cats pricked up their ears, and those that trusted him padded closer to satisfy their curiosity.

He stood looking into the empty hearth which was too far from his cold bed to be used as a fire. He lit an open fire as close to his stone couch as he dared. He knuckled his forehead, trying to remember, his eyes flickering over the array of chains and hooks. The trouble was that, and this he could recall, if pulled in the wrong order, the trapdoor locked irrevocably. So, which one was it? He walked into the hearth and gently touched each chain and hook in turn trying, through feel, to gauge a response that would tell him something. And it worked. One of the hooks, and only one, when brushed with his fingers, responded with a faint clicking sound within the stonework. Hardly audible but, even if his eyes were no longer as sharp as they were, there was nothing the matter with his hearing. He took a deep breath and pulled. As one, the cats fled as stone and metal moved against each other and the base of the hearth slid back revealing...blankets.

Chapter 18

Toletum, AD710

It happened without any warning and she was completely unaware of anything until she woke the next morning. Her mouth was dry and her head pounding. She struggled into consciousness to reach for water, and then she felt it, the pain! Suddenly she was wide awake and threw back the covers on the bed and saw the blood. The pain hit her again and she bit hard on her fist to stifle a scream. After a few moments, she cautiously felt between her legs. Instantly she snatched her hand back in disgust and knew exactly what had happened to her. Young and inexperienced she might be, but Florinda was no fool. There was always talk at the court about relationships and what could happen should a liaison become too passionate outside the marriage bed and, in any event, to have reached the age she had, without some such experience, was mostly due to the fact that she had led such a sheltered life under her father's protection at Septem. But how had it happened here? She had no recollection whatsoever of the events of last night, beyond laughing and joking with the group of unattached girls who had admitted her to their circle. After that, nothing! Frightened and confused she wondered where her assailant was now. This must be his room since it certainly wasn't hers. She bit back her tears, she had to think. Tamegrant! How had he allowed this to happen? She looked towards the door; the key was on the inside so she wasn't locked in. That was something. Her clothes appeared to be scattered all over the floor. Such was her eagerness to be out of this room, she didn't even wait to dress properly; she put on her underskirt and, wrapping her cloak tightly around her, she walked carefully towards the door in her bare feet. It wasn't locked. She opened it slowly and peered out into a passageway and there was Tamegrant, not opposite the door she had just opened, but the next one along. He was in the usual position he adopted when guarding her door at night, seated on the floor, his back against the wall, his huge arms folded across his chest. His eyes were closed but they opened as soon as he sensed her presence. Seeing her and her obvious distress, he leapt to his feet. She let out a great sob and threw herself into his arms. He pushed her away, his eyes looking for some kind of explanation from her. She dragged him into the room and pointed out the blood on the bed. He looked at her, his expression gradually changing from incredulity to shock, and finally one of rage. Suddenly, he threw back his head, opened his mouth and let out an atavistic howl of distress. The fact that no sound came out did nothing to detract from this primeval demonstration of grief, and Florinda instinctively stepped back and ran to the door to see if there was any response. There wasn't; only a silence which, to her, appeared almost as unnatural as Tamegrant's noiseless expression of anguish. She quickly closed the door and ran back to Tamegrant, who was now slumped on the bed, his head in his hands. Even seated, he was taller than her and she had to reach up to catch hold of his hair and force his head back to look at her. Using the combination of gestures and looks that passed for their common language, she asked him if he could tell her how she had ended up in this room which wasn't hers. More urgently, she needed to know who had accompanied her here. All this took some time because Tamegrant's distress appeared to exceed her own and his huge frame was being shaken by sobs, but she persevered because she had to know how she had been brought to this condition and by whom.

•

Eventually the giant pulled himself together and answered her questions in the only way he could. First of all, he pushed himself up to his full height and stuck his nose in the air in an exaggerated pose of pride. He then drew a circlet above his head with his fingers, continually flexing them to indicate brilliance. Florinda was beginning to understand this mime but let out an involuntary gasp at his next. He took a step to one side and began to imitate the mincing gait of a haughty woman. She stopped him immediately and instructed him to concentrate on her face as she slowly but very carefully mouthed, "The king AND the queen?"

He nodded vigorously and this time it was her turn to subside onto the bed. She began to think furiously, and very gradually her thoughts began to assume some sort of order. Roderick and Egolina! Fragments of memory were beginning the piece themselves together. She, Florinda, had been talking with the girls when Egolina's maid, who she decided she didn't like very much as the girl seemed altogether too familiar with her mistress, had taken her to one side and told her that the queen needed to have a word with her . She was led out of the room and, still following the maid, was taken through the palace to, what she imagined, were the royal apartments. This was an area unfamiliar to Florinda as all her other dealings with the queen had taken place in her own rooms, where Egolina had complimented her on her hair, soon after her arrival at the court.

They came to a door; the maid knocked and, on being instructed to enter, Florinda found herself not only face to face with the queen but with Roderick himself. Before the door had been closed behind her, Florinda had caught a glimpse of Tamegrant in the corridor outside. For once, she felt grateful for his presence, even though he wasn't in the same room. Roderick and Egolina had been exceedingly gracious, Roderick asking after the health of her father and saying how valuable an ally he was. He also expressed the hope that Florinda was enjoying her stay in Toletum, finding it not only to her liking but also instructive from the point of view of the history of their people in which, he understood, she was receiving some instruction. Florinda replied that life for her here was, indeed, highly enjoyable and very different from Septem which, she had to confess, had begun to feel mundane and boring. Now, still sitting on the bed, she refused to view it as her 'bed of shame,' she furrowed her brow and thought 'what had happened next?' Ah yes! Her brow cleared. What happened next was that Egolina had offered her a cup of wine, the very best wine in the whole kingdom, Egolina had said and then…then. She couldn't remember - or could she? Very dimly, as though through the shrouds of a thick mist, she could faintly bring to mind an image of Roderick, throwing off his mantle and smiling at her. Quite a pleasant smile, or was it? Try as she might, nothing else came into her head. She couldn't remember calling out or struggling. Hadn't, in fact, felt anything at all until now, when she had woken as though from a dream but, in reality, into a nightmare.

Tamegrant had now risen to his feet and was pulling her towards the door. She pulled her hand away from his and looked around the room again. Something else was wrong. She hadn't found Tamegrant outside the door of this room but the next one along the corridor. Yet Tamegrant would have stayed resolutely outside the door that he had seen her enter so there had to be another entrance to this room. Another door, connecting it with the room that Tamegrant had last seen her enter. She ran to the wall which was covered with hangings and started to part them, tugging at them and there it was, a door but one that was locked and not from this side. She gestured to Tamegrant to do something but, to her surprise, he was picking up her discarded clothing which he handed to her, miming that she should be properly attired before they met with anybody else. She shook her head at her own impatience and smiled gratefully to him for his thoughtfulness. Once dressed, however, she gestured again that he use his strength to force the door but, once more, he declined, knelt down and put his eye to the keyhole. He gave a grunt of satisfaction and produced a small dagger which he kept strapped to his forearm and, with more dexterity than she would have thought possible from such a big man, he delicately set to work to pick the lock. It took no time at all. He stood up, looked at her and she nodded. He flung open the door and they both stepped through into the other room. It was empty but, to Florinda, it brought back memories of the events of last night and she gagged at the thought of them. True, this was the room in which her recollection ceased but that was enough. Her empty horn cup was still on the table and Tamegrant picked it up and sniffed at the dregs, shook his head sadly at her, then squeezed it in the palm of his hand until shattered. Florinda held a finger to her mouth and Tamegrant gently placed the shards which hadn't fallen onto the mosaic, back on the table. There was not a sound from anywhere and suddenly Florinda made her decision.

•

She turned to Tamegrant, who was guarding the open door to the corridor which, they discovered was unlocked. Urgently she performed her mime for 'horses', one that they had used since she was a child. He nodded an emphatic agreement and, taking her hand, hurried her through the palace until he located a door leading to the exterior. Fortunately, it was still early for the privileged to be abroad and, apart from some of the lower servants, there was nobody to impede them or ask awkward questions. He opened the door and, now completely oriented, took her to the corner of the extensive stabling, held a finger to his lips and gently pushed her into a doorway. He motioned her to stay there while he turned the corner and entered the main stable block. There was the sound of raised, angry voices which stopped abruptly and, within a short time, Tamegrant emerged, leading three horses, two of which were large-framed beasts, obviously calculated to carry his formidable weight, the third, a fine-boned mare of the type that her father traded from Ifriquya and which were much favoured by the local aristocracy for their speed and endurance. Apart from getting away from the palace as quickly as possible, the next step of her plan was slightly more difficult. It would not be long before her absence would be noticed. Roderick and Egolina were not her immediate concern, they, she calculated, would not be too anxious to confront her in the circumstances, but there were plenty of other members of the court for whom her disappearance would present something of a mystery. She might not have been missed at all had she been on her own, but Tamegrant had become something of a celebrity in the court and anyone would have to be blind not to notice that he wasn't around anymore. That, however, was not her main worry. Once clear of the city, she had to remember the road to what, she hoped, would turn out to be her refuge. Tamegrant picked her up and put her on the mare's back. Her skirts up, she rode astride as she always did, and always had when they had raced around her father's lands in Septem. This time, though, it was extremely painful and she had to grit her teeth to stop from crying out. Tamegrant pulled himself into his own saddle and, leading the spare mount, they set off as quietly as they could through the narrow streets until they reached the walls of the city. Here they were challenged but the gates were open, Florinda gave the guard a cheery wave, and once clear of the poor outer limits, they dug in their heels until the city on the hill behind them was little more than an indistinct blur. They pulled up. Florinda closed her eyes and breathed in the clean air as if released from the confines of a dank, unwholesome prison cell. Tamegrant restlessly rode in a circle around her, keeping his eyes on the distant horizons, for they were now at the edge of a great plain which stretched endlessly before them. Satisfied that there was no threat in view, he dismounted and walked both his horses to her side. She looked at him and gave a wan smile which faded as she, once more, tried to gather her thoughts and remember how to get to her sanctuary. How could she get Tamegrant to understand where it was that she wanted to go and would he remember how to get there? She looked back behind her to the distant city and calculated that they had probably ridden due south. She gestured to Tamegrant to help her dismount. Holding the bridles of all three horses, he did so and she stood, looking around her before extending her arm and pointing south-west. She then joined her hands and brought them up to her shoulder, dropping her head on them and closing her eyes. The universal mime for sleep. Perplexed, Tamegrant watched her until his face broke into a broad grin and he nodded vigorously. He turned to the direction where she had pointed and, stretching out his own arm, made a chopping motion with his other hand before pointing it back towards Toletum. Florinda gave a shriek of joy, nodded at him and he lifted her back on her horse before mounting himself, and both of them turned in the direction they had indicated.

It didn't take very long before Florinda happily noticed landmarks on the route they had taken on the last leg of their journey when travelling north to Toletum, and before the sun was at its zenith they were clattering into the courtyard of Julian's friend and business associate who had proved a kindly host on their former journey. Their arrival occasioned all the usual fuss and activity brought on by unexpected visitors, but it was their hostess into whose arms Florinda threw herself, sobbing madly, who quickly restored calm and it was she who ordered her husband to see the horses looked after and Tamegrant taken into the servants' quarters and given breakfast. Florinda, she took into her own chamber and there, between sobs, was given an account, or at least all of it that Florinda could remember, of her ordeal. Instinctively and immediately, Florinda knew that she had made the right decision to come here. Not only was Camilla, for that was her name, sympathetic and caring but she was also sensible and wise. As soon as Florinda had quietened down, she sat beside her and counselled her to remain with them. She would be quite safe and no one would think of looking for her there. Unless…?

"My dear, when you arrived at Toletum, did you or your father make any mention of having stayed the night with us? Because if they do come looking for you, although we shall try to keep you hidden, this is one place they might search."

Florinda, still sniffing back her tears, shook her head.

"No! I am sure neither of us mentioned it because I didn't want anyone at court to know that I was vain enough to arrive there looking fresh and unstained by travel. All of the servants who came with us returned with my father. Except Tamegrant, of course. You are looking after him aren't you? He gets so hungry and…"

Camilla patted her arm and assured her that Tamegrant was being well looked after. Then she asked Florinda what she intended to do next. The girl was in no doubt.

"I would like to stay here, if I might although.." her voice trailed away, as though she suddenly realised her predicament. Camilla was at her motherly best and said, "If you mean what has happened to you, well we can't do anything about that. It has happened and we must pray that nothing will come of it. If, on the other hand, you mean that you have arrived with nothing but the clothes you are wearing, then I can help you.

I have a press full of clothes. Not fashionable, I'm afraid, but clean and I'm sure we can find you something that won't be too offensive to your modern tastes. We are, after all, in the country."

Florinda smiled her grateful thanks but there was something more and, again, the practical Camilla could guess what it was.

"A bath, my dear? More than anything else, I expect you would love to bathe."

Florinda let out a huge sigh of relief. "Oh, thank you. Thank you so much. I crave that above all else."

Camilla led her toward the bathing room, Roman in origin as was the villa, but still in use.

•

Some hours later, Florinda, clad in a clean if somewhat rural gown, was sitting with Camilla and her husband. The first thing she did was to ask after Tamegrant and was surprised to learn that he had left the villa and, because of his affliction, had given no idea to any of them, servants or hosts, where he was going or what his intentions were. On learning of this news, Florinda suffered a momentary panic. She had become so used to his presence and the protection it gave her. Then she thought about it a little more deeply and was convinced that Tamegrant had done the very thing that she would have asked of him, had the opportunity presented itself. She explained to her hosts.

"He's gone to Septem, to tell father. I didn't think why he took three horses but now I know. It was so he could gallop south twice as fast with a change of mounts. It would be him they'd look out for because he would be so easy to identify, but with two horses they'd never catch up with him and I could never be able to keep up. I suppose he left as soon as we got here?"

Camilla patted her on the arm. "Indeed he did, my dear. No word to anyone but then, with his affliction, he wouldn't have the words anyway, would he? By now, he will be well on his way and I think it is for the best. After all, it is important that your father knows the situation and if only Tamegrant can make him understand, at least he will be happy to learn where you are and that you are safe with us."

Florinda clutched Camilla's hand for reassurance but still looked uncertain.

"But what if they do come looking for me? By leaving the court without the King's consent, I have violated the trust my father placed in them. Suppose my father suffers for my actions. Suppose…"

Camilla broke in, "It is not for you to speak of violation is it? What Roderick did to you was unforgivable, king or no king, and trust works both ways. In any event, the shame he should be feeling for his actions should more than outweigh a mere lapse of court protocol."

At this point, the discussion was joined by Camilla's husband. Up until now he had remained silent, perhaps feeling that any comment concerning Florinda's ordeal might not be appropriate, coming from a man. Once the conversation had moved onto more general ground, however, he felt free to offer his opinion. His name was Cyprian and he had known Florinda's father since they were both boys, both subsequently becoming powerful through the acquisition of wealth and the avoidance of political associations. A polite cough announced his intention to join in the discussion and both women turned to him expectantly. He was, Florinda had learned from her father, a man of great integrity, intelligence and resourcefulness and the one night Florinda had spent under his roof had confirmed this, even though her mind then, was full of little else other than her onward journey to Toletum. Now, his keen eyes firmly fixed on hers, he said, "I think it fair to say that, at the present time, King Roderick has rather more to occupy his mind than court protocol. His enemies to the north are becoming ever threatening and the king, probably as we speak, is busy gathering a force strong enough to defeat them. I would not be at all surprised if he is not marching within the month.

That being the case, your father's anger at what happened is not going to count for much with a king faced with rebellion. True, Julian has followers of his own in the south, people of our persuasion who have small household forces but it is as nothing compared with the host commanded by the king. Therefore, my child, I would recommend, as I am sure will my wife, that you stay under our protection until such time as your father can ensure your safe onward journey to Septem."

Florinda sighed, but agreed that she could think of no better arrangement.

•

At his post, the lookout, atop the tower overlooking the Strait, knew immediately who it was aboard the vessel as it skimmed towards him. The unmistakable figure of Tamegrant stood in the prow, like an enormous figurehead, one foot on the top-rail, poised to leap off as soon as the vessel reached port. The lookout summoned the gateman who had the gate drawn up as Tamegrant raced towards the citadel, his voluminous white robes flying behind him, making him look twice as big and twice as formidable. Julian had already been alerted and ran down to meet his servant, saw the look of misery on his face and hurried him upstairs to his private apartments. This had to concern Florinda, it couldn't be anything else and his inability to communicate at all but the basic level with Tamegrant, increased his sense of anxiety. Julian gave Tamegrant time to recover his breath then mimed one of their few shared gestures, his hands moving slowly over his face and coming together in an attitude of prayer in praise of beauty, the gesture he always used to signify his daughter, ever since she was a small child. His eyes still full of a misery Julian had never before witnessed,

Tamegrant nodded then swiftly drew out from his robe a green unripe apple. Now confused, Julian watched him place it slowly and deliberately on the table. Their eyes locked together, Tamegrant then unsheathed the dagger from his arm and, without looking, brought the point down into the dead centre of the apple, splitting it cleanly in half. For a moment, neither man did anything, then Julian pointed to the apple and repeated his mime for Florinda. Tamegrant nodded, and very carefully Julian mouthed the word 'ravaged?'

Tamegrant nodded and tears started to roll into his beard. Julian took him firmly by the arms, looked up into his face and mouthed, 'who?' Tamegrant repeated the mime he had performed for Florinda, and Julian immediately interpreted it, just as his daughter had. He released Tamegrant and took a pace back before whispering, as if to himself, but clearly enough for Tamegrant to read his lips, "The King, Roderick himself?" Tamegrant nodded and started to beat himself on the temples with his fists. Julian eventually managed to calm him down but doubted if the giant understood the words "not your fault, Tamegrant. It was not your fault."

Tamegrant eventually controlled his feeling of guilt and rushed into a corner of the room where there was a stack of swords, recently returned from the smith. He grabbed one and raising it above his head, made a move towards Julian who took a moment to realise that he was not himself threatened, but was being asked by Tamegrant for permission to exact his own revenge. Julian managed to make him understand that was not what had to be done but he, Julian, would confront Roderick himself. He gently held out his hands for the weapon and, once it had been returned, gave instructions for his servant to prepare for Toletum. He would travel in the company of his extended bodyguard, all highly skilled warriors and, of course, Tamegrant.

•

That same day, a small fleet sailed across the Strait, landing at the foot of the Rock as the shadows of the day started to lengthen. Horses were ready for them and, suitably provisioned, Julian's tiny force made their way eastwards, stopping only when it became too dark for safe travelling. By the dawn of the fourth day, they were in sight of Toletum, when Tamegrant tugged on the bridle of Julian's mount and gestured in the direction of Florinda's sanctuary. Julian shook his head and pointed to the city, indicating that Toletum came first. Florinda, he reasoned, was safe where she was and could be restored to him on their homeward journey. In his heart, he knew that this would be the last occasion that he would be visiting the court at which his daughter had been so ill-used. From this time on, any affairs that needed to be conducted between Toletum and Septem would be done by messenger or other means. He was finished with his Visigoth overlords and he was confident that, such was their dependence on him for security on their southern borders, he had nothing to fear in the way of reprisals. At this point another thought ran through his mind and the more he mulled it over, the more seductive it became. First, he would see what sort of reception awaited him, and he wouldn't have long to find out for they were now at the city limits. He ordered the commander of his guard to accompany him to the palace. Tamegrant and the rest he had wait at the gate, mounted and armed. In accordance with practice, he and his commander surrendered their weapons on entry. There were, of course, no circumstances in which any weapons would ever be employed, and he had brought his small army for no other reason than to register his position, not merely as an agent of the crown but as the independent overlord of his own principality. Roderick had wronged him, but Julian was not going to appear before him as one humiliated.

·

They met immediately and the first thing that Julian noticed was a complete lack of remorse or guilt on Roderick's face. Julian did not bow and this small act of defiance actually made the king smile.

"Before you say anything, Count Julian," he said, "I do not have to remind you that I am king and that you are, if not my subject exactly, dependent upon my goodwill for your livelihood and position." This latter was not strictly true but Julian decided not to take issue at this stage.

"I grant you," continued Roderick, "that I did wrong in bedding your daughter as I did. I could have said that she seduced me and, in a way she did for I found the combination of her innocence and beauty irresistible, but the deed is done and there is nothing you can do about it. Naturally, should there be issue, I will take full responsibility for it. Now that is out of the way, let us talk business. Tomorrow I march north to teach those whelps of Wittiza a lesson they will not forget. I will not suffer insurrection from any quarter of this kingdom. In the past you have supplied me with fine hawks and spirited horses. By the time I return from the north, I would have you send me more of both. I can promise you the trade will be profitable and I trust that this lapse on my part will not affect our future business."

Julian said nothing but held the king's keen look for several seconds. Then he quietly said, "I promise you, my lord, I will send you hawks and horses such as you have never dreamed of."

Roderick merely nodded and terminated the interview.

·

It took a while and several deep breaths before Julian felt able to move and leave the room, attended by his escort commander. Once outside the gates, he brushed aside all Tamegrant's mute attempts at questioning him, mounted his horse and started galloping away from Toletum, his group of men making their way behind him in as disciplined a manner as they could manage. Eventually he calmed down, some order was established in the ranks and the small procession made its way to where his daughter was waiting for him, her pleasure at the prospect, tempered by the shame of her condition. She ran out of the gates to meet him and, both weeping, clung to each other in mutual consolation.

Much gratitude was expressed to Camilla and Cyprian for their kindness and care and, just before they left for the journey home, Julian took Cyprian to one side and whispered a few words to him, Cyprian's immediate reaction was a look of shock but, after a few more words he nodded gravely and patted Julian's shoulder. Florinda, flanked by Tamegrant and her father, turned in the saddle and waved her goodbyes, her feelings on leaving the region contrasting dramatically with those of her arrival.

Chapter 19

Toletum, Spring 711AD

The weather was getting warmer and the old man now had no need of blankets but, if he lived that long, there would be another cold winter so he needed to store them in a dry place where the cats couldn't get at them. Where better then, than the cache where he'd found them. He hadn't quite dared to go back since he had opened it. What he had discovered worried him. It had certainly not been there when the monastery had been occupied and it was obviously an object of enormous value and, consequently, of great religious significance. If not, then why had it been hidden here in a place reserved for the conservation of relics. He screwed up his brow and thought. Something filtering through from remarks half heard by him when he served here as a young noviciate. Something familiar yet never seen by him, but only bits of information swept up by him as though crumbs from a table. Table, that was it! A table, but what was so special about it? Apart from its immense value? That much, at least, he had seen. Only the top of it but, from what he could see, solid gold and gems. Why would a table…? That was it, the table, it was not just a table but THE TABLE, Solomon's Table and he had dared to look upon it. He, the lowest and least educated of the brothers, had seen the holiest of tables from the temple of King Solomon himself and he, for his own unworthy comfort, had uncovered it. He had crossed himself with each succeeding thought, but now he must repent his actions and replace the blankets which had obviously been placed there as protection. The cats reluctantly moved out of his way. By now they treated him as one of themselves; he smelled like them and, so far as they were concerned, he lived like them. They didn't like the inglenook though, that smelled of all sorts of things alien to them. Things like fire and incense and metal. They watched from a safe distance and turned tail at the sound of the gears laboriously moving the heavy slabs of stone. The old man hardly dared look but, just before he reverently laid out the carefully folded blankets on top, he peeked. That peek was to keep him awake for most of the night.

•

Strangely, the old man wasn't the only one whose sleep was disturbed by thoughts of Solomon's table. In his luxurious accommodation in Damascus, which could not have provided a greater contrast to that of the old man in his monastery, Musa ibn Nusayr could not rid his mind of the holy relic. While retaining all his customary self-confidence, Musa was still conscious that his standing with the Caliphate was not as secure as he would have liked. He had no intention of changing his character in an attempt to ingratiate himself with the Umayyad, he was far too proud for that, but to present Al Walid with a prize such as Solomon's table … Now, that would certainly put him firmly back in favour or, at least, he would prove to them that his services were invaluable. If only Al Walid were more confident of the military power at his disposal and would sanction a full scale invasion of Hispania. It only needed a sign, just some small shift in the balance that would make the action more justifiable to the Umayyad. Musa did not, of course, realise that this had already happened.

•

At home, in Tangier, Tariq was an early riser by nature. First he prayed, and then to the business of the day. He was not, however, prepared for the violent knocking on his door less than two hours after he had taken to his bed. Instantly alert, he threw a cloak over his shoulders and opened the door to his night servant, who was most apologetic for the disturbance, but the visitor, demanding to see Tariq, would not take no for an answer and insisted on seeing him without delay. Tariq, while dressing, asked the name of this impatient caller and on being told who it was, cast off the clothes he'd started with and decided something formal might be more appropriate to the occasion.

This was the first time that Count Julian had visited the fortress at Tangier so, considering the hour and the apparent urgency, it must be something of such importance that customary etiquette should be so ignored. Having ensured that his guest had been provided with suitable refreshment, whatever that was at this strange hour of the night, he gave orders that Akeem was to be in attendance at this meeting. Although still of lowly rank, Akeem was closer to Tariq than anyone else in the garrison, and he sometimes found that Akeem's bluntness often saved a lot time in circumstances when his more sophisticated officers felt themselves restricted by codes of social conduct. If this impromptu meeting turned out to be as important as he sensed it might, then Akeem's input could be an asset. On making his way to his reception room, he literally bumped into Akeem who, despite the hour, looked the same as he always did and Tariq wondered to himself if the man ever went to bed or, when he did, was he still in his military gear. Akeem put out a hand and stopped him.

"I think I might know what this is all about, my lord."

Tariq stared at him. "You do? Well, you know more than I do. My first thought was that some of the barges that ended up in our yards might have belonged to Julian and he's here to register a protest."

Akeem snorted dismissively. "You honestly think he'd wake you up in the middle of the night to tell you that? Come on, Tariq, he's an important man. If that was his problem, he'd write you a letter or something like that. No. This is big and, as I say, I have half an idea what it is."

"Well, Akeem, it's a pity you don't have time to enlighten me."

"I already have, sort of," was Akeem's reply to that.

The servant preceding them opened the door to the reception room and Tariq entered, followed by Akeem. Julian was seated on one of the uncomfortable stools as, with everything in the fortress, the room was austere and in complete contrast to the splendour of Julian's palace. He immediately leaped to his feet, and Tariq was surprised to see that he was accompanied by the commander of his personal bodyguard, a man known to Tariq from his visits to Septem and one with whom Tariq enjoyed discussing military matters or, at least, those that did not compromise the security of either party.

Tariq greeted them and bade Julian be seated but, he declined and seemed so inwardly distressed that Tariq quickly divined that whatever it was that had brought the Count to Tangier, it was profoundly important to him. Akeem stayed in the doorway and nodded to both Julian and his escort. Julian stretched out his arms in, what seemed like, a gesture of hopelessness and Tariq saw, with some compassion, that the man was close to breaking down. However, Julian pulled himself together, took a deep breath and said, haltingly, "General, I am sorry to have disturbed you so rudely but my head is so full of thoughts that I feel it about to burst and I need someone, such as yourself, to unburden them or share them, in the hope that you might be able to help resolve the issues with which I am beset. It is difficult for me but ..."

"Your daughter, is it, my lord?" The question came from Akeem and both Julian and Tariq swung around. He went on, "Toletum, my lord! Something to do with your daughter and Toletum?"

Julian turned to Tariq with a look of pure astonishment.

"How, in the name of heaven, did he know that? I have told nobody; at least nobody here."

Tariq suddenly thought back to a remark Akeem had made to him when they were returning from a trip to Septem. He turned to Akeem and said quietly but firmly, "Thank you, Akeem. Why don't you take our friend," gesturing to Julian's escort, "to the kitchens? Wake them up and ask them to prepare you both some food. That is if Count Julian is willing?"

Julian nodded his acquiescence; Akeem stifled a wink and ushered the escort, a Christian Berber as they all were in Julian's small but efficient army, out of the door.

When the servant had followed them out and closed the door behind him, Tariq gestured for Julian to take his seat and took one opposite him. For a moment neither man spoke until Tariq said, with a smile, "I have yet to witness a soldier of any army refuse a meal, whatever the time of day or night." He became serious again and went on, "Count Julian, I think understand something of your trouble and I won't inquire more deeply but, please, tell me just one thing. Is the Lady Florinda safe?"

Julian stiffened. "She is now, General. She is now." Then, for the first time he appeared more animated as he leaned towards Tariq.

"General, I know and you probably know that I know that your people have been conducting a series of raids into Hispania. Mostly small scale affairs. Until the last time, that is, when quite a large body of men, a cavalry battalion no less, crossed the Strait and rode towards the west before returning, fully intact so I am reliably informed, here to Tangier. Was this a preparatory exercise for a full invasion, or just a one-off military foray into Visgothic territory?" He held up a hand to stop Tariq's automatic response.

"I don't expect you to give me information which you might regard as a threat to your security, but I want you to know that I have come here as a friend. I realise that we enjoy each other's company but it is not as that sort of friend that I sit here. It is as an ally and, when I explain, I think you might regard me as an important ally. Now, can we talk as allies or is our conversation going to be limited to that of mere friends?"

Tariq slowly let out a deep breath and rose from his seat. For a second Julian thought he was going to be asked to leave but Tariq indicated that he stay seated. Still Tariq said nothing but was obviously thinking deeply. His brow was furrowed and his lips pursed.

It was not he but Julian who spoke first.

"Tariq, I have made a decision which future generations might see as one of the more momentous decisions ever made by anyone in recent history." He smiled apologetically, "That sounds very grand doesn't it, but I want to change the course of history and I need your help to do it. The people of your faith have performed great feats of arms and progressed enormously in a short space of time, but all that will be as nothing compared with what I am offering you. I am not asking you to compromise your security and more importantly for you, I know, your faith, so will you listen to what I have to say and become allies with me, or do we just remain friendly neighbours?"

Tariq listened.

•

Before dawn had made a reluctant appearance, the last man in a messenger relay was racing through the gloom towards Damascus. Reading the message, the recipient quickly forgot his outrage at being summoned from the comfort of his bed. In fact, as much as his girth allowed, he cavorted around his spacious chamber, clapping his hands and praising Allah, while working out in his mind how he could best present this incredible news to the Umayyad. Eventually, after more mature consideration, he decided not to. Not just for the time being. At some stage Al Walid would have to know but, first, he needed to travel to the source of the communication. Thus it was that, for the second time in a matter of weeks, Tariq found himself confronted with another illustrious visitor in the substantial form of Musa ibn Nusayr. There was little time for courtesies or pleasantries. Only the two of them seated opposite each other and, on the table between them, maps and charts.

"So," Musa rumbled, "tell me again exactly what he said."

Tariq decided that, for the moment, he would keep to himself the reason that Julian had come to his decision. He, quite rightly, assumed that Musa was likely to be more interested in the 'what' rather than the 'why', so he launched straightaway into Julian's proposal.

"He wants to help us, my lord. He wants to help us launch a successful invasion on Hispania. He claims that he can muster support for our cause in that country, will actually accompany our force with his own army which, as you well know, may be small but is extremely potent. He will provide us with any information he has, or can glean, about the tactics and strength of the Visigoth army. He is prepared to…"

Musa whistled softly into his beard and slammed a hand on the table, the maps shivered at the impact and the tea glasses rattled on the tray. Musa tidied the maps.

"Supplied you with these, did he?"

"He did, my lord, as a token of his good faith. As you can see, they show all the fortresses, together with a note of their occupied strength."

Musa stroked his beard and studied one of the maps. Tariq sensed that he was finding it difficult to contain his excitement and when he spoke again, Musa did, indeed, sound breathless although it had been some time since he'd climbed the steps to Tariq's operations room.

"This is a wonderful opportunity for us, Tariq. Septem's support is probably the one thing that the Caliph had not expected and, to be frank with you, neither had I, but it gives us an edge and it could be just what we need to convince the Umayyad that an attack is viable. They will see it as proof that Allah is on our side as, I expect you do. Is that how you see it Tariq?"

"I think that all the time, my lord. My faith is not dependent on the support of a non-believer," was Tariq's sober response which drew a keen look from Musa. There was a spark of tension between them, until Musa laughed and then went on, "You will obviously lead the army, Tariq. What have you here at your command at the moment, about ten thousand men I believe? All Berber, like yourself and don't start to look embarrassed, you know full well that they adore you and will follow you into the jaws of hell if you so order it. I might not spend as much time here as I used to, Tariq, but when I am in Tangier I talk to the men and your staff officers and they all say the same thing. Talking about numbers, that is a lot of men to get across the Strait. How do you intend getting them over? Your yards are too limited and, just now, I can't spare any of my fleet. You can't afford to spend weeks ferrying them across, and the longer transport gets drawn out, the longer Roderick and his army have to muster and cut you down as you disembark. I think that is likely to be your biggest problem. That is, of course, if we can get the Caliphate to sanction it in the first place although, as I say, with Julian on your side, the chances of a successful conclusion are more favourable than they otherwise might have been and…"

Tariq cut in.

"We have intelligence, again from Count Julian, that the Visigoth army is heavily engaged in action in the north of their country. By the time they have marched south, replenished their losses and be battle rested, we will have had enough time to land our army, not to mention the luxury of locating the best arena for the sort of battle we intend to fight. Apart from all this, Count Julian has offered us one more thing.." Tariq allowed the end of his sentence to hang in the air, just long enough for Musa to interject impatiently.

"What 'one more thing'?"

Tariq felt he could afford the faintest of triumphant smiles. "He has offered us his entire fleet of trading vessels, which means that we can transport our army across to the Rock in no time at all."

Musa shook his head in amazement and disbelief. Then he asked the question which Tariq had been expecting throughout the entire meeting.

"Did it not occur to you, Tariq, to ask Julian what had brought about this sudden change of alliance. Why should this man, who has long been known as a staunch ally of Toletum, and was actually an agent of the kingdom, change his allegiance so suddenly and so completely? Even though he rules what, in effect, is a principality of his own, there has never, hitherto, been any indication that his loyalty to the Visigoth is other than total. So what is it? He must have given you some reason for making a sudden decision of this magnitude?"

"Actually, my lord, he did…" but Tariq was not allowed to finish. Musa's mind was working overtime.

"Another thing, Tariq, have you considered the possibility of this being a trap? Suppose Julian's information about the Visigoth army fighting in the north is false and they were, instead, in the south waiting to cut down an Islamic invasion force when it was at its most vulnerable – during disembarkation? What you have told me, Tariq, is priceless news but you know full well that Al Walid will not act unless he is certain of it."

Tariq tapped the maps in front of them, hoping that he was going to be able to convince Musa, and through him, Al Walid, of Julian's honesty without divulging the fact of Florinda's rape. Obviously, this would become open knowledge in time. Akeem had rightly guessed it and, although he could be trusted to keep his councel, rumours ran through armies, of all persuasions, like wildfire. It was just that he didn't want Julian to know that he was the one to make it public. He therefore concentrated Musa's attention on the military facts at his disposal.

"These maps, my lord, have been verified by our agents as genuine. As has the fact that Roderick is now as far from our proposed landing sites as it is possible for him to be. You know Count Julian even better than I, my lord. He is a man of honour and I would trust him with my life."

Musa grunted. "That is exactly what you will be doing, Tariq, isn't it? That said, I do agree about Julian's integrity but, you have to admit, it is a considerable change of loyalties. There has to be something else behind it."

"There is, my lord," Tariq's response was immediate. "It is something personal and intensely damaging to the Count. Should he wish you to know of it, I would prefer him to tell you himself. Of course, if you were to order me, I would have no alternative but to tell you but…"

Musa laughed.

"Oh Tariq, you men of honour never fail to surprise me. Now that I know it is a matter of honour, I feel much better about it. I feel better about it because it is probably the only reasonable explanation for this sensational news. Roderick's offence must have been quite extreme for Julian to have reacted as he has but, that being the case, it all makes a lot more sense to me and here I must confess, I am not too surprised either. Roderick, by all accounts, is not the most stable of overlords. Anyway, as you can guess, I also have been keeping a close eye on events in Toletum and, while not privy to your delicate information, my intelligence is much the same as yours. I, too, have been following Roderick's northern campaign and been wondering how we might take advantage of it. Interesting isn't it? I wonder if my agents know your agents? Julian bringing his resources over to us though, that does make all the difference and I look forward to the Caliphate's response when I tell them of it. Now, you and I have military matters to discuss. That done, I shall carry the news to Damascus myself and once we have their blessing, we will hasten to make our last minute preparations for the greatest military expedition since Constantine rode eastwards."

•

Tariq, relieved that he had not been required to divulge the essence of Julian's break from Toletum, now set about determining his strategy for the coming assault on the shores of Hispania. While together, he and Musa had agreed that, with his army of ten thousand Berber troops, Tariq would sail across the Strait, courtesy of Julian's large fleet of trading barges. The inhabitants of the Rock were so used to seeing these plying backwards and forwards they were unlikely to notice anything amiss until enough forces had landed to render any retaliation unlikely. There, they would muster and, having surveyed the local area, it would be left to Tariq to select the most advantageous ground on which to fight the battle. Once he knew how the conflict was progressing and had, in his opinion, reached the appropriate phase, Musa would bring his much larger army into play and thereby achieve a memorable victory. That was the general plan and Tariq was well aware that he was being used as little more than a diversionary force and that Musa would, quite rightly, for he was the overall commander of the Umayyad army, claim the victory for himself. Thanks to Julian, his own agents and those of Musa, Tariq had a very good idea of the size of the enemy force and it was many, many times greater than his own. Even allowing for the fact that it had already fought a battle in the north and faced the subsequent long, forced march south, it would still amount to a formidable opposition. True, Julian had promised support from disaffected parties on the other side but, even if that turned out to be true, Tariq would be heavily outnumbered and, at the back of his mind, he couldn't help but wonder if Musa's participation would be in time to prevent the complete annihilation of his beloved Berbers.

•

Musa, under fast sail en route to Damascus, was pondering the same question. In his way, he was fond of Tariq and almost regarded him as a son, but this was one occasion where he could not allow sentiment to encroach upon his path to power and riches. He was not getting any younger and this was his opportunity to re-establish his standing with the Caliphate and enrich himself at the same time. If he played his hand correctly, Tariq would blunt the force of the Visigoth army, leaving Musa to finish them off and then… Why then, his road to Toletum would be clear. True, there would be other towns and fortifications on his way north but any opposition would melt away against his now superior host. Then, the royal palace of Toletum and the priceless booty housed therein! The fabled table of Solomon! It was Count Julian who had first told him of it and how often since had he, Musa, dreamed of it. He stood against the ship's prow and closed his eyes against the sun-drenched spray, thinking of Al Walid's reaction when he, Musa ibn Nusayr, presented it to him. The advantages that could accrue from such a coup were limitless and he could end his days in comfortable retirement, perhaps offering his services as military advisor-in-chief to a grateful Caliph. His boat, propelled by a helpful but kindly wind, was making her way through the blue water at a good rate but it was not fast enough for Musa who, now he had decided on how he was going to present his case to Al Walid, couldn't wait to get to Damascus.

Chapter 20

Tangier, 711AD

Julian studied Tariq's features, concentrated as they were into a frown. One hand shading his eyes against the sun while the other rested gently on his horse's neck, the reins loosely entwined in his fingers. He seemed totally focussed on the scene going on in front of him, and Julian was aware that, so far as Tariq was concerned, he might not have been there at all. He smiled to himself; such fancies as he had enjoyed over the past few weeks. This Berber, freed slave, army commander and governor of Tangier, would have been welcomed at any time as a prospective suitor for his precious daughter's hand, despite their differences in religion and in status. During the last few weeks that he had spent in his company, his admiration for Tariq, his character and his abilities, had grown, and if only... He sighed deeply and it was enough to unsettle his horse and Tariq's concentration. Tariq turned in his saddle, an enquiring look on his face.

"You are still unhappy, my lord?"

Julian, now a little embarrassed, gave a self-deprecatory laugh.

"Not at all, Tariq. My stay here in Tangier has done much to restore me, and how many times must I tell you, you need not be so formal. From now on, might we not address each other by our given names? Since my arrival we have seldom been out of each other's company and I have come to regard you as a true friend, rather than a powerful neighbour with whom it is well to cultivate a wise diplomacy. I have always been conscious of the fact that my small domain is a tempting target for your Islamic ambitions, although.." he continued, laughing, "your previous attempts at annexing my territory were never very successful."

Tariq laughed with him. "Indeed they were not, my lo..." He dropped his turbaned head in a mock bow, "Julian, possibly because I was not in command at the time, or am I being disingenuous?"

"Not in the slightest, my friend," was Julian's response. "Looking at what I see now," he waved his gloved hand towards the plain they overlooked from their elevated position, "your army is a credit to your leadership and your training. Although that particular infantry manoeuvre I see them performing down there looks familiar."

This time Tariq's laugh was unrestrained enough to cause both their horses to veer away from each other. Once standing quietly again, Tariq admitted that the particular action they were witnessing had, in fact, been copied from tactics employed by Julian's small but elite army. Tactics originating from Roman manuals and ones that Julian had successfully employed when earlier Islamic attempts to subdue Septem had failed.

Julian's head shot up. "How did you know about that, you were not even here then?"

Tariq smiled one of his more enigmatic smiles. "I talk to veterans, my lor..Julian. I talk to old soldiers and I listen. But enough of that, I need to watch these manoeuvres. I sense that we are nearly there; nearly ready but there are still one or two things I need to assess." He turned away from Julian and back towards the scene below them, where thousands of his troops were practising what, to Julian, seemed like incredibly complicated moves, but he was impressed by their energy and the speed with which they were performed.

•

Not only was the weather getting warmer but, more importantly, the days were getting longer and Tariq was making the most of them. The entire garrison, and the growing town that now supported it, were cramming more hours into their daily schedules. Manoeuvres experimenting with new formations and battle tactics were a constant activity as Tariq tested his ideas against his new-found knowledge of the Visigoth army. After hard days in the field even the cavalry mounts, sturdy Berber horses renowned for their strength and stamina, were happy to be returned to their lines for a rest while their riders, fatigued as they were, had to wait for their break until their animals had been fed, watered and groomed. Tariq didn't spare himself, and all those under him, as ever inspired by his example, did their share, happily anticipating the call to arms from Damascus, which was expected any day now. The excitement in the air was palpable and Count Julian, in many ways responsible for all this activity, now spent most of his time with Tariq going over maps of the landing sites and discussing those areas nearby which were most likely to give them a territorial advantage, once battle was joined. He pointed out the towns and villages which were administered by those with a grievance against the power of Toletum and were, therefore, more likely to offer little or no resistance to the invasion force. Julian's enthusiasm for this venture only served to remind Tariq that the man was in danger of turning a highly complicated and ambitious enterprise into a personal vendetta so, although he warmly welcomed his friend's advice and information, he was ever careful to keep it in perspective. No matter how well his army was prepared for battle, the odds were going to be overpowering and while likely sources of help, from whatever quarter, were welcome, he could not afford to include them in his calculations, so he concentrated on working his men hard, making them fit and building their confidence in their ability to defeat a superior force. Many of these soldiers had not long left their Berber villages and a way of life that had continued uninterrupted for centuries. Tariq remembered his own background, and tried to instil in the ranks the same sort of resolve that he had employed to get him where he was now, running a highly complex and growing garrison town, a small but increasingly formidable army and still managing to retain his simple lifestyle, his strong faith in his god and a mind receptive to new concepts and ideas.

•

In Damascus, in the privacy of his personal chamber, Musa ibn Nusayr, threw his headdress to the floor and ran his fingers through his hair. Still black and thick, it defied his advancing years but that was the only thing that did. He was feeling older, more tired and while he still experienced a degree of exhilaration from the business of intrigue and court politics, it was starting to take its toll. Still, he had got what he wanted. Permission to mount a full-scale invasion of Hispania.

The Caliph, Al Walid, had given his consent but only after a great deal of discussion and with one or two caveats, and it was these that now occupied the mind of Musa. Most of the discussion, between two of the most powerful men of their time, had taken place on a building site. To be more precise, the building site of Al Walid's lasting contribution to architectural history, his fantastic new mosque which was to be another five years in the building. Even so, it was, in its current stage of development, a most impressive edifice and, each time he passed it, Musa was reminded that the Umayyad dynasty was driven by faith just as much as by territorial ambition – although even that was seen as spreading the word of Islam by yet another means. As before, Al Walid had needed convincing that an incursion into another continent was likely to met with success and that there was no real prospect of his beloved northern army, under the generalship of the devout Tariq ibn Ziyad, being annihilated. Time and again, Musa had to point out that Tariq was now a complete convert to the idea, now that he had the intelligence of Roderick's campaign in the north and the tacit assistance of Count Julian of Septem. Not only that, but Tariq was ready and prepared for his part in the invasion which, Musa reminded Al Walid, would be supported, at the right time of course, by Musa's own more experienced and much larger army. 'At the right time,' was quite a nice touch, he thought. At least it would give him the chance to participate at a time best suited to him. Time to estimate the damage inflicted on Tariq, before coming to the rescue with his own battle-hardened army of some fifty thousand men, making the victory his own and sweeping north to claim the ultimate prize for himself. He mentally shrugged off Tariq's fate. After all, it was Tariq who was in Musa's debt, not the other way round. Without Musa's patronage, Tariq would probably still be herding sheep. But the fact remained that Al Walid favoured the younger man. So much so that one of the conditions of his agreeing to this expedition was that Musa supply Tariq with three hundred of his best Arab warriors, crack fighting men of which Musa was rightly proud, to sail with Tariq as his personal bodyguard. Musa grunted to himself. That was a small price to pay, and the men would be ordered to Tangier this very day. The other condition for Al Walid's agreement was that any treasures captured as a result of the invasion be offered as a contribution to the building of his mosque, and not retained as personal booty by the commanders of the Umayyad armies. This particular stipulation appeared to be aimed, rather too pointedly for his comfort, at Musa but he was left with no alternative but to agree. He rose from his ottoman and called for his adjutant to make the necessary arrangements for Tariq's bodyguard to be dispatched immediately to Tangier and, to his credit, he emphasised that they had to be of the highest quality, but then there were very few of his men that were not of that standard.

•

On the outskirts of Tangier, they took their meal in a tent. A large tent containing only those items of furniture necessary to their business. Maps and papers had been pushed to one side to make room for their food which, Julian had noticed before, was plain but of good quality and nutritious. It came as no surprise to him when he was told that the same food was served throughout the entire garrison and, no matter the rank or quality of the diner, there was no variation in their regime. Tariq, he noticed, ate sparingly and slowly and, while doing so, refrained from conversation but occasionally, between mouthfuls, he would pull a map or a message towards him and peruse its contents before pushing it away and continuing with his food. Always thinking, Julian observed. Did the man never take a break from his duties? Suddenly there was a commotion outside the door and after a sharp knock on it, Akeem entered, as he so often did, uninvited. He was, however, not alone and Julian's eyebrows shot up in surprise when he saw the young woman who followed him in. Her appearance was Berber, but more refined than most and she moved and held herself with the sort of confidence that was unusual in one of her background.

Akeem, failing in his attempt to keep himself between her and Tariq, threw up his arms in an attitude of surrender, saying, "I couldn't keep her out Tar.. my lord. She insisted on seeing you and wouldn't wait until Count Julian had left." He gave Julian a clumsy bow before continuing. "She said that…" was as far as she, Menna, allowed him to get. She gave a nod to Julian before saying, "My lord, it is essential that we talk before your preparations go any further. What I would like is for me and some of my women to accompany you on your campaign."

Tariq rose from his chair, smiled apologetically to his guest, and introduced him to Menna, according her the same degree of courtesy that he would a woman of quality. Julian, immediately interested, noted that Tariq's attitude towards her was also not devoid of charm. His smile was genuine as he made the introduction, and then went on to explain that he and Menna had known each other from childhood and that she was responsible for the lightweight leather armour, about which the Count had been so complimentary that very morning. Julian rose to his feet and bowed to Menna. It was true; one of the things he had particularly noted about the training he had witnessed, was the extreme manoeuvrability of the army, especially the cavalry who had developed the technique of riding and changing direction using knee and heel commands, thus leaving their hands free to use bows and spears. Their accuracy, admittedly on immobile targets, was almost uncanny, and Julian could see how much the new lightweight armour contributed to their ability to move freely in the saddle; less weight for their horses too, giving them more stamina and better freedom of movement.

"I must congratulate you, my lady. Your ideas will greatly facilitate the army's ability to outmanoeuvre the enemy. Believe me, Tariq will need all the help he can get if he is to avoid defeat by Roderick's superior host."

Menna wrenched her eyes from Tariq, looked down and was silent for a moment. When she spoke, Menna addressed Julian with civility and thanked him for his comments but reminded him that she was not of noble birth and, therefore, did not merit the title he had bestowed upon her. Which small rebuke having been delivered, she turned back to Tariq and, again, reiterated her request that she and her ladies be allowed to accompany the army into Hispania, as and when Damascus approved the event. She went on, "You know it makes sense, my lord. Once battle is joined, there will be a constant need for repairs to the body armour and not only the armour; what about the wounded? All of us have experience in dealing with weapon-inflicted injuries. Your insistence on making training as realistic as possible has necessitated that. Ever since you started preparing for this campaign, we have had to learn how to deal with the sort of injuries likely to be suffered during an actual battle. Not only that, my lord, there is the small matter of…"

"Menna!" For the first time that she, or Akeem, could remember, her name was delivered, not as one friend to another, but as a master to a servant. Even Julian had never heard Tariq raise his voice like this. Then the tone softened. "Menna, you must allow me to be the best judge of how we conduct this conflict. There is not only the matter of your safety but also the important matter of supplies and time. Our train must consist only of that which gives us an advantage in the field, and it is an acknowledged fact that women, who, I have to admit, often accompany their menfolk to war, do slow down the lines of supply and communication. This is likely to be a bloody campaign and I have decided that our best chance is to outmanoeuvre the enemy with our surprise and speed. I cannot afford to do anything likely to interfere with that – and that is final Menna."

For a moment it looked as though she was going to argue further, but Akeem's discreet tug on the back of her robe and the look of determination on Tariq's face seemed to silence her. Julian could not help but note that, rather than looking piqued or disappointed, her head went up and her cool stare engaged them all in turn. Before she left the room, however, she turned her attention to Count Julian and said, not with bitterness but with more than a hint of sadness, "My lord, I have heard my lord, Tariq, make mention of your daughter. He thinks her very beautiful. I trust she is in good health?"

This was said without a trace of irony but, all the same, Julian looked at Tariq who gave an imperceptible nod of his head, from which Julian understood that Menna had not been told anything of Florinda's ordeal. All the same, an uncomfortable pause occurred, before Akeem, with a gruff "Out you go, girl," ushered her out of the door. Just before she disappeared, Julian held up a hand to stop Akeem, and said gently, "Thank you, Menna, my daughter is quite well."

As Akeem followed her out, he looked at Julian and gave a resigned nod of the head. Julian looked over to Tariq but his attention was absorbed by the map in front of him. At this moment, Julian wasn't quite sure who he pitied the most, Florinda or Menna.

This unlikely sentiment was replaced by considering Tariq's next question.

"Julian, one of the problems we have encountered in the past is the loading of our horses. With the numbers embarked previously we learned some short cuts, but with the current numbers now under consideration, this could prove a difficult operation. After all, we cannot afford to spend weeks getting them over the Strait. Do you have any ideas?"

Julian was amused. "Tariq, believe me, that is the least of your problems. My business has been transporting horses across to the Rock for longer than

I can remember. The men who operate my fleet of trading barges have made it an art and, besides, my vessels are much bigger than your naval boats and better adapted for the task we have in mind."

Tariq nodded. "Good, one more thing though. This fleet of yours, how valuable is it to you?"

Julian frowned. "At the moment, I have much on my mind and trade is not the uppermost. Why do you ask?"

Tariq, abstracted, frowned. "Oh! It's nothing, just an idea." He walked over to Julian, embraced him and said, "Thank you, my lor.., sorry, Julian. Thank you for all your help."

•

Some four days later, the last of the long relay of messengers galloped up to the gates of Tangier, and the long awaited orders were breathlessly thrust into Tariq's eager hand. Not much later there was another arrival, this time not expected. This was three hundred elite Arab soldiers, well equipped and mounted on light coloured camels, and all looking as fresh as if they had just arrived from a few miles away. When told that they were to form Tariq's personal bodyguard and had been sent by Musa himself, Tariq wasn't sure that he quite understood. It was only later that he discovered the person so concerned for his well-being was not so much Musa as Al Walid, and he gratefully accepted the gesture, not so much as a bodyguard, but as a welcome addition to his army; likewise Julian's Berber contingent, who were soon happily integrated into the Tangier garrison. The Arabs took a little longer, but even they quickly subdued their feeling of superiority once they learned that they were under the command of a General who knew his business just as well as their former military leader. All in all, Tariq could muster something like ten thousand troops, all at the peak of their profession and impatient for the order to go. All of them feeling, like all soldiers before and since, that unique mixture of anticipation, fear and excitement.

•

The decision was made to march to Septem and embark the army there. Used as they were to seeing Julian's trading barges crossing the Strait, the inhabitants of the Rock, although themselves posing no military threat, would not suspect, at first, what was actually going on. Since Julian's principal business was the export of Berber horses, widely prized among the Visigoth nobility for their sturdiness, it would be the cavalry mounts going first, stripped of their military tack but accompanied by enough men to tend them while they awaited the rest of the force. This, of course, meant that the bulk of the army was faced with an easy two day march and Tariq was to oversee this part of the operation. Malik, however, was given the responsibility of commanding the first landing and of setting up defensive positions to cover the main body of men as they followed. This was not strictly necessary because any real threat was likely to materialise as the army marched further into Hispanic territory but Tariq was taking no chances, even though Roderick's mighty army was still engaged in the north. It was, he reasoned, important for the Umayyad army to suffer as few casualties as possible before facing the ultimate test, and when that came Tariq wanted to have secured the most advantageous field on which to fight.

•

From her balcony, in Septem, Florinda watched the huge fleet of cargo vessels slip their moorings and beat their way out into the Strait. On one of his all-too-brief visits, her father had kept her informed of events and the part he was playing in this dangerous game. Remembering Roderick's dismissive account of the last Islamic assault on his shores, she was fearful of what might happen this time because, if Tariq's army was defeated, and with it Julian's contribution to the cause, the revenge of the Visigoth was not likely to be pretty. A soft footfall behind her caused her to turn. It was Tamegrant who, even here in her own home, had been her constant shadow. She gestured towards the boats and he, joining her at the balcony, put both his clenched fists on the rail, opened them and scattered rose petals in the wake of the departing craft.

The normally peaceful docks at Septem had never seen anything quite like it. Line upon line of horses standing patiently as they waited to be loaded into what appeared to be an endless procession of trading barges. At least, mused Tariq, Julian had been right about one thing. His men certainly knew how to embark horses. Within less time than he would have thought possible, the first of his cavalry regiments were serenely sailing away across the Strait. In the militarised port of Tangier, Malik was mustering his force aboard their naval vessels. With further to sail but much faster than the cargo transports, they would be there to greet them as they came ashore. Meanwhile, still at Septem, Tariq, looked back towards Tangier and could see a seemingly endless, broad ribbon of men, his men, tailing back along the dusty coastal track and waiting patiently for their turn to play their part. Momentarily, his shoulders dropped at the magnitude of the responsibility that they carried. Then he collected himself, raised himself up in his stirrups and concentrated on the distant blur on the horizon that represented Hispania.

Chapter 21

The Rock, April 711AD

Tariq disembarked, looked around him and sniffed the air; only just across the water but it was different from his native Ifriquya. He was met by a smiling Malik, the beachhead already established, lookouts posted and detachments dispatched around to the other side of the Rock, to guard against any inland threat. There wasn't any but then, none had been expected and the few locals who had witnessed the first landings had been taken into custody to prevent word being broadcast further afield. It was, Tariq reflected, more peaceful than it had been in Tangier.

The two commanders walked up the beach and the lower slopes of the Rock, in order to get a better view of the remaining transports disgorging their loads. Akeem, reluctant to abandon his self-appointed role as Tariq's personal bodyguard, had been persuaded to sail on one of the last vessels to leave Tangier. Although Tariq would not have dreamed of telling him so, Akeem was proving to be an adept quartermaster and had been left behind to negotiate for certain supplies considered essential to the operation. Akeem was struggling ashore before bullying his sweating crew into unloading their bulky cargoes.

One of the first big crates to be dragged up onto the sand seemed to be giving more problems than most until it was opened and six furious apes tumbled out, saw they were surrounded by an army of soldiers and tore off up the Rock where they soon disappeared out of sight. One of them though, the largest, stopped briefly as it passed Tariq, whose hand instinctively went to his sword, bared its yellow fangs at him and decided it probably wasn't worth risking a quick nip, before following the others into the folds of the Rock. Malik observed that it was lucky Tariq hadn't been bitten, but Tariq retorted that the animal was smiling at him which he took to be a good omen. Once the animals had disappeared, Tariq was curious, as the apes had certainly not been part of any manifest of which he was aware. He therefore instructed one of his guards to bring Akeem to him. An unrepentant Akeem explained that some of the men, mountain Berbers like himself, had asked if they could bring some Barbary apes from their region since they would remind them of their homeland as they ventured into territory unknown to most of them. Despite being told that they weren't pets or of any practical use, the men persisted, saying that even knowing they were in the same country would make them feel less homesick. Tariq looked sceptical and enquired why could they not have brought sheep or goats, which would have, at least, had some value as provisions. Akeem retorted that sheep and goats had been shipped but hadn't been unloaded yet. Malik, who could never quite come to terms with this unlikely relationship between an aesthetic general and an overweight soldier with rather a lot to say for himself, smiled uneasily and wondered if they might return to the more urgent business of the moment. So, Akeem having been dismissed, they returned to discussing the security of their current situation.

Having ascertained that their landward positions were properly protected, Tariq proposed that their first night on this alien soil be passed here, facing the homeland from whence they had just sailed. He gave orders that he would address the army as soon as the sun was up and, that done, they would march eastwards around the bay, in the direction from which Malik had conducted his first exploratory raid, and that Malik's battalions would be in the vanguard while he, Tariq, would join any ensuing military engagement should the services of he and his other generals be required. As he explained to Malik and the rest of his staff officers, he needed as much time as he could to assess the quality of the opposition and the sort of terrain they favoured, before battle was joined with the superior forces of the Visigoth army under Roderick. He reckoned that he had six to eight weeks before Roderick, having received word of the invasion, mustered his forces and marched south to counter it. During that period he hoped to battle harden his troops, many of whom would be experiencing real conflict for the first time, and gain some knowledge of this country which looked and smelled so different, yet could be seen with the naked eye from the land he knew of as home.

•

The command tents were pitched on a small plateau on the lower slopes of the Rock which offered a panoramic view of the bay, where the convoy of vessels, from which the army had landed, bobbed hypnotically up and down in the gentle swell. The beaches swarmed with troops making the best that they could with their sandy sleeping quarters. Many of them, former desert dwellers, were not unused to a bed of this nature but some of the newer recruits from the mountains were not totally happy with this arrangement and grumbled to each other, until the more seasoned of the warriors told them that this was paradise to what they might expect in the future.

In his tent, Tariq was holding his final briefing with his commanders, each one reminded of his role in the forthcoming campaign and each one now impatient to be getting on with the task. Eventually they bade Tariq a peaceful goodnight and made their way down to the beaches to pass on the orders for the next morning. Tariq watched them go and breathed in the sweet evening air, scented as it was with the mixture of sea and, to him, the unaccustomed subtle aroma of spring grasses. The stars were just beginning to make their appearance and Tariq, having studied the ancient Greek texts on astronomy, wondered how his position in relation to them would have changed by the end of this adventure, assuming he survived it of course. He dismissed this last thought almost before it had taken root. He was by nature optimistic and, for reasons which he couldn't quite rationalise, he suddenly felt happier than he could ever remember, except for the one thing that seemed to be buried deep in his consciousness; something which he could never quite reach or understand. He shook his head as if trying to shake it free but, as always, it stayed stubbornly out of his reach. He stood there for a few moments longer, casting a last look at his army spread out below him. Some of the men, veterans who had known and grown to admire and even love him over the years, looked up at him and waved. He waved back at them, smiled to himself, bade his goodnights to his bodyguard and re-entered his solitary tented room.

•

Tariq was not fully asleep. Indeed, he doubted if he would attain that elusive state on this night. Nevertheless, he wasn't particularly happy to hear the word "Master", quite audibly directed at him from outside his thin walls. He groaned, raised himself to his feet and made his way to the entrance, saying as he went, "What is it now, Akeem?" It could be no one else but Akeem, because nobody else would have got past his bodyguard. He peered out into the semi-darkness and made out two figures silhouetted against the starry sky. The obvious bulk could only have been Akeem but the other figure, an ordinary soldier, could have been any one of his men. Akeem whispered hoarsely and, to Tariq's mind, unnecessarily conspiratorially,

"This man says he must see you urgently, says it's very important and can't wait until morning. Don't worry, my lord, he's not armed."

Tariq nodded to the commander of his bodyguard, who bowed and went back to his post.

"You'd better come in then," said Tariq wearily. "But, I warn you Akeem, this had better be important or you will find yourself back in Tangier with a very large broom."

Akeem looked puzzled. "Broom, my lord?"

"For permanent stable cleaning duties, Akeem, and you probably won't get a shovel either."

More feigned puzzlement from Akeem. "Shovel, my lord?"

Tariq raised his eyes heavenwards. "Never mind, Akeem, just tell me what this is all about."

"It's him, not me!" said Akeem. "Anyway, I can't stop. I have to see to my horse." And, without further explanation, he was out of the door and descending the hill at a speed which totally belied his generous girth. Tariq was then left with the young soldier who calmly proceeded to remove his tagelmust from his head and face. Tariq's groan was loud enough to bring his Arab bodyguards to the door but, before they could enter, Tariq ushered them away, telling them he was in no danger whatsoever. He pinned the woven door closed and stood there, hands on hips, shaking his head in exasperation.

"I thought I told you that you were not to come. You do realise, don't you, Menna, that you have defied, not just me, I'm not that important, but the Caliph himself. For what it is worth I am his representative here in Iberia and you have wilfully disobeyed me."

Menna looked not in the slightest contrite. Her eyes, though tearful, were smiling at him and she was holding out her hands towards him. He moved back a step and she followed him. He held up a hand to stop her.

"This is ridiculous, Menna. We have known each other since we were small children but my faith has never allowed us to be anything other than friends." She held up her own hand and placed her palm flat against his.

"I have converted, Tariq. I am a believer. I have taken all the necessary instruction and, from now on, my devotion to the cause will always be as great as yours. I don't want to be your friend. I want so much more than that, Tariq. I know you have always thought kindly of me even if I have, on occasions, been something of a nuisance, but I have loved you, Tariq, since I was four years old and I am not prepared to wait any longer."

"But…" Her finger was on his mouth and, for once, Tariq ibn Ziyad was silenced.

•

The following morning, waking before the sun was up as was his custom, Tariq was a different man. Not outwardly perhaps but, for the first time that he could remember, he sensed a fulfilment and a 'completeness' that had, thus far, eluded him. It was still dark when the commander of Tariq's bodyguard was instructed to send one of his men to the beach, locate Akeem, the General's …well, few people were really sure what Akeem's role was in life…and order him to wait on the General immediately. The unfortunate man selected for this task looked down upon an army of some ten thousand men and wondered how he was to supposed to find him but, as it happened, he didn't have to bother because the unmistakable form of Akeem was seen to disengage itself from a group on the shoreline and move in their direction. It took him a little while to struggle up the hill, much longer than it had taken him to descend it the previous evening, but eventually he presented himself at the tent, nodded to the bodyguard and gave one of his slightly mocking bows to Tariq, who ushered him inside.

Once there he ignored Tariq for a moment while his eyes flickered around the space which, apart from himself and Tariq, was empty. He looked enquiringly at Tariq who returned the look with one of his own. Akeem was the first to break the stalemate.

"Where is she, my lord?"

"He, you mean 'he'," came the reply. "'He' was escorted back down to the beach by one of my guards, a few hours after you brought 'him' up here. You see, Akeem, much as I appreciate your motives, both Menna and I have agreed that any thought of an attachment between us would best be left in abeyance until our task here is complete."

"But, my lord, I was sure that you …"

"We will, Akeem, believe me, we will but now is not the time or the place. So we have made a decision to wait until the time is right." The look of disappointment on Akeem's face was so marked that Tariq thought it only fair to elaborate, but only to a point.

"I have much to thank you for Akeem, not the least what you did for me last night, when your action, impertinent as it undoubtedly was, helped me to understand what has been secretly troubling me for so long. Don't misunderstand me. I know what it is to love. I love my friends, my religion, I love every single one of them down there," he waved his hand in the direction of the shore, "but this, this is different and finding it has struck a chord in me that has, until now, escaped me. Do you understand?"

Akeem looked away, then, in a tone even more hoarse than usual, muttered, "Yes, master, at least I think I do." He then looked appraisingly at Tariq. "But what about her, is she coming with us or not?"

Tariq shook his head. "No, Akeem, I have no doubt that when you go out of that door, you will look back to Tangier and when you do, you should see one of our transports making its way there. Menna may be aboard that ship, but from now on, she will always be with me, here and here." He tapped his head and his heart. "Now, enough of that! I want you here, by my side, when I address the army and mark the moment, Akeem, because I sense that, despite the assurances from my staff that the men are in good heart, many of the newer recruits are extremely apprehensive of what lies ahead. Your foolery with the apes was, in retrospect, not a bad idea but somehow we have to inject a little more steel into their resolve, and the sight of your comforting bulk might help me deliver what I feel needs to be said. Even now, the men should be mustering in preparation, so shall we go?"

Akeem started to follow Tariq then stopped him. "My lord, why is only one of our boats returning to Tangier? The fleet has done its work, why do we need them now?"

Tariq led the way outside.

"Patience, Akeem, patience!"

Chapter 22

The Rock, April 711AD

The first reaction came from the gulls which, disturbed from their foraging on the crowded shoreline, suddenly beat their way into the air above and squawked their indignation at the clear blue early morning sky.

"My warriors." Tariq's voice rang out from the natural platform on the Rock. He was surrounded by his commanders and his Arabian bodyguard arrayed behind, their white robes standing out starkly against the dark rocky outcrops which formed the lower slopes. They and his senior officers apart, the only other attendant upon him was Akeem, standing at Tariq's side, sternly regarding the massed troops on the beaches below, while behind them, the armada of cargo vessels which had carried them here floated serenely at their anchors in the shallow blue sea.

•

"My warriors, where would you go? Behind you is the sea and before you, the enemy. You have now only the advantage of your hope and your courage. The enemy, when we meet with him, is strong and outnumbers us many times over, and your only chance of victory is to swallow your fears and have faith in your swords. If we are resolute we can be victorious and, remember, of all the warriors in all of Ifriquya, you have been chosen by he who commands all true believers, Al Walid, our glorious Caliph, and do you know why you are his choice? It is because he believes that, through your bravery, the true word of God will resonate throughout this land and the true religion will be established here. Be assured that, through all the perils and dangers that confront you here, I will not be at your side. No! I will not be at your side because I will be at the fore. I will lead, and where I lead you will follow me to glory and to success. When, at last, we are face to face with this King Roderick and his mighty army, I will be the one to seek him out and challenge him to combat. Ours will be the glory because we will fear nothing and when we have our victory, you, yes all of you, will be the masters of this land and will share in the spoils that will fall to us. Should I be slain, and none of us can lay a claim to immortality in this life, you will continue fighting for our homeland across the water, for me and for our faith. You have trained diligently for this day and your officers, to a man, share this determination to succeed. I know that you will not fail me and, as I have already said, over there," he gestured with outstretched arm to the land behind him, "we shall be meeting our enemy, whereas there," his arm swept round to the sea, "is…" He paused and as the army turned to follow where he was pointing, there was a muffled gasp which rose in volume as ten thousand troops watched their boats burning before their eyes. Tariq had to raise his voice to make himself heard above the collective exclamations of dismay which greeted him. "There, my warriors, is the way of no return. Trust me and trust your officers and trust in your faith, *we shall prevail.*"

•

There was another moment of silence, during which Tariq was conscious of Akeem holding his breath. Then a cheer, which was tentative at first, before being taken up group after group until the Rock was resonating with cheers echoing from every fold. Akeem was reminded of that time, it seemed so long ago now, when he had first heard Tariq, as a young, inexperienced commander, use the force of his rhetoric to rally a large number of men, uncertain of their future. Many of those same men were below on the same unfamiliar beach and some, in particular the sons of Kusaila, the head of the heretic tribe, now converts to a man, had risen to enjoy key posts in the Berber army. Tariq felt a touch on his arm and looked behind him, a long way further up the Rock, to where a laughing Akeem was indicating. The apes had appeared to see what all the commotion was about, and it was almost as if they had been infected by the excitement of the occasion because they were leaping around hysterically and shrieking at each other. Only the big male was sitting quietly on a boulder, watching the proceedings with the detachment of an intelligent observer.

"Tell you what!" Akeem shouted in Tariq's ear. "If you win the big battle, they'll name this place after you."

"And what if I lose?" Tariq retorted.

Akeem thought for a moment then said, "I suppose they'll call it 'Roderick's Rock.'"

Tariq laughed. "I like the sound of Jabal Tariq better. Anyway I think it deserves elevating to the status of a mountain. It has proved, thus far, an hospitable place for us but it's time we left its shelter and started our work."

Akeem caught hold of his arm. "Just a minute, the boats! I think I can understand why you've done it but how come none of that lot down there, let alone me, knew what was going on?"

Tariq laughed again. Akeem marked that, although his master was always even- tempered, generous and kind, his mood on this morning was definitely lighter than he had ever noticed previously. One hand on Akeem's shoulder, Tariq pointed seaward with the other. The boats were still burning although, as they settled in the water, the flames diminished and a pall of smoke was beginning to spread over the calm sea.

"If you look carefully, Akeem," Tariq indicated. "Just beyond the fleet that I ordered to be scuttled, you can see a dozen small craft waiting patiently for the fires to go out. They sailed out after the rest of us had left and they are commanded by your old friend from the yards, Amayuu, or is he your cousin? Anyway, they sailed in quietly after dark and apportioned a pile of inflammable material in every boat in the fleet then, as soon as they saw my signal from up here, they raced around the fleet and torched it. I have to say that Amayuu took a lot of persuading; he hated the idea of putting good seaworthy craft to the torch, but I needed to make a point and, to be honest with you, I couldn't think of another way to impress upon us all that there is no going back."

Akeem sniffed. "Well, you've done that and no mistake. But what's Count Julian going to say about it? You've just destroyed his fleet of ships."

Tariq became serious. "No doubt I will know soon enough; I should think Menna will have told him by now." He laughed again, though, when he saw the look on Akeem's face and the comment that accompanied it.

"You got Menna to tell Count Julian that you've just set fire to his fleet? You did have a busy night didn't you?"

Tariq shook his head. "Julian will understand and I expect him to join us before too long. He, more than anyone, will appreciate that the loss of his trading vessels will be as nothing to the riches that will accrue to him, should we succeed in this endeavour.

Talking of which, it's high time we made a start. Malik!" He called to his commander of the vanguard. "A word with you, it's time!"

•

The lookout, on his tower at Septem, was worried. He had expected to see a whole fleet of ships making their way home across the Strait, but all he could see was one lonely vessel which, as it hove closer, seemed to contain a skeleton crew and, he stretched to get a better view, a solitary woman who he didn't recognise. On hearing the alarm, the first person to respond to the call was Count Julian, himself, who hurried to the dock in time to greet and assist the woman ashore. He courteously escorted her to his apartments, sat her down and offered her food, which she declined. He could not explain why, but for some reason, this woman, who he had only met on one other occasion, when she was mildly admonished by Tariq, looked different from when he'd last seen her. Before, he had been impressed by her self-assurance and her directness but now, adding to those qualities, there was a sparkle and luminosity about her which transformed her into something more than a pleasant looking, intelligent woman. Knowing from where she had sailed and remembering Akeem's look when last they had met, he guessed what might have happened and he felt an involuntary pang for Florinda. He resolved that, if at all possible, he would see that she and Menna did not meet, which, he reflected, would not be easy. Florinda, knowing of the events that were taking place, would already be aware of the arrival of this Berber woman but, for the moment, there were more important things he needed to know.

"Well, Menna – you don't mind if I call you Menna?"

She shook her head impatiently. "Why should I mind, it is my given name." She then continued with a directness that completely took Julian by surprise, "Tariq has put all your ships to the torch. He asked me to tell you that. He wants you to know that it wasn't a wanton act of vandalism but something that he considered necessary for the discipline of his army and," she paused for a moment, "he was sure that you would understand. Do you, my lord?"

Julian didn't hesitate. "Of course I understand. He hinted as much when last we were together and," he went on, "I dare say he also intimated that my subsequent loss of revenue would be more than made up by my share of the booty, likely to result from a successful occupation of Hispania."

Menna, slightly taken aback by a directness which exceeded her own, took a moment to say, yes, that was indeed what Tariq had promised. She then said, with a passion, "He will succeed, my lord. You need have no fear of that. He will succeed and this is just the beginning for him. He is destined to perform great deeds for our faith which, as you probably know, is the motivating force which drives him on. It is not commonplace ambition, it is something much more than that, moreover he…" She trailed off, embarrassed that her enthusiasm had robbed her of the self-composure she had cultivated with such care. There was not a trace of condescension in Julian's smile.

"Menna, you have no need to enumerate the fine qualities embodied by your …your master. From our first meeting, I deduced that his was a fine mind motivated by finer instincts. A rare quality indeed and I respect him totally. Why else," he continued with a self-deprecating smile, "do you think I received your news of my fleet with such equanimity? No, I am sure…" There came a knock at the door and both Menna and Julian, who were expecting a servant bearing food and drink, viewed Florinda's entrance with a mixture of surprise and, on Julian's part, apprehension, and in fact the first moments were frozen in time as all three reached for comments appropriate to the occasion. It was Florinda who first spoke and it was to Menna that her words were addressed.

"You must be Menna. My father spoke of you after he met you in Tangier. He was very complimentary. I am so pleased to meet you and I hope that we will become friends." She spoke with such candour and simplicity that Menna, for the second time in as many minutes, found her self-confidence challenged. It was Julian who came to her rescue.

"Allow me to present my daughter, Florinda. Yes, Florinda, you are quite correct, this is Menna, of whom you have heard me speak."

The two women could not have been more different. Florinda, very poised and beautiful. Menna, currently undergoing emotional turmoil and short of sleep, dressed in the manner of her race and devoid of any social artifice. Consequently it was Menna who was about to bend the knee to Florinda who, with a little cry, darted forward, raised her up and embraced her. Julian, watching this touching little pageant, could not explain the feelings that enveloped him. The two races, of socially disparate backgrounds, somehow seemed a microcosm of the changes which were about to take place in the known world. He thought, also, of how Tariq would have approved. He also felt inexpressively sorry for his daughter. He gave a little cough to get their attention and they parted, both laughing, and the irony didn't escape him. It was the first time he had seen Florinda laugh since her return from Toletum. He coughed again, this time to hide his emotion. Adopting their prevailing mood, he said, jokingly,

"Well, now you two have got to know each other, I don't suppose I'm going to be able to get a word in, but back to business. Menna, apart from what you have just told me, is there anything else I can do to help? As you might appreciate," he continued wryly, "transport could be something of a problem but anything else apart from that?"

Menna looked at him, then to Florinda then back to Julian, before saying firmly, "You, my lord."

" I beg your pardon Menna!"

"You, my lord. Tariq hasn't said as much but I think it important that you join him over there. You see, you know many of the local Visigoth nobility and, I suspect, you know their allegiance to Roderick is questionable. If you could talk to them, persuade them to join Tariq's cause or, at least, not to arm against him, you could save so many unnecessary casualties in our army. That way, our resources might be conserved for the great battle that is to come, in which, my lord," she went on, " Tariq is likely to be greatly outmatched."

At the 'Roderick', Florinda paled and looked questioningly at her father.

He gave a minute shake of the head to indicate that Menna knew nothing of her ordeal. Menna, fearing that she had overstepped her authority, noticed none of this and walked to the window overlooking the port at which she had only just arrived. Florinda joined her, took her by the shoulders and turned her round to face her. Menna could see tears in her eyes. Florinda said quietly and without a trace of bitterness,

"Don't you think my father has already done enough? By asking this, you are asking him to put himself in great personal danger." She then whispered, "He is all I have."

Menna removed her hands but continued to hold them.

"Yes, I am sorry. I should not have said anything. Please forgive me and, my lord," addressing Julian again, "it was none of my business, Tariq will be furious with me when he hears."

Julian was thinking. After a moment he joined them at the window and put his arms around them both.

"Menna," he said, "you are absolutely right. From the point of view of religion, we might be of different persuasions but Tariq's cause is, ultimately, my cause. I will join him, but on one condition. That you, Menna, stay here and keep my daughter company."

He smiled at Florinda. "It will be better for you, my dear, to have someone to talk to, other than Tamegrant. In fact, would you have any objection if I took him with me as my bodyguard? You will be quite safe here in the citadel without him."

Florinda said, "You will take care, Papa. And you must promise me that, when Lord Tariq is victorious, you will send for Menna and me to join you over there. That way I have something to look forward to and, in the meantime, Menna will have to put up with my moods and my fears. You will stay with me won't you Menna?"

Menna nodded, "Of course I will, providing the promise you asked of your father is honoured by him, for I cannot wait to get back there, for all sorts of reasons which, perhaps," she turned to Florinda, "you and I can talk about while we wait impatiently for our summons."

Julian clapped his hands. "Now that is all settled, I must prepare for my immediate departure. The sooner I get there, the sooner I can gauge the intentions of my erstwhile colleagues and the sooner I can put their resources to good use."

•

"So, we ride around the bay and west to .., what is the name of the place?"

"So far as I know, Malik, it's just called 'the port'. The White Port, I think the Romans called it but that was centuries ago. Capture it and you can call it what you like. Keep one of your fastest riders ready to come back to us if you need help, but I don't imagine that will be necessary. According to Julian it's a run-down sort of place, but we have to start somewhere and I still think that is the direction in which we need to advance. It will be further for Roderick to march and the further he has to travel, the better chance we have of choosing our ground while still being relatively fresh. This time you can make as much noise as you like, in fact the more the better, and do whatever you have to in overcoming any opposition but, and this applies to whatever we manage to conquer, no gratuitous violence. If we are to make Hispania ours, the more local support we enjoy, the easier and less bloody our job will become. Good luck and we'll meet up again on the morrow, by which time I expect to see our standard flying from the highest tower." Malik nodded his understanding of these orders, saluted Tariq with his sword, sheathed it, rode to the head of his army, roughly a third of the total force, and led it away from the Rock in the same direction that he had taken a year previously on his exploratory raid.

•

Tariq gave orders for the remainder of the army to gather together and ride inland.

As soon as they were well clear of the Rock, individual commanders took their respective divisions through a series of exercises and drills, impressing the growing number of locals and not a few Visigoth local nobles who turned up with their retinues, mostly armed with agricultural implements. These latter quickly realised the impossibility of joining battle with such a force, superior in numbers, equipment and training. This did not prevent, however, a few of them retreating out of sight of the Umayyad army and hastily organising teams of messengers to make their way north and sound the alarm to Roderick, who was still in the process of defeating the armies of the rebellious sons of his predecessor.

•

The old monk was putting on weight. He wasn't sure how it all came about, but apparently it was rumoured in Toletum that a holy man, a hermit, had made his home in the old monastery, and the faithful of the city had got into the habit of leaving offerings of food and drink at the door. Mostly these consisted of left-overs, but they were considerably better than his recent diet supplied by the surrounding hedgerows. The cats also appreciated these offerings, to the extent that the old man was forced to hide in the bushes and grab the food before the cats could get at it. Possibly, he considered, this was the result, somehow, of him being the current guardian of a holy relic. It wasn't, of course, but, he reasoned, why else should his fortunes have changed as they had? Consequently, it became a ritual for him, in the middle of the night when the cats were his only observers, to operate the pulleys and pray over the table, as it lay, faintly shimmering in the dark.

.

It was night too, when a boat, no sails in view but propelled by ten strong oarsmen, crunched onto the shingle beach and carefully disembarked its cargo of two horses and two men, one of giant stature. They mounted their steeds and galloped off into the night.

Chapter 23

Tarraconensis, May 711AD

"Clean it." The tall armoured warrior with a drooping blond moustache took the sword and, almost reverently, knelt beside the body and scrupulously wiped the dripping blade backwards and forwards over the clothing of the dead man until it was clean. He stood up, reversed it and placed the hilt into Roderick's waiting hand. Roderick sheathed it and breathed a sigh of satisfaction. It was over; the rebels in the north eastern territories had been subdued and henceforth he could forget about this bleak and uncivilised region of his kingdom, which compared so unfavourably with the sophistication of Toletum and the other royal cities of Hispania. He would spend one more night here, just long enough to collate the reports of his officers and ensure that the leaders of the rebellion had all been accounted for, then a leisurely journey back to Toletum. No rush, and ample time to enjoy the fruits of his victory, one of whom was waiting in his tent at this very moment. He smiled to himself, and stood quietly while his pages helped him out of his armour. Freed from its constriction, he ran his fingers through his long hair and started to make his way towards some well-earned relaxation.

There came, however, a diversion in the form of a messenger, throwing himself off his sweated horse at the feet of his king, who recoiled momentarily from the man who was trying to muster enough breath to deliver his news.

"The barbarians have landed, my lord."

Disregarding the man and his dramatic statement, Roderick calmly turned to his aide, the one who had cleaned his sword, and said, "You deal with it, I'm busy." With which dismissal he turned and walked away to his tent and his post-battle recreation. He didn't get far; he had hardly moved a couple of paces when the aide caught up with him and said, "Sire, my lord, another messenger has just arrived from the south and," he took a step back and looked into the distance, "I can see another, in a lather, galloping through our lines." He had hardly finished speaking when the third man, even before leaving his horse's back, was shouting out the same message.

"The barbarians, my lord. They have landed in great numbers and our towns are falling to them one day after another."

Roderick sighed and gestured for all three men to approach. When they were ranged about his feet, he said quietly, "Now, what is all this nonsense? You do realise, don't you, that we have just won a significant victory over our enemies here in the north, a victory that has almost certainly secured our sovereignty over this land for many years to come, and what do you do? You come scrambling up here like a trio of frightened schoolgirls panicking about some sort of enemy landing on our southern shores. I can only imagine that it is the Berbers from across the Strait. So what is so alarming about that? Last year, if I remember rightly, they didn't even put up a fight but turned tail as soon as my nobles threatened them. Why should I worry about some undisciplined rabble tribesmen who are some weeks' riding away from where I now stand, victorious against a real army? Why cannot our local nobles and their considerable power either wipe them out or chase them back over the sea from whence they came?"

The first messenger raised his head.

"My lord this is not the sort of raiding party we have witnessed in the past. This is an army of several thousands, armoured and trained. Our resources are not sufficient. Day after day they are laying siege to our cities and the defenders are imploring your majesty to come to their aid."

Roderick leaned over the man, placing his hand on his bared head, as if about to perform a benediction, then twisted the hair in his fingers, forcing the man's head back so that he was made to look up at him.

"Now you listen to me," he hissed. "This is what you do. You get back on that horse and you get back to where you came from. When you get there, you tell those witless idiots who sent you here to stop behaving like women, get their armies together and resist the invaders, to the death if necessary. When I am ready, and only when I am ready, I will ride south." He released the man and was about to turn away when another of the envoys, apparently less cowed than the others, rose to his feet and said defiantly, "My lord, he speaks the truth. This is nothing like we have witnessed before. These are no opportunistic tribesmen, looking for easy bounty before returning to their land across the waters. This is an army bent on occupying our land and keeping it. They are winning over the natives with promises of better lives, more freedoms than we allow them. They take nothing from them, they even treat the Jews with, if not friendship, certainly tolerance, and the consequence of this is that the Jews are handing over valuables that they have hidden from us, on the understanding that the Berbers will be there to protect them should you try to exact vengeance on them. Moreover, they…"

Without turning Roderick snarled, "Vengeance, I'll show them what vengeance is all about. I knew it," he said, turning to his aide, "I knew those unbelievers were hiding their assets from the state in order to avoid paying their taxes. I was always taught never to trust them and it just goes to show, I have been too lenient; well, not anymore." He turned back to the messengers.

"If I am to march south, I must first have more precise details of this so-called army. How many and how armed and who leads them? Well, what is your best intelligence?"

The messenger who had spoken out earlier was the one chosen to answer. "Sire, it is difficult to be precise about numbers because they move swiftly, form and reform their battalions with much tactical skill but I would estimate something between five and ten thousand men. Generally they are lightly armed, or appear to be so, but they are commanded by one, Tariq ibn Ziyad."

Roderick frowned and repeated the name. Then his brow cleared. "Ah yes! I think Julian of Septem mentioned that name some little while ago." He closed his eyes in thought then, "Yes, that's the one. Apparently a former slave of Musa ibn Nusayr, the Caliph's viceroy. I seem to recall that this Tariq ibn Ziyad was made Governor of Tangier." He suddenly burst out laughing. "Well, well, a small army under the command of a former slave; this could be fun after all. Right!" he turned to his aide, "Pass it around that we have two days to prepare to march south." He rubbed his hands. "I take back what I said about the nobility in that territory. I hope that, by the time I get down there, they will have left me something to play with. You three," he pointed at the messengers, "have the night to rest and, at first light, you'll be furnished with fresh mounts and I want you on your way. Tell your masters that King Roderick is on the march and, I dare say, once word of it gets through to those heathen hordes, they'll pack up their prayer mats and head for the coast." Shaking his head and still laughing to himself, he turned his back on them and strode away to his pavilion and the reward that awaited him there.

•

Count Julian and Tamegrant caught up with Tariq at the White Port, which Malik had captured in the face of minimal resistance and few casualties. He had also taken a quantity of booty which seemed quite disproportionate to the size and importance of the community that had just submitted to him. On receiving intelligence that the mission had been successful, Tariq, accompanied by the rest of his army, joined up with Malik and it was here that Julian, escorted by a detachment of Tariq's Arab guard, found the two generals sitting at their command table which was covered with a collection of jewellery and precious metals. Tariq leapt to his feet and, after he and

Julian had warmly greeted each other, his first words were, "How is Menna, is she safe?"

Julian gratefully sank down onto the seat one of the guards had hurriedly procured for him and was quick to set Tariq's mind at rest.

"The Lady Menna is perfectly secure and she and my daughter will, by now, be the best of friends. You, of all people, Tariq, should know that Septem is virtually impregnable, to the extent that even your mighty Umayyad army failed to breach our defences. Mind you," he went on, "should you succeed in your work here, thereby bringing the entire country under your control, I cannot imagine that women of such redoubtable character as those two will be content to remain where they are. So don't be surprised if you find them knocking on your door and clamouring to congratulate you on your victory. That is, of course, assuming that 'victory' is yours." He indicated the table. "I see you have made a good start. Is this the down payment on my fleet?"

Tariq smiled at the question which was obviously not meant to be taken seriously.

"No, my lord; some of this will be used for supplying my army but mainly as an inducement to perform bravely in the field. As you are well aware, most of my men are of nomadic stock and have little idea of value beyond that of animals upon which they subsisted. They need to learn that rewards can be theirs for excelling in a field of battle as well as in a field of sheep."

Julian wagged an admonishing finger. "At what stage in your career, Tariq, did you learn that particular lesson, or was it so long ago that you have forgotten your beginnings?"

Tariq's answer was tinged with reproach. "My lord, you should know that it is not for this that I am here," he indicated the valuables on the table, "but to serve my God. But enough of this, there are more serious questions I have for you, the first of which is why, in a town as unimportant as this appears to be, is there so much booty to be had and much of it, I might add, was offered freely to us?"

Julian laughed and took a draught from the cup that had been placed before him. "This town might appear insignificant but it is a port, and where you have a port you have merchants and where you have merchants you have wealth, especially when you have not set their vessels ablaze," he continued with another laugh. "Why much of it was given freely is because your protection is being sought. Don't forget, Tariq, that many of these people are Jews or natives who have suffered under the yoke of the Visigoth. For two hundred years they have been in thrall to a culture which, although Christian, has behaved very harshly towards them and I promise you that, when the fighting starts in earnest, you will find unexpected allies, especially if you are seen to be coming out on top."

Tariq nodded gravely, leant over the table and picked up a heavy gold bracelet, set with precious stones. "Another question, Julian; I have always been led to understand that the Visigoth set no store by beauty, yet some of these pieces are very fine indeed."

Julian took it from him and examined it. "The nobles here," he said, "might not recognise the beauty in an object but they certainly recognise the value of it. No, Tariq, this was made by a Jewish craftsman, perhaps destined for a noble house but, more likely fashioned from off-cuts of pieces made to order, probably cheating the buyer in the first place, and then hidden somewhere. Believe me; if Roderick and his friends knew of all the hidden treasure in this country, they would probably put up an even better fight for it than they are going to."

Tariq thought for moment. "Interesting," he said. "So this is true, is it, that there is treasure of which Roderick is unaware? Surely, when he acceded to the throne, the palace in Toletum must have contained priceless items that the Visigoth had acquired from their predecessors after they assumed power?"

Julian extracted a choice necklace from the chest, and examined it carefully before replacing it. "There is certainly one item that Roderick is missing, but then, I expect you already know about that?"

Tariq looked at him enquiringly. Julian laughed at him and said, "Think now, Tariq. What was it that Lord Musa always wanted to hear about on your visits to me, at Septem?" Tariq thought carefully, then said, "You're talking about that table, aren't you, the one that was reputed to have come from Solomon's temple? Interesting artefact; I did some research on that when Lord Musa seemed so interested. I have to say, the provenance seemed uncertain." His brow furrowed. "As far as I can remember, this ancient piece of religious furniture had supposedly been looted from the temple in Jerusalem by Titus who took it to Rome but that is about all I know of it. Anyway, I assume this is the object we are talking about. Why? Is it particularly relevant?"

"Indeed it might be," was Julian's reply. "I think, of all the treasure to be found here, that table is the most valuable and the most significant, if only because of its religious importance. The thing is," he went on, "it seems to have disappeared. It was certainly in Toletum in King Wittiza's time. I always saw it when visiting - indeed you could hardly miss it, but it is definitely not there now and Roderick would give half his kingdom to learn of its whereabouts." Tariq interrupted him.

"You mean, it has gone missing, literally? Does Lord Musa know of this?"

Julian grinned, "I have no idea, it is now some time since we have spoken but his disappointment, when he finds out, is going to be unimaginable. He was quite obsessed with the thing. First, of course, you have to defeat Roderick before you can even start looking for it, so what is your next move towards that end? You do realise that Roderick will have had intelligence of your invasion and, as we speak, will be riding south. I have heard that his victory against the pretenders was quite comprehensive and his confidence will be in the ascendant."

It was Tariq's turn to smile. "I have no doubt, my friend, and it suits me very well. A confident commander does not see the need to think too much and, by the time he catches up with me, I shall be even further away from him than I am now."

"Further away?" Julian questioned. "Then you are not marching to meet him?"

"No, indeed I am not," came Tariq's assured reply. "He is marching to meet *me* and that is an entirely different state of affairs. I will be ready at a time and place to suit my strategy, not his. Tomorrow we pitch some of my, as yet, untested men against the might of Gades. Then and only then will I be ready to meet the enemy."

Julian whistled to himself, "Gades eh! Rich pickings there, my friend."

Another grin from Tariq. "You'd better come with us then."

•

At first he thought it was a thunderstorm, but the thunder was too regular and getting louder. The cats were pacing around and beginning to exit the building for what they saw as the comparative safety of the countryside. The old man, too, was fearful and, after checking that the vault containing the Table, of which he now thought of himself as custodian, was securely shut, he crept out of the building and hid in the undergrowth. The origin of the noise soon became apparent as endless columns of men and horses made their way, some little distance from the monastery, towards the city of Toletum. When the army had passed in the opposite direction some weeks earlier, their progress had scarcely attracted any attention but now there was a real purpose in their marching and the old man, watching them pass some distance away, sensed that this was different, and not merely a vast body of soldiers on the move but history itself marching into a new and unexplored era.

•

Within two days Gades had fallen. The Berbers had triumphed with few losses and had emerged from the short siege, a stronger and more competent force. The spoils, as Julian had forecast, were bountiful, for Gades was a wealthy city, and now Tariq and his generals set about finding a battleground that would give them as much advantage as possible against a foe that was likely to be heavily superior in numbers and, more importantly, had a nation to defend. Eventually, Tariq found what he considered to be the most favourable. Not too far from Gades, with the advantage of an elevated position in foothills of the mountains and a river between them and the direction from which an attack was most likely. He conferred with Malik and the rest of his staff. Orders were issued; everybody knew what they had to do and what was expected of them. All they had to do was wait.

Chapter 24

Septem, July 711AD

It was a beautiful morning. Cooler than the weather that Tariq and his army were experiencing across the Strait. With the palm fronds flapping about in the cooling sea breeze, the two women were enjoying their habitual morning stroll in the castle gardens and were making their way through the gate in the fortified walls which led down to the dock. Usually alive with the bustle of trading vessels and the unloading of cargo, they were now occupied by former crews who were busy assisting shipwrights in the building of replacement vessels and the more mundane task of renovation and cleaning. Florinda, with some help from Julian's staff, had made herself responsible for organising these operations. Menna who, while liking her hostess well enough, had begun to respect her more and more as time went on and if, at first, she had looked upon her as little more than a beautiful young woman of noble birth, she was beginning to realise that Florinda possessed a spirit equally as independent as her own.

While Florinda was inspecting the progress being made under her instruction, Menna walked to the end of the dock and stood there, gazing out over the water. She had been standing there for some time before she was joined by Florinda who said, teasingly, "Still pining for him are you? Don't worry Menna, as soon as he has vanquished Roderick's army, he will be back for you."

Menna shook her head.

"Oh no he won't!" Then she laughed when she saw Florinda's smile turn into a frown.

"Of course I worry for his safety, but what I mean when I say 'he won't be back' is that he will carry on until he has brought the whole country under the Umayyad rule. Defeating Roderick is only the start of his campaign but it is also only the start of my campaign. As soon as I have word that it is possible, I shall be joining him." She smiled at her friend. "Don't worry, Florinda. You may come with me if you wish, that is if you can face being over there again, after what happened to you in Toletum."

Florinda's frown deepened. "I have to go back. Father has already said that I should join him as soon as it is safe. Strange isn't it? He said that to me once before, when they were fighting over the succession. Once Roderick was established on the throne, father thought it was safe for me to go to Toletum. Then look what happened. Anyway, this is assuming that your Tariq will win. His army is so small, while Roderick commands a force at least three times the size."

Menna shook her head. "Tariq will prevail but it is not the Visigoth that is my only concern. Among our own people there are those who do not see their best interests served by a victory. At least, not under the generalship of Tariq."

Florinda looked disbelievingly at her. "Surely not, Menna. I thought that your religion was the driving force of this conquest. I cannot believe that there are factions within a faith as strong as that to which you hold."

Menna's reply was tinged with a dry humour. "Some of us, my dear, are less wedded to the cause than others. Tariq would not look at me while I remained outside the faith therefore I…" She had no need to continue but Florinda persisted.

"Yes, yes, of course I can understand all that. That is different. But who, among your leaders, would want anything other than victory for your army?"

"Victory in this battle, yes," came the reply, "but not the capitulation of the entire kingdom. I suspect that Tariq is not fully aware of this, but I have contacts in Damascus and have had for some time. There is another army amassing there, the full Umayyad army. I think that they are just waiting to see the result of the main battle before themselves joining the fray. That way, even if Tariq should fail, Roderick's army will be weakened by the battle, thereby making it easier for the Umayyad force to triumph and, thereafter, progress victorious throughout the whole of Hispania."

"But who..?" Florinda swallowed the question as soon as the answer occurred to her.

"It's the Emir, isn't it? It's Lord Musa?" She thought for a second. "What was it my father said once? Something about Lord Musa's ambition outweighing his beliefs. I can't remember exactly but it was something like that."

Menna said, "Count Julian is very perceptive. The trouble is that Tariq always feels such a debt of gratitude towards Lord Musa. If it comes to that, so should I. My immediate concern, though, is that Tariq, should he overcome Roderick, be recognised by the Caliphate as the true victor and not Lord Musa who is poised with his mighty army to snatch the triumph for himself. Your father will not return until he is sure of Roderick's overthrow. Once he does, I suggest we beg him to escort us over there, to some place of safety, so that I can share my fears with Tariq. What do you think, is he likely to agree to such a plan?"

Florinda nodded her head enthusiastically. " I'm sure he will and I think I know the very place where he can guarantee our security. It is where Tamegrant and I took refuge after…after..I'm sorry I am trying not to be weak but my worst nightmare is that Roderick will win and, if he does, none of us are safe, not even here."

Menna's head went up. "He won't, he can't, he just can't. Tariq is a great general and destined to go down in history as one of the greatest ever." She turned to Florinda, looked her directly in the eyes and took both her hands, pressing them tightly to emphasise her faith. "Believe me, I know it, I just know it will happen this way."

•

From his vantage point on the rising ground facing the Guadelete River, which he thought of as a boundary rather than an obstacle, Tariq sat on his white horse, his Arab guard, all three hundred of them, on both his flanks. Only Akeem, immediately at his side, spoiled the picture, his bulk carried by an equally overweight dun steed and his battle gear a drab contrast to the pristine picture presented by the others. Unaware of the confidence expressed by Menna in Septem, Tariq certainly had no conscious thought of it himself. He was, however calm and, providing the enemy did what he expected of them, knew that his smaller force was capable of giving a good account of themselves.

He had already received intelligence from his scouts that the Visigoth army was only half a day's march away now, but once they were assembled, he doubted very much if they would wish to engage in battle before they'd had a night's rest. His own army was not displayed in total. Malik, controlling the right flank composed of half the cavalry battalions, was dispersed in the forested ground further up the hill, while his left flank, a mixture of cavalry and infantry, was half hidden in the folds of the hills. He commanded the centre, and, behind him and his guard, were massed the pick of his infantry, battle hardened warriors, and a single battalion of similarly experienced cavalrymen on their wiry Berber horses. They had already sat there for two hours because, Tariq reasoned, the Visigoth would also be employing scouts and it was better that they had some tangible information to report, such as a disciplined army was in place and not just a rabble army drummed up from the Atlas. There they would wait until dusk fell, at which time the dispersal would be orderly and in such a manner that they could reform in a matter of minutes.

Tariq glanced up at Akeem.

"I've been telling you for years, you could do with losing some weight.

Even that great animal of yours is beginning to look depressed. Every day that goes by, you make an easier target."

Akeem grinned down at him and growled, "Don't you worry about me, master," he nodded towards the river, in the expected direction of the enemy. "It's that lot that needs to look out for themselves, not that I shall have much of the killing, I'm here to make sure that no one kills you."

Tariq indicated his Arab guard massed behind him, the commander of which, Asad, was smiling at the conversation. "That is what this select band of warriors is supposed to be doing. Never mind me, Akeem, you just do what you do best, put that sword of yours to good use and help us win this battle. Roderick, should he make a personal appearance, is mine." He turned in his saddle and included the guard in his remarks. "Help me get close to him by all means but once I'm there, you leave him to me. That is an order."

He looked up at the sun, getting closer to the western horizon. He pointed at it.

"As soon as that touches the tops of those hills, we stand down. The rest of the army will follow our lead. All my officers know what to do and, remember, we reassume our positions, our exact positions," he emphasised, "before first light so that when they wake up, they will see us exactly as we are now."

He had hardly finished speaking when a group of his scouts came galloping out of the trees on the other side of the river, which they forded with ease, as Tariq knew they would, it being summer and the waters, though wide, had no depth. They reported that the vanguard of Roderick's force was hot on their heels but, such was the number of the enemy, it would probably be half way through the night before it was consolidated into its full strength. Tariq nodded his thanks for the information and held up his hand to remain as they were until the sun had told them otherwise.

•

The following morning presented the Berber army exactly as it had been on the previous evening, the only difference being that now the sun was behind it and shining directly into the faces of the Visigoth army on the other side of the river, and that army was huge, seemingly receding into the far distance, into the tree line and, as far as the eye could see, they were still coming. Tariq inspected them with professional interest. Everything that he had learned from Julian, from Malik and his other agents, was looking to be proven correct. The cavalry, mostly nobles he conjectured, since they were expensively and ornately armoured, looked heavy and once they were charging, would be almost impossible to stop. Some infantry units, as far as he could make out at this distance, were well armed, armoured and looked proficient, but others, and this did come as something of a surprise, appeared to be little more than peasants, whose principal weaponry consisted of implements from the farms from which they had been recruited, probably by force. He looked hard but, at this stage, could see nothing that indicated the presence of King Roderick himself.

The sheer number of the force was daunting but they had yet to form into their battle order and until they did Tariq could not be certain of the tactics they were likely to employ. He could be reasonably certain that, by making himself highly visible, and framed as he was by his highly distinctive Arab guard he could hardly have been more so, their initial assault would be on his centre because once a commanding general was taken, the rest of his army invariably capitulated. He looked around him, checking that the deployment of his men was still as it should be. It was, so he turned his eyes again to the opposing army and saw, quite clearly because of its highly elaborate construction, a chariot proceeding slowly through the ranks of the Visigoth, many of whom bowed deeply as it passed, some even falling to their knees. It was still too far away to identify the occupants of the vehicle, other than the one whose head shone as if surrounded by a halo. So, Roderick had come into battle encumbered by the full panoply of state and he was taking his time too, waving and chatting to those of his followers he thought worthy of the attention. Tariq turned to Akeem and smiled. Akeem did not return the smile. He merely pointed at the opposing army, still being reinforced by the last minute stragglers.

"I don't know what you're smiling at. They outnumber us by what, three to one at a rough guess?" He strained his eyes to see as far as he could, then pointed again, this time aiming his finger at the chariot which, the closer it came, was even more ornate than had first been thought. "Fancies himself, that one, doesn't he? Must be Roderick himself. Looking like that he makes himself a better target than you do. What happens next then, meet them head to head do we, looks a bit softer than either wing?"

Tariq shook his head. "We don't do anything, Akeem. We wait and see what he does. Judging by the way in which they are deploying, I would say they are going to do exactly what I hoped they would but, until I'm sure, we stay and we watch."

As he was speaking, the Visigoth command appeared to be reinforcing the massed units of infantry in their centre. Most of their heavy cavalry was moving outward towards the flanks. The hapless battalions of poorly equipped peasantry were being marched through the ranks until they reached the front lines of the enormous, massed square which, it now appeared, was to be a battering ram of expendable bodies destined to test the comparatively fragile looking centre of the Berber force. Tariq nodded approvingly and with a single horn blast, the front four rows of his line, all archers, prepared their weapons. Behind them, lines of warriors held their light throwing javelins at the ready. Behind them, those men for whom ordnance was their designated duty, checked their reserves of weaponry. All wore swords designed for close combat, short blades forged to stab or slash. Only officers and mounted men carried curved blades.

•

Apart from the horn blasts from both camps and the occasional whinny of an excited horse, for some moments the silence was unrepresentative of the occasion. There was none of the usual banging of sword on shield or taunts flung from one side to the other. Even the birds ceased their chorus, for it was still early on a July morning, and seemed to have suspended their rivalries in anticipation of one much greater than that ordained by nature. Then it started.

A few tentative shouts were soon magnified into a great and continuous roar. Orders were screamed out above the general hubbub, horns sounded one after the other and it was all from the Visigoth side of the river. The Berber army, mounted and otherwise, stood like silent statuary. Roderick's vanguard started to move. Slowly and seemingly unwillingly at first, the front ranks entered the river and started crossing it. They, too, had tested the depth and found that it presented no obstacle to their advance, perhaps slowing it slightly until the near bank had been gained, then they gathered pace and, driven on by their superiors shouting oaths and curses, a solid square, thousands of men deep, advanced upon the still immobile Berber regiments. At a single horn blast, the first row of archers released their arrows which went singing through the air to bring down the first few lines of unhappy peasants and thereby slowing down the advance of the rest. The archers dropped to their knees and the second flight of arrows was winging its way into the enemy lines. Similarly with the next row. Still they came on, driven by the cursing of their Visigoth masters. The Berber lines, smoothly and meticulously, changed bowmen for javelins while, at the rear, quivers were being replenished for the next fusillade of steel and feather. All the while, Tariq sat imperturbably, taking in not only everything that was going on in front of him and around him, but also what was happening across the river where the mounted wings had still to make their move.

Such was the sheer volume of numbers thrown against the Berber, hand to hand combat was inevitable, and soon Tariq, his Arab guard and Akeem were fighting. Here, with better discipline, better speed and protective armour, the Berber assault was too much for the makeshift Visigoth soldiers who had already lost large numbers to arrows and spears, and they retreated down the hill and back to the river. Once there, a number of them, having decided that sickles and scythes were no match for conventional weapons in trained hands, fled along the banks of the river and were soon lost to sight. In good order, Tariq's men climbed back to their positions to await the next attack.

When it came, it was more concentrated and, composed as it was of troops of an infinitely better calibre, proper infantrymen who knew their work, was likely to put Tariq's centre to a much sterner test than the first assault. Indeed it was. Both sides lost a lot of men but it was the Berbers who eventually prevailed and they watched the Visigoth retreat once more to their side of the river to regroup. Again, their success, this time against a more formidable opposition, was due to their speed and ability to react quickly without the constriction of heavy armour. The terrain, so carefully chosen by Tariq, was also to their advantage and Tariq was surprised that the cavalry, obviously the cream of the Visigoth host, was yet to be employed. Clearly, he conjectured, Roderick had banked upon winning an early victory on the strength of his foot soldiers alone. In this regard he had signally failed, but continued assaults upon Tariq's centre, especially by experienced fighting men, would begin to take its toll of Tariq's smaller army, as, indeed, it already had. Neither general was to learn more at this point, since dusk had already started to gather and both sides were left to contemplate the losses and gains which had been made on this first day. Tariq's last order, before standing down his men and organising pickets, was that they assemble, before dawn, in exactly the same formation as they had on that morning. Numbers forming the centre were to be made up of support units. This time there would be nobody to rearm archers and spearmen.

•

The following morning developed in exactly the same way. Roderick, like Tariq, had brought up infantry reserves from somewhere or other but, from the look of them, local rural industry seemed the likeliest source. As before, these unhappy and unsuitable warriors were the first to be thrown against the Islamic centre and, as before, were powerless against them. As the remnants retreated back to the river, Tariq noted that the left wing of the enemy, mainly heavy mounted units, appeared to be preparing for action. Pages were busy attending their noble masters, checking their armour and weapons. At the same time, the second wave of infantry was being launched against him. Archers and spearmen, barely affected by the first ineffectual strike, made ready for them. Again it ended in hand to hand combat with losses on both sides but, again, Tariq was favoured by the advantage of his elevated position, and the enemy slowly gave ground. Before they had gained the comparative safety of the wide, but shallow, river, the ground started to shake as Roderick's left wing finally made their move, at first ponderously but gathering momentum as they charged.

Suddenly Malik's light cavalry units shot out from their tree-sheltered holding position and galloped down the slope to meet them as they emerged from the river. The Berber warriors, after months of intensive training, had developed the skills of riding, using their heels to direct their mounts, leaving their hands free to discharge arrows and javelins. Much less encumbered by protective armour, save their helmets and the overlapping leather jerkins designed by Menna, they harried the opposing horsemen like terriers snapping at the heels of a bull. Because of their metal armour, the Visigoth nobles, for they were the main component of these divisions, did not, at first, suffer significant casualties but they were disorientated and confused by these tactics and unsure whether to continue their charge up the hill or deal with the new enemy. This confusion was sufficient for Malik's men to have more time to select their targets. Accordingly, they would wheel their mounts, ride out of range while they rearmed themselves, and then swarm back in, having marked their man and the vulnerable points in his armour–or that of his horse and deal with him. The damage they inflicted was not that great but it was enough to turn the enemy back and make them consider their next move. It also concluded that day's business.

Once again, the losses had to be calculated but, as he did so, it was clear to Tariq that he would probably not be able to sustain them at the present rate if this battle was going to continue for any time. While his casualty rate was lower than that of the Visigoth, he had considerably fewer men to spare, added to which he wasn't sure that he had the taste for an attritional campaign. There were few of his men that he didn't know, at least by sight, and he mourned the loss of every single one of them. Come the morning, although there might seem a few less on show, he resolved that the tableau illuminated by the rising sun would appear to Roderick just as it had on the two previous occasions.

•

Having breakfasted well, Roderick emerged from his pavilion, still arrayed in the full pomp of the royal wardrobe. Shading his eyes against the sun, he surveyed a scene that was becoming depressingly familiar to him. The infidel army looked unchanged. The ranks were, perhaps, a little depleted but then so were his and the few natives that survived yesterday's action had, so he was told, melted away in the night. He could ill- afford the resources to round them up again but one thing was certain. Once this battle was over, they would be hunted down and made to suffer for their desertion. Had he underestimated the opposition? He stroked his beard and considered. Well, if he had, it was time to put an end to this nonsense and return to Toletum. He had been away from the seat of power for too long. Much longer, and rival claimants would be lining up to take over. It was bad enough having to guard against a sullen indigenous population, many times the size of the Visigoth, when his own rebellious nobles posed such a domestic threat. "Time to send these barbarians back to their sheepfolds and in such a way that they will think twice before leaving their own shores again." The expendable peasant foot soldiers might have failed him but he had thousands of lesser nobility and landowners who could take their place. He called his generals together and issued his orders for the day.

•

Looking at what was taking place in front of and below him, Tariq sensed a change of tactics on the part of the opposing force. The centre looked altogether more formidable than it had on previous days; no farm implements this time but trained men, well armed and well armoured, while his own centre square was weaker. He called a runner to take messages to the commanders of the flanking cavalry battalions, who had resumed their former positions out of the immediate sight of the enemy, although Malik's wing was already known to the Visigoth - and to their cost. He turned to his Arab guard commander and told him that this day, they and he would be fighting at the forefront of the coming battle. They did not have long to wait. With what seemed like renewed energy and much noise, the Visigoth infantry forded the river and started their advance up the slope. As soon as they had become detached from the main body of the Visigoth army, Tariq ordered two short blasts on the horn and his cavalry charged out of their cover and hurtled down the hill towards the enemy, attacking the foot soldiers on either side and causing panic and mayhem among them. Expecting the opposing mounted units to join battle on behalf of their colleagues, Tariq watched, at first with apprehension and then with disbelief, as the left and strongest flank of the Visigoth did nothing. Not only did they not take part in the action but as, sword in hand, Tariq prepared to engage with the enemy himself, he saw, out of the corner of his eye, these well-accoutred Gothic nobles start to ride not into battle but away from it.

For a moment he couldn't believe it, but it was true; one whole wing of the Visigoth army was deserting the field. By this time, surrounded by his Arab elite in arrow formation and with Akeem stirrup to stirrup with him, he was cleaving his way through the masses of the opposing infantry to where, in plain view, Roderick's chariot, with him in it, stood glistening in the bright sunlight. That, though, was the last sight he had of King Roderick since all his energy was now concentrated on fighting his way to the river. Malik, his opposition of yesterday apparently having given up, brought his cavalry around to the back of the retreating centre and started attacking them from the rear. The opposing flank, seeing the rest of the army is disarray, was also starting to crumble and, with a final triumphant roar, the Umayyad force was at the river with Tariq leading the onslaught. For the first time he had the opportunity to look for the besieged monarch. Once he was captured or killed, the day would unquestionably be his. His horse stumbled and nearly fell in the shallows and he looked down to see that its legs were caught up in a large gold cloak which was so weighted by gold thread and water that he had to summon four of his foot soldiers to clear it before his horse could proceed. The chariot was in front of him, the ornate vehicle was empty, the two perfectly matched, cream coloured, horses standing patiently, occasionally muzzling at the water. No sign of the occupants and Tariq gave a gasp of frustration. Akeem was at his side, which he had never left, his hand pointing at the dwindling remnants of the Visigoth mighty army.

"We've done it, my lord, or rather you have." He swept his arm round in an extravagant gesture. "This is all yours now. Everything that you can see, and beyond, is all yours."

Tariq shook his head, feeling suddenly weary and, although he could not explain why, a sense of frustration. It had been a great victory, against all the odds, and he was incredibly proud of his men, but where was Roderick? His capture or death would have set the seal on everything, but he just seemed to have disappeared. Tariq turned to Akeem, caught hold of his arm and pulled it down, saying, "No, Akeem, it is not all mine, it is ours, it is the Caliph's, it is Allah's. It will be by what we do next, that we will be judged by history. One thing I need to have explained, is why a third of Roderick's army, consisting of nobles and their sons, deserted their King. It was a vile and treacherous thing to do and, even if it gave us the victory, I need to know what possessed them? I want prisoners and I want answers from them."

So saying, he left a puzzled Akeem and rode over to congratulate each one of his generals and Malik in particular, for, at the end of the day, it was his action that had precipitated the final capitulation of the enemy.

Chapter 25

July 711AD

Stripped of their armour and the trappings of fighting men, the battalion of Visigoth cavalry, some nobility, some merely landowners, looked pale and vulnerable, surrounded, as they were, by the dark, armed warriors of the victorious Berber army. Tariq looked at them with interest. Apart from Count Julian, they were the first representatives from the north of this continent that he had seen at close quarters, and the colour of their skin and hair seemed quite alien. It was interesting too, that not only had they left the field but, having done so, they had gathered at some distance from the action and made no attempt to flee the area, as did many of those who continued to fight until it was obvious that theirs was a lost cause. That part of the Visigoth force had scattered and vanished into the surrounding woods and hills, and orders were given that they were not to be pursued but that the Berber army was to re-form in good order until told otherwise. And this is what was now happening. Apart from disarming the enemy cavalry and commandeering their armour as part of legitimate booty, they had not been abused in any way and it was not long before Tariq learned the reason for their defection.

Language proved less of a problem than at first thought. A number of the Berber commanders, Tariq of course among them, had enough Latin to make themselves understood to some of the Visigoth officers even though the Visigoth version of that tongue was still accented by traces of their Germanic origins. It transpired that this wing of Roderick's mighty army had been conscripted mainly from the southern areas of Hispania and they had seen their influence in state affairs considerably diminished on Roderick's accession. Worse, they had felt that they were regarded as provincially unimportant by the powers in Toletum, illustrative of the disunity which had haunted the empire for generations. Even more interesting to Tariq was the proffered fact that, prior to the battle, Count Julian, a figure known to most of this minor nobility, had actively canvassed them, assuring them that their country, under Umayyad rule, would be a happier place for them than it was under the despotic Roderick. His success in broadcasting this propaganda was now obvious for all to see and Tariq wished that Julian could be here to witness the fruits of his labour and to be thanked accordingly. Julian, accompanied by the ever-present Tamegrant, had not been sighted by Tariq since well before the battle, and their whereabouts was something of a mystery. Of course, he could be back in Septem by now, making certain that Florinda and, Tariq hoped, Menna, were safe, should the battle not have gone Tariq's way.

Once the captive soldiers had been informed that, apart from losing their armour, they could retain their horses, would not have to submit to a new religion and would be left alone to live their lives as they chose, many of them started to drift away, but some went so far as to offer their services to Tariq. Once terms had been agreed, that is that their share of any future booty be assured, they were given back their battle gear and weapons and placed under Malik's command. On questioning these new recruits more closely, Malik soon found that there was another reason for them changing sides so readily. This was that their families' wealth, under Roderick, had been depleted to such an extent that they were left with very little alternative but to try and restore their fortune by fighting for it. From information derived from others who had been captured in the normal course of events, it became obvious that most of the inhabitants of this region, nearly ninety percent of the population, had never formed any sort of alliance with their masters, and two centuries under the yoke of the Visigoth had done little other than cultivate a deep-seated resentment. It was a combination of this intelligence that led Tariq to his next important decision.

•

Florinda and Menna were taking their usual early morning walk down to the quay, when they heard the news of the victory. Tariq, immediately he knew for a certainty that the day was his, dispatched one of his fleetest messengers with the news and only days after the battle, the lookout on the tower at Septem was shouting down to the two women that a sail was in view. They instinctively clutched each other's arms as they awaited the vessel which, once they had it in sight, seemed to be making its way with excruciating slowness.

The messenger, when he finally stepped ashore, was immediately besieged by a lack of formality that was completely unexpected but, he judged, not at all unpleasant. Both girls threw their arms about him and at the same time bombarded him with questions. Menna, the first to recover her dignity, coughed to remind Florinda that a little decorum would not come amiss and they took a pace back while the red-faced messenger delivered his tidings. Once delivered, he again enjoyed a brief moment of glory and, glancing up at the look-out perched way above him, was equally startled to see the man dancing a solo jig of celebration. Things calmed down quickly as the girls, one on each arm of the messenger, dragged him back to the fortress where, while enjoying refreshments, he was made to recount all he knew, over and over again. Of Julian, he had no news but he assured Florinda that, as far as he was aware, her father had taken no part in the fighting and was last seen, Tamegrant at his side, riding in a northerly direction before the two armies had started to engage. No sooner had this messenger delivered his news than a bugle call from the watch tower announced another arrival. Menna and Florinda looked at each other questioningly. Menna ran onto the balcony and looked out towards the quay. She immediately returned and said, "I thought so, although I didn't expect him quite as quickly as this."

Florinda raised an eyebrow.

"It's my relative from Damascus," was the answer. "You remember, the one I told you about the other day. Wait there, Florinda, I'll go and meet him."

Florinda took no notice, as Menna imagined she wouldn't, and followed her as she flew out of the door. They both ran down the stairs, robes held up to prevent them tripping, until they met a servant leading a breathless and rather disreputable looking character through the doorway into the house. Menna went straight to the point.

"Well?" she demanded. The man paused only long enough to draw a breath.

"Lord Musa is on the march, my lady. With the biggest army I've ever seen; must be at least thirty thousand men." He was about to elaborate but Menna held up a hand to stop him. She paced the room motioning the other occupants to be quiet while she thought.

Eventually, she turned to Florinda, "Are you prepared to come with me?"

Without a moment's hesitation, her companion said, "Yes, yes, yes. I wouldn't dream of letting you go on your own." Menna turned back to Tariq's messenger. "Is your craft still manned and ready to sail?" The man looked perplexed, then looked at Menna as if expecting her to provide the answer. "Well, is it ready or isn't it? Oh! And one more thing, why did you address me as 'my lady' when we met? You've never done that before."

The messenger looked down at his feet and mumbled something to the effect that he had heard that Lord Tariq and she…then recovered himself to blurt out that, so far as he was aware, his vessel was exactly as he'd left it, ready to return him to the Berber army.

"Right," said Menna decisively, "you go down to the quay and tell them we sail within the hour."

"But, my lady, does that mean you're coming with us to Hispania"

Menna and Florinda exchanged an exasperated look. "Of course, you donkey," said Menna, She then turned to her relative. "You are going back to Damascus, we are going over to The Rock."

Further discussion was cut short by a loud booming noise from the doorway. Everyone turned to see Tamegrant filling the gap and grinning widely as Florinda, shrieking, threw herself at him. Suddenly she stopped and pushed herself away.

"My father, is he safe?" she gasped.

Tamegrant's vigorous nodding told her all she needed to know and she let out a sigh of relief. Tamegrant motioned both women to follow him to the quay and pointed in the direction of The Rock. Tariq's messenger, somewhat confused by all this coming and going, mistook the gesture and looked expectantly for yet another envoy to appear.

That reminded them of Menna's cousin and she turned to him.

"Make your best speed to join up with Lord Musa's force, and if you hear anything you think I should know of, you will find me at..at… Oh, I don't know; just do your best to find me, and thank you, your information is most valuable."

All five of them descended to the ground floor and quickly made their way through the gardens down to the quays. Menna turned to Florinda.

"Ironic isn't it?" she said, "Earlier this morning there wasn't a completed vessel in sight now they're all lining up." Suddenly Tamegrant stopped, looked hard at Florinda and started an elaborate mime which seemed to have something to do with the process of getting dressed. Florinda looked blank for a second then realised what it was he was trying to convey. She blushed, waved him away and turned to Menna. "He's asking if I have enough clothes. Last time I annoyed everyone by insisting on travelling with a huge wardrobe., sorry!" Menna looked disbelievingly at her and dragged her towards the boat. Tamegrant grinned and helped them aboard. Leaving the one vessel moored, the other two slid out into the calm waters, one carrying two excited women, a tired messenger and a happy Berber giant; the other, with yet another tired messenger headed east.

•

Tariq had thought hard about his next deployment. What finally decided him was a chance remark that Akeem had made directly their victory had been assured.

"Well, my lord, we might have won the battle but guess who's going to take the credit for winning the war?"

It then occurred to Tariq that Akeem had just put into words something that had been niggling at the back of his mind since setting out on this expedition.

"You're talking about Lord Musa, aren't you, Akeem?" he said. "You think that he is going to bring his own army, the Umayyad army, over here, complete our task for us and impress the Caliph by his actions?" He paused for a moment. "If you think about it though, we may well have won the battle, as you rightly say, but we have no idea of the forces that might be ranged against us as we move north. It might be that Lord Musa's intervention could prove decisive if total victory is to be ours."

Akeem looked at him, amazed. "You mean, the fact that Lord Musa might take advantage of you had actually occurred to you? I am impressed. I never thought I'd see the day."

Tariq grinned and told him to shut up and bring Malik and the rest of his commanders to him. Once they were assembled, Tariq told them of his plans.

"It is my intention to split our army into three. You, Malik, will take command of the largest group, march towards Cordova and secure it. I understand that it is one city which is likely to offer most resistance and which, according to the intelligence gathered from our captives, is under the control of one of Roderick's relatives. Your force is now augmented by some disaffected Visigoth nobles and there could be more as you advance. By all means add them to your numbers but, and this is important, try to avoid using them in combat. I don't want Visigoth killing Visigoth. If nothing else, they will serve to make your army appear larger than it actually is, which could be enough to force the defenders to surrender."

A number of hands were raised, Malik's among them and it was Malik who put the question.

"My lord, if I am to have command of the greatest number, will that not leave you and the others dangerously under strength?"

Tariq shrugged his shoulders. "My reasons for adopting this strategy are these. Cordova, as I have indicated, constitutes a greater threat than all the other significant centres of population. The region around that city is, so I am reliably informed, extremely fertile and agriculturally prosperous. Providing you are successful, and I would not have given you this command had I not thought you would be, the provisioning of the greater part of our army will have been taken care of. The next objective will be the city of Elibyrge, and you Askil," he indicated one of his cavalry commanders, "will have the responsibility for capturing that particular hill town. As for me, I intend to make all speed with what's left of the army and my Arabs, and take Toletum. Once Toletum is in our hands, then we can truly claim Hispania as ours. Remember though, we do not kill unnecessarily and, while we can claim legitimate plunder as the just spoils of war, we do not take from those who cannot afford it and we do not feed ourselves at the expense of starving the natives. They, together with the disaffected Visigoth will almost certainly turn out to be our greatest asset in our campaign. Now we will settle the division of our army into three parts and tomorrow we march. You will all have understood by now that speed is of the essence. Small armies can travel faster and, being the smallest, mine should be best placed to cover the longest distance at the greatest pace. Speed and surprise will make this country ours." He held up a hand to stop them as they started to talk amongst themselves. "If you are still not convinced by my arguments, just consider this: my lord Musa ibn Nusayr is, by now, launching his own invasion of Hispania with a force that, I have no doubt, is considerably larger than ours. If we can secure the major cities before he arrives, there will be no doubt that it is the Berber army that will go down in history as the conquerors of the Visigoth." He paused for a moment to let his words sink in and, at the same time, caught the eye of the Arab commander of his bodyguard. The Arab, without a second thought, called out,

"We are with you Lord Tariq. It is you that has led us to victory and we will see that the world knows it."

All the Berber officers then took up the cry of "Tariq, Tariq, Tariq" and it took another raised hand from their leader to quiet them.

"One last thing; I talk about speed and surprise but we do not march on a Friday. It is our faith which has brought us this far and we will continue to observe it and respect it."

A murmur of agreement followed and, after a few more questions, the command meeting broke up, leaving a slightly embarrassed Tariq fending off the barrage of praise bestowed on him by the ever-enthusiastic Akeem.

•

Count Julian was riding his horse up and down the beach below the Rock. From time to time he reined in and, turning towards the sea, he shaded his eyes against the reflection of the sun on the gently rippling blue waters. Suddenly he stood in his stirrups and waved both his arms as a sail hove into view on the horizon. He wasn't alone! Surrounding him was a motley collection of people, some like him on horseback, some obviously better off than others but all, it seemed, in a party mood and all following his lead, first pointing as they saw the boat, then waving their arms madly at it.

On board the vessel the occupants strained to see what all the fuss was about and, for an instant, Florinda and Menna looked at each other in consternation as the display, from a distance, looked as much like a warring party as it did a welcoming one. Once closer, it became evident which it was and the two women embraced to show their relief. As soon as the keel started to touch bottom, Tamegrant leapt into the water and, one after the other, he lifted, Florinda and then Menna, onto the dry sand. Julian meanwhile had jumped from his horse and ran down the beach, ready to welcome his daughter with open arms. Menna hung back at first because, not only was she surprised to see the noble Count break into an undignified trot when he was always so urbane, but because she was disappointed not to find Tariq waiting to welcome her. Strangely, it was Tamegrant who first sensed her unease and he came back, took her gently by the arm and led her to where Julian and Florinda were still in animated discussion. Julian immediately turned and acknowledged her with a courtly bow which ended with him sweeping his arm still further behind him to indicate the happy crowd that attended upon him. He then took Menna by the hand, raised it so that all could see it and informed them that this was Menna, the lady of Lord Tariq. As one, they all cheered and clapped, then turned and indicated the Rock behind them, chanting,

"Tariq's Mountain, Tariq's Mountain, Jabal Tariq, Jabal Tariq."

It was all too much and she couldn't help the sobs that, for once, overcame her impeccable self-control, and the tears ran down her cheeks while the crowd still cheered, "Jabal Tariq, Jabal Tariq."

It was then that she remembered the importance of her mission and shaking her head, as though to shake the tears away, she implored Count Julian to take her to Tariq so that she could deliver a message of the utmost importance. Julian smiled at her impatience and assured her that he would, indeed, convey her to where Tariq's army were thought to be encamped. He led her a little way from the crowd.

"You are anxious to warn him of Musa's imminent arrival, yes?"

She searched his face for any sign of amusement but he was quite serious.

"But, how did you ..." she faltered.

This time he did smile. "My lady, you can't move an army of thirty thousand men from one side of the world to the other without everybody knowing about it."

"Yes but.." she began impatiently. "It's not just that Lord Musa is coming with a large army, it's the implications for Tariq that I have to warn him about. You see, my lord, he won't understand that Musa will take all the credit for the victory, and all the spoils," she added plaintively.

"Indeed he will," replied Julian, "But I think that Tariq will be well aware of all that, and will have taken steps to avoid being completely overshadowed by his erstwhile master."

Her reply was vehement. "He won't, you know he won't. Tariq's not like that, he thinks the best of everybody."

"I think you will find him changed, my dear," said Julian. "The last weeks have wrought many changes in the way that Tariq regards the world."

Menna was quiet for a moment, then, "And me, my lord, what about the way in which he regards me. Will that have changed too?"

This time Julian regarded her with genuine fondness. "Why don't I take you to him and let him tell you himself?"

Chapter 26

Autumn 711AD

Tariq's predictions had proved to be even more accurate than he had hoped. The hill town of Elibyrge had fallen with scarcely any opposition, and Askil's battalions had almost been welcomed with open arms by the local population who perceived the Berber force as a liberating army. So easy was it that it was only a matter of days before Askil decided that he would be safe to leave a token, albeit well armed, occupying army under the command of one of his lieutenants as acting Governor, while he took the remainder of his troops towards Cordova where, he hoped, he might be in a position to help Malik in his more difficult assignment.

He had assumed correctly for, as Tariq had foreseen, Cordova was going to be a difficult place to overcome. Malik, as soon as he entered the region, could detect hostility in the attitude of unarmed civilians and it appeared that the Visigoth here were made of much sterner stuff than that encountered at the main battle. Indeed, those renegade Visigoths riding with him had assured him that Pelayo, the incumbent ruler of the region, had made the city, with its Roman defences, virtually impregnable and any siege was likely to be prolonged and unprofitable. Why then, asked Malik, if Pelayo, a cousin to Roderick, was such a good soldier, had he not represented his side in the battle? After some knowing looks between them, his newly allied Visigoth informed him that it was all part of the constant power struggle which had served to divide the nation. Pelayo, they went on, probably even hoped that Roderick would have been defeated or, at least, weakened by the battle. Pelayo would then take to the field with his own not inconsiderable force and assume control of the country.

Malik immediately countered with, "What about us then? Would Pelayo not have the Berber army to fight as well as the remnants of Roderick's force?"

They shook their heads at that and replied that nobody in Hispania viewed an invading Muslim army as a serious threat and it was probably the decisiveness of the victory and the subsequent speed with which Malik's divisions had advanced towards Cordova that had made Pelayo think again and retrench in his own territory.

All this became obvious as Malik neared the city and saw, with some concern that any direct attack on the walls would not succeed, even with the help of Askil who, he learned, was making his way with all possible haste to join forces. The Berbers made camp at a safe distance from the city and the posted guard was made formidable enough to deal with any enemy scouting party, eager to prove themselves against the invaders.

Malik had evolved a genuine respect and admiration for Tariq's principles, and he resolved that he would keep casualties as low as possible on both sides. As his commander had stated often enough, if they were going to conquer Hispania and rule over it, then the population, native and Visigoth, would respond more favourably towards an army that displayed civilised behaviour rather than one that slaughtered, burned, raped and pillaged its way through the land.

Malik considered his options and was not impressed with any of them. His army was a mix of cavalry and infantry, although some of the latter divisions had yet to catch up. He looked up at the defences, moonlight giving the walls an even more impregnable aspect than when viewed in sunlight. He had no idea how the city was provisioned or what water supplies existed within its walls. He called over one of the Visigoth officers who had surrendered at the battle, and asked if he had any idea of how to gain entry to the city or, failing that, was a siege a practical alternative to bring about a capitulation. The man shook his head and explained that it had been many years since he had been inside Cordova and then, of course, not with a view to capturing the citadel. All he could tell Malik was that the riches contained therein were greater than those likely to be found at Toletum. Over the last twenty years, Cordova had become much more favoured of the Visigoth nobility. The region was one of the most fertile in the land and many had become rich on the resources to be found here. He then reminded Malik that one of the reasons his troops had ridden with them was because of the bounty Tariq had promised would be theirs once Cordova had been subdued.

Malik retorted tartly, "Yes, but you didn't tell us at the time how difficult a task it was likely to be." Eventually Malik decided that, if he could have a night without moonlight, he would send some of his best men to reconnoitre the site and see if any weakness could be found. A siege was out of the question. For one thing it was alien to Malik's impetuous and impatient nature and, for another he had no idea of how long it would take to starve the inhabitants into some sort of action. Once the actual fighting started, he felt reasonably confident that his men would be a match for Pelayo's power, but he needed more intelligence before the situation reached that happy stage.

This problem had not escaped Tariq, as he led his smaller force north, passing Cordovan territory to the east. In fact, at one point, he thought he could see a faint blur on the horizon, which could well have been the city itself and, not for the first time, he wondered if he had been right to split his army as he had. He then reasoned that Toletum, even though it was the capital of power in the country, had lost its king, had a much larger hostile Jewish population which had suffered more than most under the Visigoth yoke, and was the focus of discontent from several quarters. It was, in short, a city divided whereas Cordova was not.

His thoughts and his progress were interrupted by a dust ball rolling in from that very direction. This soon resolved itself into a galloping messenger who, as he neared, Tariq identified as one of Malik's officers. Obviously, then, this was important as communication was generally conveyed by a troop of specially mounted couriers, renowned for their horsemanship and ability to navigate. Qualities which were second nature to most of his Berbers. An officer though? Tariq ordered his own army to halt while he took the man to one side.

"My lord Malik," the officer struggled to get his breath, "my lord Malik says that the city of Cordova is too well defended for a direct assault, and a siege could take months, so well are they prepared inside the walls. He asked me to tell you, my lord, that despite the lack of cover and bright moonlight, he has reconnoitred the area as thoroughly as he could." He paused and quietened his horse, still excited after the gallop. "I have led some of my own men in a search of a weakness in the defences which might be exploited, but in vain, and all the other patrols have made similar reports." He went on hastily, "It is not that my lord Malik is worried by the prospect of a battle but.." He was stopped in mid-flow as Tariq leaned forward, smiled encouragingly and said, "Never, for one instant, would I envisage my friend backing away from a conflict. In fact," he continued, "I am glad he is being so circumspect." He caught hold of the messenger's bridle and led his horse a little way away from the main group, especially away from Akeem who was never happy to be left out of things. Their horses ambled a few paces in the direction from which the messenger had ridden and they both sat there, looking towards the horizon. Tariq's brow furrowed in thought, Malik's officer, nervously brushed at a soiled sleeve. It was he who spoke first. "My lord Malik wondered, my lord, if he should bring his army to join yours in your march north?"

Tariq shook his head. "I dare not risk so strong an army as Pelayo's to threaten my rear. Cordova must be dealt with. Has Askil not joined up with you yet?"

"No, my lord, although reports indicate that he is on his way to us. But even with the addition of his strength, Cordova remains still as impregnable."

"No it doesn't," replied Tariq thoughtfully. "No it doesn't," he repeated, then continued, "Tell lord Malik this; tell him that I have given him the keys to the city."

The messenger shifted in his saddle. "My lord?"

Tariq nodded. "That's all, just tell him that."

"Very well, my lord, I'll tell him. But, my lord…"

"It's all right." Tariq smiled at him encouragingly. "He'll understand."

The messenger dropped his head in a bow. "Of course, my lord." With which, he wheeled his horse around and galloped off in the direction from which he had come.

Tariq had scarcely rejoined the head of his army and was just on the point of telling an inquisitive Akeem, 'I'll tell you later,' when shouts from the opposing flank presaged the arrival of yet another envoy. Tariq sighed and muttered to Akeem that 'any idea of a speedy and surprise attack on the capital was getting less likely by the minute.' His frustration might have been alleviated had he known the meaning of this latest interruption.

•

Malik was sitting behind the table in his pavilion when the return of his messenger was announced. The man, again breathless, took a while to deliver his report, brief though it was. Malik stared at him and the man wished, for a moment, that someone else had been selected to perform his task.

"He said what?" Malik posed the question in a tone wavering between incredulity and anger. The messenger repeated it and Malik wanted to know if Lord Tariq had been made fully aware to the situation.

"Did you tell him that we have risked men's lives, your own included, in an effort to scout the walls and find a weakness?" The man nodded.

"And all he said was, that he'd given me the keys to…"

Malik rose to his feet and the man took a step back in anticipation of a verbal onslaught, but he needn't have worried. Malik's move had been motivated by an idea. He raised his eyes heavenwards.

"Of course," he breathed. Then, slamming his hand on the table, causing his envoy to retreat still further, muttered, "Why didn't I think of that?"

"My lord?" The confusion of the messenger grew in a ratio to his master's rising enthusiasm. He was, after all, an officer and curious to understand the meaning of this cryptic message. Malik immediately understood, thanked the envoy warmly for his work and asked him, as a final task, to bring the leaders of the renegade Visigoth to his tent. The man bowed and left, still none the wiser, but happy, at least, that his master seemed to have derived real intelligence as a result of his work.

•

Tariq gave Akeem the order to intercept this new emissary and hear what he had to say, so that the columns of soldiers could continue their progress without further interruption. Accordingly, Akeem pulled over to one side and met the messenger who, like the last one, was showing signs of neither sparing himself nor his beast, in an effort to deliver his report with the least delay. Whatever it was he had to say, it didn't take long for Akeem to hear his message and send the man back the way he had come. He then cantered back to the head of the army. Expecting an immediate report from the normally loquacious Akeem, Tariq assumed that he had learned nothing worthy of repeating and, having a number of other things on his mind, the problem of Cordova not being the least among them, was content to continue their march in a companionable silence.

Akeem, though, was not of the same patient mettle as his master and kept clearing his throat, as though about to say something, before lapsing once again into silence. Eventually Tariq was compelled to ask Akeem if he was coming down with a cold or did he have something he wished to say. If the latter, would he please get on with it so that, having heard him out, Tariq could get back to marshalling his thoughts in peace. Akeem feigning indignation was so amusing a picture that Tariq couldn't help bursting out laughing, and so infectious was it, that soon the laughter was taken up, first by those immediately around them, even the usually impassive Arab guard could not restrain themselves, until it seemed to echo through the entire army. Eventually Tariq held up a hand to halt the march and ordered Akeem to explain what it was he had to say. Just for a moment Akeem, unusually embarrassed at being the centre of attention, said nothing until, eventually he blurted out, "I would like to suggest, my lord, that we camp early this afternoon."

"And why would you like to suggest that Akeem?" Tariq's response was inevitable but, even so, Akeem seemed, or pretended to be, surprised by it.

"Um, because I can detect that some of our men, particularly foot soldiers, are showing signs of weariness. After all, my lord, we have made excellent progress thus far and…and…" His voice tailed away as it was obvious that Tariq didn't believe a word of what he was saying. Tariq decided it was time to put him out of his misery.

"Akeem," he said quietly, "why don't you just give me the message delivered to you by that envoy?" Then he patted Akeem on his broad shoulders and asked, even more quietly, "How far away is Menna and, I assume, Count Julian's party?"

Akeem scrambled his bulk around in the saddle. "How did you know, my lord? How did you know the message was about them?"

"Not too difficult, my friend. The messenger came from the right direction and you went to too much trouble to keep it secret from me."

Akeem lurched back and shook his head. "And there I was, hoping to give you a happy surprise. Why do you always have to be one step ahead of me? Alright," he went on defiantly, "now that you know, what are we going to do?"

Tariq grinned. "What I don't know, Akeem, is how long before they catch up with us. Obviously they are going to travel faster that we can."

Akeem brightened. "They should be here this very evening, my lord."

"In that case," said Tariq, with another grin, "we'll halt and set up camp now. It's as good a place as anywhere. At least, if we are attacked, the enemy can be seen coming from afar in all directions. See to it, Akeem."

Akeem's round face split into a toothless smile. "Right away, my lord." The order was carried on down the lines until the shouting ceased and the smallest of the Berber host put an early end to their day's march.

•

Not too far away from the relaxed atmosphere of Tariq's headquarters, Malik was hoping that his interpretation of his master's message was correct. Accordingly, he was facing a trio of Visigoth nobles who, having been assured of their future safety, were now looking apprehensive in case this peremptory summons might threaten it. Malik looked at them and tried to judge whether or not he could rely on men who had, only recently, betrayed their king. Although they had been treated, as ordered by Tariq, with every courtesy, Malik could not help but see their actions as extremely dishonourable. He decided, therefore, that an appeal to their baser instincts would probably be his best approach. He cleared his throat and said, "Gentlemen, you tell me that the riches to be plundered from this city," he waved an arm towards a heavily fortified Cordova, "are likely to be in excess of anywhere else on the continent, including Toletum. Am I correct?"

They all nodded in unison and began to outdo each other in their estimates of the wealth to be plundered from the city.

Malik held up a hand to quiet them.

"Very well, gentlemen. You already have our assurance that you will receive your fair share of any plunder and that you will enjoy that wealth without having to fight for it."

The three nobles looked at each other and started to shuffle uncomfortably, sensing a sting in the tail of that last remark. Malik continued.

"How likely is it that Lord Pelayo will have learned of your..." He hesitated, searching for words that would not carry too much offence, "your recent strategic decisions in the course of the great battle?"

The noble who appeared to have elected himself as the Visigoth spokesman, his name was Kunimund, looked Malik directly in the eye and said, "Very likely, my lord. Pelayo will have received intelligence of everything concerning our defeat and the death of Roderick. That said, my lord, his feelings on the subject of our..our decision to leave the field will probably be quite ambivalent." He saw Malik raise an eyebrow and went on to explain. "You see, my lord, the fact that he and Roderick are, or, I should say were, related, does not alter the fact that Pelayo had designs on the throne and Roderick knew he did. That is one reason why the Cordovan faction did not join forces with Roderick. So, you see, my lord, Pelayo might well see our decision as one which might have aided his own designs – had things worked out differently, of course."

Malik nodded thoughtfully. "My next question would be then, is Pelayo likely to be aware that you have ridden with us?"

Kunimund shook his head, as did the others. "Not at all, my lord; we have been most careful, for obvious reasons, to remain inconspicuous while in your company."

Malik leaned forward. "You then will be our keys to the city. There are risks but at least your portion of the booty will have been earned. My lord Tariq is most anxious that you are not involved in the fighting, nor need you be, but this is your chance to restore your fortunes and the stability of the southern regions of your land. Will you help me?"

There was no hesitation. Kunimund, without referring to his colleagues, immediately agreed and it was resolved that they, in the company of half a dozen of their compatriots, would ride away from the Berber army, which itself would be seen to withdraw, and would approach Cordova from a different direction. They would then seek admittance to the city. Having established their credibility, they would announce to Pelayo that Malik had decided to bypass Cordova with his large army and join up with Tariq on his march to Toletum. Meanwhile, a much smaller force, under the command of General Askil, was to take Malik's place and put the Cordovan garrison to the test. Assuming Pelayo accepted, without question, the credentials of Kunimund, he would hopefully decide with his commanders, that the might of Cordova's power would easily crush an army the size of Askil's and, once having done just that, he could retire back inside the ramparts knowing that he had, at least, had inflicted a defeat upon the invading force.

•

When first sighted by Tariq's guard, the party was much larger than expected. So much so that it was initially thought to be a possible hostile scouting party, but a single figure was seen to detach from the slow moving group and gallop ahead towards the camp. Once identified as a Berber outrider, the guard stood down and conducted the man to Tariq's pavilion. Tariq was already mounted and, waving away the attentions of Akeem and his Arabs, he and his newly arrived attendant cantered to meet the oncoming group.

Chapter 27

Tamegrant was the first unmistakable figure to catch Tariq's eye but it was a smaller, lighter mounted one which was seen to detach itself from the main body of riders and spur its way towards him. He urged his escort to ride ahead while he remained stationary and waited for Menna to meet him. He was not particularly self-conscious but it seemed to him better that the two of them should greet each other, if not exactly in private, but at some little distance from Count Julian and his followers. As it happened, Julian was obviously of the same mind because he halted his party, rather to the annoyance of Florinda, to allow Tariq and Menna a moment to themselves.

Almost before her horse had reached him, Menna flung herself from the saddle and ran to his stirrup, clasping it as if she was prepared to hold on to him forever. Tariq leaned down and gently lifted her head which appeared to be adhering permanently to his boot.

"You're crying?" He seemed surprised.

"No I'm not," she said.

"Yes you are," he replied, "your face is all wet. And another thing," he continued, "your horse is wandering back to your companions. The first rule of mounted warfare is never to lose your horse."

She raised a tear-stained face up to him, to see if he was being serious, and his crooked grin disarmed her so completely that more tears, this time of affection rather than relief, welled up again. Tariq gestured to the company which, having kept a respectful distance, was now ambling in their direction.

Tamegrant's giant figure, mounted on an equally enormous horse was riding alongside the equally unmistakably feminine Florinda who was flanked on her other side by Count Julian. Behind them rode a number of others. Tariq, for whom the arithmetic came as second nature, counted upward of a hundred. Some were mounted on a variety of animals, including mules and donkeys and some, obviously less affluent, were ambling along in the rear. By the time the group had caught up with them, Menna had managed to reclaim her horse and was sitting alongside Tariq, a proprietorial hand on his horse's bridle. Florinda giggled and was quietly admonished by her father, who rode up to Tariq, the two men greeting each other warmly. After all the acknowledgments had been made, Menna drew Tariq a little apart and started to warn him about her news of Musa's imminent arrival on the continent. Hearing her, Julian joined them and added his pleas that the first force to capture Toletum was likely to set the agenda for what might well be an extremely long occupation. While Tariq agreed that Toletum, as the Visigoth administrative centre of Hispania, was the most important prize and it was as such that he had evolved his strategy for a rapid advance on that city, he did not see himself as a potential rival to Lord Musa.

Directing his argument both to Menna and Julian, he said, "First and foremost, I am not a political animal. I lack the guile and the appetite for it. Being Governor of a garrison town like Tangier is one thing, no more than an extension of what any military commander might be expected to do. If and when we subdue the Visigoth and assume the responsibility for this land and its people, then the Caliph will decide how it will be done and who will do it. Lord Musa is an experienced negotiator with much experience of administering conquered territories and he has the ear of Damascus. I am a soldier pure and simple."

Menna and Julian again started to raise objections to these arguments but Tariq lifted a hand to silence them, saying, "There is one thing, however, which I would dearly like to achieve before Lord Musa takes over. He is, as you know, an ambitious and covetous man and those are characteristics not wholly compatible with the tenets of our faith. That said, were it not for his patronage and encouragement, I would not be in the enviable position in which I now find myself. I think, though, I can see a way by which I can reconcile my ambivalent feelings towards him. We will discuss it when we arrive back at our encampment." He now addressed Count Julian directly.

"My lord, it goes without saying that I am delighted to have your company. If nothing else, it gives me the opportunity to thank you again for the invaluable part you have played in our success thus far," he then turned and indicated the entourage that had been attending upon the Count, "but your band of followers, who are they exactly?"

Julian laughed. "They're not my followers Tariq, they are yours. The better appointed among them are merchants, with whom I have had dealings over many years and who are anxious to learn from you that a regime controlled by your Caliphate will not be to their disadvantage. Some of the others are disenfranchised enemies of Roderick, again hoping that you will advance their interests, and the remainder, mainly those trying to keep up on foot, are native Iberians who want to give you their thanks for delivering them from the Visigoth yoke."

This time it was Tariq who laughed. "I see I have to remind you again, my lord, that I am a soldier, not some miracle worker who has the authority, or the ability come to that, to improve the lives of these people."

Julian shook his head. "Oh yes you have, Tariq. Or, at least, they think you have. It is already known that you are not going to impose your faith on those that choose to retain their own, and your reputation as a man of honour contrasts most favourably with anything they have ever previously experienced. I do agree with you, however, that Lord Musa is unlikely to be quite as liberal once he lands with his mighty army, but much will depend, of course, on the direction he receives from Damascus. What is your opinion? Do you think that the Umayyad will want to rule with an iron fist or a velvet glove?"

Menna, riding behind with Florinda and Tamegrant, was straining to overhear the conversation and, although too polite to say anything, had to curb her impatience with Florinda's excited chatter.

Tariq considered Julian's question carefully before giving him an answer.

"Since you ask, I think it probable that Lord Al Walid will do exactly as he has done with the Christian community in Damascus. That is, allow them freedom of worship and activity, while taxing them for the privilege. The communities seem to work well together and I see no reason why a similar situation should not evolve here. Ah! We are about to be challenged."

Instantly recognised by the Berber camp guards, Tariq and the company were salaamed through. Akeem, to the fore, grinned hugely at Menna as he helped her to dismount while Tamegrant attended to his charge, Florinda. As soon as Count Julian's friends were introduced to Tariq's staff, the rest of the motley group were free to mingle with the Berber soldiers who made light of the language problems and welcomed them as friends. Once all this had been done Tariq, ushering Menna in front of him, invited Count Julian and his daughter into his pavilion. Once there, Menna and Julian pressed Tariq to enlighten them further as to his plans for Musa. He declined, reminding them that the campaign was not yet over and would not be until Toletum was under their control.

•

Having seen Kunimund and his compatriots ride off in the direction of Cordova, Malik left five of his Berbers, stripped of their battle gear and dressed as local peasants. This transformation was easily achieved by buying threadbare garments in exchange for a few silver pieces from the delighted, not to say surprised, Iberians who would probably have given them up quite happily for nothing to the newcomers, who they saw as their liberators. The five soldiers then mingled with their local hosts and awaited the arrival of Askil and his reduced force. Once sighted, Askil was to be escorted to Malik's new temporary headquarters in the low mountain range, just north of the city and out of its sight. They didn't have long to wait. Within the next twenty-four hours, Askil's force had assembled and he was riding into the mountains to meet Malik, who lost no time in explaining his plan. Really, it was quite simple. Since there was neither the time nor the inclination to conduct a siege, Askil's miniscule army was to present itself outside the city, looking as though it was intending to attack. If Kunimund and his companions had done their job and persuaded Pelayo to leave the security of his walls and join battle with a significantly inferior force, then Malik's cavalry, followed by his infantry battalions, would then sweep down from the north, join battle and defeat the Cordovans in the field, leaving the infantry to clean up the defenders remaining inside the city. On hearing the plan, Askil was not particularly amused.

"So, I am to be the tethered goat and your role is that of the brave slayer of the lion that has eaten me."

"Precisely!" was Malik's urbane response. He then went on to assure his friend that the cavalry divisions would be joining battle within hours of it having started. All Askil had to do was to make certain his army was not too close to the city, and prolong, for as long as possible, the inevitable posturing manoeuvres that presaged any conflict.

"And when exactly," Askil wanted to know, "is this sacrificial exercise going to take place?"

Malik shrugged. "How tired are your men?"

Askil shrugged in return. "Our march from Elibyrge was not difficult and a day's rest should be sufficient."

"So be it," said Malik, clapping Askil on the shoulder. "Have your men in position, looking as vulnerable as possible, by sunrise the day after tomorrow. We must lure Pelayo out into the open, it's our only chance."

And so it happened. Pelayo's army was tempted out of the city by Malik's subterfuge but the battle was a great deal fiercer than either of the commanders expected. The Cordovan army was better organised, better disciplined and better motivated than Roderick's had been and they inflicted heavy casualties on the Berbers. Eventually, however, Malik's men prevailed and the city was theirs and, when they entered it, Malik and Askil could see why the Visigoth had defended it so rigorously. Neither man, even the more sophisticated Malik, had seen anything quite like the splendour of the buildings, the richness of the ornaments, the hangings and the obvious displays of wealth. Bloodied, bruised and weary they might have been but the victors soon took comfort from the plunder they had earned. Kunimund was suitably rewarded, as were his companions, but Malik was quick to point out to the lightly wounded Askil that most of this treasure was destined for Damascus. As he drily responded, "Lord Tariq will not be slow to tell us that our reward awaits us in heaven. I wonder if Toletum will prove as valuable a prize? We shall see that the wounded are attended to and, as soon as we are sufficiently rested, we shall follow Lord Tariq, fight if we have to, and see for ourselves."

It would have been easy for Tariq to disregard the native elements that trailed behind Count Julian and who, at first sight, looked likely to represent little more than additional and unwanted baggage. Although thoroughly conversant with Classical Latin, communication presented something of a problem for him. The Count, however, with his long experience of the country, had some knowledge of their tongue, a weird kind of Vulgar Latin, and was able to translate for Tariq's benefit.

Tariq was very conscious that, with his relatively small army, he was vulnerable to attack. He had always banked on the fact that Roderick's principal military strength would be naturally centred on Toletum and would have followed the king as he marched south to confront the Berber invader, leaving the capital relatively lightly defended. It now occurred to him that, if they were willing, these native Iberians would be ideal to use as scouts, travelling in small groups as itinerant peasants. They would be less conspicuous than his own soldiers and could provide useful intelligence on any possible ambush or other hostile threat. When Tariq inquired of Count Julian if he thought these people could be trusted, Julian dismissed any such fears by telling Tariq that, such was their relief at their new-found freedom, they looked upon Tariq as a sort of god and would do anything for him. And if, as was Tariq's plan, their role would involve the use of Berber horses, their gratitude would know no bounds.

There was one other source of valuable information, of which Tariq, at that time, was totally unaware. The morning following their arrival at Tariq's encampment, it transpired that Florinda could not face the thought of returning to Toletum itself but asked, rather if she could be reunited with her friends Cyprian and Camilla and stay with them until her father was ready to return to Septem. Julian readily agreed, saying that was exactly what he was going to propose anyway. He then made his way to Tariq's quarters, where the General was engaged in a meeting with his officers.

Julian waited for him to finish his business then asked Akeem if Menna was available because he wondered if she would like to accompany Florinda to Cyprian's villa. Akeem, as usual falling into his self-appointed role of Tariq's mouthpiece, informed the Count that Menna had assumed the mantle of army tailoress and could be found somewhere in the vicinity, sewing, mending and generally doing what she considered needed doing. He further confided to Julian, as they went out, that Tariq was not especially pleased that Menna had seen the necessity of taking on any duties but she had insisted. Julian, imagining the conversation that had taken place, grinned and said that he would look for her. He soon came across her, armed with the biggest needle he'd ever clapped eyes on, sewing the straps back on some warrior's shield. He bade her a good morning but she, with her mouth full of leather lacing, merely grunted and concentrated on her work. Julian then posed the question he had come to ask and, still with her mouth full, she shook her head violently in answer. Then, she looked up at him and her head stilled while she obviously thought through the question more carefully. She frowned and removed the leather string from her mouth.

"I'm sorry, my lord. I did not intend rudeness but there is a great deal to do here."

Julian smiled at her and said, "Please, Menna, don't apologise, it is good to see you occupy yourself while waiting for Lord Tariq to give his orders to march."

Menna shook her head again, "Oh, no, my lord, we won't be marching today, not on a Friday." Julian clapped a hand to his forehead.

"Of course, of course, I quite forgot. Incidentally, Friday or not, I think the Iberian scouting parties are on the point of leaving the encampment."

"Ah yes. Last night, Tariq and I were discussing using them to spy out the lie of the land. Of course, they are not of our faith so they can carry out their duties at any time. What do you think, my lord? Is the idea a good one?"

"Of course it is," was Julian's enthusiastic response. "Tariq and I also discussed the matter and I have explained what is required of them and they can't wait to make themselves useful. Now, about my original question; my daughter does not feel able, at this time, to enter Toletum. Would you like to accompany her to my friend's villa where she, and you for that matter, would be out of harm's way?"

Once again a negative shake of her head then, again, another thought.

"This friend of yours, my lord, would he have any knowledge of the current situation in Toletum? Not only from the military prospective but also from the response of the religious leaders and the general population? While travelling with your retinue, it has seemed to me that our Berbers are regarded, if not as friends exactly, at least as something preferable to what they had before. Would your friend be a really useful source of information in that regard?"

Unhesitatingly, Julian's response was positive.

"Cyprian, that is my friend's name, probably knows more about what is going on in Toletum than the inhabitants of that city know themselves. He only survived Roderick's rule, and that of his predecessors, by oiling the wheels of their rusty political machinery. There are few people in Toletum, bishops included, who do not owe Cyprian money or favours. That is why Florinda felt safe in finding sanctuary in his house."

Menna jumped to her feet, handing her repair equipment to a bewildered warrior whose bewilderment was not lessened by her telling him what to do with it. She then turned to Julian.

"Come with me, my lord. Let us tell Tariq about this."

By the time they reached Tariq's battle table, his officers had returned to their unit lines and he was tidying up the papers and maps that had formed the subjects of their meeting. On seeing Menna and Julian together he smiled warmly at them and offered tea, but Menna waved her arms impatiently at him and said, "Tariq, Count Julian wishes to place Florinda in the care of his friend Cyprian. Apparently Cyprian's villa is not far from here and only a slight deviation from what I believe, is our intended route to Toletum."

She stopped abruptly, suddenly conscious of the limit of her authority, and Julian, sensing her discomfort, continued for her.

"The thing is, General, that this Cyprian could well save you and your men quite a lot of trouble. He has an intimate knowledge of Toletum and those who administer the city. Obviously, and quite rightly, your army must preserve its readiness for battle but it might save you a lot of time to have an accurate assessment of the current situation there." Menna then broke in, "And it's time that is important to us, Tariq, so what we, I mean Count Julian, is suggesting is that we all go over to Cyprian's villa, deliver Florinda to his care and you can discuss with him what we are likely to meet with when we reach Toletum." She frowned at Tariq, who was shaking his head.

"You are forgetting, Menna, that today is Friday."

Menna sighed. "Of course I know what day it is but we are not fighting or marching to battle, we are making a social call, that's all. Surely that does not offend against your, sorry I mean, our faith."

Tariq looked hard at her for a moment, then his gaze softened and he ended up by grinning at them both. "I think your interpretation of the word 'social', while not strictly accurate, will suffice. Give me a few moments to organise things here and I'll call up my Arab guard to accompany us. I take it that we can be there and back by the end of the day?"

Julian nodded. "Indeed we can, Tariq, by which time your scouts will have reconnoitred the direct route to Toletum. Incidentally, have you news of Lord Musa and his army?"

"Not as such, Julian," came Tariq's response. "Rumours abound and the whole world seems to know that he is coming but I've heard nothing of his precise whereabouts which, considering he's reputedly leading an army of eighteen thousand is strange. Since he is to the south of us, I imagine that Malik will have better intelligence but I can't afford to wait for him to catch up with me. I need to concentrate on Toletum, and if this little 'social call' of yours is as helpful as you suggest, then it will be a day well spent. Now you must excuse me. If you would see your daughter and, I imagine, Tamegrant, mounted and ready, I and my escort will be with you."

•

Malik was in no danger of catching up with his General. His army, together with Askil's, were making much slower progress than he wanted. The walking wounded were slowing them down and he dare not leave them behind. Although soundly beaten, Pelayo had disappeared with the battered remnants of his army which while still at large, posed a constant threat. Cordova was safe but only because the two Berber generals had depleted their forces to ensure its defence against any counter-attack. Also it was Friday, so Malik, frustrated by his faith, was forced to sit out the day although the respite was welcome to his tired but still triumphant soldiers.

•

In the abandoned monastery, the heavy heat of summer was having its effect on the one soul who was living out his life there. Change was in the air though. He could sense it and so could his feline companions. It had nothing to do with the oppressive temperature or smell, he was used to that. It was from outside. On his occasional forays, there was never anyone in sight and the distant buzz of city activity was silenced. Offerings, which had diminished over the past weeks, had now come to a complete stop so he was forced to leave the building and forage, but the pickings were meagre and he had to go further afield in order to satisfy his hunger. Despite the heat, he felt cold in his bones, and during the night he was forced to find warmth in the blankets which covered the Table. Wrapped in their folds, he found comfort in sharing the same wool which, he sensed, had absorbed some of the mystery of the piece they existed to protect.

•

The heat was even more intense in the south of Hispania and there, the sun-baked earth shook with the weight of the immense army now marching over it.

Chapter 28

Just outside the grounds of the luxurious villa, the Arab Guard did what it always did when stood down. Lookouts were posted, dried wood and scrub were collected, fires were built, water boiled and tea made. The water was courtesy of a well, just inside the walled gardens of the house which belonged to Cyprian. Inside the villa, Cyprian's guests were also engaged in drinking tea, but their surroundings were infinitely more comfortable, and Tariq was reminded of the times he had been the guest of Count Julian at Septem. The furnishings and the decor were not dissimilar, and this was not surprising since both Cyprian and Julian had known each other since boyhood, conducted business with each other and, generally, retained something of the old Byzantine tastes and lifestyle.

Tariq immediately felt welcome and at home here, which was more than could be said for Akeem and Menna, for whom the visit felt more alien and formal. It was especially difficult for Menna, who was impatient with the social formalities and eager to get on with the real purpose of their visit, which was to provide them with useful information about Toletum, its likely defences and the political implications of losing its ruler and ending two hundred years of Visigoth dominance. Tariq, who understood the value of patience, was, for the moment, quite happy to hear Cyprian and Julian discuss business and family matters. From these harmless topics, he was able to glean quite a lot about this land, its history and the potential it offered to a regime different from the repressive one that thus far he, Tariq, had been responsible for deposing. Soon though, it was impossible to ignore Akeem's restlessness, so Tariq suggested he leave the confines of the house and discuss certain matters concerning tomorrow's march with his friend, the commander of the Arab Guard. Then at the suggestion of her hostess and Florinda, and to her considerable disgust, Menna was led away to the women's quarters to admire the latest marvels of needlework and dressmaking. Menna was an accomplished tailoress and needlewoman but now preferred to practise her trade on uniforms and armour. It soon reached the stage where she found herself so frustrated by topics in which she had no interest, that she excused herself and returned to the men, hoping that she hadn't missed anything of importance.

•

The moment she entered the room, it became obvious that she had. It was the first time she had ever seen Tariq lose his composure. He was staring, open-mouthed and disbelievingly at Cyprian and she immediately ran over to him, standing behind him, a protective hand on his shoulder. The only thing that defused the moment was the broad smile on Julian's face. She felt Tariq take a deep breath and his body relaxed under her touch. He turned his face up to her.

"My dear, this is quite extraordinary. You will never guess what our host has been telling me." She gave his shoulder a pat which, from anyone else, might have been construed as patronising.

"I can guess quite easily, my lord. He has been telling you that Musa and his great army have landed here, in Hispania."

Julian clapped his hands together. "There you are Tariq, what did I tell you? Your lady is wasted with a needle. Give her a sword and make her your adjutant."

Tariq removed Menna's hand and turned to Cyprian. "What you have just told me, my lord, did not surprise me by the content but by the fact that you knew before I did. I have taken every care to have intelligence of Lord Musa's landing and subsequent movements. Relays of messengers are in place for that very purpose. Ready to bring me the news the moment his first soldiers set foot on these shores, and I have heard nothing."

Cyprian motioned to a servant to fill Tariq's glass, then said, "General, how long would you expect it to take for your messengers to ride this far and acquaint you of the news that you are waiting for?"

Tariq looked at Menna, then at a still smiling Julian, then turned back to Cyprian before saying, "Two or three days at the most my lord; two days' continuous riding by relay. Obviously, that would be in daylight and not taking into account interception or accident."

Cyprian shook his head. "I knew within half a day, General, and, what is more, within another hour I will be able to tell you where he is going and, with a little luck, what his intentions are."

Menna moved to sit at Tariq's side on the plush ottoman. She took Tariq's arm and dared to ask the question she knew he was about to ask.

"How, my lord; how would you know this, do you have spies that fly with the wind?"

Cyprian smiled at her and gave a slight appreciative nod of his head. "How very perspicacious of you, my Lady, that is exactly what I have."

By this time, Julian was openly laughing at the look of incredulity on the faces of his Berber friends. "Come, Cyprian," he said, "these are your guests and it is not polite to tease them so. It is time to show them what you mean."

Cyprian nodded his agreement and indicated that the three of them should follow him. He led them through several rooms towards the rear of the villa. In one of the rooms through which they passed, Florinda and Camilla were seated at a table, pouring over what looked like clothing patterns. As soon as she saw Menna, Florinda turned to her excitedly and said, "Menna, come quickly, come and look at these."

Menna's reply was a curt "not now Florinda" as she hurried out after the three men.

•

Cyprian led them across a large courtyard to a building, from which they could hear the soft rustling of animals, accompanied by the cooing of doves or pigeons. Tariq, his head on one side, listening, came to a sudden halt and took hold of Cyprian's sleeve.

"Pigeons, my lord, you use pigeons to bring you messages." He turned to the others. "I've read about this." He turned back to Cyprian. "Julius Caesar wasn't it? Was it not the Romans who used pigeons in battle to deliver messages?"

Cyprian gave him a bow. "Well done, my Lord. You are, just as my friend Julian has told me, a man of many parts. I have been using pigeons for a number of years now. Not as messengers in conflict of course, but as a means of informing myself of my rivals activities. As you would say, knowledge is power and, so far as my business is concerned, power is profit."

Intrigued, Tariq turned to Menna. "We must look into this." He then turned his attention back to Cyprian. "This must have something to do with the homing instincts of the birds. I suppose you transport a number of them to wherever it is that you want to receive your information and, once there, you have agents who release them. How do they carry the messages?"

"As I just said, General, I am expecting one of my birds to fly in within the hour and, if I might retain you and Menna," he bowed to her, "a little longer, you will be able to see for yourselves."

Tariq acknowledged the statement with a formal nod, thought for a moment, and then said, "We must not forget the original reason for our visit. Count Julian mentioned that, by giving us the benefit of your knowledge, you might be able to give us some idea of what to expect when we reach Toletum. The degree of hostility, the city defences, that sort of thing; anything, in fact, that will assist us and minimise the casualties we are likely to suffer. Incidentally, I ought to notify my guard that there will be a delay in our departure if we are to await the arrival of your winged messenger. Menna, perhaps you would…"

Menna, who was determined not to miss anything, started to object but

Cyprian, gave her an understanding smile and said, "If you exit through that gateway over there," he pointed out a door on one side of the courtyard, "you will find your men are waiting just outside, and it will save you having to brave the domestic perils of passing through the house."

Menna beaming her appreciation, ran to the door which, as Cyprian had said, led to where the white-robed guard were taking their tea in the company of the rather less than white-robed Akeem. Within seconds she was back and, in answer to Tariq's raised eyebrow, assured him that all was well and the company had been advised of the short delay to their return journey.

Tariq turned again to Cyprian. "Well, my lord, what am I likely to encounter once I reach the city? Is it well-defended on all sides or is there a weakness that could be to our advantage?"

Cyprian and Julian exchanged amused glances, although even Julian, whose last visit to Toletum had been when confronting Roderick, looked surprised at Cyprian's reply.

"General, I will be very surprised if you are not welcomed with open arms. Unless they have returned in any numbers, and I have heard nothing to suggest that is the case, all the fighting men in the city rode south with Roderick when he marched to repel your threat. As I say, there may be a few that are at large but not nearly enough to worry you. If anything, they might have joined forces with what remains of Pelayo's army but even that, if my information is correct, only engages in random sorties in the south of our country. Allow me to explain. There has always been a significant number of Jews in Toletum. Through successive generations of Visigoth rulers, the Jews have been persecuted and vilified. The only reason they remained at all was because the Visigoth needed them. They needed their money and they needed their expertise in fields in which their oppressors either could not or would not get engaged. That leaves the Church. The Church does retain some power, but without a Christian army to support it, that power is very limited. So, when I say that you will be welcomed with open arms, I could be somewhat over-optimistic, but I promise you, you will not suffer any casualties." He held up a hand to prevent further discourse, his head on one side as he listened. Then the others could hear it. Wingbeats in the still air which soon resolved into a pigeon, descending in circles above their heads, eventually landing on a sill of a hole in the stonework above their heads. It looked down on them enquiringly, turned and disappeared inside.

Menna, hand to her mouth, whispered, "What do we do now?"

"What we do now," said a smiling Cyprian, "is go inside and see what news it has for us."

•

The inhabitants of Toletum were reacting in different ways to the news of the imminent arrival of the invading Berber army. Such noble Visigoth that remained in the city were mainly women, their husbands having marched south with Roderick. True, a few of these men who survived the battle at Guadelete had wasted no time in returning to their home city, bearing tales of the implacable ferocity of the victors, but they were very few in number and they quickly realised the futility of trying to defend Toletum against Tariq's victorious army. The Christian hierarchy of bishops, with the exception of the Primate, unaware of any tolerance which might be shown towards their religion, were among the first to flee the city. They, together with such families who felt the challenge to their faith was too risky, made their way north, crossing the mountains into territory they knew to be friendly.

Among the Visigoth nobility who decided to stay was the Queen, if indeed she retained that title, Egolina. Her reasons for staying were more complicated than most. Whatever her moral frailties, Egolina was no fool and, even when she was sharing Roderick's throne, could see that the Visigoth hold on Hispania was slipping away. Firstly, there was the continual threat from the offspring of the former monarch. Before his demise, Roderick might have put a temporary halt to their aspirations for regaining the crown, but they were still alive and, as such, represented an on-going problem. More than that though, Egolina knew that so many of the nobility had perished at Guadelete that it was only a matter of time before control passed to another race. At first she assumed it would be the native population who would rise up against the oppressive Visigoth, but now it was obvious that the dark warriors from across the water were intent, not just to raid and plunder, but to conquer and subdue the entire nation. Well, she reasoned, if that was to be the case she would wait and see what happened. Count Julian had often spoken of his dealings with the followers of Islam and spoken well of their manners, their education and their culture, all things which were singularly lacking in her own people. If what he said was true, she might no longer be queen of a rather shaky empire but there was no reason why she should not survive in some comfort. At least she had a more realistic chance of doing so than she would have if the locals have rebelled. And if the Jews had taken over… She shuddered to think of what would happen to her. No, it could turn out to be quite interesting but even her active imagination could not foretell just how interesting it would turn out to be.

•

Menna, who couldn't wait to see how these pigeons divulged their secrets , led the way through the rough stone doorless opening in the tower. On entering the building they were met by a servant who, his finger to his lips, indicated silence. The four of them followed him up a circular stone stairway and, as they climbed, watching where they put their feet since the uneven steps were lit only by rays of light penetrating through slits in the wall, the sound of rustling straw and soft cooing became louder. They entered a landing running around the circumference of the building, which was lined with wooden cages, about half of which were occupied by the birds, contentedly preening their shining feathers and pecking about in their bedding. This chamber was lighter than the stairway which led to it because, all around the wall, there were openings in the stonework, and it was through one of these that they had witnessed the bird enter. The servant padded to one of the cages and, putting his hand through the open wicker gate, gently removed the occupant. The bird did not seem at all frightened of being handled and sat happily in his hand while, with the other hand, he teased out one of the bird's legs behind it and the three newcomers to this ritual let out a combined gasp as they saw the fine sliver of papyrus wrapped around it. All the time cooing at the pigeon in its own soothing rhythms, the servant undid the fine hair fastening around the papyrus, and passed it to Cyprian. As he took it, Cyprian smiled at his guests, saying, "It isn't magic you know. The birds are raised here from the time of hatching and, by returning here when released elsewhere, they are doing nothing other than following their natural instincts. Now let us see what the bird has to say to us." From his robes he produced a small eyeglass, smoothed the message flat on the palm of his hand, let out a quiet whistle of surprise and raised an eyebrow. This little piece of theatre was the last straw for Menna, who completely forgot that they were supposed to be talking in whispers.

"Well, what does it say, my lord?" This was enough to cause the rest of the birds to flap around, squawking with alarm, while the one which had brought the message struggled to escape from the hand of the servant in which, hitherto, it had rested quite happily.

Tariq looked reproachfully at Menna while Cyprian pointed down the stairs and whispered that they might as well go down because the light was so much better there for reading the miniscule hand in which the message had been written. Once outside, he again studied the message through his glass before turning to Tariq.

"General, it seems that the Umayyad army is not hot on your heels as perhaps you first imagined it might be."

Tariq looked thoughtful for a moment. "Don't tell me, my lord, I think I can guess the content of your message. Lord Musa has marched on Hispalis hasn't he? And that will turn out to be a more sustained campaign than was ever promised by Cordova."

He turned to Julian and Menna. "I haven't said anything before and, frankly, I am surprised that neither of you thought to ask me why, but I deliberately avoided Hispalis, despite the fact that it is wealthy and well worth the taking."

Julian interrupted him, turning to Cyprian, "Is that what your message says? That the might of the Umayyad is presently marching on Hispalis?"

Cyprian spread his palms upwards and shrugged. "Why do I bother with a network of flying messengers when your General already knows the intelligence they bring to me? Lord Tariq is exactly right. You have quite spoiled my little surprise."

Tariq laughed and said, "There is nothing magical, either, about my prognostications. It made tactical sense for me to avoid a lengthy siege at Hispalis and make no mistake about it, even with an army the size of Lord Musa's we are talking about months of siege warfare for which I had neither the time, nor the numbers, nor the inclination. If I can get to Toletum first and, now you have confirmed my expectations, I have little doubt that I will, the seat of Visigoth power and its government will be in my hands, not his. True, he will have taken Hispalis and in doing so he will have captured the body of this continent, but I will have its heart. That said, my lord, I cannot thank you enough for your hospitality. Your information concerning the situation in Toletum is invaluable. As for your messenger service, I am impressed and will develop my own as soon as time allows. Is it difficult to train the birds?"

Cyprian shook head. "No General, as long as you know what you are doing. I'll tell you what; I have two servants such as the one you saw in the loft. When you are ready, let me know and I will lend you one of them to set up your operation."

Tariq smiled his thanks, and indicated to Menna and Julian that it was time they roused their escort and Akeem from whatever leisure they were pursuing, and made their way back to the Berber encampment. The fact that the message had confirmed his suspicions proved that time was on their side, but an early start in the morning was still to be recommended. Julian, however, declared that it was time he and his daughter returned to Septem so, if Tariq had no objection, he and Florinda would depart the following day. He turned to Cyprian, "That is if my friend here has no objection? As a matter of fact we could pass the time discussing some matters of business in which I think he might be interested."

Cyprian bowed his head. " Indeed, Julian, it will be a pleasure to have your company, and I too have some thoughts we might profitably share." Tariq and Julian embraced warmly and made their farewells while Cyprian, in his turn, bade a gracious farewell to Tariq and Menna.

Tariq's parting question was, "What about Tamegrant, does he know of your intentions? He is still at our encampment."

Julian answered, "It is time my daughter learned to dispense with her nursemaid. I will leave Tamegrant in your care. I have a feeling he might turn out to be useful to you. Nothing definite, just a feeling, that's all."

Tariq thanked Julian and said that anytime Tamegrant felt the need to return to Septem, he would be free to do so. Then it was Menna's conscience that prompted her to rush into the villa to inform Florinda they were leaving so, all in all, it was a further hour before Tariq, Menna and their entourage left the property. As they rode away, Tariq told Akeem about Musa's intended siege of Hispalis but, for reasons he couldn't explain, Akeem was doubtful.

"I just don't trust that man," was his response. "He is too used to having all the glory of the conquest. He'll have something up his sleeve, you mark my words."

Events were to prove that these words were not too far from the truth.

•

With Hispalis in his sights, Musa ibn Nusayr, had made a decision of which Tariq was quite unaware. True, the great army of the Umayyad was intent on capturing Hispalis, but he would not be with them. The tiresome month's long siege would be left in the capable hands of his senior commanders while he, in the company of his son, Abd al-Aziz, would make his way north to Toletum, taking with them enough troops to clean up any pockets of Visigoth resistance they might encounter on route. In the same way that Tariq had anticipated Musa's tactics, so Musa had divined those of Tariq, although there was no question that Tariq would claim Toletum first. Still, pondered the Umayyad commander in chief as he enjoyed the luxury of an ornate pavilion staffed by many servants, his was the right to claim whatever it was he wanted and, so far as the Caliph was concerned, it was he, Musa, and not the resourceful Berber General, who would be feted as the true victor.

Chapter 29

The sun had not quite risen enough to herald a true dawn but the ripples on the deep, fast-flowing river were just discernible to the three figures, huddled in the undergrowth on the far bank. Across the water, the city was awakening to the sounds of sweeping, street cries, snorts, cackles and straw being shuffled around as domestic stock looked forward to their first feed of the day. The three looked at one another, nodded and as quietly as they were able, for two of them were big men, moved back to where their horses were tethered, away from the curious eyes of any citizen who might be abroad at this unsocial hour. Once clear of the river, they mounted and rode south until they were challenged by the scouts of the Berber army. Tired as they were, Akeem, Tamegrant and Amayuu were immediately admitted to Tariq's presence, the latter having been retained by Tariq for his skills as an engineer and technician.

"Well?"

Akeem stifled a yawn, looked at Tamegrant, then remembered that he couldn't answer, yawned again, and it was left to Amayuu to answer the question.

"The first thing to say, my lord, is that the city doesn't appear to be heavily defended, if defended at all. The second is that the river, a deep wide one at that, flows around three sides of the city which is well elevated above the water level. There are high walls, probably of Roman origin but still in good repair, and bridges on the eastern and western flanks of the town. Capable defenders would have little difficulty in keeping out an invading force and I could foresee a lengthy siege."

Akeem growled, "They won't want a siege anymore than we do. From what Lord Cyprian told you Tar.. my lord, there is not going to be any resistance so why don't we just get on with it?"

Tariq stroked his beard and then said, "No, it is not a question of resistance that concerns me, but the problem of getting my army into the city with some sort of authority. Sending them over a narrow bridge and having them file into town is scarcely going to create the sort of impression I have in mind. Apart from the bridges, is there no other way?"

Tamegrant cleared his throat and started to make unintelligible noises, but was stopped by Amayuu who made signs with his fingers. Tamegrant, concentrating on Amayuu's hands, started to smile and, nodding vigorously, moved his own fingers and it was Amayuu's turn to nod by way of understanding. This went on for some moments, while Akeem explained that his two companions had been using this means of communication for some days now. He, Akeem, couldn't begin to understand it, but it was amazing how it worked. Apparently, it was a similar language by which Florinda and Tamegrant had communicated and it was Tamegrant who had taught it to Amayuu. Akeem proudly stated that his cousin was very quick at picking it up too. He would have elaborated on this but Tariq stopped him and told him that he was already aware of Amayuu's skill, and that he too had been impressed by the speed at which Amayuu had mastered the art of sign language with a mute. As soon as the fingers had ceased to move, Tariq again asked the question.

"Well?"

"My lord, my friend tells me that the river is fordable to the north-east, and when he and the lady Florinda escaped the city, they did so by way of a large gateway on the northern side, which was open and slackly guarded. Would that suit your plans better?"

"Indeed it would Amayuu, and thank Tamegrant for the information. We are but a day's ride from the city, and Malik's envoy tells me that he and Askil are only a day's march behind us. They will be tired but I have little doubt that the thought of entering the Visigoth stronghold as one Berber army will give them energy for one more day." Tariq turned to Akeem. "Order my commanders to assemble here now. Then the three of you get some sleep, it might your last chance for some little time."

•

At the head of his battle table, Tariq outlined his plans to his officers. Menna stayed quietly in the background, frustrated at not being a part of the discussions but determined not to miss out on what was being said. Also present, and very much an active participant, was the commander of Tariq's Arab guard, Asad, a man for whom Tariq had developed considerable respect during the campaign. It was not a long meeting and, once the men had retired to their respective temporary quarters, Tariq joined Menna on the ottoman on which she had sat, listening to the discussion. He turned to her and took her hand.

"What do you think then?"

"You really want my opinion?" was her response. He nodded and she pretended to think for a while before returning his enquiring look.

"Well," she said, "I think that you are probably the cleverest man in the whole world."

He laughed, as she knew he would, and she then continued, this time more seriously, "Akeem has often said to me that what appeals to you, about warfare, is not just the tactical aspect of it, the intellectual side if you prefer it, and it is certainly not the actual business of fighting that you enjoy. No! It is the drama of the occasion that you find interesting." Tariq started to protest but she held up a hand to stop him as she continued. "Don't misunderstand me, or Akeem for that matter. We both know that you are a brilliant tactician, but somehow the tactics grow out of your sense of theatre. Like at Guadelete, for example. Akeem tells me that, every morning, you insisted on presenting your army as if it were on parade. Every morning the same formations, and he also told me about your first command, when you instructed Tala to position his troops so that the sun set behind them. Apparently, the tribe you had been sent to subdue were so captivated by the tableau that there was not the slightest hint of violence. I have watched you too, when you play with your blocks of wood and move them around on your imaginary battlefield back in Tangier. Why is it so important to present your army as you would actors on a stage?"

Tariq shrugged. "Well, that is precisely what a battlefield is, is it not? It is a stage on which the most bloody and cruel dramas are played out; and that, my love, is why I do what I do. Even before Lord Musa raised me to where I am today, I have thought deeply about this business of warfare, the cost in terms of human lives and the misery attendant on such things. Actually you were not quite correct when you mentioned my war games. That is something different. That is when I put myself in the position of my enemy and try to think how he is likely to conduct his battle. Obviously a lot of other things have to be taken into account; the terrain, of which one could never be certain, the comparative strength of the armies, the equipment at their disposal. But, even then, I find that most military commanders and, more importantly, the men under their command, experience a degree of confusion when faced by something they weren't expecting. It just gives me a tiny advantage. Not much, but in these sorts of situations it doesn't have to be much. Our dear friend Akeem, as with most soldiers in my experience, only knows one way to fight, so if he is confused by my unconventional methods it gives you some idea of how the opposition might feel. Life is sacred and it is the responsibility of any General to preserve as much of it as he can."

She nodded. "Yes, I can understand that and I admire you for it but Toletum, according to Cyprian, poses little in the way of a military threat. Why employ the same tactics tomorrow, or the day after, whenever it is you intend to march into the city? Why not just stroll over the bridge and take over?"

"Pride!" was his short answer. "We are the invading army, the army that has defeated the Visigoth and one that will ultimately settle this land. I have no wish to induce fear but I do want, and expect, respect from Toletum. I want us to look worthy of our victory, so discipline and display will play their part." Suddenly he gave her one of his spontaneous grins, one which, in an instant, changed his normally serious face into that of a naughty child and one that she found irresistible.

"Why not," he went on, "see if we can find a camel. We'll put you on it and you can be the first Berber to enter Toletum. Just like an exotic Emir-ess, or whatever they're called. " A look of horror wiped the smile from her face and she moved away from him.

"I couldn't do that, I'd be so embarrassed, I'd rather... You didn't mean that did you? You're teasing me aren't you?" The grin faded but the eyes still sparkled, so she pounded away at him while he pretended to be hurt by her ineffectual blows. Not so ineffectual because, in pretending to evade them, he fell off the end of the ottoman, she threw herself on top of him and their laughter was so unrestrained that the guards outside the tent could hardly contain their own mirth – until the laughter inside suddenly stopped, then the looks between the guards became somewhat more meaningful.

•

Musa ibn Nusayr was not a happy General. He had deliberately left his main force to conduct the potentially lengthy siege of Hispalis while, leading the lighter elements of his army, he aimed to make the best possible time to Toletum. Although he was unlikely to overtake Tariq, he wanted to get into the city before the Berber army had time to appropriate the pick of the priceless bounty rumoured to lie there. Unfortunately, before he had time to travel far, he had been attacked, frequently and quite fiercely, by Visigoth irregular units. These, under the leadership of Pelayo, mainly consisted of the remnants of the Cordovan army which had evaded Malik's successful capture of the city. Under the competent leadership of Pelayo, they made a small but formidable adversary. Not large enough to pose a serious threat they, nevertheless, were a nuisance and, by adopting hit and run tactics, delayed Musa's advance quite considerably. The fault, too, lay with Musa himself who made a point of dealing out punitive retaliation on every occasion. This took time and, although resulting in few casualties, Musa's soldiers being better armed and better disciplined, he made far slower progress than he should otherwise have done. By contrast, the armies of Malik and Askil were advancing far quicker than expected. Now into the central plain, there was less chance of ambush and the going was generally much easier. The army was provisioned from the land through which it marched and most of it was given freely by the local peasantry who, like Tariq before, saw this new Berber army as liberators rather than invaders. Again, Musa was denied this advantage. His policy was to take, not to ask and, if not freely given, to make sure the locals were punished for their reluctance.

•

Two days later, at dawn, Tariq's army was positioned outside the northern gateway in the walls of Toletum. As Tamegrant had correctly predicted, the broad, slower-running river to the northeast of the city was easily fordable and within moments the city, walled on this side but unprotected by natural obstacles, lay unguarded and open. Malik and Askil, predicted to arrive the following day, had been ordered to parade at the Roman bridge to the east, where their restricted entry would be covered by Berbers, by then already in control of the city.

•

The population of Toletum ringed the walls and stared down at the exotic sight which confronted them below. As usual, Tariq had displayed his strength with care and imagination. His Arab guard, their robes blindingly white in the early morning sun, were formed into a broad arrowhead with Tariq, dressed with care by Menna, at the point. Behind, extending the wings of the arrow, were his cavalry units and formed up in a broad line behind them, his foot soldiers, draw swords glinting at their shoulders. Leading these infantrymen, and the only ones mounted, were Akeem and Menna. Akeem had not been happy with his position, considering his usual place at the side of Tariq, to be more appropriate but Tariq had told him that Menna was now his responsibility and, since Akeem loved Menna only slightly less than he loved his master, he agreed, but not before registering his expected objection. While sitting there, alongside Menna and waiting for the order to move, he gave her a nudge. She turned impatiently, wishing to savour every moment of this historic occasion.

"What do you think that is then?"

She followed the direction of his arm and shook her head.

"It's an old church or something. Probably one the Visigoth abandoned when they changed their faith from one form of Christianity to another. Why, what's so special about it?"

Akeem tutted. "No, not the building. That old man that's standing in front of it. Looks like a skeleton and he's got that funny robe thing on, with a hood. Cats all around him too."

This time it was her turn to sound exasperated. "Really, Akeem, what does it matter? He's just one of those monks, or holy men and that's his church, monastery or whatever is. The cats are a bit odd though; anyway, what does it matter? This is what's important. Head up, try and look friendly, we're moving."

Chapter 30

For once, Tariq had miscalculated. He assumed that, on entering the city, he and his army would sweep through to a central space, where they could assemble in their customary disciplined fashion. However, on entering the gates, which were quite wide, he was met by a maze of narrow alleys running in all directions, with no indication of where they were going. He held up a hand and the whole procession came to a somewhat undignified halt. He called for the Iberians who had scouted for him and, cursing himself for not having prepared better, instructed them to lead the way through to the nearest open public area, central to the city. After much excited exchange of instructions with the locals, itself leading to a variety of directions, the army made its faltering way to the centre of the city where, to the relief of all concerned, a square appeared which was large enough to accommodate the reduced Berber force.

Tariq's first action was to call up his senior officers and instruct them to identify every church, large house or building and have the proprietors, or custodians, appear before him in the square, before the sun had started to move from its zenith. He also charged them to mark their directions in the town and avoid the embarrassment of getting lost. One mounted squad was ordered to proceed to the Roman bridge on the east of the city and, there, to await the arrival of Malik and Askil and guide their armies directly to the square. That done, his remaining troops, in particular the Arab Guard, were again deployed in exemplary fashion, their backs to a large church which was assumed to be the Central Visigoth cathedral. As on previous occasions when receiving tributes, Tariq seated himself at a large table, this time appropriated from the church behind him and covered with an ornate cloth, also taken from the building. He didn't have long to wait. Soon, his officers filtered back, accompanied by a collection of citizens who numbered in excess of a hundred people. Some looked terrified, some almost bored and some, the majority, merely curious. Tariq had them mustered in front of his table and tried to identify to which race or religion each belonged. In the end, he gave up and, still sitting, addressed them.

"My name is General Tariq ibn Ziyad and I am the commander of the Berber army, itself representing the greater Umayyad army which, as you may or may not know, is the defender and propagator of our Islamic faith. The one fact that will not have escaped you," he continued drily, "is that I defeated your King Roderick, and that our armies are now in complete control of all your territories. Or, at least those that extend this far north. I have the rest of my army arriving here tomorrow, having conquered Cordova and, behind them, the mighty army of the Umayyad itself, under the leadership of no less a person that the great, and universally feared, Musa ibn Nusayr. The reason I tell you this is that you will find me a more reasonable conqueror than Musa, although my faith is dearer to me than almost anything else," Menna, standing unobtrusively behind him was slightly disappointed not to receive any indication of what he meant, and Akeem's gentle squeeze of her arm did nothing to help, "it is not my intention to force conversion on you or indeed force you to commit to any great change in your present lifestyle, although any resistance, through force or against my instructions, will be met with a swift and unmistakable response. Do you understand me thus far?"

This speech, which had been delivered slowly in Latin, had obviously been understood by most of the crowd, who nodded and looked at one another, wondering what was likely to come next. There was one section, however, keeping apart from the rest and less well dressed, who muttered among themselves before one of them, the self-elected leader of the group, spoke up clearly and, rather to Tariq's surprise, in passable Berber.

"I take it, my lord, that your intention, as conqueror, is to extract as much in the way of valuables as you can. My colleagues would beg you to remember that we Jews have been systematically robbed by the Visigoth for the last two hundred years. We appreciate your statement that we be allowed to follow our religious beliefs without interference, but please note that we have been left very little in the way of riches, and trust that you will not be unduly harsh in your demands. These nobles and clerics," he waved his hand at the rest of the assembly, "will have much more to give than our poor people."

Tariq, who had listened to this declaration of poverty with some amusement, stood up.

"My intention is to deal fairly with you all. My men will locate a building that will remain locked and guarded. All the items of value that we will take from you, as the legitimate spoils of war, will be stored in this building. We are not, however, so innocent as to believe that all this booty will be handed over without question. All your properties will be searched thoroughly, and we have become rather good at finding the unlikeliest of hiding places. It would, as I say, be unrealistic of me to expect you to give freely of your belongings, but rest assured, we will find them and we shall take them. I'll be fair, but any attempt to obstruct our searches or dissemble with us will incur fines of a magnitude that will leave you with nothing at all. So, you will now return to your villas, accompanied by three of my soldiers who have a passing knowledge of your language." He turned to the Jewish spokesman. "In your case Rabbi, for I imagine that you represent your community in that capacity, there would appear to be no requirement for linguistic skills. For the moment, however, I would like you to remain, together with you," he indicated an individual dressed in the elaborate robes of a bishop or archbishop, "and you." This time he picked out a few individuals of both sexes, who were, by their dress and demeanour, people of substance and power.

Once the square had cleared, Tariq rose from the table and walked first to the man he considered to be the most likely source of the information he sought and also the most likely source of booty. The two men, one dressed as a soldier of Islam and the other as a prominent representative of the Christian church, looked calmly at each other before Tariq took him to one side, out of earshot of the others.

"By your dress, my lord, I assume that you are the leader of the Christian community, here, in Toletum?" The man looked him straight in the eye as he replied, "Not only here in Toletum, but the whole of Hispania. My name is Sindered and I must tell you that I will not, indeed cannot, surrender the souls of my congregation to the barbaric religion that you represent."

Tariq said nothing for a moment but the tension was palpable. When he did speak, his tone was quiet and measured but the underlying authority unmistakable.

"My lord Archbishop, had you been paying attention, you would have heard that I am not interested in souls but wealth. Your church is rich and most of those riches derive from those who can ill afford to give them. And you would call us barbaric? However, that is bye the bye. The souls of your congregation are yours to do with as you wish, but I will have your wealth and, believe me, if it is not given freely it will not be me who destroys your churches, but Lord Musa who does not share my generous spirit. If he has to extract your valuables by force then, trust me, your suffering will be proportionate."

Tariq, having delivered this warning, took a step back and awaited the Primate's response. When it came, grudgingly delivered as it was, Tariq was gratified by the abrupt change of attitude. It transpired that, not only was the Archbishop prepared to hand over the gold and silver precious ornaments and relics of the cathedral, but also offered the assistance of his bishops to locate and give up everything of value to be found in all the churches in the region. Tariq, however, had not quite finished with the Archbishop.

"My lord, there is one relic in particular in which I am interested. That is the Table, rumoured to have originated from the Temple of Solomon in Jerusalem. Are you the guardian of this table or have you any idea where it might be found?"

The Archbishop's response was so vehement that Tariq had little doubt that it was completely honest. Shaking his head so strongly that Tariq would not have been surprised to find the episcopal mitre rolling around in front of him, the Archbishop exclaimed that the Table of Solomon, the most revered and precious object ever possessed by the Visigoth, had not been seen for years. He, himself, had only glimpsed it once, when he had occasion to visit the royal palace, then occupied by King Wittiza, in the company of the then Archbishop, Gunderic. He went on to explain that, since the death of Wittiza, virtually everyone of note, the nobility, the Church and certainly King Roderick, had searched up and down the continent, but in vain. It was assumed that Wittiza's sons, on fleeing to the north, had taken the table with them and had it hidden in some remote place up there, but King Roderick, when campaigning in that region, had conducted diligent enquiries that had revealed nothing of the Table's existence. It was a mystery, destined never to be solved and doubtless one ordained by divine providence. Tariq mused over that last comment but, believer that he was, quickly came to the conclusion that most acts of providence were inspired by men rather than divinity. He had been sure that the Church would be in possession of the Table but it now appeared that luck rather than ingenuity would have to deliver it, if he were to find it before Musa arrived and, although the reason was still not clear in his mind, he knew instinctively that he had to find it first.

•

The Archbishop having been dismissed in the company of several of Tariq's officers, Tariq's attention now turned to the other notables, only one of whom was a woman; a striking looking woman who held herself erect and, alone among the Visigoth nobility, was not particularly overawed by the occasion. Partly out of politeness and partly out of curiosity, Tariq approached her next. "Madam, you are..?"

"My name is Egolina, Queen of the Visigoth." She appraised her interlocutor and saw a man who wore his authority with ease and one who did not look upon her as a woman, although she had taken great care with her appearance, but rather as an opponent to be assessed and, ultimately, defeated. She liked what she saw. But Tariq seemed oblivious of her regard. Rather, his manner was one of amusement.

"Not 'Queen', my lady. Your husband has been slain in a battle that I have won. You are, therefore, no longer a queen. Tell me, what do you know of the Table of Solomon?"

She shrugged and said that, although she had heard of it and her husband seemed to have wasted too much of his time looking for it, she had never seen it nor knew where it was. In her opinion…!

Tariq interrupted, rather rudely, she thought. "Unless you know of its present whereabouts, my lady, your opinion is of little interest to me. Presumably you have other treasures in your palace, which being the case, I shall have you escorted there by my men who will relieve you of them. The jewellery which you are wearing will not be exempted." Egolina's hand automatically went to her throat, to the heavy gold necklace that all but covered it. "Yes, my lady, that too," was Tariq's curt response. Angrily, Egolina tore off the necklace and threw it at Tariq's feet. He merely gave a bow of the head and instructed one of his men to pick it up and accompany Egolina to the palace and search it thoroughly.

•

Menna, watching from the rear, was impressed by Tariq's performance but the interchange between him and Egolina gave her a moment's unease and Akeem, although not the most sensitive of men, felt her stiffen perceptibly. As Egolina swept away from the group, accompanied by her newly acquired military escort, Menna broke ranks and, pulling a mystified Akeem with her, followed as Egolina made her way to the palace.

•

Meanwhile, Tariq continued to question the remainder of the Visigoth nobility, most of whom had long been reconciled to their fate. He then despatched them to their villas, together with the Berber officers who were to relieve them of their riches. His next move was to instructed others to find a building in which the spoils might be securely locked away and, having done so, entered the Cathedral leaving word that he was only to be interrupted in an emergency. It was not the first time he had entered a Christian church. On his progress through to the centre of Hispania, the churches were one of the best sources of booty and had been duly stripped of all that was valuable. This one was likely to be the most productive of all but, on this occasion, it was not the object of his visit. This time he needed space and time to think before the arrival of Lord Musa. It seemed that the mystical Table of Solomon was looking more mythical than mystical, yet he was becoming almost as preoccupied with it as Musa but not, he mused, for perhaps the same reasons and it was this that he wanted to resolve in his mind before he carried on with his day-to-day duties. For him, the whereabouts of the Table was becoming an interesting problem. Where was it and how had it remained hidden for so long? Somebody must hold the secret, but who, and where were they to be found? So, he reasoned, that was his problem and now that he was here, in Toletum, this was surely the best place to make his investigations. On the other hand, the Archbishop had, quite reasonably, thought the Table had travelled north with Wittiza's sons. Tomorrow, with the increased support of Malik's men, he would, if necessary, question every likely source of information here, in Toletum. More than that he could not do but what of Musa? Where did his interest in the holy relic lie? Suddenly it came to Tariq and when it did, it was blindingly obvious; Musa needed the enormous prestige that such a gift to the Caliphate would bring. Tariq had always known that his exploits in the field, his victory over the Visigoth, had not been expected by Musa, who imagined that Tariq's Berbers would prove little more than a diversionary tactic for his own invasion of Hispania. It must have been a bitter moment for his mentor to have been bested by his own pupil. Thinking about it brought a smile to Tariq's lips and then he shook his head. He admired Musa and, without his support and encouragement, Tariq would never have enjoyed the success that he had but, he reminded himself, he'd worked for it and whereas there was little he would begrudge Musa in view of the loyalty he owed him, no one, not even Musa himself, was going to deprive him of the honours he had deservedly won for himself. No! If Musa wanted the wretched Table, he was welcome to it, providing, of course, he could find it. But if he, Tariq, could find it first, then it might really result in an interesting situation!

•

It didn't take long for Menna and Akeem to catch up with Egolina and her escort. Egolina had never hurried in her life and the fact that she was about to part with her valuable possessions was, she thought, an excellent reason for delaying the unhappy moment for as long as possible. Therefore she was pleased when a female voice, in Berber, ordered her escort to come to a halt. When she turned round she saw a fat Berber soldier, of no definitive rank, and a slight, much younger soldier similarly attired. Her escort, however and much to her surprise, bowed to the unlikely pair and muttered a deferential greeting, in what she supposed to be, their barbaric tongue. Looking more closely at the unlikely couple she was intrigued to see that one was, in fact, not a man at all but a women, dressed as a Berber warrior. She snorted with derision and said to her escort,

"So you have women soldiers in your army, how quaint!"

It was Akeem who growled, in execrable Latin, "Soldier, not soldiers and not just any soldier, she is the wife of Lord Tariq and you should address her accordingly."

Egolina's mouth fell open. Still she found it difficult to keep the amusement out of her voice when she said, "The same lord Tariq who is going to rob me of my jewellery? Well, that is a surprise, I would have thought that such a man might have chosen better, but then again… perhaps not."

Menna, during this interchange, had unwound her head-dress, walked up to Egolina and addressed her in Latin, only slightly more sophisticated than that of Akeem.

"You are the Egolina who used to be queen of the Visigoth, a nation that, had our army been composed entirely of my own sex, would still have submitted to our superior moral power and intelligence. You are the same Egolina who, together with your cowardly husband, raped and dishonoured my friend Florinda." She turned to the officers who had escorted Egolina. "I want you to be sure that you miss nothing of value when conducting your search. If necessary, burn her palace to the ground and, should she still be in it, so much the better." The two women locked eyes until Egolina dropped hers. Menna then wrapped her scarf around her face and turned on her heel, returning with Akeem, a huge grin on his face, lolloping along behind.

•

At first light the following morning, trumpeters on the wall, heralded the arrival of Malik and Askil who, as ordered, drew their armies up to the eastern side of the city, by the ancient Roman bridge. Their soldiers immediately made busy, creating their encampment on the banks of the great river. Tariq had already concluded that, such was the geography of the city, the accommodation of another army inside the walls could prove a serious problem. Anyway, should he have need of more men to search for plunder or police any situation that might arise, he had men in plenty to call upon. In the privacy of his quarters, (he had elected to commandeer a large villa, formerly the property of a nobleman slain in the battle) Tariq, Malik and Askil greeted each other enthusiastically. Tariq debriefed his generals, particularly with regard to the spoils they had won and the security in which they were held. It was important, he felt, that when Musa appeared, he had a precise inventory to hand over to him. Knowing his Emir as he did, he knew it would be checked most carefully and there would be hell to pay if Musa felt that he had been cheated in any way. Tariq was quite surprised at the amount that Malik had accumulated, in excess of what Toletum was likely to produce, but he was already beginning to learn that, although Toletum might have been the seat of government, Cordova was the centre of commerce. In any event, he hoped that there would be enough accumulated treasure to keep Musa happy. Happy enough to forget about the Table? He'd soon find out. If the local notables had failed to find it since Wittiza's death, then his chance of doing so before Musa's triumphal entry into Toletum in, say, two more days, was highly unlikely. He needed more time and Sindered had, perhaps in his innocence, provided him with the idea of how he might gain it.

Chapter 31

It was two days later, early after sunrise, that the lookouts on the city walls of Toletum trumpeted the sighting of huge clouds of dust which heralded the arrival of Musa's army. Thus, Tariq surmised, the Emir had either been marching through the night or, which was much more likely, had made a very early start. In any event, he was obviously in a hurry to arrive at Toletum. Tariq's feelings were mixed. His genuine respect and affection for Musa were tempered by the intuitive knowledge that Musa's actions were not always motivated by the same moral code which he, Tariq, had always tried to follow. Musa halted his army at the Roman bridge, where his small force, Tariq calculated no more than a thousand men, joined up with Malik's troops in setting up their encampment on the banks of the river. The clatter of hoof beats on the bridge, however, indicated that Musa and his aides were riding into the city where, guided by one of Tariq's senior commanders, they were conducted to the central square in which Tariq stood, ready to greet them.

The moment Musa flung himself from his saddle Tariq was struck by how much he had changed since last they had met. Although always a big, powerful man, the old Musa always appeared to be carrying excess weight, reflective of an easy lifestyle. Now he looked, harder, fitter and, Tariq had to admit, every inch the general of legend and one who had yet to experience defeat in the field. His manner was as jovial as ever and he embraced Tariq as he would a favoured son. He then introduced his actual son, Abd al-Aziz, who had ridden in with him, and suggested they repair to Tariq's pavilion which had been set up in the square and which, under Menna's watchful eye, had been suitably embellished with bunting and banners representing the Umayyad colours. Having seated themselves, tea was brought in and, the initial courtesies dispensed with, Musa wasted no time in setting out his priorities.

"Loot! How have you determined that nothing has been overlooked and that everything is secure and correctly inventoried? My information is that Cordova yielded much wealth and, even as we speak, my transports should have emptied the vaults there, loaded, checked it, and be ready to move north, here to Toletum. Passing Cordova, that pup Pelayo has proved an irritant and prevented me from arriving here sooner and, without his interference, my light force might even have got here before you did. As it happens nobody, with access to the Caliph, is likely to tell him that I didn't."

The implicit question was not lost on Tariq who, however, bowed his head and gravely said, "Indeed not, my lord."

Musa's eyes searched keenly for any irony in Tariq's remark but, appearing to find none, he immediately reverted to his usual jocular self.

"What's this I hear about you and Menna then? Must say I'm surprised at you, my boy. I thought your strict principles would prevent you from taking a woman for your sensual comfort. Especially with her being a non-believer."

Tariq, far from appearing offended, merely laughed.

"You are mistaken, my lord. Menna is of our Faith and I did not take her solely for my comfort, but as a wife."

Musa was momentarily discomforted, not so much at the nature of the revelation but because he hadn't been privy to it before.

"You have been busy haven't you? So, when did all this happen?"

Tariq shrugged. "Oh! Menna converted before we sailed for Hispania and the marriage: well that was made on the Rock. Idir, you remember Idir, her father? Well, he died six months earlier so Akeem stood in as her guardian."

Musa smiled. Ah, the Rock! Named after you, so I hear. Something for which posterity will remember you?"

Tariq gave one of his self-deprecating smiles. "That, my lord, was not of my doing."

"No, Tariq, I don't suppose it was. Now, tell me of our booty here in Toletum. I don't imagine that it equals, in value, that which we have discovered in Cordova or, indeed, what my men will find in Hispalis, once we succeed in our siege but there is one item, in particular, that I expect to take from this city and that is…"

"The Table of Solomon, my lord?" Tariq interrupted. "I fear that it is not here, my lord. My men have searched high and low, and have questioned anyone who we suspect might have some knowledge of its whereabouts."

Musa slowly rose to his feet, the rest of the gathering hastily following suit. He frowned.

"You have not been in possession of this city for long. I suggest your inquiries be made, shall we say, somewhat more forcibly. It has to be here," his voice rose, "it has always been here, in Toletum. They are playing games with you, Tariq; this whole expedition has been partly set up in order to… in order to…" He lowered his voice again. "You cannot, in all seriousness, tell me that the most famous of all ancient artefacts has just disappeared. It has to be somewhere, it just has to be. Why I promised Al Walid myself that I would.." Again, his voice trailed away and he started to stalk around the pavilion in an effort to regain control of his temper. When next he spoke it was in a much more conciliatory way.

"Tariq, have none of the local persons of influence any idea at all where it might be concealed?"

Tariq walked over to him, took him away from the others and spoke quietly, "Yes, my lord, I have already spoken to those who are most likely to have some knowledge of the subject although they too cannot speak with absolute certainty. They think the most likely explanation for the Table's disappearance is that, when Wittiza's sons fled to the north to escape likely retribution from the newly elected Roderick, they took the Table with them. In the short period that I have been here, my men have investigated every possible hiding place and I can assure you, my lord, it is not to be found in this city."

Musa looked long and hard at Tariq but could detect nothing but candour in his expression but then, knowing his man as well as he did, he expected nothing else, so he contented himself with a "Humph" but then went on to say, "All right, I believe you but I would rather like to speak to some of these people myself. You will not be surprised to learn that I have, in any event, prepared a short list of those I wish to interview."

He walked over to his clerk and held out his hand for the rolled papyrus offered to him.

He unrolled it. "Let me see now, there is the Archbishop, Sindered isn't it? The leader of the Jewish population, sundry other princes of the church, as they call them and," he peered closely at the word, "last but not least, Roderick's widow, Egolina. I know that you have already talked to them but I would like to have a few words with them myself. You never know; they might let slip something that they concealed from you. First thing tomorrow morning would suit me. I have been in the saddle for half the night so I'm for my bed. Tomorrow morning then?"

With which, Musa gathered his group together and, with his son at his side, walked out of the pavilion, making his way to one of the more luxurious villas which had been appropriated for his use while staying in Toletum.

•

Menna, who had been making herself as inconspicuous as possible in the town, hurried to join Tariq as he left the pavilion.

"Well, what did he say?"

Tariq shook his head and steered her into the cathedral before replying, "It is as we suspected. This Table is to be his proof that he is the rightful conqueror of Hispania. He imagines, and I think quite rightly, that the Caliph will view the Table as some sort of spiritual confirmation of Musa's military prowess and will reward him accordingly."

Menna's response was predictably one of outrage.

"But that's not fair. You have conquered this land, not him. By the time he landed it was all over, well, mostly all over. What would happen if you, and not Lord Musa, gifted the Table to Al Walid?"

Tariq's rueful grin said it all. "Well, I suppose I would be the hero of the hour but there are two things you've forgotten. One is that Musa outranks virtually everyone except the Caliph himself and the other, I have no more idea where the Table is than Musa has. Oh yes! He knows all about us. Being married that is. That surprised him."

She didn't react as he thought she might. She just sat there deep in thought. "Time!"

He looked at her quizzically.

"That's what we need, time." She went on, "We need more time to look and time to question people. I know you have questioned the obvious people, the nobles and other important people but what about ordinary people; the ones who aren't obvious. The thing can't just have vanished, unless it's been destroyed of course. So why don't I, together with a few of your most trusted men, like Malik, start talking to the people in the street. Oh! And I think I know one place where you haven't looked?"

Another raised eyebrow.

"While we were waiting to make our less than grand entrance into Toletum, Akeem and I noticed an old church or monastery, or whatever it was. Anyway it was almost a ruin, on the outskirts of the city." Her brow wrinkled as she remembered. "There was an old man and cats, that's it, lots of cats. Why not send someone out to have a look. Even better, why don't I get hold of Akeem and we'll take a look at it while Lord Musa's out of the way."

Tariq shrugged. "Why not, you never know. As I keep telling myself, it can't just have disappeared. Then again, perhaps Sindered is right. Perhaps it is somewhere in the north. One thing we can find out is whether Roderick, on his expedition there to subdue the rebels, spent any time looking for it. There must be some disgruntled veterans who marched up there with him and might be able to tell us something. Why don't you and Akeem have a look at this ruin of yours while I get some men talking to, as you put it, the ordinary people?"

She gave his hand a squeeze and flew out of the cathedral to look for Akeem.

•

The next morning, Musa did more or less what Tariq had done on the day of his arrival and questioned all the city leaders. Although his technique was more threatening, he learned no more than Tariq had done in more conciliatory fashion. His mood was not improved by this although one outcome of these interviews was profoundly unexpected. When Egolina was called before him, her concentration on his questions was minimal and all she had eyes for was the handsome Abd al-Aziz standing at his father's side. He, for his part, seemed equally smitten and for several moments the mighty Emir had difficulty in getting any sense out of his witness and, as soon as it became clear that she was going to be no help with regard to the Table, he dismissed her. Abd al-Aziz leaned towards his father and whispered in his ear. Musa frowned, then he turned to his son and nodded, upon which sign of approval, Abd al-Aziz left the assembly and hurried off in the direction Egolina had taken. Musa then beckoned Tariq to his side and murmured, "You can take that grin off your face, General. Think about it; we have conquered these people and we are here to stay. Perhaps not you and me, Tariq, but at some time in the future, our people will have to integrate and mix with the local people. You would be the first to tell me that it is possible, indeed only right and proper, that non-believers can marry into our faith so why not start at the top. The Visigoth might not have much to teach us but the blood of the nobility is pure enough. I would not be averse to creating a dynasty in my name."

Tariq bowed his head and contented himself with replying, "I imagine not, my lord."

He then continued, "I have not been privy to everything that has gone on between you and these people," he indicated the notables of the city who remained, "but I gather that your efforts to discover the fate of Solomon's Table have proved no more successful than mine."

Musa groaned. "No, they have not and I am drawn to the same conclusion that I think you have reached; namely that it is not here, in Toletum, but assuming it still exists, was taken to the north by Wittiza's cubs." He looked at Tariq. "You stay here and see if you can't uncover some more valuable loot. What you have under lock and key seems little enough for a city of this importance. You have to press them harder, get more juice out of them."

Tariq bowed again. "Certainly, my lord, but will not you be here, to do… do some squeezing yourself?

"Certainly not, Tariq. We are here to conquer Hispania and, thus far, we have only conquered half of it. I shall take my army north and finish what it is we set out to do."

Tariq raised a questioning eyebrow. "But, my lord, the main body of your army is engaged in besieging Hispalis. What lies further north is unknown territory. Surely it is taking too much of a chance to…"

"To march into the unknown, Tariq? Oh no! I shall take some of your men." He waved his hand over towards the eastern side of the city. "Malik's army for a start; they are taking their ease on the banks of the river. Then there is the Arab Guard. Let's face it Tariq, they were mine in the first place. No, you need have no worries. I shall be more than adequately armed for the exercise."

"Indeed so, my lord; I shall command Malik to ready his force. When will you be starting, my lord?"

"Couple of days, Tariq. My troops are still tired and so, for that matter, am I."

Tariq thought for a moment. "In view of your earlier remarks, will your son be accompanying you, my lord?"

The reply was instantaneous. "Of course he will, Tariq. Just make sure that no one else sniffs around the old palace. Believe me, she'll keep. My boy is, by far and away, her best hope of a good future and she'll not want to spoil her chances. Now, tonight you will dine with me. Your Generals are invited as is, of course, your wife. Clever woman, is Menna. She could turn out to be the best quartermaster any army could wish for."

Tariq wondered if Musa had any idea what Menna was doing at the moment. He hoped that searching ruined churches for the cherished antiquity would not occur to him but doubted it would, so he thanked Musa for the invitation, and, leaving him, made his way to the Roman bridge to inform Malik that he was about to serve under a new commander.

He didn't relish giving the order and he was quite sure that Malik wouldn't relish following it. At least it would take Musa out of Toletum and if he did find the Table hidden in the north, so be it. If nothing else, it would give Tariq and his team more time to search in the place where it had last been seen.

•

When Menna learned of a possible pact between Egolina and the son of the all-powerful Musa, she was not particularly amused.

"That woman is a moral degenerate and any idea that she might be part of the new ruling elite is monstrous. Can't you do anything to stop it, Tariq?"

Tariq laughed. "No I cannot! And, if I were you, I wouldn't say anything to Lord Musa at dinner. Once he has an idea, he is unstoppable. He has appropriated a large part of my army and is now intent on conquering the rest of Hispania. He marches north in a couple of days."

Menna looked surprised. "I can see the sense of that, I suppose. His army in the south to consolidate our gains there and overcoming any resistance in the north secures the whole country for us." She reflected for a while before continuing, "And a rich, fertile land it is compared with many of our poor pastures at home. I'm surprised that he didn't send you though, and take his ease here, together with the credit for adding such a jewel to the Umayyad crown."

Tariq shook his head. "I think he would have done just that, but for the lure of Solomon's Table. He is now convinced that Sindered's theory is right. That Wittiza's sons spirited the Table away with them when they fled north. Talking of which, what did your old church yield up in the way of treasure?"

"Nothing!" was the laconic reply. "Nothing except a truly awful stench of cats and an old man, probably he was a priest there at one time. He wouldn't come near us and just cringed in one of the alcoves. He said nothing and we found nothing, the place is empty. Akeem has collected three or four of his friends and they are going to start knocking on the doors of humbler dwellings but nobody we've spoken to seems to have seen the Table and some even claim never to have heard of it."

"Ah!" Tariq looked thoughtful. "I'll have a quiet word with Akeem. Advise him to suspend activities until Lord Musa has left the city. In the unlikely event of him turning anything up, it wouldn't hurt to keep it to ourselves for a while."

•

The following day, Musa, Tariq and their senior officers spent most of their time discussing Musa's intended advance northwards. With Malik now under his command and the restoration of his Arab Guard, Musa was commanding a substantial force. This presented him with problems of extended communication and supply lines, to which was added a lack of strategic intelligence with regard to the territory he was aiming to invade. The Visigoth appeared to have no knowledge of cartography so even the simplest of maps was not available to him, and it was Tariq's suggestion that an attempt be made to identify and interrogate any survivors of Roderick's earlier incursion into the region. As it happened there were a few of these men still to be found, most of whom had suffered wounds which prevented them from continuing the march south to defend against Tariq's army, and they were duly brought in front of Musa. They still yielded little information. For the most part they were uneducated, simple peasants who'd been conscripted into the army against their will, but Musa did learn that the campaign against Wittiza's sons and their supporters was fought in the north-east of the country, that the terrain could be mountainous and difficult and that it had always been a problem to engage an enemy who tended to disappear back into some quite impregnable position. Sending these informants on their way, Musa seemed quite cheerful, considering that he had learned very little of real value. He turned to Tariq.

"Just as I thought! If Wittiza or his heirs wished to find a suitable hiding place for the Table, the sort of place those idiots have just described couldn't be bettered. In a city like Toletum, there are too many eyes, too many ears. Up there, in that sort of wilderness, well away from the intertribal squabbling that seemed to characterise the Visigoth tenuous grasp on power, you could make things disappear for centuries."

Tariq interrupted drily, "Would that then not make it equally difficult for you to find it, my lord?"

Musa dropped a paternal hand on Tariq's shoulder. "Nobody hides anything from me, Tariq. Not for long. In the end, I always get what I want. Now, let us talk about supply and communications. If the country through which we travel is as productive as this, there is no reason why my army cannot live off the land. If not, you will have to have ready, the necessary resources and the means to get them to me. I understand that you used native scouts to probe ahead of your march here. If you've taught them their business, they'll do for me so perhaps you'll be so good, hand them over to my men, and what's this I hear about some sort of bizarre use of pigeons? They make extraordinarily speedy messengers apparently. That being so, I'll take those as well."

Tariq held up a hand. "Whoa, slow down, my lord. I do have some birds but they are young and not yet fully trained. The scouts, though; I'll have Akeem track them down and bring them to you. Is there anything else, my lord?"

Musa shook his head. "I don't think so Tariq, just keep an eye on our treasure and, yes, there is one more thing; in the future, you can leave any communication between ourselves and Damascus to me. I'll keep the Caliph fully informed of our activities. No, I think that's all. I march the day after tomorrow."

•

Having been guests at a grand repast, grander than either of them were used to, Tariq and Menna were lying in bed. Both were preoccupied with their own thoughts and Menna, always more impulsive, was the first to give voice to hers.

"Did you notice how, across the table, Musa's son and Egolina seemed to be sharing some private joke; as if they'd known each other for ages. Do you know, I sensed that they were laughing at us – or, at any rate, me."

Tariq stifling a yawn, squeezed her hand. "Not at you, my love. Why should she? You have the advantage of her."

Menna raised herself up on one elbow. "I do? In what way? She is of noble blood, as is Abd al-Aziz. Me? I'm a nobody"

Tariq pulled her back down again, "Oh yes you are. You are my wife and the great advantage you have over Egolina is that you know who she is and, more importantly, what she is and what her weaknesses are, whereas she knows nothing about you at all. Knowledge is power and it is that which gives you power over her."

Menna nestled up to him and mumbled, "I think you've just won another battle."

She immediately became wide awake again.

"Tariq, you know that old church, the one with the old man and the cats?"

But Tariq had fallen asleep and Menna, peering into the darkness, tried to make sense of the thoughts which were tumbling around in her head.

Chapter 32

Tariq woke early the following morning and quietly got up, leaving Menna, who had been restless for most of the night, to enjoy what was now a deep sleep. He walked outside his pavilion, nodding to the guards standing there on duty. They were his own Berber men now, not the elite Arab warriors who, until yesterday, had guarded him and fought for him. These had now reverted to Musa, under whose command they had originally served until the Caliph had ordered otherwise. They were brave soldiers and he had been glad of their service and he would miss them but it was only right that he should lose them. He scarcely warranted that degree of protection, now that he was safely installed in Toletum and the enemy vanquished. He yawned and stretched in the bright morning sunlight. He was happy not to have continued the occupation of one of the abandoned smart houses in the city. There were many of these for the taking, such as the one now used by Musa and his commanders, but he always preferred to spend his nights under a tented roof. The encampment was outside the north gate, by which he had first made his entrance to the city, but there were already a number of people abroad; hawkers from the city, who welcomed the invaders and who were under instruction to be fair and honest and meticulous in their dealings with the local tradespeople. Warriors, exchanging guard duties, were marching to and from their posts, and the contented noises from the horse lines indicated that their attendants were up and about their business of feeding and grooming.

Tariq stood, taking in these sights and sounds and uttered a silent 'thank you' that his army, away from a combat situation, was still disciplined enough to go about its tasks without having to be ordered to do so. He made a mental note to instruct his commanders to revert to the same routines that they practised back in their barracks at Tangier. He continued to walk through the encampment, acknowledging the greetings of his men as he passed by them, but he was looking for one individual in particular. Not a warrior and not even a Berber, but a native of Hispania with whom he had established a respectful and friendly relationship. Eventually he found him, a little distance from the rest and under the great northern defensive wall, which was starting to crumble in parts, but remained much as the Romans had left it all those centuries ago. Here the man he had been seeking was busy erecting some sort of wooden structure in the lee of the stonework. As soon as he heard Tariq approaching, he dropped an armful of wood and bowed towards him. Tariq returned the greeting and said, "Is this to be their shelter then, the home to which their instincts will compel them to return?"

The man bowed again. "Yes, my lord."

Tariq continued, "And how are they progressing with their training; still too young to use, I suppose?"

"More important, my lord, they need to be here for several weeks yet, before they can be trusted to return, but every day now I take them a little further. When this," he gestured to the half-finished wooden structure, "is completed, it will be made more comfortable than their temporary crates and their homing instincts will be stronger."

Tariq nodded. "Of course. You say several weeks before they are ready to fly long distances? When they are ready, seek me out and I will have work for them. In the meantime, select someone from the city who you think suitable and involve him in training the birds. My friend Cyprian was good enough to send you to me but, when the time is right, I will need two of you. Will you do that?"

Of course, my lord I have already befriended a local labourer who has shown interest in my work. I will ask him today, if that is alright with you, my lord?"

Tariq nodded his approval and turned away, only to be nearly knocked over by the ever-present burly form of Akeem, who apologised and asked if there was anything Tariq wanted of him.

"Just a quiet word, Akeem." Tariq guided him to the outer limits of the encampment from where they could see, in the morning light, the sharp outline of mountains, far to the north.

"Tomorrow, or the day after, Lord Musa will be leaving us and taking his army up there," he waved a hand at the distant horizon, "His action will complete the invasion of Hispania and, who knows, whatever lands lay beyond its boundaries."

Akeem followed his gaze and shrugged his broad shoulders as much as to say, 'so what?'

He then turned to his master and said, "It doesn't really matter to us what Lord Musa does now. It was you that conquered this land, not Lord Musa, and nobody can take that away from you and," he went on, "you have a mountain named after you, they can't take that away either. Ah, there it is!" Shielding his eyes he pointed into the near distance.

Tariq, shielding his own eyes, looked hard in the direction where Akeem was pointing. "The mountain, Akeem? You're looking in the opposite direction and, anyway, you know you'd never see it from here, or is this today's riddle, because, if it is, I'm not really in the mood."

"No, lord, not the mountain, the church, religious building or whatever it is. The one that Menna and me first saw on our way into the city. We went there yesterday in case that magical table was hidden there. Hasn't she told you about it?"

Tariq dropped his hand. "As a matter fact, she has, Akeem. Bad smell of cat apparently and nothing else."

Akeem, theatrically pinched his nose. "Bad smell isn't the half of it, and not just the smell either. I thought they were supposed to be clean animals. Cats' piss and shit everywhere. Disgusting it was."

Tariq thought for moment. "While we're on the subject of that 'magical table', as you call it, I wouldn't go around asking about it just yet. Lord Musa is convinced that it's hidden in the north. I think that's one reason why it's him and not me that's taking an army up there. I can't help thinking that he exaggerates the importance of the object but he seems to put more value on that than on the territory we have won."

Akeem snorted. "Think about it, Tariq; that object is the one and only thing that can impress Al Walid more than your success as a conquering hero. Lord Musa needs it to boost his position and put you in the shade. I tell you, the thing is magical – if it can be found."

Tariq sounded resigned. "Well, there's nothing I can do about it, and if fame and fortune are so important to my lord Musa, then let him get on with it. One more thing, he wants to use my scouts, you know, the local Hispanic ones. Sort them out will you and get them over to him. I am going to break my fast. If you need me, you'll find me in my pavilion."

•

When he arrived there, he found Menna sitting outside and sipping tea, her eyes speculatively scanning the various activities taking place around her. Tariq took a drink from the offered tray and joined her.

"I tried not to wake you, you were sleeping so soundly."

She smiled at him and covered his hand with hers.

"Thank you for that, yet I thought I was never going to get to sleep. You, on the other hand, were sleeping like a baby as soon as your head touched the pillow."

He gave her one of his grins. "Clear conscience! What was on your mind that kept you awake?"

She stifled a yawn. "Oh I don't know. Nothing really except…"

"Except what?"

"I can't explain it, well, not in the logical way that you might understand."

He made a face. "Am I that patronising? Surely not! Anyway, try me."

She thought for a moment, "Well, it's that church, the old monastery, almost a ruin, that Akeem and I explored yesterday. The thing is, and this is what you won't understand, I have a 'feeling' about the place. As I told you, we searched high and low and found nothing. Nothing, that is, except an old man, as decrepit as the building and his collection of cats. It was just that he… that he was frightened. Not of us as a threat to his person, but a threat to something else."

Tariq, listening intently, broke in, "Something that you might find, for example? Is that what you mean?"

She shook her head. "No, well, yes, perhaps. When he was cowering in an alcove, he didn't once look at us but kept his eyes on something else in the building."

"Anything in particular?"

She shook her head again, "No, not particularly. I mean there's nothing else in there, just cats. No wall hangings, no decorations. The place is bare except for a hearth and some curing hooks." She took a deep breath, looked at him and grabbed his arm. "Wait a minute; that was what I was trying to remember, what kept me awake. There was no ash. Not there. I mean the place was filthy and there were old ashes lying about but not there, where you would expect them to be."

Tariq gently removed her hand. "I don't see that that signifies anything. He wouldn't need a fire at this time of year and in the winter I expect he slept in one of the alcoves and lit some sticks nearer to his bed."

She looked at him reproachfully. "You see, that's what I mean. You always find a logical solution to everything. Alright, I agree, I have very little more than intuition to go on but something is not right in that place and if that 'something' was enough to keep me awake half the night, then at least it warrants some further investigation."

Tariq waved his arms in mock surrender. "All right, all right, we'll take another look at it. Strangely enough, Akeem pointed it out to me earlier this morning but I can't say that he shares your intuitive instincts. We will take another look at it but not until we have waved farewell to Musa ibn Nusayr."

Menna grabbed his arm again. "Good! But I think that Tamegrant ought to be with us."

"Tamegrant? Why Tamegrant? If you hope to get any information from your old mad monk, Tamegrant's more likely to frighten him into a vow of total silence."

Menna tightened her grip on his arm. "You are the cleverest man I know and I love you beyond belief but sometimes you just can't see the obvious. Tamegrant is sensitive to things that we are not, and if that old man is hiding something, is frightened of something other than us, then Tamegrant is the most likely person to see into his mind."

Tariq looked unconvinced. "Uum, you could be right, but if you take Tamegrant, you'll have to take Amayuu, otherwise nobody will be able to decipher what it is that Tamegrant's found out."

Her look, this time, was almost pitying. "Of course we'll have to take Amayuu, I'd already thought of that."

Once more Tariq disengaged his arm from her grip and rose to his feet.

"Anyway, we won't speak of this to anyone at the moment. Not Tamegrant, Amayuu, Akeem, anybody. Now I have pressing things to do; a meeting with my Commander-in- Chief not being the least of them. We'll talk later. Oh, one thing more; since Musa's son seems to have discovered the doubtful charms of ex-queen Egolina, perhaps you might be a little more conciliatory towards her or, failing that, keep out of her way. As it is, I find myself having to reconcile good government with Musa's avidity. After Roderick, we stand a good chance of winning over the population of Hispania and making life beneficial for all, but we won't do it by depriving them of their every last piece of silver. So you see, my love, we both might find that we have to come to accept situations with which we are not in agreement."

Menna's retort was instantaneous and instinctive. "In that case, I'll keep out of her way. How do you expect me to befriend a woman who behaved as she did towards Florinda. I thought you were Count Julian's closest ally. How can you…?"

"Later, my love. I have to go."

Thus saying, he waved goodbye and walked off towards the city gate and left her, frowning furiously, until she turned in the direction of the old monastery and her frown turned from one of annoyance to one of thought.

•

The meeting, attended by senior officers of both Malik's army and that of Musa, was short, to the point and Musa was the only speaker. He intended to march on the morrow and a relay of messengers would ensure communication between themselves and Toletum. Tariq was to stay in the city with his remaining force to create an administration that would ensure security, a return to commercial normality and, through that, some form of taxation system. From this directive, Tariq assumed that Musa's intention was to absent himself for some period of time. How far north, Tariq wondered, was he prepared to go? Beyond the boundaries of the Peninsular and whatever that might entail from the point of view of supply and support, should it be needed? Musa beckoned Tariq to his side as the meeting concluded.

"Tariq, I have left you with enough power to govern this city and I have every reason to think that you will do so with your customary efficiency. If, by chance, I am too remote for Damascus to send a message to me, then the Caliphate will make contact through you. In which case, your only duty will be to pass the message on to me as quickly as possible. Do not allow yourself to become involved in any political discussions with Damascus. Just get word to me and I will deal with it. Is that clear?"

Tariq's face was expressionless. "Quite clear, my lord, it shall be as you wish."

Musa clapped him on the shoulder. "I know what you're thinking, Tariq. You're thinking that I don't want to risk you getting too close to our masters. You're thinking that I don't want you getting the credit for the successful overthrow of the Visigoth and you would be quite right in thinking that. I'm getting older and I need to start thinking about a comfortable old age and that means wealth and influence. I need my influence with the Umayyad to be at its peak when we return. Don't forget, lad, had it not been for me you'd still be milking sheep, so cheer up and be prepared to settle down with that new wife of yours. Don't worry, you'll have plenty to tell your children as they grow up.

Right! By the time I return I expect to see this city returning to some of its former glory and prosperity, in which I shall expect to share. Another thing, don't waste your time looking for the famous table, it isn't here. My men have turned the place upside down and there's no sign of it." He clapped Tariq on the shoulder again. "I shall expect to see you and your army cheering us on our way tomorrow. Until then!"

With an airy wave of his hand, he left Tariq standing there, contemplating the dilemma which had been occupying his mind ever since his arrival in Toletum. Did his loyalties lie with Musa, who had just reminded him of the debt he owed him, or to his Berber army which had served him so wonderfully and which had sacrificed so many colleagues to the cause of the Faith.

•

The next morning, Tariq's army smartened up their encampment and assembled in disciplined ranks to cheer off Musa's force as it left the northern gate of the city, passing through the orderly lines of Berber tents on its way to conquer more of Hispania. Tariq, Askil mounted by his side, positioned himself at the end of the lines in order to be the last to wish his Emir good fortune as he rode by, the Arab Guard just behind him, reminding Tariq of the battles he had endured with them at his side and not Musa's.

As they passed, Musa gave him a formal salutation, while the captain of the Arab Guard gave him a friendly, if regretful, smile and Malik contented himself with a conspiratorial wink, which Tariq was happy to return. It took a good time for the Umayyad army to pass through and as soon as it had done so, Tariq ordered Askil to stand the men down and follow him to his pavilion.

Once there, Tariq informed Askil that, henceforth, he would be in direct command of the Berber force remaining in the city, thus freeing Tariq to orchestrate his new administration. Obviously, should anything seriously threaten security then he, Tariq, would still be on hand to assume command. In some ways Tariq wished that Malik had not joined forces with Musa. After all, he had proved a competent stand-in for Tariq when, as Governor of Tangier, Tariq had been obliged to be absent himself for any period of time, such as when he visited Damascus. Musa, however, had seen fit to commandeer Malik so Tariq was left with no choice. Not that it was likely to prove a real problem; although Askil was not as intuitive and intelligent as Malik, he was a good disciplinarian and respected by his men. All in all, Tariq reflected, it was probably better the way it was. Askil would be ideal for this sort of situation where fighting units were going to have to assume the more pacific model of an occupying force. He would keep them trained and fit and was likely to take his responsibilities more diplomatically than Malik.

•

Before the year was out, Tariq had achieved much of what he set out to do. He held regular meetings with those elders still remaining in Toletum. He brought the three local leaders together, Christian, Jew and Iberian and instructed them to work together for the greater good of the community. He ordered them to forget their past differences and to respect the skills that each could use to mutual advantage. The Jewish population, freed from the bonds of the Visigoth tyranny, were free to practise and expand their trading expertise and were happy to pay the higher taxes levied by their new overlords. The local peasantry, who were excellent farmers, discovered that their crops had a cash value hitherto denied them, while the Christians, almost all Visigoth and indolent, soon discovered that racial and religious integration was their only hope for a better future. Menna and Akeem had visited the old monastery on a couple more occasions but had still failed to find anything. The proposed addition of Tamegrant and Amayyu to the search party had not materialised because both were too busy undertaking work that Tariq considered more important. In point of fact, Tariq had more or less given up any hope of finding the Table in Toletum and had not, despite Menna's pleas, even visited the monastery himself. Understanding that Menna needed a challenge, Tariq suggested a number of activities, and soon she was throwing herself enthusiastically into arranging classes for sewing and leatherwork. Askil, in the meantime, selected the most intelligent and educated of his troops to study the local languages and, once proficient, to instruct those interested, in the history, knowledge and Faith of Islam. Perversely, it was Egolina who proved to be one of the keenest participants in the new culture. Inevitably, she and Menna crossed paths but studiously avoided one another when it happened. Menna, Tariq thought, was becoming somewhat too repetitious in her condemnation of the ex-queen, whose sensual appetite suddenly seemed to be replaced by one for knowledge, but then, one day, Menna walked into his office with a look on her face which, well as he knew her, Tariq found impossible to interpret.

Chapter 33

"That look either means that you have had the most enormous row with Egolina or that you've found the Table of Solomon. I thought I said that if you can't be civil to her, it would be better to avoid her altogether." Tariq's tone was mildly admonitory, although he couldn't help but smile at Menna's pent up anger – or was it excitement?

She was flushed and kept turning away and looking for something outside the room. Tariq waved a finger at her. "Look, Menna, this is a situation with which we have to live. I grant you, the woman is imperious and patronising but, at least, she is making an attempt to learn something of what goes on in the world outside Toletum. Why, only the other day, she asked me what I thought of…" His lecture came to an abrupt end as Menna banged his table with the flat of her hand. He patiently began collecting the stylos and documents that the action had scattered.

"Tariq, will you just listen for a moment? This has nothing to do with that wretched woman. It's the other thing, the Table!"

"The Table," he repeated. "You mean the Table of Solomon?"

She gave a sigh of exasperation. "Of course I mean the Table of Solomon, what other table would I come barging in here to tell you about?"

Tariq rose slowly to his feet. "You mean to tell me that you've found the Table of Solomon, the one we've spent the last months looking for?"

This time she laughed. "Yes, Tariq, the one we've been looking for. Anyway, I hope there's only the one."

"And you've actually found it?"

"Yes, Tariq. Well no, not actually *found* it but we know where it is."

Tariq could not help looking sceptical. "And where would that be?"

She shook her head and looked outside again, then turned and said, "I'll let Akeem tell you. Funny, he should be outside, I told him to wait. Ah, here he comes."

Akeem then lumbered into the room, supporting an old, but powerfully built man who was handicapped by only having one leg. Akeem gave Tariq a broad grin and winked at Menna.

"Here we are, lord," he said. "The answer to all our prayers."

Tariq found a chair for the man and, once he was safely seated, turned to Akeem.

"All right, you two, what is this all about? Who is this cripple and why is he the answer to all our prayers?"

"This, my lord, is the ex-commander of the old King's guard. King Wittiza, that is, and he has some valuable information for you."

Tariq regarded the cripple dubiously. "You know something that we do not? Do we have a mutually accessible language that will enable you to share your information with us?"

Akeem broke in. "'Course he does, my lord. He even understands me."

Tariq nodded and, turning to the man again said, "Is there anything I can have brought for you? A glass of wine, perhaps, something to eat?"

The man replied in very passable Latin. "No, thank you, my lord, although," he paused as if calculating how far he dare go, "I have heard that you are a fair man, my lord!"

Akeem gave a scornful snort. "Fair! I told you he's the most honourable man you're ever likely to meet. Just get on with it, tell him what you're here for."

The man, whose name was Geberic, shifted on the chair to make himself more comfortable.

"Since you are a fair man, my lord, I shall be fair with you. I'll tell what I know and then, should you think the information worth it, I'll tell you what I want in exchange."

Tariq looked at his two companions, and then, back at Geberic.

"That is a risky strategy on your part. Once I have your knowledge, you have nothing left with which to bargain, so, obviously, I accept your offer. Tell me, then, what it is you know about the Table of Solomon."

Geberic, in his turn, looked at Akeem and Menna, before returning his attention to Tariq who, by this time, was seated back at his desk, alert and expectant.

Geberic cleared his throat. "I have seen the Table, my lord, and I know of its location."

He cleared his throat again. "What I cannot tell you is where it is hidden within that location."

Tariq nodded thoughtfully. "So, you can tell us where it is but not where it is exactly? You'd better tell us what 'exactly' it is that you do know."

Geberic then went on to explain that he had been in charge of the Guard that had escorted Wittiza and the Table. Wittiza had, by that time, become quite frail and anxious. He had gone to great lengths to emphasise that what they were doing should remain a secret and that nobody was to mention a word about it.

Tariq's interruption was quiet and civil. "Excuse me, Geberic isn't it? Excuse me, Geberic, but here you are divulging this sworn secret to us. I need to know if you have told anyone else?"

Geberic shook his head violently. "Oh no, my lord. The only reason I'm telling you now is that everything here has changed. Your people rule us. Our time in Hispania is coming to an end. The other thing is that King Roderick was responsible for this," he pointed to his amputated leg. "I lost my leg in his service when we were fighting in the north and he refused me a pension even though I'd been a faithful servant to the nobility for most of my life. I have no other loyalty now but to myself."

Tariq gave an understanding nod. "So where was this place to which you and your men escorted King Wittiza and the Table?"

"An old church, just north of the city, my lord."

Menna said nothing but she and Akeem exchanged looks which, Tariq thought, were unnecessarily triumphant.

Geberic continued, relating how Wittiza had had the escort blindfolded before they were allowed to carry the Table into the building, so that, once inside, they had no means of seeing where they were going. Wittiza guided the men carrying the two front corners of the Table.

Again Tariq interrupted. "So it was just you, your men and Wittiza present, when all this was taking place?"

Geberic shook his head again. "No, my lord. There was a priest, he went into the church with them."

This time it was Menna who broke in. "A priest? That would be the old man that's in there now."

Again a negative sign from Geberic.

"No, lady. It can't be him. You see, King Wittiza ordered us to kill the priest before we left. He was the only one, the King apart, who knew what happened to the Table once it was inside the church."

"You killed a priest?" Tariq looked shocked and Geberic went on to explain that the church in question, and the clergy in it, were representative of the old order of Christianity, considered profane by the newer Catholic order. Tariq was quite aware of the turbulent history of religion in Hispania and of the excesses committed by both sides but still, to kill a priest? He asked Geberic to continue his narrative.

"There's not much more to tell, my lord. Your man here knocked me over as he came round a corner and, after he'd brushed me down, he asked how I'd lost my leg and, when I told him, he asked if I'd heard any rumours, in the north, about a magical table as he called it. I assumed he meant the Table of Solomon so I told him what I knew. Which is exactly what I've just told your lordship; so is my story worth anything, my lord?"

Tariq said nothing for a moment but then turned to Menna and Akeem. "Well?"

They both nodded so he turned again to Geberic and said, "You have fulfilled your part of the bargain so what is it you want from me?"

Geberic didn't hesitate. "A pair of well-made crutches, my lord, and enough pension to see me through the rest of my days. Just enough to be comfortable, I don't like extravagance."

Tariq laughed. "Neither do I Geberic, neither do I." He turned to Akeem.

"Akeem, instruct our best carpenter to call on this man and tell him to make whatever Geberic wants."

Menna broke in, "I'll find the best padding and leather for the armpits."

Tariq continued, "And you may be sure that I'll see a pension is secured for the rest of your days. Akeem, help our friend back to his lodgings and, all of you, this information goes no further than the four of us. Menna, be so kind as to fetch my clerk. As soon as I have told him what I need doing with this," he indicated the pile of documents, "you and I will take a stroll."

•

As they walked out of the north gate, Tariq turned left, along the wall. Menna pulled his arm and pointed in the direction of the old monastery. He shook his head.

"We are not going to your church, at least, not yet. There are still a few eyes and ears in this city that I would prefer not to know our intentions, especially with regard to that particular business. You must not be impatient, Menna: we will go there, of course we will, but not today and probably not tomorrow. We will talk further about it tonight. At the moment I want to have a word with our friends who are training the pigeons. Now is the time that early information on Lord Musa's activities and intentions is vital, especially after the news we heard this morning. I mentioned, did I not, that Cyprian's man has recruited a local to assist him? They now tell me that the birds are ready. Lord Musa has requested we send a light baggage train full of woollen blankets. It appears that he hadn't bargained for the colder weather he was likely to encounter in that part of the peninsular. Anyway, I shall send a crate of pigeons and one of the men, with instructions that they leave the train before reaching the Umayyad army. They will, however, be making contact with Malik who will give them information on any talk of the army returning south to Toletum. This information will be relayed to us by our pigeons which, unlike human messengers, will not talk to anyone else about it. That way, we should have some breathing space which we can use to our advantage. This has nothing to do with disloyalty, it's just that I would like some time to prepare for the return of our esteemed lord and master."

Menna agreed and she was fascinated to see the pigeon loft that the men had erected against the ancient wall. She turned to Tariq.

"This is lovely. I must have passed this many, many times since we have been here and I never knew what it was for. I just assumed it was an ordinary storage shed but now I see the perch outside and the hole through which they enter and it all makes sense." She turned to the men, "May I see them?" Pleased to hear their work praised, the two men unclipped the front of the structure and lowered it, revealing the boxes inside, each occupied by a softly cooing pigeon which, associating daylight with food, cooed even louder.

Tariq spoke quietly to their handlers, informing them of his intentions, and their ready smiles indicated their understanding and willingness to undertake the task. Actually, Menna thought, they seemed pleased that they and their charges were finally going to be put to work. As they were walking back to Tariq's office, he asked Menna to find Akeem and instruct him to join them this evening, in their pavilion.

•

When the Guard ushered them into Tariq's office, they were slightly surprised to see him involved in discussion with General Askil. Tariq invited Menna and Akeem to join them and explained that Askil had been told about the monastery, the Table and, above all, the necessity of keeping it all a secret. Since Askil was the Berber commander it was, of course, only proper that he be aware of what was going on. Askil smiled at that and said, "Actually, my lord, a lot of my men already know of the old church, or monastery. It seems there's an old man living alone there. They say that he is all skin and bone and some of them leave a little food for him from time to time. When they've tried to enter the place, just to have a look around, he has become extremely agitated. One or two have managed to get through the door but couldn't get out quickly enough. Apparently the smell is enough to offend the strongest stomach."

Akeem growled that he and Menna could vouch for that but keeping anything quiet wasn't going to easy. Not if half the army was roaming around the place.

Tariq agreed that it wasn't the ideal situation, but, so long as the real purpose of their interest didn't become common knowledge, it shouldn't present too much of a problem.

In the end it was agreed that Askil would issue an order that the old building was unsound, unsafe and out of bounds to his men. When Tariq and his party searched the building, it need only be known that they were conducting a survey. The presence of Amayuu, whose engineering skills were known throughout the Army, would therefore be explained; similarly that of Tamegrant who was seldom seen apart from his friend.

The next thing was, when? Menna was all for the following day but it was eventually agreed that the search would take place within the week. Tariq wished, first of all, to have words with Amayuu about what they were doing. Amayuu would then communicate the facts to Tamegrant and, by the time they entered the monastery, each would know what was expected of them.

This Tariq did. Amayuu, and presumably Tamegrant because, with Tamegrant it was never easy to discern what he felt, were looking forward to a challenge and, perhaps, discovering some new technical principle of which he, Amayyu, had hitherto, been unaware. It was decided that noon would be the best time because of the available light which, at this time of year, was difficult to predict. The night before, Menna found it impossible to sleep, while Tariq, who was still not convinced of the Table's existence, patiently waited for her to stop moving about so that he might get some rest. He, though, had his own questions keeping him awake. Was it that important that he find the Table first? If they were lucky enough to find it, how was it to be concealed from Musa who, as the senior general, had the first claim to all the spoils of war, and why did all his closest companions insist that he, and not Musa, should present the Table to the Caliph? Well, he reasoned, that last question was easily answered, he owed it to his Berbers. It was they who had defeated Roderick, not Musa. All the same...!

·

The morning dawned bright but still cold. It was the light they needed and as they made their way to the monastery, the noonday sun, though watery and weak, should give them enough. Now that the day had arrived, Tariq found himself surprisingly elated at the thought of what they might discover. Despite any qualms he might have about the stewardship of the Table, the thought that he might actually see and touch a piece of furniture attributed to the Temple of Solomon filled him with an enthusiasm he hadn't expected. Menna, on the other hand, was unusualy quiet and yet it had been she who had talked about little else since they had arrived in Toletum. Akeem too, was in a reflective mood and Tariq, who had frequently wished for Akeem to be more reflective and less verbose, now missed the banter he had been expecting. Amayuu and Tamegrant lagged a little behind the other three, hampered by their need to converse with their hands and, in Amayuu's case, by a sack of tools he carried under his arm.

They attracted little attention from the soldiers as they passed, and Tariq assumed that Askil's explanation for their interest in the building had been successfully accepted. The monastery was larger than Tariq had expected and, as reported, was in a poor state of repair, with holes in the walls as well as the roof. The chamber into which they entered was cavernous and there were doorways in the other walls which, Tariq supposed, led to what had been the sleeping quarters of the now defunct order. There was no doubt, though, that the stinking chamber in which they now found themselves had been the communal space where most of their activities had taken place. As there had been no sign of a chapel, ruined or otherwise, as they approached, it had also served as their place of worship, and Tariq spoke quietly to the others about the need to show respect and go about their business with as little fuss and noise as possible.

At first, with his eyes unaccustomed to the poor light, Tariq had failed to notice the old man cowering in his alcove, until Menna pointed him out. Tariq walked softly towards him and held up his hands in a gesture of peace but the old man tried to squeeze himself even further into the stonework, whimpering like a small animal, his fist thrust against his mouth. Tariq tried, without success, to make eye contact and, as they had previously agreed, waved to Tamegrant to join him. Strangely, as the giant approached, the old man calmed down a little and Tariq was fascinated to observe that Menna's intuition had not failed her. It was almost uncanny how the two men, so vastly different in stature and demeanour, had struck up an immediate rapport. Menna, who had witnessed the tenderness which Tamegrant had bestowed upon the unfortunate Florinda, was not at all surprised by this side of his nature and hoped that he would able to read the old man's thoughts as he expressed them through his eyes. To this end, it had been agreed that Tamegrant would raise his right hand a little if the old man was registering alarm at the direction the search was taking. If, as they searched the refectory, his left arm was raised, it would indicate that they were moving further from their goal. At first they made no effort to move towards the fireplace at the side of the room, but confined their 'search' to the corners and to the doors which led from it. The left hand of Tamegrant remained suspended. When, however, they moved towards the enormous hearth, his right hand signalled immediately.

Tariq and Amayuu looked at one another and Tariq nodded. With Menna and Akeem as spectators, the two men walked into the hearth which suddenly lit up as the sun passed over the hole in the roof which served as a chimney. Amayuu went down on his knees and felt around the edges of the hearth. He let out a low whistle of satisfaction.

"This moves," he said. "As you can see, my lord, it is proud of the surrounding floor and my guess is that there is a system of wheels and pulleys underneath." Tariq felt Menna tap him on the shoulder and gesture over to Tamegrant, whose right hand was now moving up and down like an automaton. Tariq turned back to Amayuu.

"You could well be right but how exactly do we make it work?"

Amayuu, still on his knees, looked around him, then nodded towards the curing hooks hanging on the end of their chains.

"It's probably something to do with those, but we have to be careful. Very often these devices only work when operated in the right sequence. If you try the wrong sequence, it could lock it off forever."

Tariq let out a slow breath. "But that is a really heavy slab of stone. What makes you think that this...this mechanical device is capable of moving it?"

"Not impossible, my lord. Just think of the weight of a drawbridge or even the ramps on the boats you sailed over here. They can be lowered or lifted by just one relatively small pulley. Instead of moving something heavy through a vertical plane, this would move the slab through a horizontal plane."

Tariq shook his head and looked at Akeem and Menna, who only shook their heads back at him. "Well, Amayuu," he said, "that's the reason you're here. You know about these things and we do not, but how do we know which is the right hook to pull?"

Amayuu nodded towards his friend whose right hand was still raised but not moving.

"We keep an eye on him, my lord."

Tariq asked Menna and Akeem to step away a little, then said to Amayuu, "I suggest you do what you have to but, in order for you to concentrate, we will interpret Tamegrant's signals for you. If, as you suggest, we only have one chance of getting this right, we'd better make sure that we make no mistakes."

"I couldn't agree more, my lord," said Amayuu. But he smiled when he said it and Tariq was grateful for that small attempt to relieve the tension.

•

Amayuu slowly rose to his feet, his knees cracking as he did so. Equally slowly he approached the hooks and, as he did so, Tamegrant's hand started to move up and down. In spite of the ray of sunlight, it only illuminated the spot where the four of them stood and all they could make out were the outlines of Tamegrant and the old man, into whose eyes Tamegrant's were firmly locked. That they couldn't see, but the pale shape of Tamegrant's hand was unmistakable. Amayuu reached out to one of the hooks. The hand, on the other side of the room, stilled and remained unmoving as Amayuu slowly reached out towards another hook. Then the last hook and Tamegrant's hand became a blur.

"That's the one," Tariq had to stop himself from shouting out loud. Amayuu grasped the hook and, with some effort, started to pull it down. They jumped away as the hearthstone started to move back, very slowly, grinding on the stones over which it moved and revealing the space underneath.

•

The four of them walked to the opening and peered into what appeared to be an empty hole. Tariq looked towards Tamegrant and saw that the huge Berber was cradling the old man in his arms like a baby. He motioned to the others to stay where they were and walked over to where Tamegrant stood, sweat dripping from his brow, despite the chill of the day, holding the old man who appeared to have fainted. Tariq took off his cloak and Tamegrant laid the old man on it and quietly folded the garment around him. They found another blanket in the alcove where he'd been crouching, and covered him with that as well. Tariq indicated that Tamegrant stay with his charge until he recovered and then went back to the others. Amayuu was scratching his head.

"There's something down there but how we get it up here is anybody's guess." He nodded towards the old man. "We can't depend on his reactions now and, although I suppose it can be raised by another of those hooks, I have to say again that, if we pull the wrong one…!" Tariq didn't wait for him to finish. He strode over to the hooks, dangling from their chains and, without any hesitation took hold of one and pulled down hard on it. Nothing happened. He pulled again and kept on pulling, the chain seemed endless, and then the gasp from the other three told him what he needed to know. He turned and rejoined them, just in time to see his prize, glittering where the sun caught the gems, slowly rise above the edge of the cavity. He felt Menna's hand convulsively grasp his and Akeem let out a shout of triumph, which he quickly swallowed on catching sight of Tariq's warning glance. They heard a muffled sob coming from behind them. It was Tamegrant, again cradling the old man in his arms and making one of the few noises of which he was capable, a requiem for the old priest.

•

Excited as they all were, Tariq reminded them that, without the help of the old priest, they might never have found their treasure and he might have given up his life once he realised that his guardianship had come to an end. Their first task then, was to find the graveyard of his predecessors, doubtless just outside the monastery, and see him committed with all due respect. If any of them was reluctant to have their triumph postponed, it didn't show. The graveyard, overgrown and unkempt, was soon found and the ceremony carried out with dignity and tenderness. Tamegrant, as the only Christian, was requested to undertake the actual committal and, although he had no words to express his thoughts, the onlookers were left in no doubt of his sincerity as he bent to his task.

On their way back, Amayuu asked Tariq how he knew which hook to pull. Tariq grinned at him and said, "I didn't! To tell the truth, Amayuu, I am growing tired of the Table and the influence it seems to have on everyone who knows of its existence. I'd reached the stage of not really caring if we found it or not and had I grasped the wrong hook, resulting in the secret being locked away for all time, I would not have worried unduly. But, tell me, I think I can understand your theory of pulleys moving the stone slab but how did my hook raise the platform on which the Table was standing?"

Amayuu thought for a moment then said, "I imagine, my lord, that there was a chain or chains running up through those pillars on either side of the fireplace. Again pulleys, probably in the ceiling, did the lifting. I believe the Romans used this device in ancient times."

Tariq nodded, "Yes, I seem to remember reading something of it; the Romans again. When you think of the force required to operate their huge stone throwing machines, not the ballista but the really big ones, that was using pulleys and reducing weight through a system of wheels."

"It was, indeed, my lord, and if you recall…"

Akeem's snort of derision cut off their discussion.

"Never mind all that, Tariq." He pointed to the Table, still standing on the raised platform. "How we found it is not important but this is what we came for so what are we going to do with it, drop it back in that hole?"

Menna, excusing herself to the others, took Tariq to one side.

"Think, my love, think hard, because that," she indicated the table, "is going to mean the difference between you and our race going down in history as the true conquerors of this land or being no more than a forgotten footnote."

Tariq looked at the others, then turned back to her and smiled.

"I'll tell you what we are going to do. We are going to do this!"

Chapter 34

The five of them looked at the object with some awe, although their individual reactions to it had differed markedly. They were now no longer in the monastery but in a solid, well-built and secure house, one formerly the property of a minor Visigoth noble, right in the middle of the city. They had not been there long and had arrived under the cover of darkness which, at this time of year, set in early. The Table had been carried from the monastery in a small covered donkey cart which Akeem had borrowed from one of his many mysterious sources. Apparently the owner was under the impression that it was for carrying firewood which Akeem, groaning and holding his back, claimed was needed for heating his room to alleviate the pains with which he suddenly found himself afflicted. He, in the company of Tamegrant, then conveyed the Table to the address which Tariq had, after a thorough reconnaissance, deemed as safe a repository as anywhere in the city. Tariq, Menna and Amayuu left the building a little later and, to allay any suspicion that their activities might have been in any way unusual, they stopped and chatted to comrades, just as they would have done on any evening stroll through the encampment.

•

Now they were together again and Akeem was the first to speak.

"Phew, that was a lot heavier than I thought it was going to be. I know it's not very big but Tamegrant and me, and we're no weaklings, had quite a job getting it in here."

Menna cautiously ran her hand over the jewel encrusted top and shivered slightly. "I don't like it," she said. "I don't even like the look of it, in fact it's quite ugly, but I especially don't like the..the… I can't explain it but it radiates a feeling of sadness, of unhappiness? As I say, I can't explain it but, whatever it is, it makes me feel uncomfortable in its presence."

Tariq nodded, "I think I know what you're trying to say and I sense something of the sort, but we must not forget that this is probably the oldest and holiest object in the known world and, as such, we should not perhaps be over hasty with our criticism. Maybe the unhappy history that it has undergone accounts for this feeling we sense from it." Akeem then broke in,

"I don't really care about its history, or what it stands for. All I know is, that Lord Musa covets it above all other things and we all know why he does. If he can present this priceless piece of furniture to the Caliph, he will have made the point that it was him who found it because it was his army that captured Toletum first and not ours. So why don't you, Tariq, take it over to Damascus now, before Musa gets back here and claims it?"

Tariq smiled at this predictable outburst and shook his head. "No, Akeem, that won't work either. Lord Musa will just say that I was sent with it, as his emissary. He is, after all, the commander of the whole Umayyad army. No, I will hand it over to him when he returns from the north and he can take the Table himself."

With the exception of Tamegrant, who couldn't understand what was being said, the other three looked at Tariq with amazement tinged, it has to be said, with a degree of scorn.

"But Tariq…" Menna began but Tariq stilled her with a raised hand.

"No, Menna. If Lord Musa is going to claim the credit for the conquest of Hispania, and I have to agree with you that he will, then we have to discredit his claim. For reasons that I have stated earlier, I take no pride in doing that but it is not my pride that is at stake, it is the honour of our people, and that I will protect to my last breath."

For a moment there was silence as they all looked at one another, as if one of them might throw some light on Tariq's last remark. Eventually it was Menna who confronted him.

"But, husband, if you are going to hand over the Table, how are you going to discredit him? After all, it's your word against that of Lord Musa and you have already explained that his position, reputation and power give him an advantage over any claim you might make."

Tariq made no answer but walked around the Table, knelt and studied the underside closely, raised himself slowly, all the time without touching the relic, stood back from it and said, "Will you all please leave me alone with it."

Menna's response was immediate, "Does that include me?"

The look that Tariq bestowed on her was affectionate but tinged with sadness.

"Yes, Menna, that includes you but I will join you presently. Now, please, if you will all leave."

Akeem laid a protective hand on Menna's arm and led her towards the door. Amayuu quickly transcribed the order to Tamegrant, who nodded solemnly and they followed the other two out of the room, leaving Tariq looking at the Table and thoughtfully stroking his beard.

•

The next morning, in another part of the city, the Jewish Quarter where most of the craftsmen plied their trade, four men were gathered together in a workshop belonging to one of them. At about the same time, the first pigeon to make its way home from the north was spotted circling above before making its descent onto the perch outside the new loft. The handler, who had waited patiently for this moment, held out a palm full of grain under the perch and, while the tired bird gratefully garnered its breakfast, the small tube was removed from its leg. Once the pigeon was happily restored to its allocated nest, the man, clutching the tiny tube tightly in his fist, hurried to Lord Tariq's pavilion. Arriving there, he was informed by the guard that Lord Tariq was absent and his whereabouts unknown. The man decided to wait; he had his orders directly from Tariq himself and these were to hand over any messages directly to him and to him only. He therefore sat himself down against the wall adjacent to Tariq's pavilion, the miniscule tube still clutched in his hand.

Hardly had he made himself comfortable when, Menna, alerted by the conversation with the guard, came to see who it was that wanted to speak to her husband. The guard pointed to the man sitting against the wall and Menna, recognising him, hurried over to him and crouched beside him, holding out her hand for the message. The man shook his head and turned away from her. Menna mustered what little of the native language she had learned during her stay here in Toletum, and asked if one of his pigeons had, in fact, delivered a message for Lord Tariq and, if so, could she please have it and she would see that it was safely delivered to Lord Tariq on his return. The man shook his head again and, for a few moments, Menna was annoyed at his stubbornness, but then she realised that he was only displaying his loyalty to Tariq, so she sat quietly beside him to await Tariq's return.

She was not unduly worried but it was unusual for Tariq to leave her without some indication of where he was going and the reason for him doing so. During their working day, he went about his business and she hers, but last night was the first time he had left her in the middle of the night without a word. He had been so quiet and careful not to disturb her that she had not noticed his absence until she awoke in the early hours of the morning. She had her eye firmly fixed on the great open gate in the city wall through which she expected Tariq to emerge and when he did, instead of jumping up impetuously, which was her first instinct, she continued to sit quietly and watch his approach. He hadn't seen her and was walking slowly and thoughtfully. Menna frowned. Why did Tariq always have to look so serious? Then her look softened and her irritation was instantly replaced by the wave of love that washed over her.

Suddenly Tariq's eyes lifted and he saw her and gave one of his boyish grins. Just as she was getting to her feet, Tariq saw who was with her and the grin disappeared.

•

"Is he on his way?" Menna could feel the tension in Tariq's arm, which she held as he read the tiny message. Silently he handed it to her.

"Your eyes are better than mine but, yes. Malik tells us that he is on his way." He took the tiny scroll from her again and turned to the bearer of the message. "Will you go back to the loft and see if any more birds have arrived. If they have, please bring the messages to me immediately." The man turned on his heel and ran along the wall to where his birds roosted. He was soon back, holding out his hand, on which lay two more of the tiny scrolls. Tariq thanked him in his own tongue, handed one scroll to Menna and read the other. They looked at one another.

"Only Musa is on his way, not Malik."

Menna broke in,

"Apparently, you are to be sent north."

Tariq mused while re-reading the three notes. "It looks as though Musa is going to replace me, here in Toletum. I'm only thankful that I arranged that other business in time." Menna looked at him. "Other business? Is that what you were doing all night? I wondered where you'd crept off to. So, what is this mysterious 'other business' that has to be conducted in the middle of the night?"

Tariq shook his head. "Not now Menna. Later, I'll tell you later. Just now I have to meet with Askil, there is much we have to discuss." He started to move off in the direction of the gate but Menna ran after him and hung on to his arm. He shook her off, not roughly but leaving her in no doubt that this was not the time for further discussion between them. She watched him go through the gate, trying not to feel hurt at his rejection, then felt her own arm being gently taken. She knew from his shadow that it was Akeem who, for a big man, could move very softly.

"Don't you worry about him, Menna." Akeem turned her towards him and looked down on her with an expression, half amused and half solicitous. "If he doesn't want to share anything with you, it'll be because it's something too dangerous for you to know. And another thing you don't have to worry about are his feelings for you; feelings and, I might add, respect. So, sometimes it's best to let him just get on with his job. He knows what he's doing. As for me. Well!" He opened his arms expansively, "My job is to take care of both of you, as far as he'll let me, that is."

She returned his smile, if a little uncertainly, and they moved back to the pavilion for a late breakfast.

Tariq had not been completely honest with Menna because, although it was important that he advise Askil of the situation, that was going to have to wait until he had dealt with the other business. This 'other business' took him back to the Jewish quarter and the building he had left a little earlier, before the sun had broached the horizon. Now it was light, he did not head directly for his destination but took advantage of the labyrinthine alleyways which characterised this part of the city. The three men, with whom he had met earlier, were still gathered there and Tariq, wasting no time, told them the news which would necessitate them undertaking their task with an even greater sense of urgency; that done, he made his way to Askil's headquarters, where he informed the general of Musa's intentions.

Askil was not particularly happy to learn that he was expected to serve under another commander, especially one such as Musa who, he knew, exercised his authority very differently to Tariq. He wondered if it would be possible for him to join Tariq when he marched north to join Malik, thus completely uniting the original Berber army, but Tariq was doubtful.

"We will have to see but, mindful of our success thus far, I expect Lord Musa will wish to see more integration between the Umayyad army and ourselves and I can't say that I blame him for that. We can but wait and see when he gets here." He nodded in the direction of the Visigoth palace. "Bearing in mind the plans he has for his son and Egolina, he might decide to leave Abd al-Aziz to take over from you, in which case…

Whatever, I want you to see that he is royally feted on his arrival. Make sure that your men are smart and co-operate with whatever force accompanies him. I am aware that some of our men are unhappy that we are allowed insufficient credit for our exploits but, at the end of the day, we are all on the same side and Lord Musa is our commander- in-chief and, as such, commands our ultimate loyalty."

Askil nodded resignedly and, after discussing one or two other issues relevant to the new city order, Tariq took his leave. He was tired; recent events had taken their toll. Not only the responsibilities of his position but the doubts about the course of action he had decided upon. He tried to shake them out of his head but, even in sleep, they gnawed away at him, and Menna, not knowing exactly what it was that troubled him so deeply, smoothed his brow and murmured endearments to try and calm him.

•

It was some three weeks before Musa re-entered the city, together with his son and, Tariq calculated, about half the power with which he had ridden to the north, less Malik and his Berbers. His coming to Toletum was predictably regal, and trumpets announcing his imminent arrival could be heard long before the procession came into view. Askil had paraded his men immaculately and Tariq stood on a podium at their front. At his side stood Egolina, an arrangement that annoyed Menna beyond belief but, as Tariq had warned her, the object of her intense dislike was the chosen bride of Musa's son, while she, Menna, was merely the wife of a soldier serving under the Umayyad commander. The fact that Egolina was making the most of her new-found role and informally, even intimately, engaging Tariq in whispered conversation, did little to improve Menna's temper as she stood at the back of the podium. Akeem, at her side and with a restraining hand on her arm, could almost feel the heat of her anger and continually 'shushed' her when her comments became uncomfortably audible.

Once the ceremonials had come to end, to the relief of all except those closest to Musa, the Emir motioned that Tariq should join him and give an account of his stewardship, here in Toletum. Efficient as ever, Tariq produced statements of tax revenues, up to date records of valuables uncovered and seized as bounty since Musa's departure and…

"Perhaps you would like to see for yourself, my lord?" Musa, intently studying the figures which had been passed to him, looked up.

"See what Tariq?" He waved the parchments in front of him. "I'm more than happy looking at these at the moment. I must say, your administrative powers almost exceed your military prowess. I am impressed."

"Thank you, my lord, but there is something else; something that does not appear in those figures." Tariq's tone was enough to hint at something extraordinary. "I truly believe that you ought to…"

Musa slowly put down the reports. "You have found it, haven't you? the Table, King Solomon's Table?" He clutched Tariq's robe and pulled him towards him. He was nearly forty years older than Tariq but still the more powerful of the two. "Just tell me I'm right; I am right aren't I? You've found the table?"

Tariq respectfully removed Musa's hand, and nodded.

Musa's voice was pleading, "Take me to it, please. Please let me see it."

Tariq nodded again, then said, "Later, my lord. We should not yet be seen together, skulking around in the dark. What we are discussing is the existence of an iconic item of religious and political significance. It is important that only you and I know of its existence and its whereabouts. It will be safer if you are settled here for a little while first; that way the sight of us walking unescorted through the city will be a commonplace one. Believe me, my lord, I have given much thought to this, and a little patience on your part, if you will excuse the impertinence, will be invaluable in order not to compromise the whereabouts of the item."

Musa looked puzzled. "But surely Tariq, when it was discovered, there must have been others than yourself involved. A piece like that cannot be …!"

"It can, my lord." Tariq was whispering now and drew the side of his hand across his throat.

Musa, so far as he was capable, looked almost shocked. "You mean that you actually..?" Then he started to chuckle. "My word, Tariq, you have learned a lot. I would never have thought it of you."

Tariq said nothing, but his relief at Musa's agreement to his suggestion was heartfelt.

•

The next morning, Musa called a meeting of all the senior military staff to explain his plans for the immediate future, and they were not exactly as Tariq expected. Musa was, in fact, intending to march north again as soon as his army, or at least the bulk of it, had reached Toletum from Hispalis, which city had finally fallen to the successful Umayyad siege. That his main army was on its way to Toletum was not a surprise to Tariq as Cyprian had only ridden over a few days previously with the news, but he had not expected that, accompanied by Musa, it would continue northwards. Nor did he suspect that Askil, with his followers, would be added to Musa's power while Tariq would have command of Malik and the rump of Musa's units still camped with him. The gap left by Askil would be taken over by Musa's son together with whatever numbers were deemed necessary to preserve a peaceful, and profitable, regime in Toletum. The onset of this activity was not expected to take place until the main Umayyad force had reached Toletum, been rested and prepared for their onward advance. This, Tariq calculated, would take about another month and into the onset of spring weather. Enough time? He fervently hoped so. One event he would not be able to postpone for long was the introduction of Musa to the Table and so, taking the initiative, he proposed to the Emir that they leave it for a couple more days and then, should they enjoy the necessary privacy, he would take Musa to it. This was agreed and, accordingly, a few nights later, there being no moon and a heavy overcast sky promising heavy rain which should keep most, if not all, of the locals shut up in their homes, they made their way to the secret location.

Their route was as circuitous as Tariq could make it. By now he knew the city like the back of his hand and he was counting on the fact that Musa, not a man given to walking, would not remember the house to which he was being taken. They arrived without seeing anyone and, as far as they could tell, without being seen themselves. Tariq unlocked the entrance door, then the door to the room in which the Table stood covered by a cloth, on top of which various items of domestic utensils, bowls and such, had been carelessly distributed. Tariq explained that, in the unlikely event of anyone obtaining access, it would appear to be an ordinary piece of furniture. Musa nodded his head approvingly and helped to clear the artefacts away. His response on seeing the Table, lit dimly by the lamp that Tariq had brought, was, perhaps, the most surprising thing of all. After all the excitement he had shown of being told of the Table's discovery, his reaction on observing it was something of an anticlimax. He stared at it for a long time, hardly laid a hand on it and merely expressed his breath in a long, drawn-out, sigh.

Tariq understood immediately. The historical, religious and philosophical implications of the piece escaped Musa completely. He saw it merely as a means to an end. It was a tool, nothing more than an object he would use to ensure his glorification in the eyes of the Caliph. Any misgivings that Tariq might have felt for his actions were immediately dissipated and it was with some relief that, after restoring the Table to the condition in which they had found it, they left the building.

•

Within an hour of their leaving, a lone figure emerged from the shadows and the two locks were changed.

•

Reports from Malik, in the north, indicated that the weather was on the mend and, if anything was going to hamper a further advance by the combined armies, snow and ice were unlikely candidates. The Umayyad main army now at Toletum, that part of it chosen to march were preparing for their departure with Musa at their head. Askil, now back under his preferred command of Tariq, had already left and was due to link up with Malik in a matter of days. Menna was happy to observe a change in her husband's mood as they rode side by side through unfamiliar terrain; Tariq seemed more composed than he had been at Toletum and she had assumed it was because he had returned to his favourite occupation, that of soldiering and in command of his beloved Berbers. She was partly right; but what she didn't know was that which, for her own security and safety, Tariq had kept to himself. He had been happy to pass over the keys to Musa when ordered to do so, but he need not have worried on that score. Apparently Musa had contented himself with the secure location of the Table and, as Tariq's agents had informed him, had not returned to the building since. Musa was in no hurry, he had his campaigning in the north to do and, once finished there, he could return to Toletum to collect his prize and deliver it to Damascus. The building in which it was hidden was commonplace, as far as he could judge, and unlikely to be disturbed by anyone else, even if stumbled upon by accident.

Chapter 35

Malik, as with Askil, was pleased to be under Tariq's command once more and even the section of the Umayyad army assigned to his leadership seemed happier with their new position than they had been under Musa. As Malik explained to Tariq, "The problem with the Emir is that he likes to kill too many people. Any group, village or town that he fancies a threat, he puts them to the sword and then to the fire. As you know, my lord, I am an uncomplicated soldier, not as subtle or forward thinking as you, but if there is one thing that you have taught me, it is that co-operation and diplomacy make soldiering a lot easier and a lot more productive."

Tariq laughed and said he thought he'd never see the day when the impetuous Malik owned up to ideas such as these, but he was pleased and, as they fought their way towards the great mountain range that separated Hispania from Gaul, Tariq towards the west and Musa towards the east, it was discernible that Tariq's army disposed of its foe and resettled the somewhat bleak landscape with far fewer losses than Musa, who continued to fight an attritional campaign.

•

They were on the march for nearly three years, when the Umayyad order came for them to return to their base at Toletum and thence to Damascus, where they were expected to report on their exploits and make good account of their spoils.

The two armies were making their separate ways back to Toletum. Both, in their own way, had conducted successful campaigns but their supply lines were stretched and, unlike their arrival in the south, it was not so easy to live off the barren lands of the north.

Tariq, Menna and Akeem, as they did most of their time travelling, were riding three abreast and, while still days from Toletum, Akeem suddenly said to Tariq, "Ever since we have been away from our base in Toletum, I've noticed something odd. I haven't said anything up until now but.." Menna, laughing, broke in, "I know what you're going to say, Akeem. I've noticed it as well but the reason I haven't said anything is that, if my lord and master had wanted me to be informed, he would have done so. Shall I ask him or do you want to?"

"Alright," came Akeem's answer. "Ever since we've been away, we've been carrying three locals from Toletum with us. They haven't done any fighting or, as far as I can see, done anything to support our cause so, who are they exactly and what are they doing here?"

Tariq said nothing and they rode in silence for a while, but both Akeem and Menna could tell that Tariq was quietly amused yet still not ready share the joke. Eventually he did say, "Trust you two to notice three very inconspicuous individuals among an army of, what, upward of twelve thousand men. I suppose that, while we campaigned, you've noticed that I've exchanged a few words with them and yes, they are with us at my behest and that is all I'm prepared to tell you about them. I imagine that you can question them as much as you like but you will get no answers from them; that much I can promise you."

His two companions looked at one another and admitted that they had confronted these men but on being questioned they just acted either as mutes or as if they didn't understand the question. Tariq nodded.

"Good, I'm pleased not to have misjudged them. All I will tell you at this stage is that they are here under my personal protection and for the safety of all of us.

For the time being, you'll just have to be satisfied with that and, yes Menna my love, that includes you."

The rest of their journey proceeded peacefully and their entry into the city of Toletum, while not accompanied by the same degree of pomp that would be extended to Musa on his return, was friendly and agreeable. Abd al-Aziz, Musa's son, formally welcomed them, although it was noticeable that Egolina and Menna took care to maintain a frosty distance. Then the armies built their encampments outside the northern walls, a territory rapidly becoming over-crowded. As soon as night fell, Tariq left Menna, as she suspected he would, and walked into the city prepared to meet up with the three mysterious individuals who had accompanied them throughout their long absence.

•

It appeared that Damascus was impatient for the return of the victors and Musa, as soon as his triumphal entry into Toletum had been suitably celebrated, summoned Tariq to his side, fumbled for the keys on his belt, handed them to Tariq and ordered him to return to the building and confirm that the Table was still where he had last seen it. Tariq deftly changed the keys for the new set and, together, they set off. This time ignoring the precautionary measures they had taken on their first visit together. The Table had gathered three summers of Hispanic dust but, that apart, it sat there, exactly as they had left it. Then Musa took over. He had Tariq write him directions to the house from all the central areas of Toletum so that it could be easily located. He called up half a dozen of his Arab guard to supervise security, had special packaging arranged and an ornate cart on which to convey it into the presence of the Caliph. Once he was satisfied that he had done everything in his power to allow for a truly dramatic presentation, he called Tariq to him and asked if he could think of anything that might, conceivably, have been forgotten. Tariq replied shortly, that he could not!

Chapter 36

Damascus, 715AD

Menna had never seen anything like it and Tariq, gratified by her interest, did what he could to explain the wonder that was Damascus. They were strolling, alone and unescorted, through shaded alleys thronged with people, which were intersected at right angles by other alleys and wider thoroughfares. She had already noticed that the roads were laid out as a grid, leading north, south and east, west and Tariq explained that it was an urban system initiated by the Greco-Roman civilisations that had inhabited the city so many centuries earlier. This made the process of location so much simpler than, for example, the haphazard layout which had grown almost organically in Toletum, a city which neither of them was sorry to leave. Here, Menna was captivated by the sheer energy of the city, the commercial activity and, more than anything else, the ethnic mix of peoples all blending, conversing and engaging. She had, of course, been used to the frenetic atmosphere of Tangier but that had been more of a huge open market whose only function had been to serve the growing garrison. In Toletum, despite Tariq's best efforts, segregation was still practised to an overwhelming degree and this had resulted in small, ghetto-ised enclaves of industry and commerce but here, here in Damascus, the whole population seemed to be occupied and engaged as one. Tariq felt bound to explain that it wasn't quite all as it seemed. True, Coptic Christians, Jews, Arab Christians and Muslims all worked together and were allowed to pursue their own faiths but, in reality, the Umayyad family had instigated an Islamic coinage and Islamic commercial rules which placed other faiths at an economic disadvantage. Nevertheless the system seemed to work and everyone could profit from it, if not to the same extent as the Umayyad and their followers.

•

The situation in Toletum had become unhappy for both Tariq and Menna. For her, it was the dignity bestowed upon Egolina and the autocratic way by which she exercised it and, for Tariq, it was the visible increase in the levels of cruelty and bloodshed which were a mark of Musa's methods for dealing with a vanquished nation. He could see that, despite all his efforts to bring the people together to work for their own prosperity and culture, Musa had caused further division and stress. But that was now all behind them. They had been in Damascus for some days and were now awaiting a summons from the palace to meet with Al Walid, an occasion much anticipated by the victors in the expectation of their exploits being justly rewarded. Not so Tariq, however. He knew that his role would be marginalised by Musa, had prepared himself for it and taken what steps he could to ensure that the Berber army would, in fact, be justly recognised for the feats they had performed. He was, however, genuinely looking forward to another meeting with the Caliph. Their previous meetings, brief as they had been, had convinced Tariq that, exalted as he was, the Caliph was a man not dissimilar to himself. A man who put his faith before all else but, when required, had the capacity to administer his ever-expanding territories with a dispassionate and clear logic. He was also a man who had ensured his place in history by his Great Mosque. Although it was close to completion on his last visit to Damascus, Tariq had yet to see the finished building. As they neared the site, Tariq asked Menna to close her eyes and be guided by him. He hardly dared open his own eyes but, as they entered the huge square, Menna felt the grip on her hand tighten and heard the audible gasp that involuntarily escaped Tariq. She opened her eyes, and saw what she thought was the most beautiful building she had ever seen. For several minutes neither spoke but just stood there, and they were not alone. Even the citizens of the city, who saw the Mosque every day of their lives, were still compelled to stop and drink in the spectacle. Tariq was explaining to Menna what it had looked like when he'd last seen it under construction, when he felt a light tap on his shoulder. Instinctively his hand went to his belt but, on turning, he saw the beaming, black-bearded face of Asad, the commander of the Arab guard that had accompanied Tarik's Berbers as they fought their way through Hispania. The two men had built a mutual respect for each other's talents in the field which had developed into a genuine friendship, and both were sorry to be parted when the Guard was reassigned to Musa's command for the northern campaigns. Menna too, was happy to be reacquainted but, the greetings over, they learned that Asad had been ordered to seek out Tariq and deliver the summons which had long been expected, if not quite in the form delivered by Asad.

It transpired that Al Walid was unwell, indeed quite possibly terminally so, and was anxious to debrief the victorious generals and receive the rich bounty resulting from their successes. Upon questioning Asad, Tariq learned that Musa was planning his triumphal entry into Damascus and had invited Tariq to join him. Tariq shook his head.

"Thank your master but, as you know, Asad, I have few followers here with me in Damascus and I have no doubt that the Emir will have no need of me to celebrate his great victories."

Asad gave a wry smile. "No, General, you and I both know who inflicted defeat upon the Visigoth and we equally know who will take the credit for it. Yet I am instructed, not by my master but by the Commander of the Faith himself, that your presence is ordered at the same time as that of the Emir. So am I to report that you will proceed to the palace accompanied only by your personal staff?"

Tariq nodded. "Thank you Asad and thank the Emir for his offer to include me in his train but I'm sure he won't mind me following behind. I take it that he will be accompanied by, if nothing else, the Table of Solomon suitably wrapped for the occasion."

Another wry smile from Asad, "The packaging is almost more sumptuous than the Table itself, my lord."

Menna started to say something but Tariq pressed her hand gently and she swallowed her remark. Asad bowed his farewell and turned, immediately to disappear into the crowd that thronged the square. Menna, still frowning, said, "How did he know where to find you, in the middle of this frenetic city?"

Tariq smiled. "Nothing magical, my love, I assure you. I knew that Musa would want to contact me at some stage, if only to know what I was up to, but I also had word earlier that the Caliph was planning to see us both at the same time. Either would make a rough guess that, at some hour of the day, I would be here in this square, worshipping that beautiful building. Asad would also know where to find me because this mosque has always been a keen topic of conversation between us. Anyway, we had better make our preparations, or rather, my preparations to appear before the Al Walid. I only pray that he is still alive to see me."

•

Preceeded by Musa, Tariq was ushered into a large room which, dark as it was, was furnished with an opulence which surprised him. His previous meetings with Al Walid had indicated that the Caliph was a man of austere taste, a characteristic with which Tariq could happily identify. But this was not the Al Walid of Tariq's memory. The Caliph was obviously a very sick man and showed little of the absolute authority that he had enjoyed previously. Instead he reclined on a divan, propped up with pillows, his eyes which before radiated intelligence were now half-closed and unseeing and his breath was rasping in his chest. In fact Al Walid was still alive but only just, and it soon became obvious that it was his brother and successor, Sulayman, who was going to be in charge of the proceedings and it was he who opened the audience by remonstrating with Musa for putting on such a display of triumph, at a time when the Caliph was on his death bed. Al Walid waved a tired arm at his brother, at the same time bestowing a weak smile on Tariq and congratulating him on his marriage. That done he fell back on his pillows, using the last of his strength to indicate to Sulayman that he should continue. Tariq could see immediately that this brother, soon to be head of the Umayyad clan, was not of the same material as Al Walid. His eyes, although equally intelligent, were cruel and vindictive and Tariq saw that there was not to be the instant rapport that he had enjoyed with Al Walid.

Sulayman wasted no time in coming to the point. Waving a sheaf of finely written vellum in front of him he said,

"Very well, this is an inventory of the bounty that you have liberated from the Visigoth but it is the only one that we have been given and it is Musa ibn Nusayr who has submitted it." He turned, abruptly, to Tariq, "And what about you? Have you no treasure to declare to us?"

Tariq bowed and replied that all the treasures collected in the course of his campaigns had been handed over to the Emir, together with the supporting inventories, at which point Musa interrupted saying that, although the Berber army had fought valiantly, it was, of course, he and the Umayyad army that had conquered Hispania for the cause. It was he and the Umayyad army that had captured Cordova and the capital, Toletum, and it was he that was the bearer of treasure such as the Caliphate could only dream of and moreover…

At this point, Al Walid, painfully raising himself on one elbow raised his hand to still Musa and, mustering the little strength that remained to him, spoke for the first time.

"It was my understanding that it was the Berber army that defeated Roderick. Your army, my lord Musa, did not reach the shores of Hispania until after the battle had been won." The effort of delivering this one sentence was too much and, scarcely able to draw breath, he fell back on his pillows.

Sulayman went over to his brother and gently wiped his brow with a sweet-scented cloth and, for an instant, his eyes softened as he spoke.

"You must not tire yourself, my brother. Conserve your strength for prayer." He straightened up and immediately resumed his businesslike and cold demeanour.

"Well, Musa, does the Caliph speak true? Which of you can justly claim the victory?"

Musa, without a glance at Tariq, repeated what he had just said, adding "and my proof, lord, is the most valuable item of treasure it is possible for me to bestow upon your mighty family. So valuable is it, that it has not been included in that inventory that you hold in your hand, and why, my lord? Because it is beyond price; it is unique and the most sought after piece in the religious history of the world." He waited for his declaration to sink in, then continued, "Had my worthy colleague, the Governor of Tangier, reached Toletum, the Visigoth capital, before my armies and procured this item, he would have made certain that it was he who had the honour of presenting it to you, my masters, rather than your humble servant."

For a moment nobody said anything, then Sulayman said, "To all intents and purposes, Tariq is your vassal and it would have been his duty to pass over this… this wonder of which you speak into your keeping. That is, of course, if he had found it before you did, which would surely mean that he was in Toletum before you."

Musa gave a vigorous shake of his leonine head.

"Not this, my master. This piece, as a gift to the Umayyad exceeds anything your illustrious family has been fortunate enough to possess in the past. It would have assured your favour for the rest of his days."

Sulayman's smile was anything but amused. "Which, we presume, is what you expect of us. Very well, Hispania is ours so I don't suppose it matters greatly who it is we have to thank for it. You have succeeded in engaging our curiosity, so what and where is this piece that is going to earn our undying gratitude?"

Musa bowed again. "If you will permit me, my lord." He walked to the door and whispered his instructions to whichever attendant awaited his orders. Within moments, the door opened and two of Musa's personal guard appeared, dragging behind them a small cart, sumptuously decorated. Once in the room, they made their obeisance to the Umayyad brothers, removed the cover from the cart and, with some effort, lifted the Table to the floor. They then hastily threw the cover back on the vehicle and took it outside. Sulayman glanced at the Table, then at his brother who merely groaned and covered his eyes.

"Is this what I think it is?" The question was peremptory and fired at Musa. The Emir nodded and Sulayman stretched out a hand, touched the Table and snatched his hand away again, as if he'd been stung. He took a deep breath.

"The Table of King Solomon!" The words were breathed out rather than spoken. Then, "You have succeeded in pleasing us Musa and.."

The interruption came in the form of a polite cough from Tariq, who all this time had been standing in the background, his existence apparently forgotten by everyone.

In a flash, Sulayman's eyes were turned on him, cold and dispassionate.

"You wish to say something?"

Tariq walked towards the tableau formed by Sulayman, Musa and the Table.

Without a trace of deference or apology in his voice, Tariq said firmly, "My lord Sulayman, might I ask you to examine the Table closely, in particular the legs."

Sulayman looked as if he was about to order Tariq from the room but a whisper from the sickbed took him to his brother's side. He bent down, the better to hear the dying man's words. He then nodded to his brother, walked back to the Table, bent down and inspected the four legs. Suddenly his back visibly stiffened and he turned to Tariq, his voice neutral.

"One leg is different. The arrangement of the stones is slightly different and the chamfered grooves differ in length. What does this mean?" His voice rose slightly. "What are you trying to tell me?"

Tariq calmly asked permission to leave the room, did so and was back within seconds. He was holding a long thin object parcelled in skins, which he started to remove. He held up a table leg. "Might I ask your lordship's indulgence once again and request that you match this leg with the matching three on the Table?"

Sulayman glanced at the recumbent form of Al Walid before stretching out his hand for the proffered leg. Taking it, he walked back to the Table and did as he was requested.

It took him no time at all to confirm that the leg given to him by Tariq was the original and that the odd one was a clever copy.

He cradled the leg and looked from Musa to Tariq and then back to Musa. Eventually he addressed his next question to Tariq. "If this leg is the original, it would suggest, would it not, that you came into possession of it when it was attached to the Table? It would be too much to ask me to accept that it was found separately. In other words, that Lord Musa found the Table while you found a leg originally belonging to it. So, what are the facts of this beguiling mystery? No! Don't tell me, let me tell you what I think. I think that the Berber army was victorious over King Roderick, and that the Umayyad army, under your command Lord Musa, arrived after the event. I have no doubt that your army which, incidentally was at least double the size of yours, Lord Tariq, then marched north but, by the time you reached Toletum, Tariq was already in control of the city, had secured the Table and it is therefore in his gift and not yours."

"But, my lord, it is I who command your army, surely I have the right to…"

"To what, Musa? The right to deceive us and claim favours that rightly belong to others? No, you have forfeited any rights you might have imagined to have been yours."

Sulayman's words were delivered like whiplashes and he went on, "This is not the first time that you have attempted to cheat our illustrious family but, rest assured, it will be the last. Because of your advanced years and the undeniable service you have given us, your life is spared and you will receive a small but adequate pension, on which you will live in exile."

Tariq's feelings were mixed but, to his surprise, Musa did not storm out. Quite the opposite; on his way, he had to pass Tariq who he embraced warmly, whispering in his ear, "I should have known, I taught you too well."

Sulayman had not quite finished and this time the accusatory finger was pointed at Tariq.

"You have been duplicitous and that I do not like, whatever your reasons. Why did you feel you had to go to those lengths to make your point?"

Tariq explained that it was not his honour but that of his people that was at stake. His Berbers had received little in the way of reward for their service. Many had chosen to remain in Hispania, especially in the south where the land was that much more fertile than at home. As for himself, he asked for nothing.

Sulayman nodded and, for the last time in his life, Al Walid smiled.

•

"He did what?" Menna stared at Tariq, disbelief written all over her.

Tariq gave her one of his grins and said, "He gave me a hug and wished me well."

Menna shook her head. "I don't understand it. You deprived him of a supremely comfortable future and he wished you well?"

Tariq sat down heavily on the bed, suddenly very tired.

"The truth of the matter is," he said, "Musa is a very old man, strong as he is, and when I did what I did, he looked over to where Al Walid lay dying and felt mortality enter his own bones. In the end I think that he probably thought to himself, 'Well, what does it matter anymore?' I think he truly regards me as a son and loves me accordingly."

Menna thought for a while, before saying, "Well, at least it explains your mysterious behaviour. Not saying anything to Akeem or me and those three strange Iberians who seem to have been following us around for years like stray puppies. What was their role in all this and what's going to happen to them now?"

Tariq stifled a yawn. "Well, two of them have already found work here and it won't be long before the other one gets hired. Three gifted artisans, a silversmith, a master carpenter and a locksmith, there's plenty of work for their sort here in Damascus, and they'll make a better living here than they ever would back in Toletum. Toletum is fast losing its prestige and being superseded by Cordova, and the harsh measures introduced by Abd al-Aziz and that dreadful wife of his won't make it any easier for the natives."

He swallowed back another yawn but Menna, by now, was wide awake.

"What's going to happen to us now, Tariq? Is it the first boat back to Tangier for us?" Tariq pursed his lips and said nothing. "Well?" Menna pressed him further, "What about us?"

Tariq's immediate response was to pull her to him and hold her tightly but she pushed him away, the question still posed by her expression. He let out a long sigh.

"If you must have answers here and now, my love, my greatest wish would be to remain here, in Damascus. You see, there is so much to learn here and so many better ways of acquiring knowledge than I could ever hope for at home. But of course," he went on hastily, "if you are unhappy with that idea, then, naturally we will return to Tangier as soon as we can."

Menna put her finger to his lips. "Can we afford to live here, as comfortably as we could at home with your Governorship to support us."

He shook his head. "No, but I have been granted a small pension and a house. It will be enough for my needs, so long as you are at my side."

"Then, of course, it will do for me too. What about Akeem, what will he do here?"

Tariq smiled at her, "I imagine the same as he always does, he'll get under our feet and worry about us."

This time it was Menna who yawned. "We're both tired, come to bed."

Just as he was nodding off to sleep, his mind clearer than it had been for many months, she turned to him.

"Tariq, I'm with child."

His response was no more than an imperceptible snore.

-//-

Notes and acknowledgments

The leading protagonists of this book, Tariq, Musa, Julian, Roderick, Egolina, Malik etc, are all historically recorded characters. There are, however, no contemporary accounts of their activities and the earliest available to researchers is that of Abd al-Hakem, an Egyptian scholar, whose history of the Islamic invasion of Hispania was written one hundred and fifty years after the event. The decisive Battle of Guadelete is now universally accepted to have been fought in either 711AD or 712AD and it is generally agreed that Tariq (whose origins are also veiled in obscurity) was the commander of the Berber forces who emerged victorious against overwhelming odds. There is no doubt that Tariq has since enjoyed the status of an Islamic folk hero.

It is, perhaps, not unexpected that the nineteenth century pre-occupation with Gothic Romanticism found these events, and the characters that inhabited them, of particular interest. For example, we have Robert Southey's epic poem about Roderick, Walter Savage Landor's piece on Julian of Cueta and the somewhat overblown painting of Florinda being spied upon by Roderick, from the brush of Franz XavierWinterhalte. If the research channels of documented history are not readily available, there is no shortage of legend, as the above mentioned have already illustrated and it is two of these legends around which this novel has been constructed. It is unlikely that the army of Titus liberated the Table from the Temple, if it ever existed in the first place, since the Temple was sacked by the Babylonians some four hundred years previously. Whatever the facts, the Table has been central to Islamic lore and has featured prominently in most of the stories concerned with the tensions between Tariq and Musa. The rape of Florinda, or La Cava as she is sometimes known, does not seem to have seen the light of day until the 11th century, since when paintings, poetry and other works have made the connection between her and the downfall of the Visigoth. That said, it is not known if she was the wife of Count Julian, his daughter, or even if she existed at all.

In view of all the above speculation, this cannot honestly claim to be an 'historical novel' by any standard. Rather it is a drama constructed from the few 'known' facts available and legends which have transcended time to become a central tenet of Islamic and Hispanic folklore.

•

My grateful thanks to the following. Pauline Dowsett who, despite our mutual affection for the 'Oxford Comma', wielded her red pen like a broadsword. She has lived with this book almost as long as I have, and it is largely due to her that the narrative makes any sense at all. Then there is John Wheeler, whose editorial input has been inspirational. I am also deeply grateful to Leslie Stephens, for his time spent on the manuscript and Guy Deverre who generously allowed me access to his academic notes on Islamic History.

About the author

John Hallam Lott has a degree in History and studies philosophy. He has written a number of short stories for radio and is a prize-winning poet.

He lives with his wife in a particularly beautiful region of Northern France and does much of his thinking and planning while walking the surrounding countryside and, from time to time, some of the sunnier parts of Europe.

•

Also by John Hallam Lott

Designed to Deceive

1077, Dover Castle - William 1st, King of England and Duke of Normandy is captivated by the presence of a stranger in the Great Hall. This young man does not know himself why he has been summoned or by whom. Nor could he guess how his incredible talents will be employed in the ensuing weave of murder, deceit and betrayal.

FICTION / HISTORICAL FICTION

•

Winter Beach

A collection of poetry designed to make you laugh, cry and think – but not all at the same time!

POETRY

NON-FICTION

Make Do & Cook

Learn the secrets of 10 important foods and how to cook healthy, delicious meals on the smallest budget

by Patricia Mansfield-Devine

Make Do & Cook teaches you how you can eat well on a budget. Whether you're a student, a pensioner or a parent with a family to feed, this is your guide to making tasty, cheap and nutritious meals without spending hours in the kitchen. It includes chapters on savvy shopping, menu planning and budgeting, essential ingredients and 100 simple and delicious recipes.

NON-FICTION / COOKING / FOOD

.

For more information, go to: www.webvivantpress.com

www.ingramcontent.com/pod-product-compliance
Lightning Source LLC
Chambersburg PA
CBHW021520240626
47154CB00002B/713